COALESCENCE

COALESCENCE

THE VIEW WITHIN

A NOVEL BY

M. DANIEL SMITH

Published by Bay Ledges Press
www.bayledgespress.com

ISBN (paperback): 978-1-7377843-2-6
ISBN (ebook): 978-1-7377843-3-3

Edited by David Aretha
Book design by Christy Collins, Constellation Book Design

Printed in the United States of America

Dedication

I would like to dedicate this novel to my Yvonne, a willful, intelligent, and vivacious lady. The universe sending her my way. Showing up in my story one full year before we met, her energy reflected in the women inhabiting the world my words have created.

PROLOGUE

MAN IN THE SHADOWS

Now....

He could hear waves reaching for the shore. Fingers of foam in clinging grasp, dragged away by the next in follow. Each making their claim with a whispered name uniquely their own. He sighed, worn down by mental fatigue, beyond reach of the rhythmic sound. Beyond reach of the soothing beat of the ocean's eternal heart, wishing to be freed of his own inner metronome in steady clench and release. Maintaining his life in a ceaseless throb, wishing it would halt its faithful duty, allowing him to slip away into a dark and soundless void where the curse of searing memories would never haunt his endless dream again.

The sound of his name floated through the press of heated air, beneath a sun frozen in eternal hang. He listened to the rich vibration of an angel's voice: soprano notes edged with a husky rasp, worn down by years of uninhibited laughter. A playful tone, born from years of carefree observations tossed like acorns in the air. He could feel her essence as she came to him from out of the sea, drinking in the image of her lithe, toned body. Long-legged and limber, like her mood, most times.

She reached for him. He stood up and backed away, seeing a confused look spreading across her face when he refused her hand, aware her image would disappear in a glow of flickering light. That her hair, thick waves of burnt gold the color of the sun, would dissolve beneath a relentless heat, along with her eyes: hazel-green, a match to the color of the water parted by her upper thighs. His heart swelled with unendurable pain, knowing everything she had ever been, or would ever be, would disappear the moment she touched him.

He refused to let the scene play out, running past her into the water, arms thrust forward, fingers in joined point, diving in, driving himself deeper and deeper into the sheltering abyss.

CHAPTER ONE

RESEARCH FACILITY, MARYLAND

Arrival

Doctor Cheryl Atkinson stared at a set of doubled doors as if she could force them to open with her will alone. The clock perched above the opening showed that the moment of anticipated arrival had come and gone, leaving her chewing the inside of her cheek, her small hands clenched in frustration. A military officer stood on the opposite side of the vestibule from her in a relaxed mood, despite his ram-rod straight posture. He noted her glance in his direction and returned a friendly smile, poised beneath a pair of light-blue eyes, a fan of fine lines radiating from their corners.

Cheryl forced a tight-lipped greeting in return, aware he was an officer in the Marines, responsible for the security of the facility she was working at. Then she turned her head and stared at the doorway, exasperated, the test subject selected for her by the government, overdue. Delivery expected ten minutes ago. She glanced up at the clock again, then glared at the doors until shadows appeared on the other side of the thick security glass.

The major, middle-aged with a stocky frame, stepped forward, nodding at two military orderlies as they passed by. They were pushing a gurney with a man strapped to it, a young lieutenant following close behind who stopped to salute the major before holding him a release. The major signed it, then presented it to the doctor, watching as she did the same with perfectly formed whorls and a single dot. The lieutenant recovered the clipboard, removed two copies, handing one to each of them. Then he stepped back, waiting.

Cheryl took a moment to stare at the comatose man. He appeared to be in his early thirties. His eyes closed, a thin shadow of black hair covering his head and gaunt cheeks, recently shaved. She turned around and looked at her assistant, a seven-foot-tall albino man with wide-shoulders, and light-gray eyes. Cheryl nodded, watching as he escorted the orderlies down a long hallway leading to the section of the building where her research facility was located. The lieutenant pulled a sealed binder with the patient's medical records from beneath one arm, handing it to her, then following the others.

Cheryl stared at the dense collection of files, knowing the government would have followed her directive to scrub them, removing any personal information related to the man on the gurney. She was the director of a restricted access project dealing with the visualization of people's thoughts. As the leading expert in her field, having developed an advanced technology able to reach deep into the minds of those unable to respond, her goal was to help guide them out of their mental traumas, whether caused by extreme physical injuries or emotional stress.

Cheryl opened the thick binder and started to scan through the first few pages. The major, noticing the packet was difficult for her to manage, reached out, hands spread, providing a place for her to rest it on. She tossed him a smile of thanks, setting the binder down and pulling out a section of pages detailing the man's injuries, without any indication of how they had occurred. She scanned through them, then nodded, recovering the binder while giving the major a warm smile that crinkled the edges of her full lips.

"I appreciate your patience. Just wanted to get a sense of his medical history."

The major nodded, turned away and started toward the doors. Then he stopped, looking back at her. "Do you know how soon you'll have any—"

He hesitated, his voice soft. "I know it's not my place to ask about your work." Cheryl returned a stare, causing him to blush. "I apologize, Doctor Atkinson. For any violation of protocol."

Cheryl pursed her lips, having noted his name tag, along with the sprinkle of thin scars etched along the edges of his weathered face and neck, and lines of pain painted into the expression in his eyes. "The only protocol *I'm* concerned with Major Kelly, is that existing between those who are suffering—and those who care about them." She eased her tone as he nodded in response. "And I promise I'm going to do *everything* possible to help them heal. *All* of them."

Then she turned away and headed down the corridor, side-stepping the orderlies and young officer returning with the empty gurney, their black-soled boots squeaking on the polished linoleum floor.

"Had them put him in here, leaving his arms and legs free." Cheryl's assistant, named Isaac, was an enormous man with a gentle demeanor and light touch. He tilted his head to one side, knowing something was bothering his employer: a much shorter woman with mid-length, curly brown hair, showing the first hints of gray.

He'd had been working for Cheryl for two years as a minor player on a large team of support staff. During that time, he'd watched her hold her tongue when questioned by governmental over-sight personnel invading her workplace, making dozens of uninformed comments and suggestions. She would face them down with a calm expression, nodding her head while leading them in circles before ushering them back through the entrance, commanding her entire staff's respect, his included.

Isaac was still uncertain why he'd made the cut, Cheryl having invited him to join in her latest effort: a scaled down project, the other members of her team released back into research labs or academia. When she'd asked him to stay on, he'd been happy to sign up, securing a position with a substantial increase in pay, far beyond what someone with his limited experience and academic background deserved.

Isaac gave Cheryl a considered look, noting her silent mood. "Are you okay?" He watched as she shook her head, eyes narrowing in concentration the way she would get before making a snap decision, most often the correct one, selected from a host of options conjured up by her fertile imagination.

"I'm thinking—the major might be a better man than I was expecting."

Isaac shook his head, his voice high-pitched, breathy, with a soft southern accent. "Don't worry. I'm sure he'll make you angry at some point, proving you were right about him the first time. Which you usually are." He paused, glancing toward the patient resting in his bed, eyes still closed. "What about our guest—regarding his nutrition intake and elimination capabilities?"

Cheryl stared at the patient. "His records show him to be ambulatory, capable of eating with little help needed. And zero issues with evacuation regimen." She paused, looking up at the man she'd selected to work with her. "We'll need to monitor his basic hygiene, though based on the report, it will be less of an effort *this* time. Not like the last subject, although he came around quickly enough once we got him zeroed in and were able to start leading him back into the world."

Isaac raised a hand, stirring the air with a forefinger the size of a sausage. "Yay. No more diapers."

The facility cafeteria was almost deserted, a handful of soldiers sitting together at a table in one corner, along with a scattering of civilians, their noses poked into notebooks made of plastic and glass. Isaac referred to them as *data junkies*, pointing out to Cheryl they probably considered everyone else in the room as minor characters projected into their own versions of an artificial universe.

"Nerd alert—coming in on your six." Isaac smiled as Cheryl ducked her head, his boss unwilling to listen to another inquisitive mind detailing how her unorthodox methodologies might be better used to create a fully immersive virtual world. He chuckled. "It's only the major, heading to grab some coffee." Isaac gave her a wide grin. "You should go over and see if you can help him out. Maybe give him some cream and a little *sugar*, then offer to *stir* it up for him."

Cheryl returned an icy stare. "Have you *noticed* the latest unemployment numbers, man-mountain?"

Isaac picked up his fork, pretending to stab it into his heart. "Ouch. Too cruel by half." He frowned, a serious expression on his lips. "But it *is* your turn to bus the table. I did it earlier."

Cheryl eyed him as she considered delivery of another of her patented glares, realizing it would just bounce off his alabaster skin. She shrugged, stood up and collected their dishes, heading to the rectangular opening of the cafeteria's service window, just to one side of a counter holding several coffee dispensers.

The major's full name was Jean Kelley, known as Dancer by the men who'd served with him overseas. With twenty-seven years of service behind him, he'd earned a reputation among his peers as a courageous leader, with multiple tours of duty served in places with tortuous terrain. Always in the field, he supported his men as they faced daily pass-fail tests. His innate instincts, hard-won skills, along with an immeasurable will, helped inspire them to endure oppressive heat, the mind-fogging-stress of patrolling roads, waiting for the blinding flash of an IED, along with countless close-quarter firefights. And then there was the bane of every soldier's existence: endless hours of tedious boredom standing watch, unable to find a reason for being there. Young men, having shipped out believing what recruitment personnel had told them, only to discover upon their arrival in-country that it was a false reality. Hard-eyed men with knowing smiles etched on sun-bronzed skin, shaking their heads as they marched by, dismissing the weakest among them who they knew would soon melt away.

Jean pursed his lips, his eyes narrowed as he considered what the doctor had just shared with him about her project. "So—it's like a virtual reality setup." He paused, his eyes pinned to the doctor's. "Like what we're doing with our latest training setups, simulating rapid reaction drills during live-fire events using headsets and goggles. Like what you're doing with your—skull caps."

"My people call them Tee-Cee's, Major. Short for thinking caps." Cheryl winced as she used the expression.

Jean leaned back, a grin on his face. "You just reacted like I fed you a mouthful of—" He raised his cup of black coffee. "This, or something just as runny, but with *far* worse flavor."

Cheryl nodded, matching his expression. "I'll have to take your word on *that*."

Isaac came over, letting Cheryl know he was heading back to the lab to check on their guest, telling her not to stay out too late, it being a school day tomorrow. He moved away before she could find something to throw at him.

Jean cocked an eyebrow as he watched the big man with a jovial demeanor saunter off. "I thought he worked for *you*."

Cheryl stared at Isaac, knowing his methods of interaction were different than most others. "Me too—once." She hesitated, taking a sip of her coffee, the taste of it bitter despite the cream she'd added. "Isaac is his own person. Guess he's had to be, growing up like he did. Ostracized and isolated." She paused. "His mother always—"

Jean coughed, stopping Cheryl who looked over with raised eyebrows. He leaned back. "Might that not be considered—confidential information?"

She reflected for a moment, then raised her cup, toasting his comment with a slight nod.

Cheryl sat up in her bed, one of two spare rooms at the facility. It was early, her internal clock prodding her from a lazy dream where she'd been clinging to a tree-limb ten feet off the ground, holding on for a slow count of one hundred while her older brother, Robert, stood below tossing acorns at her, trying to make her fall. Anti-diversion training, he'd been saying to her, his deep laughter letting her know he was enjoying the game. The sound of it caused her to join in, falling, waking up just before she hit the ground, with the smile still painted on her lips.

Cheryl left her room, going down the hallway and stopping at the dormitory sized bedroom next to her own. She opened the door, checking in on the subject. He was lying beneath a sheet, eyes closed, the sigh of his breathing barely perceptible in the still air. His chest rose and fell as if the wings of a newly hatched butterfly slowly opening and closing. His appearance seemed peaceful enough for now, though Cheryl knew it was a facade: the left side of his upper chest, visible in the open neck of his hospital gown, heavily scarred, the result of a forceful collision between soft flesh and a solid object. Along with the injury to his head: a slight indentation on the left side of his temple showing an inter-cranial penetration, indication of a severe head-wound, now fully healed.

The cause of his injury was unknown, though Cheryl was determined to reveal it in time by use of her innovative technology in a carefully designed double-blind study with the subject's identity and cause of injuries erased. If successful, she'd be able to prove her technology would work under the most adverse conditions, before releasing it for widespread use.

There was a soft knock on the door, followed by Isaac, having to duck his head as he entered with a nod of greeting, his huge hands at his side, a clipboard held between thick fingers. He went over and leaned forward, gently opening one of the supine man's eyelids, angling his head to check on dilation. "Our guest seems to have settled in okay. Appears to be responsive."

Cheryl nodded; arms crossed on her chest. "He's a perfect candidate, the selection requirements having been *very* specific."

"Then we can start the calibration sequencing today?"

"Yes."

Isaac nodded. "I'll go summon the orderlies."

Cheryl stopped him with a raised hand. "There are to be no outside influences *this* time. No other voices, vibrations, or even thoughts, other than our own."

The large man angled his head, staring at Cheryl. "Eliminating any chance of unintentional informational exchange between—" Isaac smirked. "Our uniformed overlord and his superiors."

Cheryl frowned. "Don't—call him that. The major seems okay. And the military's been *more* than generous in supporting my research."

"Because they're eager to use your solution to their *own* ends."

"As is their *right*." Cheryl looked at Isaac, knowing he'd always had her back in arguments with close-minded bureaucrats, moving to stand beside her when he sensed she was about to lose control, looming over them, proving himself an immutable force of nature, one she'd leaned on in times of trembling frustration at the shortsightedness common in such people. "We're doing important work here, no matter the source of investment or potential for misuse. *Important* work, Isaac—intended to help hundreds of people suffering from PTSD, and those who—"

"*Thousands*, boss." Isaac gave her a solemn look. "More of them coming along, every day."

Cheryl looked down at the comatose man's face, his life altered by what had happened to him, with injuries beyond measure of blood, bone, and flesh. She knew if she were going to provide him a pathway back, it would require continued support from those who may have been responsible for sending him to wherever he'd been and was now unable to return from.

Isaac looked at her, able to see her unspoken thoughts, ones that mirrored his own. He lowered his voice. "Then we begin. Again."

Cheryl nodded, forcing a confident tone. "Yes, Isaac. We do."

CHAPTER TWO

LAB, RESEARCH FACILITY, MARYLAND

Patient

It was sunny. He could feel a gentle brush of warmth on his exposed skin, along with the scent of sand and salt with a hint of a breeze. The keening cry of gulls and gentle wash of waves mixed with the laughter of children calling out in joy-filled chorus from somewhere long ago and far away. Tears fell from his closed eyes, trailing down cheeks raised in a grimace. Waiting, waiting for the inevitable throb of jagged pain as glass-edged memories rose in waves of countless needles, sharp, jagged pieces lurking somewhere in the shadows, harsh reminders of flayed flesh. Everything he loved, siphoned away, leaving behind an endless scream as he fell into the depths of a bottomless well of immeasurable loss.

There was a sudden shift. Thoughts pulled into a vortex of swirling sounds, images, and feelings. His father calling to him. A familiar voice, released from the folded strands of memory. Added to a handful of other voices in wax and wane, drifting in and out of the eternal fog of his thoughts. "Catch it, son."

Green color flooded his senses as a half-cut lime landed in his hands. Followed by the tart-sharp flavor as he took a bite, scalding his taste buds with an acidic onslaught. His throat constricting, trying to refuse the intrusion, rejecting the assault. Succeeding as green slowly faded away, replaced by orange.

Calming and reassuring. Reminiscent of an endless summer day spent with his grandfather in vast groves of fruit trees. A freshly picked globe of gold kissed by weeks of sunshine. The thick skin ripped apart. Lips opening. A gush of juice as warm pulp was crushed between his teeth, releasing sweet and sour. Gone.

Replaced by brown. The scent of wet dirt. Loamy, black, and rich. Fertile, pungent, with the scent of peaty decay, a delicious fragrance to a gardener's nose. The smell of ripe potential, waiting press of seed, spill of water, stroke of sunlight's gentle hand. And time. Then he heard a plaintive bleat of lamb, in chorus with the croaking saw of ravens. Whinnying notes of greeting from a horse. Angry bark from a startled dog. Crunch of gravel, his father home, toss and laughter, hug and teasing words, hand in hand crossing to an open door and the yeasty scent of baking bread. Lemonade, ice-cold in a sweating glass. Biting, acrid overlain with achingly sweet. Back home once more.

Though he knew it for the lie it was, his childhood centered inside a mansion dungeon. Private schools. Carefully screened friends and endless exhibitions underneath the thumb and watchful eyes of parents eager to use him to further their own ambitions. He allowed the charade to continue, prepared to leap away, back to the sandy shore where he'd been plucked from. Back into the bottomless sea. Away.

Isaac shook his head, staring at one of several large high-definition monitors. "He's responding at the upper end of the spectrum, well above nominal baseline parameters." He spun in his chair, waving his hand at the screen, freezing the display. "Hitting on *all* targets. The fidelity is—beyond excellent. You can almost see the images, even in the raw data. Even through the background noise."

Cheryl nodded. "Agreed. Bring him out."

Isaac stared back. "*Really?* He's stable. Not even close to—" Noting the expression in Cheryl's eyes he reached over, tapping a key, reducing the signal strength until it zeroed out.

Cheryl leaned back against the edge of her desk, hands on the surface, supporting her as she considered the results of the first calibration effort.

"We've collected enough information for now to establish his basal response rate *and* get a measure of internalized perception to external stimuli. We'll assess the data streams, then move ahead again—after we see how quickly he recovers. How fast his mental patterns settle out."

"Yeah." Isaac shifted his immense weight in the over-sized office chair he was sitting in. "I get that, but you've got to admit—he's gonna be a perfect candidate for Tee-Cee therapy." He angled his head. "Right?"

Cheryl frowned, hating the term used by her earlier team for the unique piece of technology she'd spent a large part of her professional life developing. The basic structure, referred to by the diverse group of developmental engineers she'd worked with over the years as a 'thinking cap', was fabricated from multiple layers of silicon, seeded with thousands of wireless sensors of her own design, creating a flexible array. The inch-thick membrane contained pathways for a conductive gel that circulated through the interior, helping to cool and power each tiny sensor, the signals collected by dozens of wafer-thin receiver blocks positioned along the outside surface.

"He seems to be, Isaac—so far. But we've seen that go to heck in a hand-cart when pushing ahead too quickly, knowing *who* the patient was, along with their personal history. Which we purposely don't know—this time."

Isaac shrugged. "So, it's slow and methodical that wins the race."

Cheryl nodded, an uneasy feeling crawling up her spine. "For now."

He was aware of vibrations striking the outer layer of his senses like distant rumbles of thunder, resonating deep inside his mind. Instinct urged him to flee as the clamor of footsteps approached, the sound rising to a volume his physical ears could detect. Not enough information available to inform where to run to, or from what. As if something had suddenly sprung from the edge of woods alongside a wilderness trail. Creating a need to escape, feeling the pressure of an intense focus, his heartbeat racing, his breath a sawing gasp as he spun away. A compressive force wrapped around his chest as the unknown predator leaped, responding to his attempt to evade. A blossoming memory of a father

lurching through the door, alcohol breath on his age-thickened face, holding him.
Tightly. Too tightly. His body reacting, eyes fluttering as he sought to get away!

Isaac clamped his arms around the patient, a much smaller man, barely able to hold him in place, surprised at the strength in his thin body. He looked over at Cheryl, mouthing an apology, his metal clipboard having dropped on the tile floor, the noise creating an instant reaction in the semi-comatose man. A monitor posed above the chair was displaying a jagged line highlighted in red, sign of the patient's extreme anxiety.

"*Release him!*" Cheryl ran over, putting her hand on Isaac's arm. "Keep him from hurting himself—but *let* him go. He's *fighting* you! Fighting your embrace."

Isaac released the patient's arms, his cheek struck by a flailing fist. He ignored the blow, watching to make certain the panicked man didn't fall out of the reclined seat, no armrests or side rails in place to keep him from hitting the floor. Cheryl glanced at the readings on the bio-monitor, watching as they shifted from bright red through amber, then fading to rose, before falling back into a dark green. His emotional readings remained high, though his physical responses were returning to normal, his body no longer in panic mode. "He's already finding his way out of it."

Isaac straightened up, face bright red with embarrassment. "The same way a professional soldier would behave."

"Perhaps." Cheryl let out a deep breath. "First responders have the *same* capacity for rapid absorption of stress." She paused, her lips drawn into a compressed line. "Not the way I'd have chosen to establish—"

"I already said I'm sorry." Isaac reached out and squeezed Cheryl's arm, then pulled away, watching as she brushed back a curl of hair dangling alongside one eye.

"I know, Isaac. It's just that we need to be *careful* with this one. His response rates and mental recovery times are impressive, but we don't know what he's been through. This could turn into a setback. One we simply *can't* afford."

Isaac shrugged. "It's already happened. We've collected vital data, even if it was outside of standard protocols." He pointed at the display. "And he's back to baseline again, just like a real pro." Isaac leaned over and gave the patient a pat on his shoulder. "Good boy, JD. You just earned yourself a gold star."

Cheryl frowned. "Personification of a subject is prejudicial to process." She looked at Isaac, noting the swelling on his cheek from where the subject had struck him. "Why are you so determined to identify him prematurely, considering where we are with—"

"You're right." Isaac shrugged. "An old habit from when I worked in rehab facilities. Makes it easier to relate to people in vegetative states by talking to them as if they understand." He lowered his voice. "One I'll be careful to avoid in the future."

Cheryl shook her head. "It's fine, Isaac. *Really*. And I understand the benefit of talking to people in that condition. Believe me." She paused, reflecting on a memory of watching her brother's face, head swaddled in bandages, eyes open, staring at the ceiling while she rambled on about one thing going on in her life or another, hoping for a flicker of response. "But it's imperative we maintain *strict* adherence to the protocols I submitted to the oversight board." She bent down, touching the subject on his cheek, checking for a response. There was none, his expression fixed, eyes staring at something only he could see, blinking every few seconds. "We should move him back to his room, then review the data and put together an incident report."

"For immediate submittal?" Isaac looked at Cheryl, concern in his eyes.

"No." She pursed her lips. "I can hold off for now. No need to send anything to the major, *yet*, though we will have to include it in the weekly briefing."

Isaac eased the Tee-Cee from JD's head, noting the swelling on the side of his frontal lobe had decreased somewhat over the past few days. He hung the cap on one of the support arms framing the top of the chair, then slid his arm under the man's shoulders, helping him to sit up. "He's more mobile now. Glad you decided to take him off the sedatives."

"Don't really need them. Not in here." Cheryl leaned back; her voice focused. "The staff at the rehab facility, or wherever they gathered him up from, would've been required to administer them, due to him presenting with mesencephalic kinetic mutism, along with elements of dis-inhibition because of the severe damage to his frontal lobe."

"Enough with the mumbo-jumbo, boss lady." Isaac shook his head, looking at Cheryl with a grin. "And call him *JD*. We're gonna be spending enough time with him, and it won't affect the data if we normalize the relationship. At least a little."

Cheryl sighed. "*JD* has the typical symptom tree, though he's more mobile than most cases, along with an ability to perform basic exercise programs, which explains his retention of muscle tone, helping him stay healthy."

Isaac smiled, enjoying it when Cheryl used any one of the half-dozen doctorates earned by the time she was in her early thirties. He lowered his voice, speaking in a serious tone. "I concur, Doctor Atkinson. Your assessment is spot on. He's the perfect test subject. Especially since I will not be needing to change his sheets, or spoon feed him." Isaac reached out and touched JD on the shoulder. "Good little *lab-rat*."

Cheryl shook her head, trying not to smile. "And how is *that* helpful in normalizing—"

"Just good-natured ribbing, Doc. Encouraging an environment of comradery." Isaac pointed at the large scar on JD's upper shoulder. "It's obvious he's seen action. It follows he'd be used to a little bantering with his buddies."

Cheryl crossed her arms, her face in a serious pose. "*Nothing* is obvious, Isaac. There's a host of explanations for his injuries, whether from exposure to combat or from any of a hundred other causes." She watched as Isaac led JD back to room one, appreciative of his easygoing, effortless way of engaging with patients, the much larger man holding JD's shoulder, patiently guiding him as he shuffled away. It was one of many reasons she'd asked him to stay on, his limitless empathy. Another being that he reminded her of her brother Robert, who'd been nearly as tall, though much leaner, with a deep, resonating voice.

Cheryl smiled, recalling her older brother's good-natured manner. Robert had been a real outdoorsman, and an extremely gifted climber. Left wasting away, his active mind trapped in a comatose state caused by a traumatic head injury suffered while climbing a new route. She'd spent two years at his bedside, watching as her older sibling's strong, wiry frame slowly dissolved away to little more than a sheet of flaccid skin draped over a framework of bony sticks, housing what little remained of her brother, He'd been seven years older, always tossing her high into the air, catching her every time without fail. Cheryl looking down, sighing, wishing she'd been there to do the same for him.

CHAPTER THREE

MILITARY FACILITY, LAB, MARYLAND

Cheryl

Cheryl stabbed a finger at her keyboard, making a change to her program. "Shoot! Looks like we're losing him. Again!" She slammed her hand on top of a wide desk, causing her keyboard to bounce away. "Darn it!" A whirl of auburn hair, cut mid length and curly, swept across the corner of her cheek. Her eyes, hazel-green, glared at JD, resting comfortably in his chair a few feet away. "What the fudge is he hiding from?"

"You mean—fuck?" Isaac sat in his chair, the frame creaking with his every move, doing its best to contain his massive frame. His skin, perfectly white, looked like a color swab of Chantilly lace held up to the harsh light of fluorescent fixtures lining the ceiling of the lab. "And what makes you think our friend is hiding?"

"Because I do, that's why." Cheryl let a part of her anger drain away, exasperation rushing in to fill the void. "All we're trying to do is help him find his way back. If he'd only let us!" She went over and leaned down, studying JD's face, his body loosely strapped into a dental chair, with several modifications made.

She rested one hand on an articulated arm holding an instrument package positioned to one side of his head, staring at its beady green lights, blinking away. Cheryl knew it was sending gigabytes of data over a fiber-optic cable into a large server bank, humming away along the wall of the lab, digesting rivers of data being collected. Her unique program, even more innovative than the Tee-Cee, was hard at work teasing out the images, along with JD's thoughts and emotions, helping to paint hundreds of high-definition electronic patterns per second onto several monitors, revealing what their patient was seeing, feeling, touching, or being touched by.

She lowered her head, staring into his dark eyes as he blinked, every few seconds, her own eyes narrowed in concentration, her voice low. "Why are you fighting us?"

"You. Not us."

Cheryl, still leaning over JD, turned her head. "Yeah, Isaac. Just me." She straightened up, hands on her slim hips, firing off a glare, watching as it bounced off his stoic expression. "Like you're not as eager as I am to get inside his head and—"

"Nope. Not in the least." Isaac lifted one hand, inspecting the cuticles of his thick fingers, using an edge of a thumbnail to push them back. "If JD wants to be left alone, I'm all for doing that. Let him figure it out for himself—if he even wants to come back."

"Oh, come on." Cheryl straightened up. "You're not immune from curiosity. No one is. Not if they're working with a full set of emotions."

Isaac held up one hand, squinting his eyes, inspecting his handiwork. "Didn't say I wasn't curious. Just not enough to force open the door. Not when there's someone standing on the other side, trying to keep it closed."

Cheryl frowned, her lips forming a pout, which elicited a grin from Isaac, who never grew tired of watching her work through a problem, her face expressing every one of her many moods. None of them hidden from view, not while she was in the lab. Her ever-active mind driving her in a blur between multiple keyboards, as if a skilled pianist playing songs on them no one else could hear, or even imagine. Changing her innovative code on the fly, bypassing every standard of practice sacrosanct to programmers the world over: save, change, test, then save again, mindful of the need to protect the master code, preventing introduction of errors or omissions from fumbling fingers, coffee spills, or keyboards flung across the room in exasperation.

"Maybe we should break for the day." Isaac checked the clock on the wall, neither of them bothering to wear watches. "The evening, I mean—seeing it's just hitting six."

Cheryl glanced up, verifying how late it had gotten, knowing she'd upset a good friend. Again. "Fudge!"

There were plenty of empty booths in the restaurant, most of the patrons seated at a long bar, their focus locked to multiple television screens hanging from the ceiling, voices rising and falling in time with events happening on bright green playing fields in a city far away.

Laura stared at her watch, its dial a picture of a small rodent, one-half of a famous duo popular with children back when she'd still been one. The eyes smiled back, gloved hands pointing to late, again. Her cousin Cheryl was overdue, never on time, Laura knowing she'd arrive with a flurry of apologies and explanations. It had always been the same, ever since the two of them had been old enough to make plans to meet up.

They'd grown up in central New Hampshire, their families' homes tied together by a trail through thick woods serving as a thoroughfare for bikes, sneakers, or bare feet in summer. Clad in boots, snowshoes, or cross-country skis in winter. The two of them were as close as sisters, bound by a rubber band stretched thin at times by Cheryl, her restless mind shifting on impulse as she stopped to consider one odd thought or another, found along the pathway. Laura having to abide the frequent delays to their plans, sighing heavily—as she was doing now.

"I'm sorry." Cheryl slid into the booth. "I got caught up with something. No excuse, I know, but I'm here now. Have you ordered?" Cheryl put her purse on the table, reaching for a menu.

Laura pointed to a glass holding a drink with a small paper umbrella tucked into the crushed ice. "Your usual. I ordered it as soon as I saw you pull into the parking lot. The server brought it over while you were still deciding where to park, driving around like a dog spinning in circles before finally plopping down."

"OCD. Just one of my idiosyncrasies." Cheryl reached for the drink, removed the decorative adornment, and took a healthy swallow. "Or idiot-syncrasies, like you always called them."

Laura shrugged, sipping her drink, watching her cousin from over its rim, a pale blue paper umbrella centered between her eyes. She lowered her glass. "I was only pointing out how foolish it was, people always trying to identify you by—"

Cheryl reached over and touched the back of Laura's hand. "I know. I was just making a poor joke. Out of my being pistachio'd off, for having let you down." She paused. "Again."

"You've never done that, Cheryl." Laura leaned forward. "You've never let anyone down."

Cheryl pulled her hand away, then picked up her drink and took another healthy sip, enjoying the sour taste, along with the lingering twist of tequila as it slid along the surface of her tongue. It was the perfect medicine for what had turned out to be a frustrating day, JD proving to be elusive, staying hidden in the shadows, refusing to come into the light. She knew something was keeping him there, like a wounded animal in a dark cave, wishing to be left alone.

Her frustration had built up into a need for physical release, how she'd dealt with her emotions since childhood. By running, leaping, and climbing anything taller than herself to help combat the chaos of twisting thoughts and spinning images sleeting through her mind, morning, noon, and night. Populating her dreams with vibrant, richly colored worlds of rocks, trees, and granite walls, climbed with ease before leaping from their tops, swooping through the air, arms outspread as she landed in a laughing rush into the waiting arms of her brother, always there to gather her in. Every time, without fail.

Until he wasn't. Injured during an ascent of a virgin climbing route, his helmet removed to adjust its strap, his head slammed by a falling rock, left with a flap of torn skin hanging from his shattered skull, a concave dent leaving him pinned in a hospital bed in critical condition. Her parents had moved him to a long-term-care facility out of state, then moved him again to a nursing home in the town they lived in. Robert ending up in a bed on the ground level, his eyes blinking slowly when Cheryl made twice-daily visitations during the week, speaking to him non-stop in quiet desperation, hoping he would wake up and tell her to be quiet. That it was his turn to tell her stories, soothing her active mind, her small hand in his as his deep voice lulled her off to sleep.

She spent weeks, then months regaling him with adventures of the two of them, far away, climbing impossibly high mountains with mystical names in mythical places. Pretending she could hear his voice, his laughter rumbling in her ears. Memories of his muscular arms hugging her once again as she reached the top of the ledge he was standing on, telling her she was as good a climber as him. Better, her young life filled with countless dreams yet to come true as she waited for him to wake up. Willing to wait for as long as it would take. Waiting until people with no imaginations yanked him away, seeing only the body and not the mind. Leaving her to fall out of her dreams, landing with a thud on a cold bedroom floor, lying in a puddle of tears with a bruised head. Just like his.

Laura could see her cousin had slipped away, again, back to where her brother had lain for so many months. She reached over and took her hand, squeezing it slightly, then letting go. "You didn't let Robert down, Cheryl. There was nothing you could have done. It was their decision. Your parents." She leaned back. "Robert was a wonderful brother to you. An incredible brother, but—" She paused, knowing the pain her cousin had gone through. "He was their son, forcing an impossible choice on them to have to make. I'm sure you can see that by now."

"No. I can't." Cheryl stared at her cousin. "They let him die, giving that bastard permission to pull the plug." She took in a deep breath, then released it in a burst of anger. "They gave up on Robert." She leaned back in her seat, arms crossed, shaking her head. "And when they did that—they lost him. They lost us both!"

JD

Now....

He was back in balance, the surface of his mind no longer being probed, left free to roam the corridors of his interior world, opening doors to multiple lives where he was in control. Each of them holding fragments of his thoughts, memories, and reflections of people he'd met throughout his life. Loving one of them more than all the rest. Cherished. A light in the darkness that had helped guide him out of a labyrinth of multiple addictions, providing a protective web of fresh memories, experiences, along with an enduring love.

One kept safely locked away, unwilling to allow himself to be dragged back into memories of the life they'd shared, fleeing in dark despair, his soul shriveled by pain. Wanting the comforting oblivion only death could provide. Saved, by people offering themselves as friends, companions, and guides, helping him find a measure of balance again. Seeking it, needing it, wanting it. Making a slow journey back to his former self, his will to live regained, then taken away by a large shadow of a man with a damaged soul, lashing out in misplaced love, placing him in the prison of a damaged mind.

He fled the light, swimming deeper into the abyss, releasing himself into a world where he could find what he craved: a place filled with stories. Other people's stories, now made into his own. Altered. Added to. Belonging only to him.

CHAPTER FOUR

SOUTHWEST DESERT, CALIFORNIA.

Twain's Story

The sun was a slab of heated iron on Twain's skin, searing his thick neck and shoulders with its relentless touch. He squinted, eyes closed to slits, peering to see if the rifle shot had been true. A last second gust of wind had twitched the image in the scope, causing the crosshair to flutter up and to the right with the jolt of recoil against his shoulder, followed by the sight of the target falling away from view, over three hundred paces away.

A small outcrop of tumbled rocks was shielding his primary target now, the shorter of the two men who'd been arguing, their lips moving silently in the scope while they had a heated discussion, ending with a sudden exchange of close-range gunfire. The taller man down, having lost the draw, leaving the other smiling in victory until hit somewhere in the chest by the long-distance shot. Now lying dead, or still alive waiting below, looking to return fire at his unseen assailant.

Twain was close to the end of a six-month long pursuit of the men responsible for having taken something from him that could never be replaced: a pregnant daughter and her husband caught up in the chaos of a back-street suburban shootout between rival gangs. Three innocent victims knocked from the false perch of their carefully planned lives by a racing vehicle that had forced them off the road, their car striking a tree head on.

A large red German Shepherd huddled at Twain's feet, lying in a thin slice of shadow, looked up at him, pink tongue lolling between white canines, panting but alert. It tasted the air with its nostrils, with nothing untoward to report, its tail slowly wagging as Twain slid down from his firing position and joined the large animal behind a shelf of sandstone.

Twain leaned against its surface, feeling its warmth through the thin shirt he was wearing, matching the color of sand and sun-bleached rocks in the hills surrounding the meeting place below. The hat he had on was the same color, pulled low, helping to reduce his profile as he'd lain in wait on the windswept ridge. He knew he had to move. His quarry was an experienced killer and could have marked his location by measuring the time between hiss of passing round and delayed sound of the shot if he'd missed. Though there was little concern if the bullet had struck anywhere in the man's upper chest: his target not long for the world.

With a frown of concern on his face, Twain started working his way down from the rock lined ridge, the dog staying close to his heels as he used a narrow defile in the surface of broken ground to circle around, making his approach to the target from the opposite side. When he reached the edge of the killing zone, he stayed behind a line of large rocks and used a small mirror, held out with his left hand, inspecting the thick-set body of the stocky man lying on the ground, eyes open, pointing up at a sky he could no longer see. The other combatant, a slim Anglo man with graying hair, was lying against a boulder a few yards away, hands clenched against his upper chest, air leaking out of a punctured lung in a shallow wheeze.

Twain knew the wound would prove lethal if left untreated. Time enough to worry about that later, he told himself, using a large canteen to re-hydrate himself and the dog. As for the wounded man, Twain noted the bunch of loose fabric in his lap, a potential hiding spot for a pistol that prevented a safe approach. He twisted the cap of the canteen back in place, then called out, his rough-toned voice breaking the silence. "I have water." He paused. "You'll have to manage it by yourself."

When there was no answer, Twain moved to the opposite end of the boulders then risked a quick glance. The man was staring back, blood seeping from one corner of his mouth. His right hand fluttered, signaling acceptance of the offer. Twain tossed him the canteen, watching as it landed just out of the man's reach. "*Fuck.*" He looked at the shepherd. "Go and take it to him, boy."

The large animal stood up and moved around the end of the pile, head and tail held low. Moving with caution, aware of his owner's concern. It grabbed the strap and slunk forward, dropping it into the man's outstretched hand, then backing away. Twain's eyes focused on the slow movement of the man's free hand as he worked the cover open and lifted the canteen to his mouth, taking a drink, coughing, water-thinned blood pulsing from the corner of his mouth.

"Thanks." The word took two tries to come clear. "Wish it—were booze" A slight pause followed as the man took in a rasping breath. Twain smiled, then leaned out, counting on the dog to growl a warning if needed. "You must be wearing a vest."

"Yeah." There was another bout of guttural coughing before the pinched voice called back. "It slowed the round down. Kept it from—" Silence followed. Twain stood up, pistol in his hand as he stepped around the rocks, eyes on the wounded man who was staring straight ahead, chest barely moving. He started over to him, stopping when a sharp voice cut through the air.

"*Cut*! God *damn* it! Mother *effing* son of a *bitch*!" A tall, thin man rose from his seat beneath an awning set off to one side of the rock pile. He threw a clipboard through the air, pages fluttering as it sailed end over end, landing a few feet from the dog, back arched as it took a huge dump in the middle of the shot. The director, a skinny man in his late thirties and normally even mannered, looked around, face beet red, hands clenched in anger. "Where the *fuck* is the *fucking* handler?"

Twain patted his leg, calling the shepherd over, who was looking around, unaware of having caused all the excitement. It sat down beside him, then licked his hand, used to being at his side for hours at a time during the past two days of shooting. The two of them watched as the director stomped his way across the set, eyes fixed on a large, thick shouldered man with a cell phone pressed to one ear, leaning against one of a dozen or more portable generators.

The other actor signaled for water and a sunshade to be brought over. Twain and the dog joined him beneath it, leaning back as the stagehands arranged protection from the bright noon-day light.

"Wonder if they'll keep the set hot." James mumbled the question, his face angled up, a make-up girl cleaning the fake blood from his mouth and chin. She shrugged, an intense look on her face as she daubed away. "We still have plenty of light—but Phil sounds pissed!"

Loud shouting echoed from the edge of a roped-off section of desert located two hours from the L.A. basin. The director was in the handler's face, leaning in while three security men held his arms, trying to keep the situation from becoming physical. They failed, the heavily muscled dog handler swinging a fist, hitting one of the security men in the side of his eye. A scrum ensued, the director standing back, smiling as the three men picked the handler up, hauling him away toward the car lot. The unscripted scene played out in front of half a hundred people. And one curious dog.

"What's his name?" The makeup girl looked over at Twain, her face clear skinned.

"The handler? I don't really know him."

"No. I mean your dog."

Twain glanced at the animal, its tail wagging, stirring the dirt. "No idea. He's not mine. More of an acquaintance."

The three of them looked over, watching the security team return, one rubbing his eye, scowling, while the other two were laughing. They walked over to the director and started to fill him in when a loud racing sound came from the car lot, followed by a crunch of metal and the sound of broken glass, causing everyone to look in that direction.

"What the hell was that?" Twain stretched his neck, trying to see through a cloud of dust rising in the lot. James chuckled. "It sounded like a pickup truck—running into a Lamborghini."

The security men started sprinting toward the sound, followed by the director and a handful of assistants. The make-up girl packed up her case and went over to where the rest of the support crew were milling around.

"So—about your dog." James nodded. "He'll need a name. You decided what you're gonna call him?"

Twain shook his head. "I don't have a clue. Besides—he's not mine."

"Does he know that? Seems happy enough, sitting there beside you."

Twain looked down at the dog. It leaned forward, nosing his hand as he scratched it between the ears. "I guess I could look after him—at least until his owner comes back looking for him."

CHAPTER FIVE

PARKING LOT, MID-COAST MAINE

Calvin's Story

A large red shepherd with a thick glossy coat kept nosing Calvin's closed hand, trying to work a small dog-biscuit free, using just enough pressure with its large canines to cause some measure of discomfort. Calvin pulled his hand away. "Knock it *off*. You'll get it when we reach the truck." He shifted a large bag of dogfood he was carrying to one arm, his fingers slipping into his pocket to retrieve the key to his old, rust stained Ford truck.

"Nice looking dog."

Calvin glanced over, watching as a young woman stepped out from behind a newer model Toyota Tacoma, her narrow face lined with a smile, a smudge of dust on one cheek, hair pulled back in a thick braid. Her vehicle, covered in a layer of dried mud, sported a drop-down trailer hitch slung beneath a local license plate: agriculture issue. She was of an age to him, wearing close-fitting jeans and an untucked flannel shirt showing signs of having met with long hours of hard work.

The shepherd perked its ears forward, tail wagging. Calvin looked down. "Don't let it go to your head." He shifted the bag of dry food, setting it down as she came over.

"Is it okay to pet—" She hesitated, glancing at the animal's hindquarters. "Him?"

"Sure. As far as I know. He seems friendly enough—with most people."

"Hey there, big guy." She knelt, taking the dog's head between her hands, fingers rubbing the base of his ears as she stared into his eyes. "As far as you *know*?" She paused, looking up, her eyes amber brown, a close match to the shepherds. "He's *yours*, right?"

Calvin shrugged. "For now, I guess. He showed up at my place a couple of weeks ago. I put some fliers out. No one's stopped by, able to make a legitimate claim to him."

She returned to rubbing the dog's ears. "Surprised. A dog like this is gotta be worth a *butt-load* of money."

Calvin shrugged. "There were a couple of guys showed up a week ago, wanting to claim him. He growled when they approached, so I told 'em to shove off."

"What's his name?"

"Been calling him dog. Figured on using it until his rightful owner comes along."

"Hello, dog." The shepherd lifted one paw, waiting for her to take it. She looked up at Calvin again. "You can do better than *that*." She stared at the large canine, his tail wagging in response. "At least call him *Dawg*, with an A and W in the middle."

She stood up, holding out her hand. Calvin took it, noticing the close-cut fingernails along with several scratches on the back. "I'm Jemma. I bought a small farm a month ago—just down the road a bit. The one with a country store attached." She waited, her grip firm on his hand.

"I'm Calvin."

"Nice to meet you, Calvin. And you too, *Dawg*!" She released his hand. "Got to be going. I'll see you around, it being such a small town and all." Then she walked away, her long braid swinging in time with the swaying of her hips.

Calvin picked up the bag of dog food and dropped it in the bed of his truck. He opened the driver's side door, waited for the shepherd to jump in, then tossed him the biscuit, watching as he snatched it in midair. He climbed inside and started the truck, then looked over at the shepherd. "You all set—*Dawg?*" Getting a woof in reply, Calvin pulled out and drove away.

The music playing on an inexpensive CD player was a rich blend of acoustic guitar and raspy, bass toned vocals. Calvin stood in front of a small gas stove, stirring a pot of homemade stew, thick with chunks of venison from an autumn hunt the year before. He'd added fresh vegetables, home grown, harvested from a moderately sized garden out behind the house. It had been his aunt's home, left to him when she passed with no one in her immediate family making a claim against his ending up with it. Those with any axes to grind having slipped away to their final resting spots beneath upright slabs of granite, laid out in neat lines in a family plot nearby.

Calvin cocked his head, looking over at Dawg who was lying in the doorway of the small kitchen, nose between his paws, dark eyes watching every move he made. "You hungry?" The large dog wagged his tail but didn't bother sitting up, knowing it was only a tease. No venison allowed, ever. Only beef, along with chicken or pork.

A soft knock at the front door raised the shepherd's ears. Calvin heard it too. He frowned as he lowered the flame under a small, heavily dented metal pot, then motioned to Dawg, letting him know he should stay as he made his way down a narrow hallway and opened the door.

Jemma was standing there, about to knock again. She lowered her hand, smiling. "I knew you were here. Saw your truck in the driveway." She paused. "My neighbor told me where you live. I wanted to stop by and make you a proposition." She hesitated a moment. "A *business* proposition."

Calvin stepped back. "I have stew, heating on the stove. It's almost ready if you want to join me and—" He grinned. "Dawg."

Jemma pushed past him, heading along the corridor to where the shepherd was standing, tail wagging, thumping both sides of the narrow hallway.

"Hey there, *big boy!*" Calvin closed the door, then worked his way around the two of them, heading back into the small kitchen.

"It's venison stew. Not bad, if you don't mind the taste. A bit strong for some unless you've grown up eating it."

Jemma glanced over, her fingers working on the base of Dawg's ears. "Yours?"

Calvin considered for a moment. "You mean the deer? Yeah. A nice fat doe, taken out back last fall. She was feeding on the last of the Winesaps. They're an old strain of—"

"I know what they are." Jemma angled her head. "You couldn't have caught a *boy* one?"

Calvin grinned. "I could have taken a *buck*, but the local herd needs thinning." He shrugged, stirring the stew, releasing a waft of scent that swiveled the shepherd's head around, nosing the air. "Just doing my part to help balance things out."

"It smells *great*." Jemma stood up and came over, leaning against the counter, arms crossed, watching as Calvin set out another set of silverware and a chipped edge bowl. "I haven't eaten since morning. Been on the road all day." She watched as he sliced a loaf of homemade bread. "You're not the least bit curious about my proposal?"

Calvin grabbed two beers from the fridge. He looked over at Jemma, getting a nod, setting them down on the small kitchen table. "Figure you'll fill me in when you're ready. Besides—not sure I'd be able to *hear* you, over the sound your stomach's making. Even Dawg's getting nervous, what with all the growling going on."

The CD player began another run through of the music: the second time since they'd begun their meal. Jemma used a thick slice of homemade bread to daub up the last of the stew, grinning at Dawg who was watching her closely, head and tail lowered, a concerned look in his eyes. His tail fanned the air as Calvin went over and added a spoonful of gravy onto his evening meal, his nose diving into the mixture, eating it with gusto while the two of them washed, then rinsed the dishes, stacking them in a wooden rack to dry.

Once they finished, Jemma sat back down and leaned forward, her elbows on the small kitchen table, chin in her hands, enjoying a cool breeze slipping through a small window. She closed her eyes as it started to sweep the heat from the kitchen, listening to one of the songs that had caught her ear the first time it had played: a compelling ballad about life's uncertain path, exploring the twist and turns, choices made, and opportunities spurned. The bass notes and gravelly vocals clutching her heart.

Jemma opened her eyes and looked over at Calvin, who'd tilted his chair back, leaning against the kitchen counter. "Who is this?" She paused, the emotional lyrics causing her to sigh. "The singer?"

"Someone from the local area. Popular enough—before he died." Calvin leaned forward, the chair legs thumping the linoleum floor. "Coming up on twelve years now, end of the month." Dawg came over and sat down, his muzzle pressed into Calvin's lap, receiving a gentle rub of his neck and ears.

Jemma straightened up, her voice soft as she probed Calvin's quiet mood. "A friend, I take it—with you knowing the date."

"My cousin. Carl. With a big, bright future ahead of him. Loaded up with opportunities." Calvin looked away, his eyes measuring the angle of the setting sun, the sky glowing with golden light. "Just like in the song."

Jemma nodded, crossing her arms below her breasts, looking at Calvin with an expectant look. "So—what do you think?" Calvin swung his gaze back toward her, then looked down at Dawg, who stared back, mouth open, tongue dangling. "About your proposal?"

"My offer." Jemma grinned. "Well?"

Calvin shrugged, considering what she'd asked him earlier, her words squeezed around mouthfuls of stew while she told him of her plans for the property she'd bought, asking if he'd be willing to drop by her place and help her decide what to tear down and what might be worth trying to save. Her plan: to modernize the farmhouse and store, turning it back into a fully functioning business again. Calvin hesitated, of two minds about what she was asking him to do. Willing to help with the design and planning, but reluctant to take on any of the work, with a dozen older couples around town needing his help to get them through the winter. Putting in wood. Making minor repairs to roofs. Driveways to be plowed, walkways shoveled, and the like. Along with flues that needed cleaning and groceries picked up in foul weather.

Jemma grinned, her perfect teeth a gleam of white in the dimmed light of the kitchen, framed by full lips. "You're interested. I can tell."

"I am." Calvin met her grin with one of his own, a rare occurrence over the past few years. "I'll be short on hours—for any work needing to be done."

Jemma shook her head, having undone her braid before sitting down to eat. She ran her fingers through it, leaving it hanging over her shoulders, catching the glow of the setting sun, twists of red and gold highlights running through a sea of dark brown. "I have all the help I need. I'm interested in getting ideas on the best way to move ahead." She tilted her head, the movement causing the ends of her hair to brush the front of her shirt, top two buttons undone, catching Calvin's eye. "And you're the person everyone says I should be talking to." She leaned back, the tip of her tongue revealed between her teeth, curls of hair framing her high cheekbones. "So, are you in—or out? With me being one of those opportunities spurned, like in the song your cousin was just singing?"

CHAPTER SIX

COMPANY HOUSE, MARYLAND

Jared's Story

Jared sat his suitcase down, taking a moment to look around the company house assigned to him. He was standing in a sunken living room with large ceiling to floor glass windows covering an entire wall. The curtains were open, revealing a spacious, fenced in lawn edged by hardwood trees and mixed shrubs, bordering a small forest.

He went over to the large windows and stared at a full moon rising over a small ridge that framed the backyard of the spacious house. It was a single-floor structure, laid out in a series of half-levels. There were two large bedrooms, along with a study and a large kitchen that opened into a dining and living room. It included a decent sized sunroom with a Jacuzzi, looking out over a small lap pool running along one end of the lawn, along with a two-car garage, attached to the main house by a side entrance, opening into a foyer. The house was sitting at the end of a long, winding driveway, part of a neighborhood dotted with comparable homes. Thin ribbons of paved sidewalks lined the edges of a wide, private road, perfect for biking, jogging, or walking. The development was gated, with an on-site security office, located in a rural area just outside the business district of Baltimore.

Jared changed into sweatpants and a work-out shirt, then went into the garage. He swung his leg over the seat of a rented bicycle, intending to go for a quick ride around the local area. He hesitated, a dark shape materializing from the shrubs lining the walkway, heading towards him, forcing him to let go of the bike to free his hands while backing away. Then he stopped, recognizing it was a dog. A large dog with a pronounced limp, its head hanging, tail wagging, as low whimpering notes slipped through the evening air.

"'He's going to be okay. Hindquarter bruised up some, but the x-ray didn't show anything's broken. He's lucky—most likely hit by a car." The elderly veterinarian cocked his head to one side, his hand resting on the injured dog's shoulder. "His front paw will be sore, but the toes will heal soon enough." He gave Jared a satisfied smile. "He's young and healthy, other than having missed a few meals."

Jared looked at the vet. "What about shots? I understand there's a risk of—"

The vet's smile widened. "I gave him a full set of boosters. He's a purebred, not some stray left to roam the streets. *Someone* owns him." He paused, looking at the dog, rubbing his neck. "I'm surprised there's no chip."

"In his tooth?" Jared eyes narrowed, wondering about the cost of dental work for a dog.

The vet grinned, shaking his head. "No. In his *neck*. To identify him. I mean—he had to cost a thousand dollars or more, *minimum*, when a pup. Chip's a standard practice with these kinds of dogs, in case they get stolen or go missing—like this big guy did. His owners will be along shortly to gather him up once they know where he is."

Jared nodded, a relieved look on his face. He'd never had pets and knew nothing about caring for them. "So—you'll be keeping him *here*."

"There's no need. The x-ray shows he's fine. Just feed him the food I'll give you and make sure he gets plenty of water. And be sure to check his stool tomorrow, or whenever he has a bowel movement. If you see any red spots, especially *dark* red spots, call me before bringing him in. And grab the sample. Use a baggie turned inside out. Or a zip lock if you have any."

Jared's voice wavered. "I—don't have time to deal with this." He saw a frown developing on the vet's face. "I mean, I need to get supplies. Put out notices. I just moved into the area, so—"

"You can't leave him here. Sorry. You can take him to a shelter in the morning. I'll give you the address of one." The veterinarian stared at him; his words having lost their former warmth. "I'm sure they'll be happy to take him off your hands."

Jared raised his hands, palms out. "It's okay. I'll keep him with me. I'm only trying to get up to speed, that's all. It's the last thing I was expecting to have to deal with tonight."

"The dog too, I imagine." The vet shook his head, mild disapproval still showing on his face. Jared looked at the dog, who stared back, eyes dull from exhaustion and stress. He nodded. "Yes. For him, too."

The shepherd held its injured paw in the air, whining as it waited for Jared to open the door, wanting to come inside and get the treat held in his hand. A smile tightened the corners of Jared's lips as he regarded the large animal. Its paw had healed over the past week, allowing for the speedy chase of any gray squirrels foolish enough to come into the enclosed yard. None caught to date, though the small rodents had learned to be alert when trespassing on the dog's domain.

Jared opened the door, the dog limping in, head down, a whimper in its throat. Jared grinned, holding the treat behind his back. "You're a real actor, pretending to be hurt, looking for sympathy." He looked at the animal, meeting its steady gaze. "I'm not blind. I watched you chasing those squirrels all over the place. No problem with your paw then."

He held out his hand, the treat pulled from his palm by the flick of a warm tongue. "And still no response to the flyers I put out at the guard shack." He reached out and ran his hand along its back. "Your owner's not looking too hard for ya. Not if they're living in the neighborhood."

The dog nosed his hand, looking for another treat. Jared rubbed him between his ears, following the advice of the veterinarian's office manager who'd told him to talk to it, giving him plenty of attention, as shepherds could be a handful if not properly entertained. "I'll have to look into running an ad in the local paper, I guess." Jared frowned, aware of the hassle that would ensue, with dozens of people making false claims of ownership, with the dog constantly stressed out until the rightful owners showed up. The large dog licked the back of his hand, then went over and curled up on the couch, ignoring its new bed. It picked up its favorite tooth-worn toy, chewing it, trying to make it squeak.

JD

Before

"Seriously?" She eyed the small office trailer, head angled to one side, hair done up in a careless twist, secured by a blue piece of frayed cloth. Her hazel-green eyes staring into his. Tall, a match to his own height, willowy in build. "What if we get caught?"

"No one's going to go in there, except us. Not my first time using one on remote shoots. Its small, but clean. Delivered an hour ago." He considered her reluctance, about to let her know it was his trailer. Wanting to avoid doing so, letting her think they might be found out, helping to heighten the excitement "I promise. No one will know."

She raised her eyebrows, a scar on the side of her face joining in the movement. It drew his eyes, along with every imperfection on her angular face. Along with her unkempt hair and misaligned teeth. Her rough-edged fingernails, trimmed to different lengths. She didn't wear make-up. Nothing to shield her skin from being seen or touched.

He reached out and touched it now, his need for her increased by every one of her perfect imperfections, as if beacon to a sailor lost at sea. A lost soul on a sinking ship, craving the arms of a sheltering cove, safely away from a storm-tossed sea. Craving her.

"Is it what you expected?" She wore a crooked smile, framing the edges of her unevenly spaced front teeth, her voice husky. It was hot in the trailer, the power not connected yet, the air-conditioner silent. Sweat beaded her forehead, her cheeks, neck, and chest. Beads of it dribbled down her exposed breasts as he traced their curves with his tongue.

"More." He felt himself falling, lost in her irregular beauty. He placed her hands on him, his on her. "More," he whispered, then shouted, her hand covering his mouth as he pressed against her body, her own a willing accomplice to the

assault. Losing himself again. No drug he'd ever taken, shoved in his nose, mouth, or injected inside of him could hope to match the joy of his shuddering release. Tears fell from his dark eyes, mingling with his sweat. Its salty taste in the corners of their mouths, pressed together in need. His, desperate. Hers, as smooth as the honeyed color of her sweat-beaded skin.

CHAPTER SEVEN

RESEARCH FACILITY, WASHINGTON D.C.

Cheryl

The screen showed a sea of red sand, with a turquoise sky, arced above an orange-red ball of light, sinking behind a blurred horizon as the approach of dusk formed shadows across the desert floor. Twisted roots of sun-bleached trees were poised along the sides, angled down, as if reaching out to grab small white rocks.

"It's *breathtaking*." Cheryl grabbed a screen shot, adding it to a file she'd set up. Isaac stared at her, shaking his head, his bald head reflecting the overhead lights of the lab.

"Why are you doing that? Everything's going into the database."

"It's a work of art, you *philistine*. No different from any other, whether created from his memory, or by a brush. It's still incredible—the blending of colors and textures."

Isaac leaned in, studying the image. "Looks like any of a dozen or more I've seen him do. And you promised to call him JD."

Cheryl ignored him, her fingers flying across the keyboard on the terminal. The resolution wavered, then sharpened as the imaging program manipulated the stream of data coming from the man lying in the chair a few feet away. Isaac frowned. "You shouldn't make changes like that. Not live. There's a good chance of corrupting the base code."

"*You* shouldn't. But *I* can." She glanced at him, sensing his mood was off. "Are you okay?"

"I'm fine. Had hoped to get things moving, that's all." Isaac shrugged. "Wonder how many more levels we're going to need to wade through before we get to the core. *His* core."

Cheryl grinned, a bead of sweat dropping to the end of her pert nose. "You mean JD's core?" She stepped away from the desk. "It's intriguing—the complexity of what he's showing us. As if he's trying to hide from reality by creating diversions. Mental projections." She hesitated, biting her lower lip. "Like he knows we're trying to break through to him and is showing us—" She pointed at the screenshot. "Things like this, trying to throw us off his trail."

Isaac shrugged, then muttered something under his breath as he turned and walked away.

Major Kelly studied the report, printed out in single-spaced lines of text covering three sheets of paper, front and back. He reached up, adjusting a lamp on his desk. "Three possibilities?"

Yes."

"Are you certain that's *all* of them?"

Cheryl waited a moment, looking at the older man, his back ramrod straight, sitting forward in his chair. "There are only *three*. No more—or less." She paused. "As I stated in my report."

Jean sniffed, marking her irritated tone, then nodded as he initialed each page, signing the last one, placing the report on his desk, a desert of polished wood with nothing other than the report adorning its surface. "Why?"

"A diversionary tactic." Cheryl paused. "I think."

Jean allowed a slight smile to lift the corners of his lips, betraying his pleasure at her direct manner and open approach to uncovering the subject's identity. He nodded, a sign she should continue. Cheryl took a deep breath and began explaining what the subject was doing, and why.

When she was done, Jean shrugged. "So, you believe the trauma the subject has suffered, physical or emotional, is preventing him, this JD as you're calling him, from coming back. Forced to deal with whatever it is that happened to him. Correct?"

"Yes. Leaving us to try and unravel the various stories he's presenting. Trying to collect then *connect* the common threads, helping determine which one of them, if any, is his actual identity."

"Proving your process works." Cheryl nodded. Jean lowered his eyes, studying the report. "Why JD? Assume it's for John Doe."

Cheryl grinned, her posture relaxed. "Helps to avoid, as my assistant calls it, *lab-rat* syndrome."

Jean lowered his head, staring at the surface of the desk, seeing a topo map from long ago, reflecting a battlefield with small rectangular markers representing companies in the field. Tokens used by military planners. Nothing more to them than groups of numbers and letters. Information. Line officers looking over their shoulders, knowing them as columns of dedicated men. Field officers, like himself, out in the dust and dry, aware they were individuals, known by their first names, along with those of their loved ones at home. Knowing each of them were one moment of inattention or careless mistake away from disfigurement, or death. The faces of those he'd lost to disabling injury, or placed into aluminum caskets, still haunting his dreams, patrolling the edges of his memories, faces flashing in and out of focus, leaving him to bear their scars along with his own.

He grunted in understanding. "You seem to have things well in hand." He was about to dismiss her, falling into old habits, her demeanor professional though unbowed by his authority. It reminded him of a young lieutenant he'd commanded. A bright man who knew he was smarter than those above him, enjoying the game of testing the limits of military boundaries, unfazed by occasional reprimand. His torn, lifeless body borne back by hollow-eyed men, their grimed faces distraught, wills undone. "An excellent report, Doctor Atkinson. We'll talk again in a week."

"It's Cheryl—to those I work with."

Jean nodded without speaking, watching as she stood up and left the office. Once she'd closed the door, he touched a button on the phone sitting on the desk, signaling an office at the far end of a heavily secured hallway. A few minutes later, a young woman entered carrying a small attaché case. She walked over to his desk, reaching to take the report he held in his hand, flashing him a tight smile. "Thank you, Jean." She pronounced it with a French intonation, as John, the way his parents had intended.

"It's Major Kelly—to *you*." He held onto the folder, preventing her from taking it, watching her eyes widen in surprise. He cut her off. "I do not agree with this. *Any* of this." His eyes glared at her from behind his desk. She smiled, tugging the papers free, slipping them into her case and closing it with two sharp clicks.

"Noted, *Major* Kelly." She gave him a pretense of a smile. "I suggest you file a report to that effect." She nodded and left his office, leaving Jean to wonder when the world had tilted on its axis, with multi-national corporations calling the shots, leading the military by the nose into the new millennium, driven by pursuit of money and the power it produced.

JD

Now

He was uneasy. Too long the master of his own domain, unwilling to accept the possibility of being nudged from his position as ruler in his self-constructed kingdom. There was knowledge seeping in from outside. An awareness of a determined mind beyond the thin veil separating him from them. The ones seeking him, teasing him with colors, tastes and textures as if extra balls tossed into a juggler's hands, forcing him into a twisting retreat, having to shed his dreams to avoid being stranded by an out-going tide, left to shrivel in the heat of horror-filled memories. He was aware someone was shadowing his movements, able to keep up. Knew he couldn't outpace them while swimming on the surface, so he drew an unnecessary breath into imaginary lungs and dove into the comforting surroundings of a dark and bottomless depth.

CHAPTER EIGHT

RESTAURANT, ARIZONA

Twain's Story

Twain shook his head. "No. I don't think so." Phil, his Lamborghini repaired, nodded, a glass of iced tea in his hand, sunglasses covering his eyes. They were sitting outside at a small diner, just beyond the outskirts of Phoenix. "Yes, you can. You're a natural and the role is *perfect* for you. A few more lines this time, with *lots* of action scenes. They even wrote a part in it for your dog."

The shepherd perked up, hearing his name. Twain reached out, rubbing his thick neck, thinking about what the director was offering: a healthy paycheck for a few weeks of steady work balanced against increased exposure in an industry compelling most people to shameless self-promotion. Or prostitution, depending on personal inclination and financial circumstances.

"How many?"

"Lines?" Phil hesitated. "Not *too* many."

"Sounds like a lot."

The young director smiled. "You'll have a coach. Someone to run lines with. Besides—the writers will allow you some leeway in your presentation." Phil smiled. "Just be yourself."

Twain stared back. "Then it's not really acting, is it?"

Phil paused for a moment, taking a sip of his tea. "It shouldn't be a problem for *you*, living the part. Taciturn. Letting your actions speak for themselves." He grinned, reaching out to pet the large dog, then hesitating.

Twain looked down. "Say hello, Dawg." The shepherd raised one leg, waiting for the director to shake it.

Phil complied. "The owner—he never came looking for him?" He cocked his head to one side.

Twain shrugged. "Heard he's still in jail."

Phil hesitated, his face reddening. "I—didn't know that. My people took care of all the paperwork, with the insurance company."

Twain shrugged. "And with the police too, I imagine."

"I assume so." Phil took off his glasses and stared at the melting cubes of ice in his drink.

Twain leaned back, crossing his arms. "He was wrong, Phil, to have wandered off the set like he did. But not wrong enough to justify your over-reaction to it. It was just an animal, answering nature's call."

"I take it he's a friend of yours?"

"Not at all." Twain relaxed. "Fact is, he seemed like a real asshole. But still."

Phil pursed his lips, considered for a moment then nodded. "I'll look into getting him released. Set him up with a good job." He paused. "And I'll make him a generous offer for release of the dog to *you*, if you'll agree to doing the film. *Deal?*" He held out his hand.

Twain looked down at the shepherd and rubbed the base of one ear, Dawg stared back, wagging his tail. "Sure. Why the hell not?"

Janice scratched her head, eyeing a piece of white, sun-bleached cedar root sticking out of a patch of sunbaked earth at an angle. Curved on the end, the thin sections of white wood were angled down as if fingers reaching to pluck a small, white rock from the surface of the ground. She was in her late sixties, hair gone over to silvery gray, with light-colored blue eyes framed by a sea of wrinkles earned from countless hours working outside, most of them under harsh sunlight.

"So, about the dog? Is it gonna be alright? Him staying here with me?" Twain waited, wondering if the older woman had heard him. She was his landlady, renting out a section of her home an hour's drive north of Phoenix. The apartment provided a decent sized bedroom with full bath and large living room, along with kitchen privileges and a separate entrance. Ideal for someone like him, popping in and out between weeklong stints of stunt work, or longer periods of time, now he was being asked to add acting to his limited resume.

"What dog?" Janice turned around, still scratching her head, gray hair hanging in limp strings over her thin shoulders. It needed washing, her eyes dull, like her mood most days. Twain pointed at the shepherd, sitting beside him, its eyes focused on the woman's face. "Him? *He's* fine. More human than most folks, hereabouts."

"He'll either be going with me, or I'll board him at a kennel. That way he won't interfere—"

Janice cut him off. "He has a home here with me, same as you. Now—come help me move this *goddamned* rock!"

The chicken soup was cold, a thin layer of oil and tiny pieces of fat coating the surface. Janice had forgotten to turn on the gas burner before going to take a shower. Twain twisted the control knob, waited for the burner to light, then adjusted it down. He started putting a salad together, finishing up as Janice came into the kitchen wearing a threadbare bathrobe buttoned up out of order. A loose flap of fabric dangled just below her jaw, a clump of her hair clinging to it, wet and stringy, having forgotten to use shampoo again during her weekly stab at personal hygiene. She stared at the kitchen table.

"Where's the damn soup?"

"Still heating."

"It should have been hot by now." She looked at the pot. "Must be *weak* gas. Told you them chiseling *assholes* are trying to cheat me."

"I'll talk with them." Twain stepped around her and checked on the soup. "And I'll see about getting some cash back on your latest bill."

"You *do* that." Janice frowned. "If *I* go, I'll carry a *gun* this time."

"You don't have one."

"I'll *get* one."

Twain smiled as he stirred the soup. "Could you let Dawg in? He'll be needing a drink by now."

Janice nodded, making her way to the door, having already forgotten about the weak gas. "Not very original. The name." She opened the door, watching as the large shepherd came bounding in. "You'll need to put in one of those doors for him to use."

"Are you sure? I'll need to cut a large hole."

"Wouldn't have said it if I wasn't."

Twain nodded as he ladled soup into their bowls. "I'll get one in town. Tomorrow."

CHAPTER NINE

FARM, MID-COAST MAINE

Calvin Story

The old tractor belched a cloud of smoke, the engine stuttering to life in grumbling protest. It had sat idle in a sway-backed barn for several years, Calvin having to drain the old fuel and oil, replacing all the filters, and installing a new battery and cables, getting it done in a less than a day.

"Engine sounds okay." He glanced at Jemma. "They made these to last. It's a Farmall Model C. Not much to look at, but it'll get the job done." He pursed his lips. "Dangerous to operate, though, if you don't know what you're doing." He stared at Jemma, noting her narrow wrist and waist. "Ever use something like this?"

Jemma frowned. "I'm familiar enough with running all kinds of construction equipment."

"With power steering, right?" When she nodded, Calvin turned his head to one side and spit. "Ain't the same thing. And it's not something you'll pick up easy. Not on the fly." He looked at the tractor, missing Jemma's glare. "It'll take ya hours of driving the damn thing to learn where it wants to keep heading off to, with no warning given." He faced her once again, arms crossed on his chest. "You'll tear up your hands, trying to keep it going straight."

Jemma opened her mouth, prepared to argue her cause. Calvin cut her off. "Nothing against your capabilities, okay? Just a matter of muscle and experience. And you're not exactly overburdened with either one. Especially with something *this* old." He paused. "At least, that's how I see it."

"Might be you need *glasses*, then!" Jemma spun around, heading toward the farmhouse. Calvin caught her halfway there, touching her shoulder, coaxing her to a stop, letting go and stepping back when she turned around.

"I'm sorry. And you might be right. We can take it down to the field and see if it'll obey your orders." Calvin's voice was soft, blending with the sound of the old diesel engine thumping away in the background. "Long as you make them *reasonable* ones. Okay?"

Jemma shrugged, a frown on her face. She finally nodded, then turned around and led him back to the old barn.

"Not as easy as I *thought* it'd be." Jemma shifted into neutral, the tractor left idling. When she jumped down, her foot slipped on the freshly turned ground. Calvin grabbed her upper arm, helping her regain her balance.

"You'll be needing a pair of farm boots. Rubber ones, with thick treads. You'll be working in the wet most times unless there's a drought. And that'll bring a host of other issues for you to have to deal with."

Jemma looked at the plowed section of field. "How'd I do?"

Calvin looked across the fresh turned earth. He'd shown Jemma how to get the tractor moving, the steering wheel bucking in her hands until she learned to stop fighting it, finding the sweet spot whenever a sudden twist from the narrow front wheel's over-rode the grasp of sweaty palms: the intended line of direction left hovering in the balance. It had gone much better once she'd listened to Calvin and let the tractor find then follow the natural slope of the ground. The front wheels knowing where to go, informing the faded black steering wheel in Jemma's relaxed hands, letting the tractor do the work.

"Good. Not great—but a decent enough job." Calvin smirked. "For a *rookie*."

Jemma ignored his jibe, rubbing her sore hands together. "I'm *starving*! It's time for some lunch."

Calvin followed her back to the house, leaving his rubber farmer's boots on the back steps alongside her sneakers, both muddy, same as her feet, not having bothered to wear socks. Calvin had washed everything clean with a stream of icy water from a hose, fed from a spigot on the spring fed well, the primary reason the farm had been located there over a hundred years. He'd enjoyed the sound of Jemma's laughter as he'd sprayed her toes, ankles, and calves, especially liking the view as she'd leaped up the back steps of the farmhouse, her lithe body moving with liquid grace.

Calvin coiled up the hose, then headed into the farmhouse. Dawg thumped into him from behind, his thick shoulder hitting the back of one knee, almost spilling Calvin to the ground. It was a trick the large animal pulled from time to time, always catching him unaware. He stepped aside, making room as the large shepherd ran up the steps and nosed open the screen door. Calvin smiled as he listened to Dawg slurping water from a large ceramic bowl, then shook his head and followed him inside.

Jemma was bent over in front of a large refrigerator, her jeans tight, Calvin looking away while she moved things around. "I have some leftover grilled chicken. And there's fresh bread. Mayo, okay?"

"If you don't have any Miracle Whip."

"So, you're one of *those*!" Jemma stepped back with a platter in her hand and flashed him a dimpled smile, then nodded at a loaf of bread sitting on the counter. "Knives are in the middle drawer. Plates up in the cupboard, overhead."

They worked together, preparing the meal, Calvin watching in awe as Jemma consumed her portion with enthusiasm. He'd sliced the bread into thick pieces, used by Jemma to wrap around generous portions of grilled meat, the sandwich barely able to fit into her small hands. Two glasses of iced tea helped them wash it down, with a thick wedge of apple-pie for dessert. Eagerly accepted by Calvin, Jemma's eyebrows raised when he asked for a chunk of cheddar cheese. Only thin sandwich slices available, refused by Calvin with a sorrowful expression.

"Must be a family tradition." Jemma grinned. "The cheese?"

Calvin finished chewing, then swallowed. "It is, from when my aunt was still kicking. She always had a slice of pie waiting for me whenever I dropped by." He angled his head, fork filled with another shovel sized load. "Never thought about it before. I mean, it must seem odd to you, coming from away." He swallowed, then wiped his mouth with the back of his hand. "Speaking of which, you never told me exactly where it is *you* come from."

"You never asked." Jemma flashed a grin. "I'm from Medway, a small town—outside the Greater Boston area."

"How did you end up finding this place?" Calvin took their plates over to a large soap-stone sink in the kitchen, rinsing them off.

Jemma looked through a small window, her eyes tracing the length of an extensive field that stretched for over a thousand yards, bordered on one side by a small creek. "Came up here on vacation. A few months ago. Needed to get away, so I booked a week at a cottage, down near the beach." Her voice softened. "My girlfriend came along. To help me celebrate a nasty breakup."

"And?" Calvin leaned against the counter, watching as Dawg went over and placed his muzzle in Jemma's lap, nosing her hand until she began to rub his ears.

"We stopped in here for lunch. On our way home. The owners, two women, were arguing. My friend and I standing right over there." Jemma pointed at the door leading out to the attached storefront section. "We waited, listening to them for a few minutes while they yelled from in here. In the kitchen. We assumed they were having a lover's spat, so we left." She leaned forward and took Dawg's head between her hands, looking into his eyes. "I went online a few weeks later, checking properties in the area. Saw it listed, so decided to come back up with my grandfather and check it out."

"Were the two of them still arguing?" Calving grinned. "They had a reputation for fussing. That and supplying healthy, home cooked food from local grown produce. Not much of it farmed here, though the soil's plenty good enough."

Jemma released Dawg. She stood up and came over to where Calvin was leaning. "I didn't meet with them. An older man showed up. Took us around. Some local guy. An artist, he said. Spent most of his time relating stories from his past, rather than giving any real guidance as to the property. But he was *beyond* interesting. Saw some of his works displayed at a small diner we stopped at on our way home. Watercolors. Of seascapes and local houses."

Calvin nodded. "I know who you mean. Not many people of note from around here. Bev being one of the finer ones."

"Anyway, I went home and thought about it for a few days. Talked it over with my grandfather, then took the plunge." Jemma looked at Calvin. "Crazy, right? A suburban girl like me, buying a run-down place like this. Needing work everywhere you look. I mean, I came into this with my eyes open. My grandfathers in construction and I worked summers and school vacations with his crew, so I understood the work needed to get it where I wanted it to be. A working farm again, with everything organic. Using low-energy equipment, completely off the grid—if possible."

Calvin nodded. "Green energy used to produce organic food. A great idea, though a lot of work needed getting it there. And money." He glanced toward the window, seeing a red squirrel in a tree that had caught Dawg's attention. The shepherd came over, Calvin letting him out, watching as the large animal bounded down the steps and raced around the corner.

Jemma smiled. "Then you'll let me hire you to help with the planning?"

"Okay." Calvin hesitated. "Though I can't guarantee regular hours. People relying on me to drop by whenever things come up."

"Heard that about you—from the painter guy."

"Bev."

"Yeah. From him." Jemma grinned as she saw Dawg chase one of the resident red squirrels up a large oak tree, his paws on the rough bark, nose in the air, tail wagging in satisfaction. "He stopped by a week ago. *Bev.* To see how I was doing. He had good things to say about you. Told me you were someone who knew what they were doing. That you were someone I could count on."

"There's a dozen in the area, good as me." Calvin paused. "Or better."

Jemma turned and looked at him. "There's one right here. Standing in my kitchen."

Calvin stared at her, noting the look in her dark eyes, her mouth set in a firm line. He nodded. "Yeah. I suppose there is."

CHAPTER TEN

ART GALLERY, MARYLAND

Jared Story

A painting of yellow flowers in an alpine field coaxed Jared to a slow stop, the image finding him from behind a thick, plate-glass window of a small gallery. It was compelling, the canvas positioned at a slight angle, begging the eye to move further into the strategically lit interior. A faint waft of a floral bouquet welcomed him as he stepped inside, matched by a series of similar paintings lining two long walls of the narrow room.

Jared stared at the painting that had caught his eye: a field of wildflowers in soft pastel watercolors, undulating along a slight rise framed by hardwood trees bathed in golden sunlight. Some of the delicate leaves bore traces of a faint rust-rose color, their faces curled in as if bowing to the seasonal transition between late summer and early fall.

A soft voice, underlaid with faint Hispanic notes, floated across the interior. "It's a—subtle work." Jared turned around: a slim-bodied woman in a simple black dress coming over and standing by his shoulder. She was of a height with him, with dark eyes, hair closely cropped, her skin a shade darker than his own. She crossed her arms and tilted her head, eying him up and down. "And still available, if you're interested."

Jared found the sound of her voice enticing, bearing a slight huskiness as it slipped through the hushed confines of the narrow space. He looked up at the other paintings, similar in style to the one that had caught his attention. "I'm just looking. Never been in here before. Not really my thing—buying art." The young woman looked at him, Jared noticing the natural color of her lips as the ends curled up in a soft smile, drawn to her eyes, framed by long, thick eyelashes, without any sign of make-up, masking her natural beauty.

"Looking is the *first* step." She came closer, her shoulder brushing his. The delicate scent of her perfume stirred a memory Jared quickly brushed aside. "Coming to an understanding of what it *is* that draws your eyes—the second."

"And the step after that?" Jared turned and faced her again, having found a measure of emotional control. She gave him another warm smile, her eyes narrowing as she stared directly at him. "Deciding on whether it speaks to you. Enough to convince you to part with a sizable amount of money, allowing me to make a decent commission." She extended her hand. "My name is Teresa. I run the gallery, providing creative support to those looking to enhance their lives, seeking a piece of art that speaks to their innermost selves."

"Must be difficult—" Jared returned her appraising gaze. "Getting all that down on a business card."

Teresa smirked. "And who is it *I'm* speaking with, standing in my gallery, looking at a painting of day lilies?"

Jared reached out and took her hand, feeling its warmth, having noted there were no rings on her fingers. "My name is Jared. A wandering soul, new in town." He paused for a moment, then let go of her slim hand. "I'm looking for something to fill a blank space on the wall of my unadorned house. Or rather, the company house I'm staying at for the next year. At least."

"And does a field of lilies meet your need for *adornment?*" Teresa raised her hand, cupping her narrow chin as she stared at him. "Don't see it. You seem more of a landscape kind of guy."

"Really?" Jared leaned back against the frame of the window, smiling, relaxed, enjoying the exchange.

"Definitely. Shorelines or sand dunes. With crashing waves or shifting—" Teresa eyes widened slightly, her full lips parting as she looked toward the back of the gallery. "There's coffee in the back. Or tea. And *cake!*"

Jared noted the diversion, letting it go. "What? No wine?"

"Just coffee, or tea. But the *cake* is fantastic. Made it myself." Teresa turned away, moving toward the rear of the space, expecting he would follow. Jared hesitated for a moment, then moved to join her there.

"It's absolutely *breathtaking!*" Jared leaned in, angling his head as he sighted across a canvas filled with a south-western landscape. He noted the layers of pigment, adding a subtle texture to the image of a series of gnarled roots out-thrust from the ends of sun-bleached trees, curled above a swirled surface of multi-colored sand with an assortment of small rocks strewn in careless piles. The artist had positioned the scene beneath a sky in sunset glow: richly hued colors blending the top half of the wide canvas into the blue-black edge of night.

"I knew you'd love it." Teresa paused. "It's not for sale."

Jared straightened up and stared at her. "Then why—"

"Because I wanted to share it with someone who would love it as much as *I* do." Teresa frowned, looking around the cramped space of a small office area. "It's a shame I have to keep it tucked away back here, out of sight."

Jared looked at the painting, mounted in a protective outer frame of wood with a thin layer of craft paper undone and pulled back, revealing the canvas beneath the dim light in a cramped storage area. He felt a twinge of regret, realizing it would need to be covered up again. "Would the owner—" He gave Teresa a searching look. "Could you convince them to let it go?"

Teresa shook her head. "I know her pretty well. And, with all she had to go through to purchase it—I doubt *that's* going to happen."

Jared stepped back. "It's yours, isn't it?" When Teresa nodded, he eyed her, considering. "And you don't have a place with a wall large enough to hang it on."

Teresa lowered her head, her voice soft in the hushed confines of the back room. "No. I don't. I share a small apartment with a friend, renting out one room. Her spare bedroom. Not exactly suitable or large enough for a work like this."

"Yet you bought it, knowing—"

"I *had* to have it, despite the cost. Figured I'd work out how to pay for it later. And to display it." She pursed her lips, looking at the painting. "Somehow."

They were sitting at a table in a small restaurant Teresa had recommended. A group of younger people were gathered at the bar, their voices blending into a laughing banter. The sound of jibes and quick-witted responses in full flow, raised the eyebrows of several older couples camped out in shadowed booths along one wall, shaking their heads as they ate their dinners in silence.

"One of my personal fears. *That.*" Teresa leaned across the table, a tiny silver cross slipping from the opening of her blouse, swinging in the dim light of an overhead lamp. Jared followed the movement with his eyes, then turned to look where her chin was pointing, noting a couple tucked away in one corner of the dimly lit dining room.

"Of getting old—or getting too used to one another's company?"

"*Both!*" Teresa shrugged her shoulders, the movement pocketing the fabric of the dress she wore, exposing the cinnamon-colored skin of her upper chest to a wash of the yellow-toned light. Jared averted his eyes, Teresa noticing, letting a sliver of a smile cross her lips. "I watched my parents doing *exactly* that, falling into the *same* routine. Dinner out, twice a month. Evenings in between spent at home in semi-isolation, each claiming one end of a long couch. Recliner sections shoved back, television on, with sporadic outbreaks of mumbled observations offered during the commercial breaks."

Jared nodded, turning his attention back to the menu he was holding.

He could feel her eyes staring at him, and waited until Teresa spoke, her voice tightened. "*Well?*"

"The pasta dish looks interesting." Jared continued to study the menu, ignoring her comment. Teresa stared; her full lips drawn into a tight line. "You're *kidding*. Right?"

"I'm *hungry*." Jared lowered the menu, finding her eyes. "And *yes*, I'm kidding. I just happen to see it through a different lens than you." He looked past her, watching as another couple stood up at one end of the dining area, the man helping his wife into a coat, the two of them holding hands as they headed toward the door.

Jared followed them with his eyes. "My parents were seldom in the same room, let alone the same area code. Or country." He leaned back, crossing his arms. "My mother was a professor of archaeology. My father: an ambassador at large, assigned overseas. They were always traveling, the two of them. Each to their own sections of the world, most of the time."

Jared stopped, taking a sip from a glass of ice-tea, licking his lips dry. "Would've given anything to see the two of them together, sitting on a couch, watching TV, whether they had anything to say to one another or not. Better than the tight-lipped bouts of carefully coded language used in front of me when I was a child. Becoming more open, or honest, I guess—in their feelings *toward* one another when I was older. Not that *I* cared, too busy with my own life to care about theirs."

Teresa nodded, taking a sip of her wine: a dark maroon color matching the shade of her lipstick, applied before leaving the gallery. She savored the deep bodied flavor for a moment, then swallowed, giving Jared a sympathetic look. "Well—that must have *sucked*!"

"You think?" They both looked up as their server stopped by the table and flashed a perfect smile, without making eye contact, leaving as soon as they'd placed their dinner order. Jared shook his head, joining Teresa as she took another sip of her wine, then he sighed. "My parents spent plenty of time with me, *individually*. I got to travel with my father while he was serving in a handful of the smaller African countries, living in gated housing near the embassies, attending private schools, meeting hundreds of people." He paused, resetting himself in his chair. "Formed a few close relationships with some incredible people."

Teresa leaned back. "And your mother? I'm getting the sense she didn't go with the two of you."

Jared shook his head. "Rarely. Between teaching at the university and doing field research, there was little time for anything like that. I mean, the two of them managed to find a week here or there, the three of us doing something together on occasion. But most times, she'd collect me up and spirit me away to someplace remote, handing me a shovel or a trowel, encouraging me to put my hands in the dirt and, as she put it: 'feel the history' waiting to be revealed."

Teresa's eyes widened in amazement. "That must have been an *incredible* opportunity for you. One parent, helping to form history. The other, trying to recover it."

Jared sighed again, deeper this time. "Would have preferred less opportunity and more normalcy. A trip to a family resort or a camping trip. You know—something normal, like other families did."

"Boo-*effing*-and-*hoo*." Teresa grinned, softening her remark. "Can't work up any sympathy for you, my friend. I'm sure it helped get you where you are today." She paused. "Which is?"

Jared nodded. "Working as a consultant for a multi-national corporation, specializing in reorganization of business practices, pertaining to design, manufacturing, sales and installation vectors."

Teresa took another sip of her drink, looking at Jared over the rim of her wineglass. Then she lowered it, a smile spreading from one corner of her perfect lips to the other. "And how many cards do *you* need—to get all that written out?"

The dinner was perfect, their choice of food pairing well with the half-bottle of house wine Jared had ordered. The two of them shared semi-intimate tastes of the various textures and flavors of their meals, between in-depth discussions of art, music, and the possibility of Jared renting her painting: a suggestion currently under silent consideration by Teresa, pretending to study a dessert menu. When she finally responded, Jared could hear the edge of doubt in her voice.

"Seems a bit pricey—just to hang it on a wall."

"It's a fair price to *me*. The house came fully outfitted, with a decent budget to redecorate as I see fit."

Teresa looked away, staring at one of the walls of the restaurant, a large seascape with crashing waves along a rock-toothed shoreline. "It would definitely *help*, financially. But leave me with no *visual* stimulation, which I count on whenever past life decisions start weighing me down."

Jared nodded. "The house is only a few minutes away from your gallery."

Teresa swung her eyes back to his. "Is that an invitation for me to visit it?"

"Someone has to find the perfect place to hang it, then stop by now and then to verify it's being properly cared for."

"It's tempting." Teresa placed the dessert menu on the table, her mind made up. Then she looked at Jared and smiled.

He leaned forward. 'Then you agree?"

"To dessert. Yes."

"And as to the other?"

Teresa hesitated, feeling a rush of warmth spreading through her face. "I'm leaning towards it—along with the crème brûlée."

Jared raised his hand, catching their server's attention.

JD

Before

"You'll never find what you're looking for. Not in me." Her fingers traced a delicate line on the skin of his chest, weaving through fine strands of dark hair. "I'm not what you're looking for. Not what you think you need." She twisted around, one of her long legs slipping across his lower body, looking down at him.

Waves were a rush of constant sound in the background. Pacific waters stroking Mexican sand. Resort sand, raked clean each morning, removing overnight deposits of natural and man-made litter. Returning it to brochure perfection in thin wavering lines, ending up a false representation of natural beauty. Like polished fingernails drawn across smooth masks of make-up, worn on vacant-eyed faces of models marching stiff-lipped down a runway pier with stiff hair, stiff bodies and closed minds, their emotions tucked safely out of the way. Mirrors reflecting innocence lost, shattered to pieces, their unlined foreheads pressed against make-up-table tops, left to wonder if they could go back and reclaim it in the eyes of loved ones, friends, and that one special person who'd they'd carelessly tossed aside.

"Let's just stay. Let's just stay, you and I and—"

Her lips touched his, silencing him. "Let's not—and pretend we did. You, back to your world. Me, to mine." She stood up, naked, the rising sun back-lighting her as she walked away, wading into the surf, her body fading into the rays that stretched from shore to the edge of the sea. The lithe lines of her body dissolving as she slipped from view, the sunlight and water carrying her away. He ran to catch her. His mouth twisted open, calling her name. Screaming, as strong currents ripped her away. Torn from his straining arms. From his burning hands. Cursing the men who were trying to save him. Cursing them to the lowest depths of Hell. Fighting them with useless arms. With broken bones. Losing to their insistent pull as night reached out and claimed his soul in a shadowed spin.

CHAPTER ELEVEN

AUDITORIUM, GEORGETOWN UNIVERSITY

Cheryl

"There are core responses. Autonomous responses, inherent in all humans, based deep within the brain. Fight or flight. Avoid or strike. Encoded in our DNA. Hard-wired, if you will, none of us immune from the effect." Cheryl paused, searching the sea of faces in the small auditorium. She heard a voice call out, one of the bright lights sitting up front, taking her advanced bio-physics class: a bi-weekly commitment that helped to keep her hand in educational waters.

"But there *are* people who *don't* react that way. Able to assess the situation, then—"

Cheryl cut in. "Professionals. Conditioned by training and long-term exposure to deal with stress. Able to absorb the initial adrenaline rush, converting its biochemical influence into directed action based on an instant analysis of the situation. Athletes. emergency personnel, firefighters, police." She lowered her voice. "And soldiers."

"And *mothers*. With children."

A voice from the back row provoked waves of reflected laughter, causing Cheryl to join in. "Agreed. Parents often need to make snap decisions when dealing with sudden and oftentimes *drastic* changes in their local environment." Cheryl glanced toward the back of the hall, unable to locate the woman who'd spoken up. "The goal is to minimize a portion of the *negative* effects of constant adrenaline secretions resultant from continual exposure to excessive stress arising from physical and/or emotional traumas. Leading to mental burnout, fatigue, obesity, prescription drug abuse, psychological issues such as social withdrawal, self-damage and, in extreme cases—suicide."

"By utilizing desensitizing methodologies, like the ones you've recently published on." The speaker revealed herself, standing up behind the furthest line of seats: a middle-aged woman with her arms crossed on her chest, without a laptop or tablet in her hands.

Cheryl nodded. "Yes. Coupled with *other* successful coping mechanisms, natural to our ancestral programming. Seclusion sought in natural environments. Working with soil or animals. Our bodies and minds exercised by the parallel routines of hunting *and* gathering."

"Holistic healing."

Cheryl nodded as she stepped away from the lectern and approached the front row. "Technology is in a constant state of rapid advancement, with breakthroughs happening at an accelerated pace, leading to applications being provided without consideration of their potential for misuse. Like the over-prescription of antibiotics when they became readily available, leading to a decrease in their effectiveness. Trying to cure infectious diseases grown resistant to them. The same true of opioids, used to replace more traditional pain medications. Again, with predictable results leading to expansive abuse." Cheryl lowered her voice again. "With tragic consequences to thousands of otherwise healthy people."

"With natural cures pushed aside. Or worse—ignored." The two women settled into the flow of conversation, the class of students looking from one to the other, furiously scribbling notes with pens or styli, trying to keep up.

Cheryl nodded. "The price of chasing the latest innovation, happening on a global scale. Our increasingly interconnected society turning a blind eye to ancient lessons. Ancient cures." She clapped her hands together. "We've gone past the top of the hour, again, as usual. My apologies to those with tight schedules. Please read the next selection from the syllabus and prepare a spirited rebuttal to Miller's tepid dismissal of Selec's excellent treatise on the effectiveness of Neolithic through seventeenth century use of homeopathic cures."

The middle-aged woman who'd spoken up approached the raised section of the auditorium and waited as Cheryl collected her things. She stuck out her hand. "Sorry to have interrupted, but it seems to be your modus operandi."

"It is." Cheryl reached out and returned her handshake. "Encourages interchange of ideas in real-time, helping to keep everyone engaged."

"My name is Mari, spelled with an I. Mari Coleman. I asked your department head if I could stop by and audit your class." Mari hesitated. "I know Chancellor Jannsen—or rather, I attended the same school as his *daughter*, many years ago. I used to stay with them from time to time. I hope you don't mind."

"Visitors are always welcome to stop by at any time. And encouraged to take part." Cheryl considered a moment. "Is your interest in the subject matter personal, or professional?"

"Both." Mari smiled, her hands holding a thin notebook, spiral bound, a pen inserted in the binding. "The concept of mind-to-mind communication has always fascinated me. I used to wish I'd been born a twin, just to see if the stories are true."

Cheryl studied the other woman, drawn to her open, laid-back manner. "I've tested my theories and technologies with twins. The connection is there, to a degree. More pronounced in females than males. Above standard deviation in all those we worked with." She paused. "And your professional interest?"

Mari nodded, holding out a business card. "I work for a corporation. A multi-national doing research in application of emergent physiological interactive technologies. Focused on the medical community, supporting research into—well, what you're working on."

Cheryl looked at the name on the card: Nascent Industries. "The name suits them since they must be new to the industry. *I haven't heard of them, and I'm familiar with all the major players.*"

Mari shrugged. "They've only recently incorporated, having operated under a host of names and research grants these past few years."

Cheryl glanced at the wall, eyeing a large clock. Mari took notice and stepped back. "I should let you go. I'm sure you have more important things—"

"More pressing. Not more important. But yes, I do need to head out." Cheryl shook Mari's hand. "It's nice to have met you, Ms. Coleman. I hope to see you here again."

Mari watched as the renowned researcher quickly ascended the stairs, heading to the exit. She nodded; her thin lips fixed in a firm line as she murmured beneath her breath. "You can definitely count on that, Doctor Atkinson."

CHAPTER TWELVE

ON LOCATION, WEST-COAST

Twain and Miranda's Story

A knock on the door of Twain's trailer caused him to look up from the script he was holding. He was in a sour mood and responded in a frustrated tone, framed around a growl that raised Dawg's ears. "Come *in*. It's *open*." The door swung back, revealing his actor friend James, from the movie set a few months before. His white hair, backlit by the bright, mid-afternoon light, framed the same neatly trimmed beard. He was holding a worn cowboy hat in one hand, a six-pack of beer in the other.

"*James!*" Twain's face brightened. "I didn't know *you* were on the shoot. Come in and sit down. I'm just going over my *damn* lines. Supposed to be someone coming by to help me with them."

James nodded to one corner of the small trailer. "See you still have the shepherd." Dawg stood up and looked at Twain. Getting a nod, he went over and sat down in front of James, holding out his paw. The man knelt, shaking it. "Pleased to meet you—" He looked over at Twain, waiting.

"Been calling him Dawg. D-A-W-G."

"Creative." James shook the offered paw. "Hey there, Dawg." Then he straightened up and glanced at the pages in Twain's hand. "Got another set?"

Yeah. They dropped two of 'em off, an hour ago. But you don't have to—" Twain stared at his friend. "You're the one gonna be helping me."

James grinned as he reached out for a chair. "Phil called me a while back and offered me the job. I said I'd take it, long as I get to do a scene or two with you."

"You can have 'em all. I never wanted to be out in front of the big glass eye. Was happier off as a stuntie. Part of the support crew. There's way less pressure in crashing cars, jumping off buildings, fight scenes and the like."

"The money's a lot better, though." James pursed his lips as he looked at the script. "Are you ready to get started?"

Twain nodded his head, watching as Dawg returned to his corner and laid down, muzzle stretched between his paws, keeping a close watch on his every move.

A rental car with a thin coating of red dust on its surface eased into the end of the driveway leading to Janice's house. Twain stood outside, supporting the older woman by her elbow, helping to steady her, like he'd been doing for the past twenty-five minutes, Janice insisting on being outside when her only child, Miranda, arrived home. Her daughter, a few years older than Twain, was known to him by a scattering of pictures posed in random places throughout the interior of the house, one of her in a cheerleader's outfit mounted on the wall of his bedroom, at the foot of his bed. Janice had insisted it belonged there, telling him not to touch it if he knew what was good for him.

Twain had never met Miranda, though he knew her by the sound of her voice: low in tone, with a soft south-western twang. He'd made several late-night phone calls during his first few months living in the attached one-bedroom apartment, letting her know what was happening with her mother. Wanting clarification on whether he should contact emergency personnel to help with Janice's occasional spells of dementia. Having to embrace her when she started flailing away at imaginary people trying to *fuck-her-over*. Giving her *huggies,* as the older woman called them, when needed. Twain holding onto her until her spasms subsided and she was back to what passed for normal again.

"You must be Twain. It's so good to finally meet in *person*." The woman's face was lean, wearing a lopsided smile beneath a light spray of freckles on high cheekbones, framed by shoulder-length auburn hair. She was close to his height, with a slim build and firm grip, matched by the direct look she gave him from hazel-green eyes.

He released her hand. "And you must be Miranda."

She nodded, then took her mother by the arm and guided her inside, out of the late afternoon sun.

Twain was at the sink, finishing the dishes. Miranda had cooked a traditional Spanish dish for the three of them, Janice complaining it wasn't spicy enough, shaking an unopened can of chili powder over her plate, tasting it, then shaking again, with nothing coming out.

Miranda reached over and touched him on his upper arm, feeling the play of his muscles through the thin fabric of the shirt he was wearing. "Thank you. For all the work you've been doing around here. And for helping my mother through her—" She paused, her eyes glancing to where Janice was sitting, staring out at a large backyard filled with roots, stones, and small piles of natural items used to keep her once creative mind occupied. "Through her rough spots."

Twain finished rinsing the last of the dishes. He wiped his hands, looking at Miranda as she leaned against the counter beside him, holding out a drink. "It's been my pleasure. In getting to spend time with her, as well as the other. Not much of that needing to be done, her project out back keeping her busy. And I'm able to be here often enough, and capable enough of helping with minor projects, so—"

Miranda nodded. "Still. It's appreciated. *Greatly*." Twain tossed the cloth onto the counter and took the drink she'd mixed for him, touching it to the side of hers. "To your mother. To Janice."

The television volume was on low, Janice off to bed, leaving the two of them sitting on each end of a large, overstuffed sofa in Twain's living room. The television screen was immense, covering half the wall. A present from Phil after their last shoot. Delivered a few weeks earlier, confusing Janice who'd railed at the delivery men, cursing them up one side and down the other as they carried it inside and set it up. Telling them it was a mistake, and that she wouldn't pay them one *God-damned-dime*, come hell or high water.

Miranda picked up the controller, searching for and using the mute button, cutting off the sound from a set of large speakers. "Are you interested in any of this?"

Twain watched as a pride of hungry lionesses chased down another doomed animal. He shook his head. "Not really. Reminds me of being on the other side of things. With me in the gazelle's role. Or the wildebeest they were just chewing on."

"*Other* side of things?" Miranda tilted her head. "What's that mean?"

Twain shrugged. "Being shoved out in front of the cameras. You know, from being in films."

"I *didn't* know." Miranda gazed at him, her eyes lighting up as she took a sip from her second drink of the evening. "Anything I might have seen you in?"

"Maybe. I've done over three dozen scenes the past few years. Most of them as a stuntie." Twain shut off the display. "A stuntman—in the background." He picked up his glass. "But my opportunities for on camera work have expanded of late. Been in two recent shoots with speaking roles. Nothing out yet, not due for release for another year. But I saw the dailies. The daily takes." Twain shrugged, his wide shoulders rising and falling as he glanced toward the door leading into Janice's side of the house. "I guess I probably did okay, considering."

"So—you're a *movie star!*" Miranda shook her head. "I've never met one before." She grinned. "You're my very first."

"Not really one of *those*. I've been in a scene here and there, stuck safely away in the background. Usually ending up dead."

"Still, it's quite an accomplishment." Miranda touched her glass to his.

"Okay. I'll agree to that if you'll tell me what you do. Janice hasn't exactly filled me in."

"I'm an editor, and a writer. For a publication house in New York. Used to be a field reporter."

"Now *that* takes real talent."

Miranda frowned. "My mother—she hasn't told you about what I do?"

"No. Only that you live all the way to hell and gone in New York." He paused. "You sound surprised. I mean—Janice only deals with what's happening to her in the here and now. Never mentions the past. Same as it was with my—"

Miranda waited, her expression open, inviting him to continue. Twain sighed; his hands clenched. Dawg came over, nosing in between his legs, head wedged in his lap, looking up. Twain rubbed him behind his ears. "My mother—she had the same type of thing. Not true dementia. There were days on end when she was in her right mind."

"And you took care of her. So, you understand—"

"No. I didn't. My brother put her in a facility while I was overseas. With me having no say in it." He paused. "No letter from him either, letting me know. Not even a phone call."

Miranda leaned in slightly, her expression focused on his face, seeing the lines embedded in the corners of his eyes. "Overseas?" Twain nodded, remaining silent. "Military?" Dawg whined, sensing the change in his owner's mood, using his teeth, tugging at his hand, trying to pull him to his feet.

Miranda slid back. "It's okay. Don't feel that you have to explain." Twain took a deep breath, letting it out. He turned his head, looking through a sliding door letting in angled rays of sunlight as dusk arrived with a red-yellow glow. "Let's talk outside. Dawg needs a walk and it's a nice evening for it."

The streetlights were on, of little use beneath the overhead display of sunset colors painting the sky. Miranda looked over at Twain as they walked along the sidewalk bordering a wide street. "I meant to ask you something—when you invited me over to your side of the house." She gave him a quizzical look. "What's the reason for my picture—hanging on the wall at the foot of your bed?"

"Saw that, did you?" When Miranda nodded, Twain shrugged. "It was there when I moved in. Your mother insisted I leave it the *hell alone* if I knew what was good for me. Said it was your bedroom once you came to your senses and moved back home."

"It *was* my room until I moved to New York." Miranda shook her head. "And I'd never come back here to live. Not that it isn't a suitable place for her." She added in a soft voice. "Or you."

"Seemed to make her happy, my leaving it there."

"What about any *friends* you invite over? Doesn't that picture kind of—I don't know, *cramp* your style?"

Twain angled his head, looking straight into her eyes. "No one's ever been in there." Then he grinned. "Do you *still* have the outfit?"

Miranda looked away, a blush coloring the edges of her tanned face. "No. Not that it would still *fit* if I did." She could feel his eyes on her, a tingling sensation running down her spine. "So, you end up going to *their* places." She tapped the side of her head. "Smart."

Twain shrugged. "I've learned a lot over the years. Army didn't just teach me how to shoot."

Miranda turned her head, her eyes on his. "Which theater?"

"Both of them—spread out over three tours."

She nodded. "I was there too. Covered Iraq during the invasion when I was starting out. Wetter than a weeping fish behind my ears. Then went into Afghanistan and spent seven years off and on doing embedded pieces. Wrung completely dry by then. Not one tear left to shed after my—" She trapped her lower lip beneath her upper teeth. "Last trip there."

Twain shook his head. "Would never have guessed it. You don't exactly have the *look*."

She forced a grin, unable to get it to her eyes. "Same secret as with you and your current occupation. Tons of make-up and great acting—whenever it rises up and grabs me by the heartstrings." She released her lip, twisting her hands instead. "Happens at the oddest moments." Her voice dropped to a whisper. "They're the walking wounded. Those who serve behind the wire or out beyond the berm. Wearing their scars, inside and out. The few, following in the footsteps of the many. Weary, worn, bowed down, but—"

"Seldom beaten, and always proud." Twain finished the sentence. "We posted that on our PNN board." He noted her look of confusion. "Private news network. Cut from an article someone wrote about our outfit." He paused. "Yours?"

Miranda nodded. "Written during my last trip over there." She smiled, her eyes glistening. "Pulled into the senior editor's office when I got back. A good friend and mentor recognizing the signs, taking me out of rotation."

Twain reached out, touching Miranda on her shoulder. "Thank you. For what you did. What you wrote. It helped, knowing someone understood what we were going through. Trying to take some of what we were dealing with back to the world, even if it was mostly a one-way street."

The bedroom window was open. Cool evening air wafted through Twain's bedroom. An occasional vehicle passed by in a rush of sound that quickly faded away. Twain lay on his side, watching Miranda as she slept. Thin lines creased the corners of her eyes, her make-up scrubbed clean when she'd joined him in the shower. Both naked, open, and vulnerable. Each seeking something the other had to offer and desperately needed in return. An emotional connection beyond the physical. Beyond words. Making love then lying back, holding each other as they quietly worked their way through troubling memories beneath a blanket woven from a common thread.

CHAPTER THIRTEEN

FARM, MID-COAST MAINE

Calvin and Jemma's Story

Calvin had a satisfied smile on his face. "The solar array will provide enough power to feed both the house and store, with battery backup good for a week, even with minimal sunlight. Solar water heater on the roof will cover all your needs, with enough capacity to tide you over for a couple of days even under overcast skies. The biofuel generator in the new barn will use natural gas from animal waste and other organics to provide power enough to cover running the pumps, small appliances, and other equipment."

"It looks—complicated." Jemma leaned over the drawing Calvin had prepared, the end of her braided hair brushing across the back of his hand. She held a mug of coffee in her hands, palms wrapped in cloth bandages with a home-made salve supplied by a local naturopath to help heal her blisters, result of having driven the old tractor a few days earlier. Jemma reached out, pointing with the cup. "What's with the *tent* thingies?"

Calvin's face grew into a smile that stretched his lips from corner to corner. "They're the incubators—heart of the biogenic system. With scrap food and animal waste going in one end, getting broken down by the conversion process, producing the gas used to power the genset. Then *that* charges the battery banks, with enough power produced to run everything. Any extra gets sold back into the grid. Plus, the process leaves behind a high grade, all-natural compost for use on the fields. With enough left over to sell."

Jemma looked at him, a frown pinching her narrow face. "How much?"

"Compost produced—or the cost?"

She hesitated. "Both, I guess. Although, if it's *too* high—"

"Seventy-five. Grand."

"Seems expensive, just for the tent—I mean for the *incubators*."

Calvin shook his head, his smile firmly in place. "That's for the *entire* package, including the genset, battery banks, system install and setup, and tie-in to the grid." He paused. "Should cover some, if not all the construction costs for the new barn."

Jemma stared at him. "And it can really take us off the grid?"

"Yes. Except in extreme situations when, with a bit of energy management, you'll still be able to run at close to eighty percent of normal. Just have to cut a few corners." Calvin pointed to a column of figures. "Plus, there's value in recycling waste to compost. You'll have more than enough for your own use, with plenty left over to sell. I'll help you get a bagger system set up for that."

"This is amazing. And very doable, Cal. I'll have enough funds left over to put a new roof and solar panels on the main house *and* build the new kitchen. The remodeling of the house can wait."

"Is your grandfather still an active part of the construction business?"

"He's retired but owns a majority share of the company." Jemma smiled. "He can help with materials and labor, sending a few trailers up, along with a crew." She rubbed the fingers of one hand together. "At a *substantial* family discount."

"There you go. You'll be able to add low energy appliances. More efficient refrigeration units, along with a new pump for the well. Before you know it, you'll be selling fresh organic produce. And *meat*!"

Jemma looked at him, a shocked expression on her face. "I'm not—*killing* any of my animals."

Calvin raised his eyebrows. "Why raise them then?"

"For milk, wool, and eggs."

"And the pigs?"

Jemma bit her lip. "I don't know. Maybe I could—"

Calvin rolled up the drawings. "A farm isn't a nursery, Jemma. Or an animal shelter. Plenty of them around to handle cast-off pets." Calvin stared at her. "You're venturing into a new market, with *great* upside. Naturally grown food stuffs, organically produced with no pesticides or other chemicals used. Supplying restaurants, and *schools*, if you can get them signed up, having to wade through all the red tape from the government. Then there are the hospitals and nursing homes to go after."

"Yes, but—"

"They're *pigs*, Jemma. No different from deer or rabbits. They *all* die, eventually. Pigs have an easier go of it, with a less painful death at the end—when it's done right."

Jemma's hands were trembling, the coffee in her mug sloshing over. Calvin moved the cylinder of drawings to one side, then took the cup and sat it on the table. He held her hands, squeezing gently before letting go. "Let's just skip the meat part for now. No room for them here anyway, not until next Spring."

"Okay." Jemma's voice was low. "When can we, I mean—how do we begin?"

"I'll get a list of materials put together. Draw up some detailed plans. Start getting the paperwork for the permits going. You can take the preliminary numbers I've come up with to your bank, applying for the grants I mentioned. Those will help defray costs and lower the interest rate. You can plan on breaking ground for the power plant in a month. Then tear down the old barn and build the new one. Start in on the other structures over the winter. Be ready to plant crops as soon as the ground thaws."

Jemma picked up her mug, holding it out, waiting for him to do the same. She touched it to his with a solid clunk of kiln-fired clay. "Here's to North Brook Farm and Country Store. Soon to be producing the finest organically grown food—with no carbon footprint. Thanks to *you*."

CHAPTER FOURTEEN

COMPANY HOUSE, MARYLAND

Jared and Teresa's Story

"I have a dog. Or rather—he has me. At least for the moment." Jared pulled into the driveway of his house, waiting while the garage door opened. He looked over at Teresa. "Just wanted to let you know, in case you're allergic." They were nearing the end of their third date, still early in the evening, the two of them having spent an hour enjoying pizza and a single glass of wine at the gallery, after she'd closed it. The landscape was sitting in the back seat, ready for transition to his house.

Teresa stiffened slightly. "I'm not allergic—but I don't exactly like them." She looked over at him. "One bit me when I was a child. Left a scar on my cheek." She reached up, touching the side of her face.

Jared leaned in, the glare from the garage painting her ivory skin in a white glow. "Where?"

Teresa took his hand, placing his finger on her upper cheek. "Right here."

He could feel the warm pulse of her breath on his cheek as he traced the smooth surface of her flawless skin, feeling no sign of a scar. He pulled away, reluctantly, her delicate scent sending signals he knew were unintentional. "Yes. I can see why you have an aversion to them."

"Is it a big dog?" Teresa looked toward the door leading into the foyer.

"I'm afraid so. He's a German Shepherd."

"Oh." Teresa relaxed. "*That's* not so bad. It's the *small* ones I have an issue with. With them always wanting to jump into my lap."

"Dawg won't be a problem. He waits to be asked." Jared paused. "*Most* of the time."

"You haven't named him yet?"

"Calling him Dawg, for now. With an AW in the middle. He—" Jared shrugged, a smile on his face. "Kind of named *himself*." He pulled ahead and shut off the engine, pushing a button on a small controller, shutting the garage door. "You'll understand once you meet him."

"Poor thing! He's *hurt*!" Teresa watched as the shepherd limped across the living room floor, whining in pain as it came to a stop several feet away, its paw held out. "You didn't tell me he was injured."

"He's milking it. Trying to get sympathy. Hasn't slowed him down any when chasing squirrels out back." Jared snapped his fingers, calling Dawg over, rubbing his head. "Say hello to the nice lady, Dawg."

Teresa leaned down, keeping her face back as she reached out, accepting the raised paw, shaking it gently. "Hello." She smiled. "Aren't you a *handsome* boy." Dawg opened his mouth, appearing to grin, panting with pleasure as she scratched behind his ear. "He's so *cool*! No wonder you call him that." She straightened up, looking at Jared. "Where did you get him?"

"I didn't. Not exactly. He found me." Jared sat down on a large couch. "A car had hit him, according to what the vet said. Or grazed him, there being no actual damage done, other than a bruised hindquarter and sore front paw. Fully healed now, despite his attempts to curry treats with the wounded warrior act."

"Can I give him one?"

"You'll only be reinforcing inappropriate behavior."

"Or—" Teresa gave Jared a coy smile. "Letting him know I'm a *friend*."

"Do I get a treat, too?" Jared raised a hand. "Didn't mean it to sound like that." He headed into the kitchen while Teresa continued to stroke Dawg's neck and ears. Once Jared was gone, she leaned down and looked directly into the animal's deep brown eyes. "He'll just have to wait and see. Won't he, boy?" Dawg lifted his muzzle and gently licked the side of Teresa's face.

The painting found its way to the perfect location, chosen by Teresa without hesitation: centered on a long wall perfectly matching its wide dimensions, reflecting its energy into the space, filling every corner of the living room. Teresa sipped her wine, drinking in the mixed colors of the painting while sorting through the various notes, tones, and flavors of the dark red liquid in her glass. A moderately priced blend of three varietals from the west coast. She sighed, feeling perfectly balanced between two pleasures, her eyes glistening as she looked at the painting, happier than she'd felt in years.

"Are you okay?" Jared was standing beside her, a glass in his hand. "Not having second thoughts about letting go of it, are you—even though it's only a *temporary* loan?"

"These are tears of happiness." Teresa shook her head, then sighed again. "It's absolutely *perfect*." She looked over at him, a smile turning up the corners of her full lips. "Don't you agree?"

Jared nodded. "I do. And thank you—for lending me the painting." He hesitated, looking into her eyes. "And for the pleasure of your company this evening."

Teresa nodded, then sat down in the center of the couch, patting the cushion beside her, inviting Jared to sit down. He hesitated, knowing a line was about to be reached, and possibly crossed. Dawg came into the living room, water dripping from his mouth, nosing Jared's hand, looking for a treat and coming up empty.

Disappointed, he moved past, bumping his new owner behind the knee, causing him to stumble. Jared caught his balance, keeping the wine in his glass from spilling over as he stared at the shepherd, muttering under his breath. Dawg ignored him, going over, circling around, then lying down on the floor in front of Teresa, looking up at her, waiting for her to reach out and rub his ears.

JD

Before

"You won't find any answers in there." She ran her fingers through his curly dark hair, twisting strands together, pulling them until he was forced to look up, into her eyes, his head resting on her flat stomach. He was listening to the murmuring just below the surface of her warm, velvety skin, the scent of her body filling him with joy. "You will never find your solution in me."

"I'll be okay—once I get back on top. I just need to work my way through all the shit. And you're the reason I'll make it. This time."

"No. I'm only a diversion, that's all. A lie you tell yourself at night, knowing its only that. One more lie, told true. Like the bottles of alcohol on your shelves, letting them slip through your fingers when they're empty, dropping them into the trash, telling yourself it's the last one. The last time. Same with the plastic vials tucked away in your medicine cabinets, with a dozen different doctor's names on the labels. The same with all your excuses."

"No! I've stopped. I told you. I'm not on—"

"They're your lovers. Your real ones. Used to fill a hole you imagine is there and keep trying to fill. Wanting to feel whole again. Which you can never do because it doesn't exist."

"It does!" He reached for her face, cradling it between his hands, lying as honestly as he could. "They drilled the hate into me! Sending everyone who ever cared for me away. Every time. Leaving me all alone."

"No. They didn't do this to you. You did it to yourself. Still doing it, with every imaginary excuse you can think of. Every perceived slight, magnifying your need to duck away. Leaving you in a puddle on the floor craving answers you'll never be able to find, in a desperate search to uncover a conspiracy that never existed. To find the source of your pain, hoping it might lead you closer to the person you thought you were, once. A creative young man who learned to crawl, walk, leap, then soar. Rising too far, too quickly while daring to touch the sun. Falling, your wings in tatter, feathers in flame. Too much, too soon. Too high, too often."

CHAPTER FIFTEEN

RESTAURANT, WASHINGTON D.C.

Cheryl

"There's something you're not telling me." Laura gave her cousin a firm look of reproach, as close to her as if a twin. Born the same day, though she was younger by three hours: a fact she was quick to point out, always teasing Cheryl for being the older woman.

"There's a *ton* I'm not telling you—and won't be able to." Cheryl gave her a firm look. "You know that."

"Not about the *work* you're doing." Laura paused, angling her head slightly. "About the new *man* in your life."

"There's no—new man." Cheryl looked down at her menu.

Laura raised her eyebrows, staring at her cousin. "Of course. My mistake."

Cheryl sighed. "Laura. I promise you. There *isn't*."

"Sure." Laura lifted her glass of iced coffee, slipping a metal straw she'd brought with her into the cocoa-brown mixture, then sipping, eyes wide as she continued to stare at her cousin.

"There *isn't* one." Cheryl tossed down the rest of her ice-tea, wishing she'd ordered a margarita instead. "I *swear*. Not anyone now, and not going to be anyone later."

"Okay." Laura leaned back, looking over as several small children ran past their table, leaping down a set of steps and racing along the sidewalk with a harried mother close behind, leaving a breathless apology as she ran past. The disruption to all the diners sitting outside soon faded away, replaced by a soft breeze, the day unseasonably warm.

"I mean—" Cheryl sighed.

Laura lowered her glass, a wide smile framing her face. "I *knew* it!"

"He's not—" Cheryl hesitated. "I mean—it's not like *that*. He's—" Cheryl fought back the urge to continue. "I really can't talk about this. *Any* of it. You know the position I'm in."

Laura nodded, used to playing hide-and-seek when dealing with Cheryl's interactions with members of the opposite sex. "Then let's move the conversation to hypothetical land, like we used to do when we were younger."

"We're not kids."

"Speak for yourself. *Granny*."

Their server came by, delivering two plates filled with an organic salad. It looked fresh and healthy, though not substantial enough to Cheryl's practiced eye to satisfy her appetite, having come from a work-out at her favorite place: a local rock-climbing gym. She grabbed a second roll and took a large bite, chasing it down with a sip of iced tea. "Okay, then. In hypothetical land I've met a man. A remarkable man with an interesting story to tell. Several of them, actually."

Laura, the meal forgotten, shook her head, her face lighting up with excitement. "You're seeing him? This hypothetical man?"

"Daily. He's at the center of some extremely important work I'm doing."

"Hypothetically speaking, of course."

Cheryl shook her head. Her hair, freshly showered, formed a dense halo of tight curls around both sides of her face. "No. He's *real!* Helping me prove the validity of what I've been working to accomplish over the past thirty years."

Laura paused, her voice dropping into a whisper. "Ever since—"

"Yes." Cheryl nodded, a look of firm conviction on her face. "Ever since Robert passed. Before that, even. Since his accident."

The afternoon sky was gray, overcast, with a light rain falling from a thin blanket of clouds racing by as if animals fleeing a forest fire. Several weeks had passed with no significant amount of rain in the New England interior, relief promised by the local forecast, calling for showers throughout the day. Cheryl was sitting on the hood of her brother's jeep, left parked near the edge of thick New Hampshire woods, wearing a large, sweat-stained sweatshirt that hung from her narrow shoulders, her arms clasped, shivering as the thick material absorbed moisture from the late October air.

Her brother had left her behind at his friend's house, telling her to play with the other boy's younger siblings while the two of them headed off to claim another new climbing route. One Robert had described to her during the drive over. She'd nodded from time to time, half-listening, caring only that he would come back in one piece and pick her up, tossing her high in the air, his face beaming with pride at having claimed another one of his 'maidenhead' routes. Whatever that meant.

"I don't *want* to play with them." Cheryl stamped her foot, the effect diminished by the sole of her sneaker and thick grass lining the side of a gravel driveway. "They don't *like* board games, and I'm *sick* of pretending to be a *horse*."

Her brother pulled climbing gear from the back of the vehicle. "It's good for you to run around. Besides, it'll toughen you up for when I take you climbing."

"When?" Cheryl's eyes lit up. Robert looked at her, his seventeen-year-old face tan, unblemished by acne. His eyes, ice blue in the gray light of the mid-morning sky. "Soon. If you can get to your tenth birthday without breaking curfew, *or* your foolish neck." He shook his head. "What was the idea of climbing the side of the old quarry like that?"

"I didn't *fall*. And there was plenty of water below me in case I did." Cheryl pouted. "And my birthday's a whole month away!"

"I'll take you on a practice climb next weekend. I promise. A *special* route that needs muscular legs to get up." He grinned. "Not chicken-legs, like yours."

"I've been doing those exercises you showed me. Every day."

"Then do some running today and build up your wind. Like a *horse!*" He smiled, his teeth a gleam of white between his lips, a stain of black hair on his upper lip and jaw, newly shaven, a mane of thick black hair trapped in a twist of leather, tied back in a ponytail.

Cheryl gazed up at him, knowing his choice of hairstyle upset their parents. Unable to make him cut it, his grades perfect, like everything he did. She ran over and hugged him, wishing she could go with him. The two of them standing side by side, looking toward the far horizon and its snow-capped mountains.

The children collapsed in a loose pile of laughing, sweaty faces, and old clothes, forming a tangle of quivering legs and heaving lungs. Cheryl, first to reach the top of a small hill, looked at the light-colored moss islands surrounding them, sprinkled between glacier smoothed boulders of granite. She smiled, happy in the natural playground, the other children gasping while trying to talk over one another, their words cut in half as they struggled to form words. They were all giggling, as only children at play can do, lying on their backs and staring up at the overcast sky.

Once they'd caught their collective breath, the eldest, a boy slightly older than Cheryl, rolled onto his side and looked at her, a warm smile on his face.

"You're really fast! I name you *leader* of the horses."

One of the other girls protested. "I stumbled, or I would have—"

"First is first. No excuses." The boy shut down any further argument with a stern look. "She's leader for today. Her turn to decide where we go next."

Cheryl returned the smile as she wiped a runnel of sweat from her forehead with the back of her hand, warm despite the cool air. Lunchtime had come and gone; her brother due back soon. She stretched her arms over her head, about to suggest a new game, when a piercing whistle caught their attention, followed by a high-pitched shout. They all sat up, swinging their heads around and looking down the hill. The children's mother waved up at them, calling them back to the house below.

The County sheriff tried to coax Cheryl down from the hood of Robert's jeep, wanting her to get into his car, out of a steady rain starting to fall. Cheryl refused to move, staring straight ahead, her tears dammed behind a wall of solid will. They finally seeped through as she saw a forest ranger coming over, his face drawn, worn-out from helping to carry her brother out of the woods: his body, limp, strapped in bright orange stretcher with a bloodstained bandage wrapped around his head, his arms crossed on his chest.

Cheryl looked away, wanting to refuse the image, telling herself her brother, tanned, strong, with nothing able to faze him, would soon come find her, a lopsided grin on his face, eager to bounce back from a failed attempt to find his way up an unclaimed route. Determined to pin his name to it on the next attempt. She knew he wasn't going to do that this time. Whisked away in a large helicopter that landed on a section of cleared ground. People kept back by a fluttering ribbon of yellow tape, placed there by two State Troopers who'd arrived to support the afternoon long rescue effort.

Cheryl heard the soft cough of the ranger, a mentor and close friend of her brother. She looked up, noting the name stenciled on his uniform. Rick. Ranger Rick, the name usually making her smile, recalling the stack of Ranger Rick magazines her brother would read to her when she was young. She looked at him now, her tears released as he opened his arms, taking her into his sweaty embrace. The scent of pine needles and pipe tobacco bringing her little comfort as he pulled her close, then released her, touching her cheek, wiping tears away with a blood-stained hand. The rust-brown color caught her eye, holding her attention.

"He's alive. His breathing's good. Color, too. Although he took a hit to his head." He looked at the back of his hand. "That's where the blood came from. It's a scalp wound, which bleeds like—" He stopped himself, his eyes glancing away. "The helicopter's transporting him to the hospital in Manchester. I'm going to drive you there. To meet up with your parents. Okay?"

"He *didn't* fall." Cheryl clenched her hands into two tight balls of denial. "My brother *never* falls."

"You're right. He didn't. A small rock came down the wall. Hit Bobby in the head and knocked him out. Then broke a bone in Tommy's shoulder, putting it out of joint. He'd taken his helmet off—your brother. To adjust it, most likely. Or trying to fix something. Took a wallop, cutting his scalp up pretty bad." The ranger hesitated, then looked away. "Tommy was able—somehow—to get the both of them down." The ranger shook his head. "I don't know how he managed it—with only one good arm."

"Because he's *Tommy*! Second best climber in the *world*." Cheryl reached out, taking the ranger by his blood-stained hand, allowing him to lead her to his vehicle.

Laura cleared her throat, sensing her cousin's withdrawal into the past. "And this man—he's helping you with your research?"

"Yeah. Kinda." Cheryl picked at her meal, her appetite gone.

"What happened to Lurch?" Laura spooned a large helping of salad into her mouth.

"Don't call him that." Cheryl gave Laura a sharp look. "Isaac's still working with me, until we get this project ironed out and ready for implementation." She stared at her salad for a moment, then lowered her voice. "We're getting close."

Laura considered for a moment. "He's a patient, isn't he? This unknown man of yours?"

"Patient, or subject. Yes."

"Like Robert was. For several years. Until—"

Cheryl looked away; fork poised over her plate. "Yes." She sighed, nodding her head. "Just wish I could go back and be able to *reach* him. Let him know I could hear him—now. See what he's seeing. *Feel* it."

"Hypothetically, right?" Laura reached over and touched Cheryl's hand.

"No." She looked at her cousin. "I've *solved* it. Just need to refine the resolution, adjust for latency. But it *works*. Mind-to-screen communication, both ways. With full recreation of the subject's senses, providing *immersive* feedback."

Laura leaned back, her meal forgotten. "Should you be telling me this?"

"No." Cheryl grinned, her eyes still holding a shadow of pain. "But when has *that* ever stopped us? We've always been close—as close as sisters."

Laura nodded. "I appreciate you trusting me, not that I have any idea how any of it works. Just like when we were kids, and you'd be sitting on Robert's hospital bed, telling me what he was thinking or feeling. As if he were speaking directly to you."

"It always felt like he was." Cheryl looked down, her hands slipping into her lap.

Laura smiled. "And now you know it was *true*. That he could hear you. Knew you were there."

Cheryl's voice was a whisper. "Too late to save him."

"But leading you to be able to help others. Right? Because of *him*. Because of what happened to Robert."

Cheryl looked up and nodded. "That's right. *His* legacy, based on my inspiration."

The monitor was showing a scene of an old farmhouse, its roof newly repaired. Sunlight was shining in large pools of light where several large oak trees once stood, exposing new shingles fastened to the southern exposure of the large roof. Cheryl noticed dozens of metal frames laid out on the ground, recognizing them as mounting brackets for solar panels.

She realized they must be the work of the man currently walking along the eaves of the house, twenty feet or more in the air, heading toward a ladder leaning against the edge. A slim woman was already halfway down, being watched by a large red and black dog. The same breed in each of JD's three data vectors.

She held up one hand; the motion freezing the image on the high-definition display. Then she leaned in, noting the markings of the large shepherd, its thick shoulders wearing a black saddle over reddish hair running along its side. Isaac leaned forward, spreading his fingers, causing the image to enlarge. "Same markings. Consistent with the other two scenarios. A different pairing up of men and women, but the same dog."

He unfroze the data feed, watching as the woman reached the bottom of the ladder and knelt beside the shepherd, her face centered in the frame. She leaned back slightly, looking up and smiling. Isaac froze the image again, his lips pursed. "Still no match in any of the facial recognition databases we've searched. And I've accessed them *all*, other than the secured ones." He paused, wondering if Cheryl would relent and let him rummage around in the government's restricted files.

She ignored his comment. "No place names, street signs, or last names being used. Nothing to help us define specific locations, only regional inferences based on angle of the sun

Isaac shrugged. "Need more specific data points."

"Doubt that'll happen." Cheryl pursed her lips. "JD's being careful not to tip his hand."

Isaac stared at her. "Meaning?"

Cheryl shrugged, then pulled a chair over and sat down. She stared at JD, his eyes open, though unfocused, lips parted slightly, hands hanging loose in his lap. "It's as if by showing us multiple storylines, he's hoping to keep from being discovered. Hiding his identity, preventing us from finding out what happened to him. Burying it beneath the noise he's putting out, aware we're trying to get to the truth. That's why he's weaving these—movies, deflecting our attempts to pin him down."

Isaac raised his finger, pointing at the people on the monitor. "Or maybe—he's hiding in plain sight."

Cheryl followed his finger, watching as the slim bodied man descended the ladder. "You might be right. Blending his identity among the others, with their emotions, able to express his own through them. In some residual desire to hold on to something he's lost, being told in three alternate lifelines."

"And the dog?" Isaac leaned back against the front of an enormous desk that held an assortment of data storage units, tied to servers humming away in the background. He crossed his thick arms. "Why show such consistency there?"

Cheryl sighed. "Unknown." She leaned in, watching as the scene played out, the data stream being captured, spinning up again. The woman in the scene rubbed the shepherd's neck in a reassuring touch, its tail wagging now that its two pack mates had made it back to level ground. "But he's *freaking* cute!"

"He?"

"Definitely a male. You can tell by the way he moves, how he's always keeping watch." She pointed. "And then there's the more obvious indicator, hanging below his belly." The dog's head swiveled as it watched the man cross the lawn, joined by the woman, the two of them heading toward the front door of the farmhouse.

CHAPTER SIXTEEN

RESIDENCE, ARIZONA

Twain and Miranda's Story

The house was silent. Absent of the routine of life. Curtains closed. Refrigerator emptied and unplugged. Air conditioning turned up. An empty shell, no longer home or nest, bereft of the quirky energy of the previous owner.

Twain stood outside, missing Janice. She'd passed away two days earlier, while he was finishing his latest shoot. It saddened him, beyond a level he'd ever felt before, even after learning of the loss of his mother. He sighed as he looked across the front yard, expecting Janice to come around the corner of the house, hands in a worn pair of work gloves, bitching about something. A wave of one hand bidding him to come out back and help move another rock a few inches to either side or dig a new hole to embed a chunk of sun-dried wood, with no apparent rhyme or reason for it.

He held a certified letter from a local lawyer in his hand, notifying him that Janice had turned the house and property over to him. He stared at it while he listened to a message left on his phone by Miranda, letting him know how sorry she was at his loss, as well as her own. That she would be there soon, boarding a plane to come be with him, to help plan her mother's service and go through her personal effects, deciding what to keep and what to let go of.

Twain had received a call from the home-care provider he'd hired to check in on Janice twice daily, letting him know she was in the hospital, unresponsive. It had come in the middle of a boisterous wrap party with dozens of extras taking advantage of the director's largess, ingesting copious amounts of food and booze at a local hotel over-flowing with people. He'd been fending off several advances from hungry-eyed starlets, his opportunities having increased significantly over the past nine months, leading to as many refusals, stirring rumors of sexual ambivalence. Not that he cared, having made a few trips back east to see Miranda, or heading off on week-long forays into remote mountain campsites, Dawg in tow, joined by Miranda when her schedule allowed. The two of them had been able to spend enough time together to keep the flames of their mutual attraction lit, their passion reaching then maintaining a level each was comfortable with. He sighed again, sensing it might be different now with Janice gone, knowing change was inevitable. Questions waiting to be asked, and carefully answered.

"Strange—how I keep expecting her to come through the door, sweat-stained hat pulled down. Hands scabbed, her fingernails broken, palms stained red with dirt." Twain reached up, rubbing his forehead, using the ends of his fingers to drag tears from the corners of his eyes.

"*Pissed* off and cussing." Miranda leaned against him, sliding under his upraised arm, pressing her head against his chest, listening to the steady throb of his heart. She tossed her arm across his lap, pulling herself closer to him. The air was beginning to cool, the windows open, a light breeze threading through the interior of the house.

"Yeah. That too." Twain leaned his head down, kissing Miranda on the back of her neck. Dawg came into the room, having used the new pet door. He walked over to the couch and paused, measuring a small sliver of space beside Miranda, deciding he'd fit. Then he leaped up and turned in a tight circle, dropping into place, pushing with his hind leg, forcing Twain to slide over. With a satisfied sigh, he placed his head across Miranda's lap, closing his eyes as her fingers gently scratched between his ears.

Twain reached up and grabbed the end of a white rope, pulling an attic stairway down. He stepped back, eyeing Miranda, who stared up into the dark recess, her hands shaking. He grinned. "It's gonna be worth the effort—*believe* me."

Miranda shrugged, regretting her remarks, made a few minutes earlier when she'd joined Twain, standing outside in the back yard, commenting on her mother's deteriorating mental condition over the past few years.

"I always admired her, but the creative side took a back seat to her emotions over the past few years. Difficult to watch, considering how great an artist she was." Miranda stood beside Twain, staring across the large backyard, shaking her head as she stared at the assortment of odd-sized pieces of wood and stones embedded in the dry soil, scattered about in a haphazard pattern.

"Gifted, though."

"Yes. She was." Miranda looked at Twain. "Not a trait passed on to me, unfortunately."

He shrugged, pulling her in, his arm draped across her shoulders. "Creativity is a medium for the expression of emotions, when done right. Doesn't much matter what's used to paint a picture, whether it's with pigments, or pieces of nature." He looked down at Miranda. "Or words."

"And film." Miranda squeezed Twain's hand. "On the back of good acting."

"Touché." Twain waved one hand. "And you're wrong about your mother. What Janice created here is without doubt her finest piece. Her final canvas, using every square foot of the yard to craft an incredible work of art."

Miranda stared at the clutter of oddly placed stones, surrounded by half-buried limbs and twisted roots of western cedar trees. There were lines of cacti and other plantings flung into place across the parched sand as if remnants of wind-torn spider webs. A disordered scene, mirroring her mother's tortured mind. "It hurts. Seeing this. Nothing but—"

"*Perfection*." Twain's voice was a whisper in her ear. He pulled back, clearing his throat. "Believe me, I helped with the larger pieces, with no clue to what she was trying to do. Placating a friend, without seeing the artist beneath the surface. Until I stumbled on what she'd been doing these past few years."

Miranda stepped back, staring at Twain, her head tilted to one side, giving him an inquisitive look. "Could be *you're* the one needing help, spending so many hours out here with her, in the hot sun."

Twain grinned, then reached down and gave Dawg a rub of the neck, feeling the solid muscles beneath his thick coat. "How are you with tight places?" He waited a beat, seeing Miranda's eyes widen in confusion at the sudden change of topic. "I mean—do you get claustrophobic?"

Miranda shook her head. "No. I've spent plenty of time hiding in holes, bunkers, or under rocks when the bullets were flying."

Twain took her by the hand, leading her back inside the house. "Let me show you something that will open your eyes to the miracle of your mother's mind. Help reassure you she'd lost nothing of her true self, even while the rest of her was slipping away."

Miranda's feet trembled as she climbed the narrow-framed ladder. The wooden rungs squeaked in protest as Twain followed her up, his hands on her hips as he guided her toward a small window at the end of the cramped space. Both windows were open, helping allay the press of heated air, reduced to survivable. Miranda reached up and wiped away beads of perspiration on her forehead, questioning Twain's mental state. He pointed, directing her to look through the small opening.

Miranda leaned forward, uncomfortable from the heat and confined space. "Now what?" Twain whispered in her ear. "Lean forward, turn your head to the left and look down." She braced her forearms on the windowsill, a layer of fine sand coating her sweaty skin. The back yard looked different from the elevated perch: the vast collection of natural objects now revealed as intricate patterns whose shapes, shadows and textures resolved into several pairs of circled arms with bone-white hands reaching out with thin-limbed fingers, caressing the sides of small stones as if belonging to an ancient sect of wizened gatherers, reaching to pluck them from the ground.

Tears fought for space with the sweat dripping down her cheeks, Miranda's breath coming in shuddering gasps of awe, the creative dance her mother had been doing for so long fully revealed, her artists soul hovering over the baked sand of her canvas, able to see how it would look from above, angled slightly to one side. "How—" She twisted her head around, gazing at Twain. "Did you discover this?"

"I was up on the roof a few months back. Had to replace a tile where water was getting in. That's when I saw what she was doing, though I never let on. Figured she'd tell me when she was ready—or finished." He paused. "Guess she got it done enough to suit her. Before—"

Miranda stood up and turned into his arms. He pulled her in, his body a furnace of heat, unbearable for long, both reluctantly pulling away.

"I'm glad my mother left you the house. You earned it, being here with her. Helping her to see it finished— before."

"You're not pissed?"

"I'm pleased, knowing you'll be—" Miranda slid around, facing him. Her robe parted, revealing her body, recently cooled by a shower and the mechanical hum of the air conditioning, working overtime. "You'll be *keeping* it. Right?"

"Of course." Twain shook his head, frowning.

"I wasn't suggesting you wouldn't." Miranda took his hand, holding it to one breast. "Just expressing my concern—without stopping to think."

Twain smiled, placing his free hand on her other breast. "Understood. And I like it when you speak without stopping to—" He paused.

"Editorialize." He reached for her, his upper body bare, a towel wrapped around his muscled waist falling away as he pulled her into his lap, leaning in, his lips on hers.

Miranda pulled back slightly, looking at him for one long, searching moment. Then she touched his face, his chest, hungry for his body. Missing her mother. Uncertain what might happen next, her eyes gazing at Twain as he leaned forward and picked her up, carrying her into the bedroom.

CHAPTER SEVENTEEN

FARMHOUSE, MID-COAST MAINE

Calvin and Jemma's Story

Jemma stood in the doorway and watching as Calvin stopped to get a drink from the well. She frowned, bothered by the thought despite his insistence the water was perfectly safe to drink. A shiver ran through her as she recalled looking inside the narrow opening when Calvin slid the moss-lined granite cover back, sunlight pouring in, revealing webs of translucent threads clinging to the tightly stacked stones lining the interior. She'd flinched, pulling back when she saw tiny insects trapped within, providing ready to eat meals for spiders lurking in the shadows. There had been more than a few panicked awakenings from dreams turned to nightmares ever since. One of her startled reactions providing Calvin a bruise on his cheek, her elbow catching him as they lay together on her couch, napping after a long day of hard labor.

She sighed, watching as he lowered a pail into the well, wondering as he pulled it up and took a long drink when he would give in and accept her standing invitation to spend the night. She was eager to test the level of their compatibility in areas outside of the constant planning and hours of hard labor. "I'm heading inside to take a shower." Jemma was leaning against the side of the back door, arms crossed under her breasts, one leg cocked against the frame. "You could join me. Help save the world—sharing the hot water."

Calvin smiled, wiping his mouth with the back of his hand, used to Jemma's teasing remarks of late. He cupped his hand, pouring cold spring water into his palm, Dawg eagerly lapping it up. "You go ahead. I'll start putting some lunch together." He leaned over and slid the well cover back in place, missing the exasperated look on Jemma's face as she spun around and headed inside. Calvin wiped his hands on his faded, work stained jeans, knowing Jemma counted on his reluctance to join in with the teasing banter. Their arrangement was simple: she paid him for his professional advice and occasional help on the project, in between his other commitments. The bruise on his cheek had been a fair price to pay in having weakened, allowing her to share the couch with him one afternoon. A serious lapse in judgment, one he was still kicking himself for. Their business relationship was important to him, and he didn't want to lose her trust.

He straightened up and headed toward the front steps. Dawg ran up from behind, his shoulder hitting Calvin in the back of one knee, spilling him to the ground. The shepherd reached the top of the steps, then looked back, head tilted to one side, as if letting Calvin know how foolish he was being.

"Are you sure about this?" Calvin stood in the door of the bathroom, hands at his side.

Jemma closed her eyes, the shower stall filled with warm mist rising around her angular body, visible beneath a thick layer of soap suds. She didn't turn around, only nodded, trembling as a wave of cool air slipped in when Calvin closed the bathroom door.

"Why the change of heart?" Late afternoon sunlight was streaming through Jemma's bedroom window, filtered by a thin curtain that fluttered in a gentle breeze. Her head was resting on Calvin's chest, her eyes centered on his face, her heart beating faster as she watched the play of soft light on the two-day growth of beard thickening his chiseled cheeks, helping to soften the sharp angle of his jaw.

Calvin was silent, his lips parted slightly before finally answering. "I was lying on the ground, hands in the dirt, Dawg looking at me like I was the biggest damn fool he'd ever seen." He rolled onto his side, slipping his hand over, brushing back a thick curl of hair from Jemma's forehead. "I realized that if *he* felt that way, I must seem an even *bigger* one in your eyes."

Jemma nodded. "That's pretty close to the way I've been feeling."

"So, I decided to take you up on your offer." His finger brushed the side of her cheek. "For the good of the environment."

Jemma wriggled in closer, squeezing her arm around his muscular chest, her mouth close to his, eyes dark. "And the rest of what happened—once we were clean?"

"It just seemed—" Calvin sighed. "Inevitable." He noted her expression harden. "I mean, it was something I'd been thinking about ever since I met you—the second time. At my aunt's house when you asked if I was gonna let you be a missed opportunity." He paused. "And the answer is no. Never again." Then he leaned in and kissed her.

JD

Before

"It isn't the end, just because you say it." She shook her head, arms crossed, looking down at him as he lay on the bed.

"It is! I swear. I promise—never again."

"And when I'm gone? What then?"

"Don't."

"Don't what?"

"Don't go. Don't say that. Don't leave me."

"Reverse everything you've done and said."

He returned an empty stare, his body shaking in withdrawal. Skin itching beneath his constant rub of fingers, feeling as if he might erupt into flames at any second. She came over, placing her hand on his cheek, her touch spreading a thick blanket of warmth. His need for her, all-consuming. A different fire. One he knew would heal him. Make him whole again.

"It's not an ending, only a beginning. It's not about what you don't want, but what you do. Not out of fear, but fearlessness. That's how you begin. As if a babe learning to crawl. By yourself. Until you're able to stand, then walk. And when you're finally free—come find me."

He watched her walk away. Struggled to stand up and follow, unable to move, his feet growing into the floor as if roots, binding him in place. Watching as she cleared the doorway, her yellow sundress gleaming in the light. His eyes overflowed as he reached for her, silvery tendrils of light trailing behind as she walked away, all that remained for him to hold on to, to cherish. Loving her for all she'd offered him, asking nothing in return. Knowing, as he wrapped his arms around himself, he would see her again. Soon. Whole again. Healed.

CHAPTER EIGHTEEN

APARTMENT, MARYLAND

Jared and Teresa's Story

Teresa angled her head and slipped an earring into her earlobe, then straightened up, brushing back her dark hair with her fingers, admiring how the diamonds looked. She knew she couldn't keep them, the gift a generous mistake made by Jared with honorable intentions as a thank you for letting him rent the painting. Unaware of the emotional message being sent, his social intelligence lacking when it came to women, based on their conversations about each other's past relationships. She smoothed her dress, twisting to check it in the mirror: a new acquisition, splurged on when a client purchased two of the more expensive paintings from the lily collection, her hefty commission check allowing the indulgence. A knock on the bathroom door was followed by her roommate letting her know there was a phone call for her.

"Yes, I tried them on. They're perfect—and will have to go back. Tomorrow." Teresa sipped from a bottle of water, then stuck out her tongue, responding to her roommate's rolling of her eyes. "Because, Jared, it's not acceptable. Diamonds are too extravagant a gift between friends." She paused, then cut off his response. "I appreciate the gesture but won't be able to keep them. Okay?" Her roommate picked up a cushion and tossed it in her direction, her jaw open, shaking her head as she walked away in disbelief.

Jared frowned, sitting outside her apartment in his car, hoping to be invited up. The jeweler had let him know about the delivery of the earrings that afternoon, and he'd been expecting a different reaction when he called. "I'm sorry. I didn't mean to—"

"It's not a problem, Jared. And I appreciate what you were trying to do. It's just—too much." Teresa paused. "You can stop by and pick them up at the gallery tomorrow. Okay?"

"Can't I come by tonight?"

Teresa hesitated. "I'm getting ready to go out. To celebrate. I sold two of the lily paintings today."

"That's great. I mean it. Really." Jared waited, unsure what to say, staring up at the window of the third-floor apartment.

"Jared?" Teresa walked over and pulled the curtain back, looking down at the parking lot.

"Yes?"

"You're outside, aren't you?"

"Yes."

She sighed, a smile sliding across her lips. "Come on up—and I'll let you in."

Jared stared at Teresa, eyes wide in appreciation. "You look *incredible!*" He nodded at her roommate. "It's nice to finally meet you." Teresa made a quick introduction, then elbowed her friend out of the way, taking Jared by the hand and pulling him into her small bedroom, closing the door in the other girl's face. Then she gave Jared a searching look. "You look nice." She noted the color of his shirt, not quite coordinated with that of his pants, though his belt matched his shoes, this time.

"I hope you understand—about the earrings. They're perfect, but not—"

Jared held up a hand. "It's okay. I get it. I'm just glad I get to see you wearing them, before having to take them back." He raised his eyebrows. "You said you were going out?"

"I am. It's a tradition whenever you sell a painting. To go out, treating everyone to dinner."

"Everyone? I thought you worked by yourself."

"I do."

"Then it's just you—going out."

Teresa lowered her eyes, nodding her head. "Afraid so, unless–"

"Yes?" Jared stepped forward, an eager look lighting up his face.

Teresa's roommate, standing outside the door, raised her voice. "Stop being such a *bitch*!"

Teresa grinned, ignoring the interruption. "I knew you'd be coming by, wanting to surprise me." She came over and kissed him on his cheek. "Give me ten minutes. I already made reservations—for two."

The music was low, barely reaching them as they sat on the couch in his living room. Dawg was lying in the room's corner, yawning, well past his usual bedtime. He looked at Jared, waiting for him to head to bed.

Jared turned his head and looked at the diamond in Teresa's ear. "Do you really have to give them back?"

Teresa nodded, then pressed her head against his upper shoulder, enjoying the feel of his body, her hand in his. The meal, wine, conversation, and music at the restaurant had caused a rush of heat to stir within her, one that had continued to build during their quiet drive back to his house. It was their fifth date and there was an unspoken promise in the air, both of them aware a boundary was about to be crossed. One Teresa knew would prove to be an issue down the road. She took in a deep breath, the smell of Jared's cologne and natural scent driving the thought away. She stood up, taking his hand, leading him to the bedroom, Dawg left looking on from the hallway, the door gently closed in his face.

Jared ignored the dull ache in his left shoulder as he lay in bed, his arm curled around Teresa's ribs, the edge of a firm breast cupped in his hand. His breathing was slow, measured, in time with her own. He sighed, thinking of how things had changed, the feel of her body against his stirring him again as he stared up at the ceiling, painted with rose-colored light filtered by a thin chemise draped over the bedside lamp. Teresa had placed it there, wanting to see him. For him to see her. The sight of her body had driven him to a place he'd never experienced before, encouraged by her eager responses to his every touch, pulling them both over the edge of control. Falling, then recovering, then falling again. The second time allowed to stretch between denial of release and then letting go, ending with shivering climaxes for them both.

He heard a scratching on the bedroom door as Dawg sought claim to his bed on the floor. A soft whine built up, ending in a whimper. Teresa stirred, rolling onto her side, and opening her eyes. "Should I leave?"

"*No!*" Jared climbed out of bed and crossed to the door, letting Dawg in. He turned around, looking at Teresa. "Do you need anything? Water? More wine?"

"No." Teresa sat up and stretched her arms above her head, her upper body exposed. "I'm replete. *Completely.*"

Jared crossed back to the bed and slipped in beside her. He hesitated, then pulled her against him, his arm sliding around her waist. "Is this, okay?"

Teresa nodded, enjoying the feel of his warmth against her skin. "You don't need to do that."

Jared started to loosen his grasp. "Do what?"

"Asking me if everything you want to do is okay." Teresa took his free hand, placing it on her breast. "Just go for it. I'll let you know when I'm not comfortable with something—believe me."

"Like with the earrings." His fingers began to gently massage her.

Teresa spun onto her back, her full breasts exposed in the diffuse light. "Yes. *Exactly.*"

"I get it. I mean, I don't regret buying them." Jared reached up and touched her ear, brushing back her hair. "They're perfect for you." He traced the curve of her face, ending at her chin, then leaned down and kissed her. "I got that right—even if it was too early." He waited for her to respond. "Right?"

"I'm not into timelines, Jared. Not with something like this."

"Sex?" He pulled back slightly.

"No. *Relationships*." Teresa saw the look of confusion in Jared's eyes, mixed with an awareness he might have misread her feelings. "I enjoy spending time with you. I do. It's easy, so far—being with you."

"As friends." He looked away. "With benefits."

"That works for me. For *now*."

"And later?" His tone let her know he was not happy with the direction of the conversation.

Teresa reached over and touched him on his cheek, encouraging him to look at her. "A few weeks ago, you were a stranger stopping by, coming inside to look at a painting of day lilies. And now—you have an incredible painting hanging in your home. An incredible canine companion, who showed up out of nowhere. And me. In your bed with no ties or expectations. Willing to share my art *and* my body with you. The second one—rent free."

"But not your *soul*."

"No."

Jared nodded, trying to hide his disappointment. He failed, looking away again, his voice soft, and determined. "Not yet."

Teresa smiled. "Okay. Let's go with that for now." She pulled him down then slid up against him as he stared at the ceiling. Silent. Considering. Teresa turned her head, studying his profile in the dim light. "Should I go?"

Jared reached over and slid his arm under her shoulders, pulling her into his embrace, kissing the side of her neck. "No—not yet." He hesitated a moment. "But if anything changes, I'll let you know."

Once Teresa's breathing had settled into a slow rise and fall, Jared turned his head, drinking in the aroma of her hair, her perfume, the delicate scent of her body. He whispered, his words barely more than a sigh of air. "I know one thing. I'm falling in love you—no matter how you feel about me." Then he closed his eyes, fatigue reaching up to carry him off to sleep.

Teresa lay beside him, tears forming in her eyes, her lips trembling as she struggled not to cry, knowing nothing he did would change her mind. Unable to offer what he was looking for: someone to share his life. To be there for him no matter what. Something she'd promised herself never to do again. One life, her own, enough of a burden to carry, knowing two would be more than she could handle, having tried a long-term relationship before and failing, miserably.

"But you *can't* leave me! We're in *love*. I *know* it." The young man looked at Teresa with an anguished expression in his eyes, his voice quivering. His glasses reflected her face: a cool, distant look in her eyes. She reached out, touching his cheek, wanting to take away his pain, knowing there was nothing she could do. Her need to move on greater than her feelings for him. Unable to resist the pull to leave, heading off to somewhere unknown. Her instincts whispering that somewhere just beyond the walls of his apartment, beyond the outer reaches of the city, just over the curve of the horizon, she'd find her way clear of her mother's raspy, tabaco roughened voice in her youthful ears.

"Women like us, Teri, real women and not those clueless fools with moody eyes, latching onto some *asshole* of a man, willing to swallow their daily ration of *shit*. We're *different*. Not staying 'round, listening to their stories, and their empty dreams. To their whining and demanding. Not sticking around until it starts up again, finding its way to an ending at the point of a sharp tongue and angry fists. Putting each other down. Tearing each other apart."

"But *Daddy's* not like that. He's *different*." Teresa turned a teary-eyed face toward her mother.

"No, he ain't, baby. He ain't any different. Just another *weak-ass* boy, trying to be a man." The claw of her mother's fingernails hurt when they found her shoulder, digging in. "We got to get *moving*, baby. I met a man gonna give us a ride outta here. In a big ass truck. With a *bed* in the back. Imagine *that*! A bed—inside a *truck*! He's gonna take us outta here—all the way to California. Maybe even all the way to *Disneyland*. How's that sound, baby? Would you like that? To go there and see them princesses?"

When Teresa protested, her mother's smile hardened like a freshly poured sidewalk in the heat of a summer sun. Teresa braced herself, expecting the slap to her face, welcoming it when it came. The pain reassuring. The words that followed from the same tired script. "I'm sorry, baby girl. Mommy needs her medicine, that's all. Just need to go find the guy, the one who's taking us outta here. You and me, going all the way to California. You'll see. It's time to move on, like the gypsies we are."

The news of her actor boyfriend's suicide reached Teresa a few weeks after she'd moved out. A note attached to his last paycheck, mailed to an ex-girlfriend's house. A small news clipping included of how he'd thrown himself from a bridge, along with a letter left detailing his last wishes. The note had driven Teresa into a deep depression and when she finally climbed out, she'd promised to never attach herself to a man again, no matter how much they deserved the love she had to give. Deciding to live down to a family legacy, one of constant betrayal, running deep within her veins.

CHAPTER NINETEEN

RESEARCH FACILITY, MARYLAND

Cheryl

Cheryl reached out, adjusting the field of the Tee-Cee with several jabs of a finger on an abused keyboard. The image on the monitor remained razor sharp as a screech of variant noise continued to sleet through the speakers, overwhelming a whisper-thin thread of speech. The high-pitched sound rising and falling as waves of data washed across the curved shoreline of sensors in the silicon cap. She was having difficulty trying to bring coherence to the scene as two people stood side by side, exchanging words.

Isaac shook his head, watching as Cheryl continued to make rapid fire changes. "Why do you do that? Take such a risk, reprogramming on the fly? Counter-intuitive to how it's usually done." He frowned.

"It's a special language. My *own*." Cheryl scrunched her eyes, the tip of her tongue caught between her teeth as she considered several options at once. She made another change to the vast array of odd symbols ranged across her laptop display, the sound from the speakers wavering, then settling back into whispers, barely loud enough to be heard above the irritating whine in the background. Swearing under her breath, she tried filtering it out again as Isaac leaned closer to the speakers.

"Sounds like a table saw, running just outside visual framing."

Cheryl looked at him, her mouth falling open. "Of *course*! That's *it*."

She gave Isaac a wide smile. "*Thank you*! It was driving me nuts, trying to work that out."

Isaac nodded, leaning back. "A fluke. My granddad used to mill lumber from trees on his property. He'd draft me to help him, seeing how big I was." He paused. "Always assuming, as he put it, that I needed to find something *useful* to do. Rather than hanging around with my mother all the time."

Cheryl missed Isaac's emotional glimpse into his life, her fingers dancing on her keyboard, filtering out the higher frequency bands in the sounds being projected, glancing over at JD, watching his face for any sign of change now that the words from his mental projection were reflecting from the walls of the lab. He continued to stare straight ahead, eyes blinking, without any awareness of the world around him, still safely locked away within the multiple storylines of his damaged mind.

Isaac shrugged, then lowered himself into his large chair, memories of the scent of freshly sawn wood permeating his mood, a smile spreading across his pale face.

"There's satisfaction to be found in hard work." The old man reached for another slab of wood. Isaac, on the opposite end, helped him feed it onto a long metal frame. A large saw blade hummed away at the far end, the scent of hot oil mixing with the resin-sweet odor of the sawdust from the southern yellow pine they were sawing into boards. "Better you aim your sights in that direction, rather than them books you've got your nose shoved into all the time."

Isaac grinned, enjoying the banter and the work. His grandfather was the only person who looked at him as a person and not an oddity of nature. "I read to learn. Every book: a window into other worlds. Other places. A variety of other people's opinions on life—and death."

His grandfather grunted as they wrestled another large piece of heavy, densely grained wood into place. "The real world has enough of that *crap* already built in. Along with the stain of sweat, stink of fear, and loads of *bullshit* being spread around." He gave his over-sized grandson a searching look. "As I'm sure *you've* learned, judging by the bruises on your arms and face."

The thick slab of wood inched ahead, pulled by series of teeth into the saw rig, fed in at a measured rate, the blade singing as it touched the leading edge.

"This programming language that you developed—" Isaac worked the beginning of a question around a large helping of pasta. "Are there *other* people using it?" He paused, another forkful of spaghetti halfway to his mouth. "I mean, it seems incredibly flexible. Must be useful for all kinds of things. Like advanced research projects, quantum computing, and helping to develop artificial intelligence."

"It's *my* baby." Cheryl took a large helping of the spaghetti and shoved it into her mouth, chewing noisily, ravenous, the two of them having skipped lunch, eager to delve further into JD's recorded thoughts. She took a swallow of lukewarm coffee, then looked across the empty cafeteria, muffling a burp with her hand. "Been improving it since I was—practically a baby myself."

She looked over, wondering if Isaac was just making small talk or if he really wanted to hear the story. Their relationship had never strayed too far from professional lines, salted with occasional back and forth bantering. She watched as he put a moderately sized forkful of food in his mouth, chewing slowly, nodding, a sign she should continue.

"I began thinking about how to create it, back when I was in school, learning how to program." Cheryl hesitated. "In college, I mean. When I was thirteen." She blushed. "Though it seemed like a regular school to me—with the same lack of friends." She lowered her fork. "I don't mean to sound like I'm boasting. They selected me because I was good at math and science. Poodle-pee poor in history, though decent enough in languages. Especially Latin. That always came easy for me."

Cheryl paused, glancing down at her plate of food, toying with asparagus sprouts, hating the thought of putting them in her mouth despite knowing how beneficial they were to her health. "I was absolutely *horrible* at social skills. Like I said: no friends, other than my cousin. Not that I missed having any. Too focused in on my—" She stopped, having tripped into areas far outside the original question, her emotions having risen to her mouth before she could rein them in.

"You need to show your work, Ms. Atkinson. It's not enough to provide the correct answer without showing a solution."

"Why?" Cheryl slouched in her chair, arms crossed on her chest, her face pinched in exasperation between two mismatched pigtails, a glare of determination in her eyes as she faced down the professor.

The elderly man reached up, adjusting his glasses, sighing loudly. "Because that's the only way I can mark your progression, matching *cause* to *effect*. Like everyone else taking this or any other class, Ms. Atkinson."

"But—" Cheryl slunk lower in her over-sized chair, her feet barely touching the floor. "I'm not *using* what everyone else is using. I have my *own* way of getting there, and it's a *hell* of a—"

"*Language*, Ms. Atkinson." Her professor looked at her over the rim of his glasses, his eyes set in a firm stare. Cheryl eased her posture of resistance, aware, barely, which side of the line she was on.

"Sorry. My way is just quicker—that's all."

"I can't grade *quicker*. You'll need to share your work, even if it is as unique as you claim it to be." The professor watched the young girl sink down in her chair, head barely at a level with the large wooden desk. He leaned forward, trying not to grin. "Are you willing to do that?"

"No." Cheryl huffed for a moment, chin down, frown on her lips. "But

I'll show my work. Use one of the *stupid* solutions. Just like all the rest of the lemmings."

"Then we've reached an accord. And I have another appointment. So, you'll turn in your amended assignments by end of day, tomorrow. Correct, Ms. Atkinson?"

Cheryl stood up, hesitating a moment, wanting to stamp her foot in frustration. Instead, she nodded politely and walked away, swearing under her breath, hearing the faint sound of her brother's laughter in her mind's ear.

"What is it?" Isaac leaned forward. "Cheryl—are you okay?"

"I'm fine." She pushed her plate away, no longer hungry. "I absorbed what they were teaching me, though it seemed frustratingly *linear*. I kept wondering why no one was interested in pursuing a fresh approach."

"How so?"

Cheryl reached into her purse and pulled out a small, multi-colored cube of plastic, Isaac watching as it dangled from her fingers on a thin silver chain, fastened to the corner of one of the smaller cubes. "I developed a unique way of coding. Like *this*."

"A child's toy?"

"No. It's a Rubik's cube." She spun the sides, mixing the colors, then handed it to Isaac, the small device all but disappearing in his large fingers. "You twist it, trying to put all the colors back in order."

"I *know* what it is. Always thought of them as nothing more than a childish diversion."

"They *can* be. But when you see the faces as if they're ordered data bases, or arrays, you realize how powerful it would be using a similar concept to rearrange disparate data points—" Cheryl's eyes lost their focus as she stared at the cube Isaac held pinched between finger and thumb, watching as it swung back and forth. "Into a coherent form of inter-connected, or cross-connected groups of data sets."

"And you came up with a solution? Some innovative way of doing that?" Isaac held the cube out, seeing it in a new light. "Like this?"

"Kinda." Cheryl looked down and stabbed her fork into the slimy stalks of healthy food, shoving them into her mouth in one fell swoop, closing her eyes while she chewed, hating their texture. "I used a hybrid approach. Morphing the cube into a helix pattern with three twisted strands, not two. Like a collagen molecule, which I used as a model for my design."

Isaac continued to stare at the cube, tempted to twist it, afraid he'd end up breaking it. "Which is a perfect solution path for what we're running into with JD, with all the various data vectors spun about—" He stared. "JD. *He's* the core. Everything running through him. The real him."

Cheryl nodded, then reached out, reclaiming the cube. "It would seem so. He's pushing three story-lines with dozens of concurrent elements, or spokes, strung between all three of them."

"The animal, for one. And the coupling up of male and female projections, another." Isaac leaned back, no longer interested in his meal.

"Yes. As well as a host of other things in the foreground, or tucked away in the background, hiding in the shadows."

Isaac narrowed his eyes, waiting as a group of security personnel walked past, making their way to the service windows. He lowered his voice. "Like multiple windows, opened up between each personnel grouping."

"Exactly. And my unique program, if you will, operates like this." She rolled the cube between her fingers, further mixing the colors. "Disorder." Then she quickly realigned the faces. "Into order."

Isaac nodded. "It seems simple enough, filtering everything we're gathering through your special program, with it manipulating the data feed, finding the constants, then tracing them back to the source. To the true source of who it is we're dealing with. Identifying which of the projections is the real JD."

"If any one of them *is*." Cheryl grinned. "Although it's a bit more complicated than only having three sides of a cube to work with." She lost her smile, lips pursed as she considered the work ahead. "There's also the *emotional* side to consider, with distinct empathy elements in each pathway, affecting all his character's behaviors. I mean—we've only been seeing them as images, up to now. Shallow viewpoints to work from."

"And when we move into the full immersion phase, once you're ready, you'll be able to deepen the emotional feedback loops. Correct?"

Cheryl pursed her lips. "Or muddy them up, preventing his recovery—if we're not extremely careful."

"You seem—" Laura eyed her cousin, sensing a change in her demeanor, as if Cheryl was both slightly depressed and excited at the same time. "*Unusually* disconnected, and it's seriously freaking me out! So, *stop it*!" Laura took a sip of her drink, a perfect mix of sweet and sour, the umbrella sticking out at an angle, lightly grazing the surface of her cheek. "Is it something to do with your mystery man?"

Cheryl shrugged. "Yes—and no. Just going through some personal reflection."

"Having to do with him?" Laura grinned as she looked over.

"Not everything is about him."

"Really?" Laura reached over and touched her cousin on the hand. "Drink up. It's Friday. You're done for the week. Your class, taught. And your work—" She pulled back. "Will *still* be there, waiting for you when you get back."

"I met a woman." Cheryl paused, looking over, seeing her cousin's eyes widen. "Not like *that*! Stop being—"

"I'm just teasing you. Blame it on the booze." Laura took another sip, deeper this time. "I'm on my second, you slowpoke."

"Lush."

"Workaholic."

Cheryl raised her glass. "Touché." Then she bottomed her glass, recalling her recent meeting with the younger woman who'd been auditing her class.

Mari had stayed behind after the class ended, having attended several times over the past two months, sitting in the back of the hall and abstaining from offering comments. She'd just handed Cheryl a single piece of paper detailing an idea she'd been working on, waiting as Cheryl read it, then handed it back.

Mari blushed. "Is my concept sound?" She folded the paper, tucking it away in her purse. "Or am I out of my league?"

Cheryl nodded; her eyes centered on Mari's. "It's solid, but you knew that already. Before asking me to review it."

Mari smiled. "I did. Even wrote a paper on it—just as an exercise."

"Do you have it with you?" Cheryl watched as Mari slipped a thick envelope from the back pocket of the light-colored slacks she was wearing, complementing a red silk shirt, its tones contrasting with the ivory shade of her flawless skin, indicative of her Asian bloodline.

"You can take it with you." Mari nodded toward the small backpack slung over Cheryl's shoulder. "I'm sure you have places to be."

"Not for another hour or so." Cheryl held up the envelope. "I can look at it now, discuss it with you over coffee, if that works."

"I'm all yours." Mari nodded, a wide smile on her thin lips. "And thank you. I appreciate you taking the time to do this for me."

"Your basic premise is fine." Cheryl folded the pages together, slipping them into the envelope and handing it to Mari. "As far as it goes." She leaned back, taking a bite of a bagel. "And familiar enough, in my having considered it a few years back."

Mari lowered her eyes. "Then it would seem I'm late to the game."

"Not at all." Cheryl took a sip of her coffee, black with a dollop of cream, no sugar, the way her brother used to make it for her, their parents none the wiser. "No one else has arrived—yet. Other than me."

"Other than you?" Mari's eyes lit up, her hand squeezing the envelope, wrinkling it.

Cheryl nodded. "I've been fortunate to have government funding behind me for the last five years, allowing me to develop the hardware and programming needed to make it a reality." She lowered her cup, holding it in both hands. "Which, to date, has *not* happened."

"Then I'm heading in the right direction. Right?"

"Again—you knew that already." Cheryl stared at the younger woman, the surface of her wide cheeks flushed with excitement, though her expression remained quiet. "You don't strike me as someone who seeks or *needs* external validation."

"I'm not. Usually. But getting it from *you* helps me cope with a lack of vision from the people I normally deal with, lacking the capability to grasp what's possible until someone comes along and makes it real."

"Visionaries—like us?"

"Like you. Or so it would seem, despite your previous denial."

Cheryl reached out and stirred her coffee, her voice low when she finally spoke. "I'm in a bit of a quandary. Unable to discuss this any further, or in more detail."

"Because—?"

"There are certain legal entanglements."

Mari widened her eyes. "Then you're saying it's possible!"

"No. I'm deliberately not saying that."

"I understand." Mari's hands shook as she lifted her cup, taking a sip of the tea she'd brewed, using boiling water from the shop and a special blend of tea leaves pulled from her purse. She'd placed them in a silver diffuser with a hinged cover attached, small holes on top and bottom to let the water in. "You're morally and contractually bound. Still—the thought that someone is working on this—"

"Hypothetically."

"Of course. *Exactly!*" Mari smiled. "Only an exercise of what ifs, and nothing more."

Cheryl leaned forward, her eyes lighting up in excitement. "Then under those conditions, let's take your reasoning and expand the realm of potential for good and harm that might arise from being able to use this hypothetical technology to reveal the workings of the inner mind. In real time."

"Really?" Laura frowned. "You took a stranger—to *our* special place?"

Cheryl frowned. "We didn't discover it, Laura."

"But I'm the one who first mentioned going there."

Cheryl considered. "Okay. I'm just saying, we weren't the first to plant a flag and claim it in the name of some King, like Christopher—"

"Queen. Not King." Laura smirked. "Isabella."

"Okay. Queen." Cheryl grinned. "I always sucked at history. Never much interested in looking back, I guess."

"Because you were always leaning into the next day. The next new thing. Eager to leap ahead, bypass obstacles. Just like your—" Laura paused, seeing a flicker of pain cross her cousin's face.

"You need to rest." Robert grabbed Cheryl by her shoulder, pulling gently, stopping her from leaping onto the next boulder. "For a few minutes. Okay?"

Cheryl shrugged off her brother's hand, then looked up at a rise of rock bordering the trail they were on. They'd been following a riverbed of tumbled stones, pinched between the shoulders of a granite ledge. The water was running at a decent flow, slipping between gravel-based pools: crystal clear and shockingly cold. The sky was a wedge of deep blue directly overhead, no rain in the offing, a perfect day to get out and work legs and arms until they quivered from fatigue. Left to collapse in a meadow of summer grass along the way, blooms of Queen Anne's lace and brown-eyed Susan's dancing in a light breeze. Robert had given her a few moments to recover, rousing her before she fell into a state of exhausted bliss.

"Can we climb the ledges?" Cheryl turned around and looked up at her brother. "Please! Just a little way. Up to the—"

Robert tilted his head, looking down, his lips pressed in a tight line. "We can turn around and head back."

Cheryl shook her head. "I'm sorry. I promised. No asking."

Her brother reached over, tousling her short-cropped hair, barely longer than his own. It had been a self-administered shearing that had upset their mother, leaving her speechless. Their father had stepped in, imposing a suitable punishment: two weekends with no outdoor activities. Robert had used the time to discover and climb three maidenhead routes in the local mountains, adding to his growing reputation as one of the region's top climbers. He'd finally relented to her endless wheedling, agreeing to take her out for a training run, their parents none the wiser, off for a day of berry-picking. "It's okay. I like how eager you get. Reminds me of myself, at your age."

"But *you* got to climb." His sister looked down at the toes of her hiking boots, an old pair of his that she'd insisted on wearing even though they were a size too large. She had on two pairs of socks, her feet swollen, blisters forming. "You were always sneaking away and doing it, with no one knowing where you were, except me."

"And falling, then punished while I was waiting for my leg to heal."

Cheryl lifted one foot, balancing like he'd taught her to do. "Learning what not to do. Like you always say—failure oftentimes the *best* teacher."

Robert knelt, meeting her eyes. "That's why I'm in charge of *you*, because I know all the tricks."

She nodded, then looked up at the ledges again, her eyes tracing the line she would use to get up to the top. "Can we get going? I'm not tired."

"Yeah. If you're ready." He gave her a broad smile, aware her feet were in pain, proud of his kid sister and her indomitable will. "Lead on, Chipmunk."

"What is it?" Laura was sipping at a glass of ice water, foregoing a second drink, having given up on her distracted cousin catching up.

"He always called me Chipmunk. Robert."

"That's because you had fat cheeks."

"*No!* It's because I was a great climber. In trees, which my parents allowed me to climb for some stupid reason. Just as likely to have gotten hurt doing that."

"True. Though the risks were less if you fell." Laura reached over, touching Cheryl on her face. "But you have to admit, you *did* have fat cheeks back then."

"And you're *still* a large-mouth Bass." Cheryl lifted her glass, clinking it against Laura's. "Here's to young girls everywhere—with fat cheeks and big mouths."

CHAPTER TWENTY

BUILDING, L.A. BASIN

Twain and Miranda's Story

Rain fell in a warm pulse of moisture filling in the holes in an empty parking lot. A tall chain-link fence with razor-wire strung along its top framed a two-story metal building standing at the back of the parking area: the front edged in yellow light from a single streetlamp. Two armed men flanked a garage door, opened to let in a white Mercedes SUV. Now closed, cutting off the interior view.

Twain lowered a compact pair of binoculars, wiping the lenses dry with a cloth, his head angled to one side as he considered how long to wait before making his next move. The head of the local drug cartel had arrived, no doubt delivering insulting accusations, berating his foot soldiers for their inability to remove a growing irritant. Valuable assets, lost to violent assaults. Money and product gone missing. Rumors spreading throughout the drug community of the head of operations having lost his touch, becoming weak, vulnerable to replacement from within or without.

Twain knew the building held what remained of the people responsible for moving a large percentage of the illegal drug trade into and through the greater LA Basin. Millions of dollars at stake, with a dozen lives already lost to a shadowy presence. His, lurking in the background, deadly and professional. The head man thinking his unknown enemy must be in the employ of a competitor, looking to force him into a merger.

Twain smiled as he shook his head, raindrops dripping from his chin with two days growth of beard staining his cheeks black. The end of the long hunt almost at hand. The man responsible for his pregnant daughter and her fiancé's untimely death enclosed within the trap he'd prepared. He watched with cold eyes as a light come on, erasing the shadows of a second-floor window, letting him know the group had moved upstairs. No doubt leaving a small security team below, woefully unprepared for what would happen next.

The thud of metal on metal drew the attention of the two men standing at the lower end of stairs leading up to the second-floor office. One of them moved toward a small door while the other slipped to one side, gun aimed, ready to cover the other man as he opened the door with a sudden jerk. A sudden flash of light filled the doorway, blinding both men. Another flash-bang grenade came through, exploding, adding to their disorientation as Twain, dressed in black, slipped inside, sliding a knife across the throat of the man closest to the door. He reached the other one a moment later, the point of his blade opening his jugular, releasing a thick rope of blood that arced through the air, splattering on the concrete floor.

Twain wasted little time in moving the armored SUV into position, its keys left in the ignition. He backed it against the bottom of the stairs, then reached underneath, puncturing the fuel tank with a sharpened rod, using the haft of his knife to pound it through the metal lining, allowing a steady flow of gas to escape. It spread across the floor, mixing with the pools of blood from the two men. Twain moved back toward the door, lighting a flare, and tossing it toward the vehicle. The gasses ignited, the echo chasing him across the parking lot where he took up position by the end of a shipping container, the door open, a firing slit already cut into it. He inserted the barrel of a high-powered rifle with night-scope attached, centering the glowing lines of the crosshair on the fire escape door of the second-floor office. Then he waited, safety slipped off, finger lightly caressing the curved shape of the trigger.

The first two men who exited the office via the emergency exit fell back inside, their chests punctured, spines blown out by hollow-point rounds. A handful of others, faced with daring the raging flames from below or risking a run through a gauntlet of aimed shots, made their decision, rushing through the door onto the metal landing, A few of them leapt over the railing, willing to risk broken bones, while the rest jumped down the steps, two at a time, falling in a sea of tangled legs as bullets thudded into their bodies. Twain cut down the men as they reached the ground and hobbled or crawled away. Two survivors on the stairwell shoved each other, trying to shield themselves. To no avail, both men dying from well-placed shots to their upper chests, leaving one more. The leader, standing in the doorway, arms crossed, a wry smile on his lips as he nodded. The fact he was still alive let him know the time for negotiations had arrived.

"A wonderful performance. Executed to perfection." The short, thick bodied man eased out onto the escape platform, the heat at his back reaching an uncomfortable level. "I am prepared to offer you and your employer *generous* terms."

Twain kept his scope centered on the man's lower body. He gently squeezed the trigger, placing a bullet through his spine, dropping him to the metal slats of the landing. He watched without emotion as the man struggled to move, his arms trying to pull his unresponsive lower body away from the inferno raging inside the building. Failing. The blistering heat igniting his pants, shirt, then hair, the same way his daughter had died, pinned inside a burning car, her husband alongside her. Both their hands on her pregnant belly, trying to shield the child carried in her womb.

Twain pulled the rifle from the slot and removed the scope, wiping it dry. Then he rubbed the rifle with an oiled cloth before putting it away in a reinforced carrying case. The keening wails of excruciating pain from the drug lord echoed in the night air, bringing a smile to his face as he strolled away. Once clear of the parking area, Twain stopped, listening to the crackling of the flames as he waited for the director to call out, ending the long take. He continued to wait for the hissing spray of fire retardant from safety personnel moving in to douse the controlled burn. Continued to wait for the stunties to rise, laughing as they wiped away layers of artificial gore from their hands, arms, and f aces. Waited with a puzzled expression on his face for the artificial rain to cease. For towels to be brought over to dry his hair and face.

The flames continued to build, the wall of the building supporting the fire escape falling back, pulling the stairway and charred body of the drug lord with it. Rain started to fall with greater intensity, dampening the sound of sirens building in the distance. No one stood up. The director didn't yell cut. There were no towels. No one else left standing there except him.

Twain spun around, facing the dark hillside, the flashing lights of emergency vehicles rapidly closing in. He slipped away, trying to make sense of what was happening. Wondering if Phil had left him out of the need-to-know loop, and the scene was supposed to continue. The performers led safely away. Equipment, trailers, and dozens of production people hidden somewhere in the darkness, just out of sight. Twain bowed his head and stumbled away, confused.

The smell of blood clung to him, his hands and lower arms coated in sheets of dried, rust-brown flakes. The smell of burning gas was in his nostrils, on his hair. He clenched the steering wheel of his truck, fingers cramping as he squeezed it as hard as he could, trying to wake up from the nightmare. Locked inside of it. White stripes in the road flashing in the headlights as he followed the signs leading him back home. He was racing the approach of dawn, waiting for the alarm beside his bed to ring. For Dawg's paws on the side of the mattress, his long black nose probing to find a patch of skin to lick.

The false memory of the loss of his daughter covered his cheeks in tears, with the last page of the script turned. A mile marker flashed into view: one hundred miles left to go. Twain opened his mouth as wide as he could and screamed.

Miranda opened the door of her mother's house, now belonging to Twain. She slipped inside and reached down, rubbing Dawg's head as he followed her through the door. He'd been standing outside, waiting as she pulled into the driveway, as if sensing her approach. Her calls to Twain had gone unanswered, made in response to a strange message left in the middle of the night. His words garbled, unclear. A frantic call to the neighbors verifying his vehicle was in the driveway, the large shepherd going in and out of the dog door, acting nervous, unwilling to come to them when called. She'd booked a flight and come as soon as possible, wondering what had caused the sudden shift in Twain's behavior, concerned it might be a delayed response to what he'd faced overseas.

When she reached the living room, Twain's eyes were open, staring at the ceiling. He was lying on his couch, a flutter of air from an overhead fan stirring the ends of hair, matted by sweat. His chest was barely moving, face gaunt, shadowed by several days of dark growth. Clothes stained, the rank odor of cold sweat and fear hanging in the stuffy air.

Dawg went over and sat down on the floor beside him, head in his lap, watching Miranda as she came over, his eyes full of concern, as were her own.

Twain rubbed his eyes, a headache throbbing inside his skull. "I've got no idea what the hell any of that was. Or if it even *was*." Still shaken by what he'd experienced, Twain grimaced, the smell of burning flesh in his nose: a familiar stench from years spent overseas. Miranda had helped him to shower, washing his hair and shaving him, helping him to dress and convincing him to eat. She was sitting beside him, holding his hand, silent, letting him find his way back to a semblance of his former self. His eyes had started to clear, his mood improving as he tried to explain the recent confusion. "I mean—I honestly thought it was the final scene. Right until the end when it all fell to shit." He turned his head, facing her. "I remember nothing after seeing the mile marker letting me know how far away I was. From home."

Miranda hesitated, then squeezed his hand, her voice soothing. "That's when you started to scream?"

"Yes." He paused, shaking his head, staring into her eyes. "It felt like someone was trying to yank my mind out through the back of my skull. Worst pain I've ever felt. Worse than being shot." He lowered his head, his free hand reaching up to touch his left shoulder, probing the thick scar hidden beneath his shirt. "It seemed so real, especially the pain of having lost my child." He shook his head. "It was more than I could take."

"But you know it's not real." Miranda touched his cheek. "That you've never had a child. Right?"

Twain touched the side of his forehead, rubbing with his fingers as if searching for the headache he'd been suffering from over the past two days. Dawg, his head wedged in Twain's lap, lifted his paw, pulling at his arm, trying to elicit a response. The request for attention worked, Twain reaching out, rubbing his ears. "I know it wasn't real. None of it was. But I can't shake the feeling of loss, no matter where it's coming from." He looked at Miranda, his eyes full of shame for having caused her to have to fly out. "I don't remember any of the rest. Nothing after that." He looked down, giving Dawg a forced smile. "Not until you showed up."

Miranda reached out and touched his shoulder. "You went through hell overseas. Enough to cause a delayed reaction from having lost friends, as close to you as—"

"This isn't—I mean it wasn't *anything* like that." Twain's voice tightened. "I've been through the flashbacks often enough, learning how to deal with the aftereffects. Been through counseling. And getting off the happy pills the doctor prescribed." He squeezed her hand, then let go, disentangling himself from Dawg's paw and standing up. He walked over to the window and looked out toward the backyard, staring at the artwork Janice had left to him to deal with: a local university contacted, with an entire department of creative people working on a plan that would allow people to see it without interfering with his privacy. "This was different. Like a bad dream. One I couldn't find my way out of."

Miranda came over and stood beside him, watching as a handful of people, most of them students, took careful measurements. She hesitated, then reached out, touching him on the shoulder. "What can I do? What can *we* do?"

"I honestly—don't know."

"Is there someone you can call? Ask them if there was a scene being filmed? If you were there, then left, after—"

"I went crazy?" Twain shrugged, stepping away from the window, pulling Miranda into his arms, drinking in the scent of her hair; savoring it. "I could reach out to Phil, I suppose." Twain kissed her on her cheek, looking into her eyes. "Or better yet, James."

"And if he tells you it happened. Or worse—" She paused. "That it didn't?"

Twain took a deep breath and let it out, resting his chin on her shoulder, eyes closed as he held onto her. "I don't know. Either way, I'm in trouble. With no obvious answer as to what happened, or what I'm going to do about it."

Dawg came over and nosed his way between the two of them, tail wagging, whining softly, letting them know it was time for his afternoon walk.

CHAPTER TWENTY-ONE

FARMHOUSE, MID-COAST MAINE

Calvin and Jemma's Story

Bacon was frying on a large gas stove, filling Jemma's kitchen with a mouth-watering scent, along with the smell of fried onions and green peppers. Calvin watched as Jemma used a long-handled fork to flip the thick strips of meat so they wouldn't burn. She winced as a drop of hot fat landed on her wrist, muttering a curse between her lips.

Dawg lifted his head, eyes glued to every move Jemma was making, knowing she was an easy touch. He looked at Calvin, measuring his mood, then lowered his head between his paws and sighed, knowing there would be no bacon for him this morning.

Calvin stepped over and circled Jemma's hips with his hands. "Can I help you with anything?"

She used an elbow to wipe a bead of sweat from her forehead, her hair piled in a knot atop her head, several strands having slipped loose, trailing down the line of her neck. "Pour some juice. And more coffee." Calvin moved to comply, then stopped and leaned in, kissing the back of her neck, small spirals of hair tickling his nose. "Smells good. So does the food." He turned away, heading toward a large refrigerator. Jemma smiled as she reached out and took a piece of bacon out of the sizzling fat, letting it cool off for Dawg.

They finished their meal: thick omelets stacked with fresh vegetables and locally produced cheese, bacon on the side. Accompanied by thick slabs of homemade toast, laden with home-made preserves. Dawg's patience had been over-rewarded with a slice of crisp bacon, along with a few drops of slightly congealed bacon grease that raised a growl of protest from Calvin, ignored by Jemma and the shepherd, his nose buried in his bowl, tail wagging wildly.

"Have something to ask you about." Jemma looked at Calvin. "It's not anything you need to answer right away, if you want to wait."

Calvin shrugged, then took a sip of his coffee. "Won't know until you pull the trigger. Fire when ready."

"About the scar. On your left shoulder." Jemma paused, gauging Calvin's reaction to determine whether to stop or press ahead. When he didn't flinch, she threw caution to the wind. "How did that happen?"

"A moment of inattention—along with a boatload of bad luck." Calvin angled his head, looking at Jemma with a quiet expression. "Happened a long time ago." She stared at him, waiting while Dawg finished his treat and came over to thank her, his head in her lap, licking her hand. She leaned back in her chair, rubbing his ears until Calvin took in a deep breath, letting it out slowly with a loud sigh. "It was an accident. Out on the neck road one-night, late in the fall. There were wet leaves on the road and a deer standing in the middle of it. At the sharp corner near the ledges. A huge buck." Calvin shrugged. "Could have hit it head on, but we swerved instead, losing control. The truck plowed into the side of the ledge, then rolled down an embankment, landing in a beaver pond. On the driver's side."

Jemma winced, imagining the scene. She pulled Dawg's head out of her lap. "I'm sorry. I didn't mean to—"

"The singer, the one you were asking about." Calvin snapped his fingers, calling Dawg over. "He was with me when it happened, both of us coming back from a get together at the local fire station. It was his birthday—just turned twenty-one."

"You were driving?"

"No. My cousin was." Calvin hesitated. "But I *should* have been. I hadn't been drinking, still two months away from legal age." He stood up, going over to the window and looking outside. "I was thrown clear when we hit the ledge. Seatbelt let go and I ended up going through the windshield. My left shoulder took the worst of it. Broke some ribs; chest tore up a little. Broke my arm too." He stopped, turning around, his face calm. "But I survived."

"And your cousin—didn't."

"Ended up stuck behind the wheel, engine almost in his lap, his legs trapped. The truck—" Calvin swallowed then looked down, his fingers kneading Dawg's neck, who'd come over and sat down beside him. "It was sinking into the muck. I tried to pull him free—but couldn't do much with only one arm.

Jemma leaned forward, seeing Calvin's jaw clench as he continued to look outside. "It wasn't your fault."

"I realized that, later. But it didn't feel that way back then. Blamed myself, right along with most of the people in town, having let him drive."

Jemma stood up and came over, giving him a hug, her face pressed against his chest, kissing the large scar through the fabric of his flannel shirt. "I'm sure they came to understand what happened."

Calvin snorted, pulling back slightly as Jemma looked up, a pained look in her eyes. He shook his head. "Most people don't understand shit, Jemma. Never have. Never will. They just form an opinion and hold tight to it. Forgiving, eventually. But never forgetting. No matter how long you try making amends, or how much you do for them."

"That's not fair. Of *them*, I mean." Jemma stood on her toes, kissing Calvin on his cheek, shrugging out of his embrace as the oven beeped: loaves of fresh baked bread needing to be pulled out.

Calvin gathered their dishes, taking them over to the sink and rinsing them. He turned around and leaned against the kitchen counter. "It's not about being fair, or unfair. It's about how you choose to deal with it. Any of it. Good, or bad. Right or wrong. You can't control what happens or how people choose to react. Whether a car crash or cancer. Good luck or bad. Just keep walking your path, chin up, as my aunt used to tell me whenever I got down on myself."

Jemma listened as she slid the loaves onto a rack to cool. When Calvin finished speaking, she wiped her hands, aware his moment of reflection had ended. "So, we're going to put the mounting brackets for the panels on the roof today?"

Calvin studied her for a long moment. "Yeah. That's the plan." Then he grinned.

Jemma looked at him, a drop of sweat hanging on the end of her nose. "What?"

"Just trying to figure it out, that's all."

"Figure what out?" She swiped at her nose with the back of one hand.

"How I ended up with someone as incredible as you."

Jemma's cheeks turned red, a flush of warmth coloring her face. "A series of bad decisions, most likely."

"Yeah." He looked at her with a soft smile. "That's probably it."

A large, silver pickup truck eased into the gravel driveway, its deep treads grinding their way across the crushed-rock parking area in front of the farmhouse and small store. Dawg came running out from behind the building, sliding to a stop as the vehicle door opened. He lowered his head, growling a warning as Jemma finished lagging the last bracket in place. She straightened up, a frown pinching her lips before swearing under her breath, recognizing the driver.

She called down to Dawg, letting him know it was okay, watching as he sat down, his haunches pressed into the dirt, another growl rumbling in his thick chest as a tall, wide-shouldered man exited the vehicle and made his way around the front of the truck. He looked up, a smile on his tanned face.

"I see you haven't changed. Still the same Jem—up to your elbows in work."

"Still the same Tom, pointing out the obvious." Jemma made her way over to the ladder and climbed down. She dropped her carpenters' apron on the ground then wiped her hands on her tar-stained work jeans. "Forget how to use a phone?"

"Nothing's changed." Tom shook his head. "Still breaking my balls." He grinned, his teeth white, a perfect match to her own, hidden behind her clenched lips. "Good to see you haven't changed, despite moving all the way up here to Goober-Town."

Jemma snapped her fingers, calling Dawg over and rubbing his neck, reassuring him she wasn't in any danger. "You've found me. *Why?*"

Tom shrugged, scuffing the toe of a polished boot on the crushed rock surface. "Maybe I came all the way up here to apologize."

"Did you?" Jemma kept the anger out of her voice, not wanting to upset Dawg.

"Guess so." Tom paused, a scowl on his lips. "I mean, we *both* said things we regret. Figured I'd give you a chance to cool off, wait until you were ready to get back to where we were." He looked around the large yard, noting the signs of new construction. "Your father thought it would be a good idea to come see you. Find out what you're up to."

"My father's an *asshat*." Jemma frowned. "The two of you make a good pair."

"Come on, Jem. Leave off with the insults." Tom spread his arms and stepped forward. "I drove all the way up here. Least you could do is give me a hug and hear me out."

Dawg stiffened at Jemma's side. She knelt, her arm draped over the shepherd's shoulder. "And then what? You'll turn around and leave? Head back home. Hatchet buried. All forgiven. Is that it?"

Tom lowered his head, shaking it back and forth. "For your information, *I'm* the one who'll be leading the install crew your grandfather's sending up. Came up a few days early to make sure you were ready for us." He glanced around the work site, eyeing the stack of solar panels. Then he looked up, seeing the brackets lining the roof. He nodded at an angular-framed man standing there, looking down. "Hey. My name is Tom. You must be the guy helping Jem get things going."

Calvin nodded. "I am." He made his way over to the ladder, lugging a bucket of tools, lowering them to Jemma on a rope. Then he climbed down and reached out, taking Tom's hand, matching his overly firm grip. "I'm Calvin. Good to meet you."

"Tom."

"Right." Calvin slapped the side of his leg, calling Dawg over. He reached for the bucket Jemma was holding. "I'll put these away and get going." He saw her open her mouth to disagree, interrupting her with a calm tone in his voice. "I need to get going. Have to take care of a few things." He gave her a warm smile. "I'll be back tomorrow morning."

Tom stepped forward. "*Great*! Look forward to going over things with you. Show you what I'm planning to do." He lifted his hand, intending to clap Calvin on the shoulder: a growl from Dawg stopping him. Tom backed away, eyeing the large animal before continuing. "We can go over the plans Jem sent down to her grandfather. I have a few revisions to make. Nothing major. Just a couple of improvements I came up with."

Jemma opened her mouth, her eyes narrowing, hands clenched in anger. Calvin cut her off again. "Thank you, Tom. There's nothing I'd rather do—truly." He gave Jemma a quick nod, then turned and walked away. Dawg hung back, staying beside Jemma, ignoring Calvin's call to heel. She knelt, taking his head between her hands, looking him in the eyes. "You go ahead. I'll be fine."

Dawg licked her cheek then bounded away, leaping into the open door of Calvin's truck.

"A total *asshat*!" Jemma's eyes gleamed in anger. She slammed her coffee mug down, rattling the large kitchen table in her kitchen. "He actually thought—*assumed* I'd let him spend the night. As if *that* would ever happen."

Calvin grinned. "Where did he end up sleeping?"

"I don't know and don't care." Jemma walked over and poured herself another cup of coffee. "Hope he headed back home." She turned and leaned back against the counter. "I'm calling my grandfather and insist he send someone else."

Calvin shrugged, taking a sip of his coffee, studying Jemma's face, enjoying her display of emotions, her feelings always near the surface. "Just let it go. I'm sure you two can work it out."

"Have you met me? Letting go of things is *not* one of my strong points."

Calvin came over and placed his arm around her, pulling her in. "I've more than met you, girl. And I *like* your weak points. And your strong ones, too. They help make up for more than a few of my own."

"We make a good pair." Jemma pulled away slightly and looked up at him. "Right?

Calvin nodded, resting his forehead against hers. "Yes."

"Then I want you to sign something." Jemma shrugged out of his embrace and went into the living room, returning with a sheaf of papers, placing them on the kitchen counter. Calvin looked down, frowning as he picked up the top page, scanning through it.

"No." His voice was firm.

Jemma crossed her arms, a scowl on her face. "Why the hell not?"

"This is *yours*. Your home. Your idea. Your money being spent. As well as all the sweat, bruises, and blood you've already invested."

"It's only a *small* share. Enough to let you know how important you are, having helped make this happen for me." Jemma gave him a searching look. "It's not much. Not enough you should feel uncomfortable. Or pressured." She hesitated. "I gave this a lot of thought, believe me. And I *want* to do this."

Calvin gave her a quiet stare. "To tie me to it."

"It?" Jemma's eyes filled with anger. "You mean me?"

"No. I mean *exactly* what I said. Tying me in to making this a priority over other things I have going on. The same things I had going on before you showed up at my door." Calvin kept his voice steady. "I was clear about that—from the very beginning."

Jemma spun around, going over to the door and staring outside, watching as Dawg chased a red squirrel up a tree, barking in reproach before lifting a leg to wet down the trunk, sealing the deal: no red squirrels allowed near the house, ever. "Got it. Forget I said anything. It was a stupid idea, anyway. And you're right—you were perfectly clear with me, from the start."

Calvin came over, approaching with a small measure of caution. "I was. And it's not a stupid idea. Far from it. It's a generous offer, one made in friendship, not partnership. No need to put anything in writing." He reached out and gently pulled her around, leaning forward, looking into her eyes. "I'll always be here to help where and when I can. You know you can count on me for that." He leaned in, pressing his lips against her neck. "I swear to always listen when you speak, no matter what crazy idea you've come up with and won't stop yakking about. To wait for you to find your own way out of things when they start to go south. To lend a hand when you reach for it, and not before. Argue with you, when you need me too, even when I know you're right. Be silent—when you know you're wrong. Wait until you find your way to apologizing." He leaned back, taking her face between his work-hardened palms. "But there are two things I will never do. And the first one is signing that paper."

Jemma reached up, finding his hands, squeezing them, her eyes overflowing with tears. "And the second?"

Calvin smiled, wiping her cheeks dry with his thumbs. "To never again spray you with a hose. Definitely learned my lesson there." He opened his arms, inviting her in, holding her while she released her pent-up anger at Tom, the man who'd once been her partner, until he'd violated her trust. A sad story told one evening, a few weeks earlier. Relationship notes exchanged between the two of them in a reflective mood. Hers, a long and convoluted tale to tell. His own: painfully short, mixed with bittersweet memories.

CHAPTER TWENTY-TWO

COMPANY HOUSE, MARYLAND

Jared and Teresa's Story

Jared held the door of his house open, waiting for Teresa to step through. He lowered his gaze, staring at her lower body as she passed by, Teresa noting his admiring look with a smile. Jared blushed as he closed the door behind them, following her into the living room. Dawg was pawing at the sliding door leading out back, a woof letting Jared know he wanted to be let in. Jared ignored him, his arms filled with a large cardboard box filled with make-up, toiletries, and a few items, unfamiliar to his eye. Teresa led him to his bedroom, towing a large suitcase, having agreed to making a small move in his direction, agreeing to move in enough things to stay for a day or so at a time. Jared's offer to move her in permanently made the previous evening. One Teresa promptly refused.

"You can use the spare bedroom if you prefer. There's plenty of space, and I can take you to work then pick you up on the way home." Jared leaned back against the desk in the small office of the gallery. Arms crossed, staring at Teresa in confusion. She shook her head as she finished rinsing out two wine glasses, setting them aside to dry.

"We already discussed this."

Jared frowned, unable to understand her reluctance, having told her of his intention to stay in the area for at least one more year, willing to commit to a new contract when it came up for renewal. "I'm not looking to pressure you. Just trying to save you money."

"Really?" Teresa came over and leaned in, kissing his pout away. Moving her lips to his ear, her voice lowered to a whisper. "Just want to save me money, huh. You sure there's no other reason?"

Jared slipped his arm around her waist, pulling her in, his head pressed against her upper shoulder, enjoying the warmth of her toned body against his cheek. "Just trying to simplify things. I mean—it's only a matter of time, right? Before we end up crossing that bridge?"

Teresa stiffened, then pulled away. "Simplify things for you, not for me. As to the crossing of any bridges, we have a difference of opinion on where and when that might come into play."

Jared watched as she walked away, uncertain of what had just happened, sensing the change in her mood, wondering what might have caused it. He stood up and followed her through the door, the two of them heading to a concert she'd invited him to, a few days ago.

People in the crowded auditorium were singing along with the band made up of five men well into their sixties, playing a selection of their greatest hits to an appreciative audience of older couples, along with a surprising number of young people who were in attendance. Old songs had become new again as a wave of retro-popularity occurred, helped along by easy access to on-line videos and a recent release of a 'best of' album.

Jared grinned, watching Teresa's face as she swayed in motion to the heavy bass beat, her lithe body moving in graceful circles; eyes closed as she lost herself to the flow of the music.

"Dance with me!" Jemma's mood had improved, her slim fingers pulling at his hands, guiding them to her hips. She grabbed him by his waist, encouraging him to join in with her rhythm, her lips pressed against his ear to make herself heard above the amplifiers. "Like making love. While standing up."

Jared leaned forward, forming his body to hers, ignoring the crowd, focusing on matching her movements. A wash of heat coursed through his body as he drank in the delicate scent of her perfume, mixing with the scent of her hair, his lips brushing along the line of her neck.

"Easy there! Still have a ton of music to get through." Teresa pulled her head back, smiling. "I love this song."

Jared nodded. "Me too. Remember watching my parents dancing to it when I was a kid. Had to leave the room when they forgot I was there and started taking it to the next level."

"Like you just did." Teresa grinned. "Must be a family trait—inherited from your father!"

"A good memory. With the two of them together. One of a handful." Jared paused, shaking his head. "Can you blame me?"

"No. Not at all. Just save it for later. Okay?"

"Buzzkill."

The music shifted tempo, heavy on instrumentals, less encouraging of languid swaying. The two of them separated, their hands joining as they faced the stage, the lead guitarist beginning a long riff played on a well-used guitar. When it finally ended, the band stopped for another break: age and the grind of a long concert tour given as an excuse.

"I'm sorry." Teresa leaned over, her head resting against his shoulder. "About bringing up your father. I know it's a somewhat of a sore subject." Jared tilted his head, having a hard time hearing her words over the increased volume of crowd noise. She looked up at him, squeezing his hand, leaning in. "Amazing—how well you turned out, with role models like that. Such a lack of empathy for each other, on their parts."

"They weren't always like that. They were close to the people they worked with. It was when they were together that things started to get tangled up." Jared tightened his lips. "I mean, individually they were completely different people. I spent a lot of time with them, one on one. Getting to see them in their natural environments. My father was extremely open-minded toward others, with a genuine interest in those he was trying to help. Seeing them as equals in intellect and ability, unlike most of the others. Embassy turtles, with their heads stuck up each other's asses. Or worse, the ones who withdrew into depressive shells of indifference, stacking up hours until their next posting opened up." Teresa waited while Jared paused again, his eyes reflecting a deep sadness as the lights from the stage painted his face in a wash of colors.

"And your mother?"

"She didn't really *see* people, not the ones she was working with. But when you saw her walking around the archaeological dig sites, you could tell she was visualizing the movements of those who'd walked and worked the land thousands of years earlier. Knowing where to dig and what would be there. Untouched for countless generations. As if she'd been the one to leave it behind."

Teresa touched his arm. "Like—a form of residual empathy. Like staring at a painting and being able to feel what the artist was feeling when they placed brush to canvas. Reflecting their emotions."

Jared reached up, brushing his fingers along the side of her face. "Exactly." He hesitated. "Do you want to leave? Go get a drink. Or something?"

Teresa stared at him. "Something?"

"Not that." Jared lowered his eyes. "Somewhere quiet. Where we can talk."

Teresa reached out, taking his hand. "Got the perfect place in mind."

The security system was beeping, the lock released in the door frame, allowing Teresa to push it open. The gallery was lit in a dim tinge of yellow security lighting, bleeding the colors from rows of paintings as the two of them passed by on their way to the small office.

Jared held Teresa's hand. "Wouldn't think you'd want to come here, seeing how many hours you've been putting in with multiple showings these past two weeks, back-to-back."

Teresa squeezed his hand, opening the office door. "A girls got to make money when the canvas is moving." Teresa shut the door once Jared stepped through, letting it close behind them with a soft sigh of air. "And I have the open bottle of wine here, compliments of the owner. Appreciative of how well sales have been."

"Because of you."

Teresa nodded. "Because of me." She opened the bottle they'd sampled before the concert, tugging the cork free with a muted pop, holding the bottle to her nose, nostrils flaring slightly as she drank in the scent. Then she closed her eyes, imagining where the vineyard might be, picturing it on a hillside with clusters of grapes, tugged from their hold on vines by nimble fingered hands. Teresa could feel Jared's eyes on her, sensing he was close to revealing something personal that had been working its way to his surface. Aware of his need as if it were her own. Familiar. Haunting. Difficult to face. Impossible to look away from. She opened her eyes. "Glasses?"

Jared held them out, watching as she poured a small amount in each, setting them down to breathe. He leaned back. "What is it? Another French varietal?"

"A Cabernet Franc, from the Loire Valley. A Chinon, bottled fifteen years ago. It'll need to wait twenty minutes to calm down. Be a bit easier on the tongue with some food. I have a brie in the refrigerator. Just need to take it out and let it warm up."

Jared looked past Teresa, eyeing a small landscape hanging on the wall. It was of a ridgeline, topped by scraggly pines with clusters of blue blossoms threaded through fractured lines of out-thrust stones. "That's new."

"A gift—from the owner. By the same artist as the one hanging in your house." She picked up a glass, swirling the dark red wine, savoring the rich scent. "Here, hold it below your nose. Close your eyes. Drink in the scent and tell me what you see."

Jared took the glass, gently stirring the liquid, his mood subdued. He held back a sigh of exasperation, wishing it were a bottle of ice-cold ale instead. Then his nose began to capture the notes rising from the aerated wine, scenting red peppers, berries, and a hint of wet sand. "Everything. From vegetables and fruit—all the way to dirt."

Teresa grinned. "Dirt, or gravel?"

Jared narrowed his eyes. "Gravel, like a riverbank. And raspberries. Red ones." He took a sip, the acidic flavor biting at first, then fading to a smooth aftertaste. "It's strong. But good."

"You mentioned wanting to talk." Teresa tested the wine, making a face, walking over to a small fridge, and pulling out a wedge of wrapped cheese. "About anything in particular?"

"Yes. And no." Jared looked down, regretting where the evening had led them to, uncertain if this were the time and place to bring up the memory that had tugged at his heart back at the concert. A memory kept in the shadows of his youth, as if a wounded lion in its den. Safe, if left alone.

"That certainly narrows it down." Teresa put a plate with the brie and assorted crackers between them, then leaned back against the front of her desk, matching Jared's pose, side by side, each of them sipping from their glasses, looking at the painting. He was first to break the silence.

"It started when we were talking about my parents. Got me thinking about how lucky I was to spend so much one-on-one time with them. And how much it hurt when—"

"When your father died." Teresa saw him nod from the corner of her eye. "You mentioned that to me, the morning after our first time together." She touched his hand. "You didn't say how. Only that you were young when it happened."

"Fifteen. Just turned." Jared shrugged, then held up his glass. "Same age as the wine."

Teresa nodded, silent as she reached for a cracker with a smear of brie. She took a small bite, mixing it with a sip of the Chinon.

"It was a plane crash. Caused by an accidental observation of, and lethal reaction by a group of poachers caught in the open when we flew over. They panicked, firing at our plane, hitting the pilot in the thigh."

A wide stretch of African plain basking in harsh sunlight had over-heated the air, unsettling it, causing a small plane to jounce as it flew through the twisting currents rising from the ground a few hundred feet below. Jared's father sat up front, alongside the pilot, with Jared curled up behind their seats, wedged among duffle bags stuffed with their belongings. The bags had been tossed on top of gunny sacks holding supplies for dozens of the park ranger's campsites. Serious-minded men, tasked with patrolling the game park, hunting for poachers.

Jared tried to relax, his stomach unsettled. He'd been through rough flights before and had planned for the nausea: a large plastic bag in his hand in case his stomach rebelled.

"Are you okay?" His father twisted in his seat, looking back, sunglasses raised to his forehead, headset pressed against his ears. Sweat beaded his tanned skin, bushy eyebrows arched above light blue eyes: visual links to his Scottish heritage. His hair, a faded yellow, had streaks of silver running through it, earned by his years as a career diplomat for the government. Forty years old, specializing in South African regions, embassy personnel often accused him of having gone native Over-dedicated to the local people. Fluent in several languages and a half-dozen regional dialects. Admired by local officials for getting out and learning first-hand about the difficulties they faced.

Jared regarded his father as a hero figure, more so than a parent. Especially now, invited along at the last minute. One last adventure before his mother would swoop in and collect him up, returning him to Washington, D.C. Back to school and another group of part-time friends. He raised his thumb, a smile on his face, matching that of his father's.

A sudden drop in altitude woke Jared from a dream: the boat he'd been riding in dissolving to a blur of brown and red streaks. The ground outside the small Plexiglas window of the plane racing by beneath the angled wing of the plane, sliding away to one side as the pilot leveled out of a banked dive. Jared could hear the tension in his father's voice, cursing in excited anger, a microphone pressed to his lips, relaying their location and details of what was happening on the ground to the nearest ranger's camp. The pilot began arguing in broken English they should leave the area. His father ordering him to go around again.

Jared opened his mouth to ask what was wrong, closing it as a spray of warm liquid covered his cheek, the salt-copper taste of it on his tongue caused his stomach to lurch, the plastic bag placed against his lips just in time to catch the warm contents of his mid-morning meal. Two thuds pounded from beneath his legs, curled atop the canned goods, followed by a high keening sound he couldn't place. A geyser of bright red mist filled the air, his sleep-shocked mind realizing it was blood, the plastic bag in his hand stained with it. He leaned over and was sick again as the sounds from the cockpit lowered in intensity. The plane began to slew from side to side, weaving its way in a halting turn toward the west, sun flooding the windscreen with a golden glow.

Jared obeyed his father's barked command to burrow into the luggage. Frightened, he watched him fight for control of the plane, rounds from a high-powered rifle having penetrated the cockpit, the pilot shot through the thigh, bleeding out. The man's body slumped to one side while his father sought somewhere level to land the plane. It settled toward the ground, the engine coughing, then coming to a sudden stop, the silence deafening. His questions were batted aside, his father explaining what was going to happen. Soon. And what would need to be done if they survived the crash.

It was later now; the end having come with a jarring thud, followed by a grinding slide into a rise of earth dotted with outcrops of large rocks. Several of them formed a wall that the nose of the plane mashed into, pushing the engine back into the narrow cockpit. Jared had been forced to worm his way out of the plane via a small opening, the door torn away during the crash. He was sore in chest and lower legs, but nothing seemed to be broken. He moved to the front of the plane; climbing up on a rock to check on his father, trapped inside the cockpit, head bent forward, one arm thrown up to protect against the sudden crush of metal and plexiglass.

Jared hesitated, afraid to find out his father was dead. The moment passing quickly, his training in first aid coming to the fore. He stretched his arm through the side window, ignoring the jagged edge of fractured plastic, finding his father's neck. A shuddering sigh of relief ran through him when he felt a steady pulse. His father reached up, finding Jared's wrist. His voice weak, the words difficult to hear.

"You'll need to—find wood—for a fire. Several piles. Enough to—to last the night." His father forced compressed words between lips tightened against waves of pain. Jared leaned forward to hear them, hands clenched to the side of the window frame, wishing he had the strength and tools to cut his father free from the collapsed cockpit, his lower body trapped, the jutting fist of stones having punched the nose of the plane back and to one side.

The pilot was dead: the cockpit torn open around his body, still strapped into the seat. Jared released the harness, working the stiffening body of the slender man free from the wreckage, wishing it was his father he was removing, injured but alive. A wash of shame warmed his face as he pushed the thought from his mind, placing the body in a thin slice of shade, crossing the arms on his chest, closing his eyelids as if he were sleeping. His body was unmarked, other than the torn flesh of his inner thigh where the bullet had ripped through, severing his artery, his death finding him moments before the crash.

Head-high piles of dry wood stood at four corners of the crash landing, spaced several paces from the crumpled remains of the plane. Jared had stacked smaller piles near each corner, readied for quick lighting if help didn't arrive before night, with larger pieces used to feed the flames. His question to his father about the need for the wood answered in a series of whispers.

"Blood. Sengi's body. Hyenas."

Jared stood under the shade of the plane's undamaged wing, staring at the pistol he held in his hand. Heavy. Large caliber. Holding five rounds. His father had directed him to pull it out from under the pilot's seat, along with a handful of flares and a large plastic gun. Jared had removed the pistol and box of ammo from an oiled pouch, frowning, knowing it was not powerful enough to stop a hyena or a lion. Its usefulness called into question. His father refusing to respond, waving a hand toward a nearby rock formation, telling him to locate a small crevice large enough to store the containers of water and medical supplies inside, helping to keep them cool. Jared tugging the supplies into place, then returning to take up position in the shade under the tilted wing of the plane.

Dusk was an hour away, with no sign or sound of the helicopter his father promised would be coming. No sound, yet, of hyenas calling to each other as they made their way onto the stage of stunted trees and thorny brush. Jared looked over at a slow drift of prey animals passing by, indifferent to the metal wreckage. The smell of leaking fuel from one of the wing tanks caused a few of them to wicker as they came too close, before turning away, tails raised in temporary alarm before they returned to their endless quest for fodder, plucked from the dry earth.

The flames were thigh high, sending their flickering light several paces into a thick blanket of ebony darkness. Nothing threatening had revealed itself, though Jared sensed something was out there, watching and waiting. He stood on a tall rock, the touch of the cool metal of the gun in his hand, reassuring. He wondered if he should carry it with him. Whether it might be better to slip inside the plane, joining his father, closing his eyes and praying for the rangers to get there as soon as possible.

His father's voice reached out, teeth grating from pain. Jared rushed over, a small flashlight in his hand, shining it to one side, not wanting to blind him. "Need. More. Wood."

"There won't be enough to last through the night—if I use it all now."

"Won't matter—if you don't. They will come—from all sides."

Jared rushed to comply, stoking the flames until they reached head high. He retreated to the false safety of the plane, leaned against the side of the cockpit then reached in, taking his father's hand. The squeeze in return was weaker than before. Ice formed in Jared's heart as he cursed, frustrated at not being able to free his father's legs, wondering how much blood he'd lost in the hours since the crash.

"I got a reply—from the ranger camp. Before—" Several moments passed, leaving Jared holding his breath. "They will—have radioed. For a helicopter. Then started here—by truck."

"How will they know where we are? By the fires?"

"From the air—yes. From the ground. No. Not large enough for—that." His father's voice faded, the labored sound of his breathing growing weaker.

"Dad!" Jared squeezed his father's hand. There was no response. He reached in, feeling for a pulse. It was weak and erratic. He slammed his free hand against the side of the fuselage, panic welling up, tears filling his eyes and spilling down his cheeks.

"I'm okay. Just had to—rest for a bit." His father's voice had steadied, his pulse firming up beneath the press of Jared's finger. He wiped his eyes with the back of his other hand. "You scared me. I thought—" Jared paused. "They'll be here soon. I promise."

"You've haven't called me that—Dad." His father's voice sounded stronger. "Not since you were a boy. It's always been father." There was another pause, the sounds of the fire beginning to die down as the wood turned to coals, his father's words fading again. "So—formal."

"Don't talk. Save your strength. Try some more water." Jared picked up a two-liter bottle, holding it to his father's lips, watching as most of it slipped back out, spilling down his neck, staining the fabric of his shirt black in the cone of silvered light from a small flashlight. A sudden shift in the firelight drew his attention, a shadow passing in front that caused Jared to freeze. Jared let go of the bottle, turning around, the flashlight gripped in a trembling hand, its bright beam revealing a large gray and black shape with high shoulders angled down to its low-slung hindquarters. Eyes and teeth gleaming in the reflected light of the fire. He pulled the pistol from the belt around his waist, the front sight snagging the leather as he jerked it free and fired, the shot missing, hitting the dirt, the sound chasing the cackling hyena away.

There was a moment of time when Jared thought it would all work out, dashing between the four fires, keeping them burning as the calls from the four-legged predators increased in intensity. They prowled the edges of the light from the fires, urging one another on. Jared held the pistol in one hand, a flaming length of wood in the other, waving it back and forth as if a wand, able to hold them at bay. The alpha male made a run, angling across the opening between two of the fires, dashing in to test the resolve of the two-legged beast. It received a thrust of fire at its face, forcing it to angle back into the shadows, chattering away in clipped notes of frustration.

Jared ducked beneath the angled wing of the plane, holding the flaming stick to one side, careful to stay clear of the damp spot where gas had been trickling from a dented section of metal, trying to guess where the next rush would come from. He raised the pistol, wanting to fire it. To strike back, but holding off, realizing it would be a hollow gesture. Better to save the bullets, he thought, blanching at the idea of finding himself in the slavering jaws of the ravenous beasts. He heard his father call to him, in a voice strong enough to be heard over the crackling of flames that were starting to die down, the last of the wood used up.

"Dad! I don't know what to do. They're coming closer. There's no wood left for me to—"

"Give me the pistol."

"What?" Jared shook his head, crowded up against the damaged cockpit, his eyes widened in fear.

"Hand it to me. Then go to the rocks. Where you put the supplies. The hollow you found. Get inside and use the supplies to block the opening."

"No! I'm not leaving you!" Jared glanced over, eyeing the dark slit, understanding that his father had prepared for this possibility. He hesitated, torn between obeying him and running away to the promise of safety, or staying by his side, defending him until the hyenas overwhelmed them both. The sound of several hyenas moving in as the fires died down overwhelmed his ability to move.

"The torch. Drop it. Now!"

The shout jerked Jared back into focus. He stared at his father, seeing the desperation in his face. "What? Why?"

"Hand me the gun, son. Then toss the torch under the wing and run. It's—time."

"I'm staying with you. I won't leave you!"

"You're going to do this." His father reached out, touching him on his upper arm. "I'm where I am because of my own actions. My decisions—not yours. There's still a chance for you and you're going to take it. It's a—last request." He paused, tears in his eyes. "And you'll honor it. Now—while there's still time."

The bright flare of light from the fuel saturated ground beneath the tilted wing of the plane spread with a ferocity matched by the protesting howls of the hyenas as they scampered away. Jared watched from the narrow opening of the small opening as his father held out the flare gun and fired into the night sky. Reloading with difficulty, then firing again. He dropped the flare gun, looked toward Jared, and waved as a wall of flames closed in around him. The loud shot that followed, cracked through the air, causing Jared to flinch. Staring. Silent. Alone. Numb with shock, as if watching a movie, knowing the end was coming soon. The pile of rocks all that stood between him and the determined beasts, slinking up the small rise, their heads low to the ground.

The sound of engines from two large vehicles approaching the flames built into a roar of racing engines and excited shouts, followed by several shots from rifles, fired to deter a snarling knot of hyenas poised before a wall of boulders, driving them away. A tall, thick shouldered man leapt from the lead vehicle, running across the fire-lit scene, skirting the burning wreckage of a plane.

He hesitated as he stumbled across the torn remains of a man barely recognizable as his friend: the pilot of the small plane. Then he glanced at the burning cockpit, seeing the dark shape of a body inside, closing his nose to the smell as he swept the line of rocks, searching for what had drawn the large animals' interest. A searchlight from the second truck flashed into life, framing a narrow opening where a pale, youthful face was staring back, blood streaming from a gash torn through his shoulder, tears coursing down his pale cheeks.

Jared lifted his glass of wine and drained it, then wiped his mouth and looked at Teresa, wondering how she would react. The memory was still difficult to deal with. Therapy sessions, provided by the government, along with his mother's constant attention over several months, had helped him learn how to cope, the two of them drawn closer by what had happened.

His father's memorial service had been attended by a host of dignitaries, foreign and domestic. All offering their condolences and admiration for the work his father had accomplished. Words that winged past Jared's ears as if birds in the sky, their shadows moving over the sunbaked ground, holding no weight against the hollow sense of loss he felt. The rangers who'd rescued him had invited him and his mother back to their camp after his release from the hospital. The two of them had spent two weeks with them, listening to their stories about the man they'd known and had great respect for. Learning more about the man his father had been from the rangers then he'd ever learned from hours spent at his side during embassy gatherings.

"It's impossible for me to understand what you went through." Teresa came over and wrapped her arms around him, head pressed into his neck, trembling as emotions coursed through her, absorbed by his embrace, as if she were the one who'd lost a father. Had suffered the trauma, shared the same pain.

"I didn't tell you to elicit sympathy." Jared pulled back slightly. "I only wanted to let you know why I feel the way I do. About you. Why it's so important to me to hold on to someone I—"

Teresa touched his lips with her finger. "I understand, Jerad. I do." She leaned back, brushing his cheek with her fingers. "And I appreciate you being patient, even though you don't understand why I've resisted moving further ahead." She took his hand, holding it. "I've suffered loss, too. Not to the same degree—but deep enough to realize how hard it is to open myself to losing someone again. To risk the pain that comes along with the joy."

"Once burned, twice shy." Jared nodded, squeezing her hand.

"Many times, burned. And scared to go through it again."

Jared brought their joined hands up to his mouth. He kissed the back of hers, then let go. "I'll back off. Take what's freely offered, without placing any demands on—"

Teresa's lips met his, pressing firmly, tongue probing the line of his teeth. Jared's arms crossing behind her shoulders, pulling her in, his need overwhelming. They both gasped, bodies shuddering as the heat of their kiss spread throughout their bodies. Her hands found his belt, undoing it while he did the same for her, his movements timed with the sound of her moans as he clung to her. Her words slipped past his ears, their meaning lost in the surge of his need for her in his life. "I'm falling, Jared. And you've got to promise to catch me—to keep me from hitting the ground." He closed his eyes, flowing into her, his love for her beyond all measure of the word.

JD

Before

He was thin, but healthy. A look of happiness on his red-cheeked face, framed by a close-cropped beard. "You weren't easy to find."

She stood in the falling snow, her breath fogging the air "Yet you did. Find me. And yourself too—somewhere along the way."

"Took your advice and followed the sun. Walked directly toward it each day, until the ache finally disappeared."

She tilted her head, one eyebrow cocked, knowing it would trigger him like it had the first time they'd met. "You finally reached my cousin, after calling everyone in the county with the same last name."

"It worked. You're here, meeting me where I told her I'd be, come rain or shine."

"Or snow." She was cold, her coat not thick enough to protect against the sudden change in weather, grabbed as she'd hurried out the door while scolding herself for going to him. "You're shivering. Your lips are turning blue."

He shrugged, his shoulders shaking beneath the thin sports coat he had on. "I'm trembling." He grinned, his teeth chattering. "Out of my love for you."

"I'm not going back."

"Not asking you to."

"Then why did you come?"

"Because—you know. Love."

She considered a moment, then left it up to chance, flipping a one-sided coin, coming up him. "Okay."

"Okay?" His mouth fell open in surprise.

She nodded. "Why not? You're here, looking clean. What could possibly go wrong?"

CHAPTER TWENTY-THREE

RESEARCH FACILITY, MARYLAND

Cheryl

Cheryl chewed her lower lip, eyes focused on a spiraling column of symbols displayed on the screen of a monitor. She followed the twisting pattern, knowing one of the three helical lines held an error. It was the latest variation of her unique code, helping to increase the computational power. She muttered to herself as she punched away at a keyboard in her lap, strengthening a weak association showing in one of the cross-modulation points of reflected energy waves, stabilizing the signal fidelity, a solution she'd been tracking down for the past hour. She yawned, shaking her head, refocusing on the hunt.

It was late, the numbers on the clock on the wall slipping from oh-one hundred and fifty-nine, to two. The hum of electronic equipment, air handling units, and other undefined mechanical vibrations created a muted soundtrack as Cheryl manned the effort. Alone in the lab, Isaac having headed home hours ago, leaving her to continue her dogged search.

"There you are—you little imp." Cheryl's finger flashed to a control key, reprogrammed to her own specifications, pressing it twice, changing one of the odd symbols from a square with a dot in the center into one with an x. The image on the monitor refreshed, showing a clearer representation of JD's thoughts, her unique program back at work processing the data feed from his afternoon session. As she reached out to close the screen, she hesitated, leaning forward to look at the latest results.

The screen resolved into a desert scene, revealing a treeless expanse, devoid of life. Scattered clumps of sagebrush were lying in careless spirals, clinging to the sides of serpentine sprawls of red rock. There was a blue sky above, with rose undertones, the result of wind driven dust in the atmosphere. A pulse of light caught her eye, flashing into a gout of gray cloud rising in a spreading arch, centered by red and yellow colors as if a flower forced from its roots, reaching up with outstretched petals, seeking the sky. A shudder of sound overcame the background noise of the lab, the speaker volume turned down, dimming the effect as a computer-generated wave of sand rippled across the ground.

Cheryl leaned in, her fingers gently touching the screen, tracing the supine form of a German Shepherd lying next to the curled-up body of a man. The view was from an overhead perspective, as if filmed from a crane. Or a drone, she mused, wondering if the man was JD, one of several male figures being projected from his tortured mind as if actors thrust onto the stage while the director stayed hidden in the background, cloaked in shadows, unwilling or unable to step back into the light of his life.

Cheryl reluctantly powered down the monitor, knowing the program would continue to churn away at the volume of data, sifting through the various bits and pieces, collating, correlating, and assigning each to where it best fit in a three-dimensional data cube with three faces assigned to each of the three separate storylines being monitored. The fourth side of her innovative programming code used for analytical processing, while the fifth sorted through billions of data points, searching for commonality, shoving them on through to the sixth. Cheryl hopeful the results would open a window into the identity of the man now lying in the bedroom next to her own. She yawned again, shutting off the monitor, then left the lab and walked toward the small dormitory where she'd been spending most of her nights. She stopped by JD's door, hesitating, wondering if she should check in on him, then yawned again and moved on.

Cheryl knew she was dreaming. Knew the small home on top of a grassy hill was not real. A familiar scene, drawn from a painting that had captured her imagination many years ago when a child of eight, her feet planted in front of a framed expanse of canvas, devouring the scene of another young girl, lying in a semi-reclined pose, gazing at a house on a hill. Her parents had urged her to move on, their time in the city limited with other works of art waiting to be seen. A reasoned argument falling on deaf ears. Robert had stayed with her. Silent. Patient. Aware his sister was standing inside the painting, her mind running ahead to gaze into the dark windows, reflecting the sky.

It was a church in her dream, now. Basic in construct, with simple stained-glass windows and one tall door that swung open as she approached, closing behind her as she slipped past rows of empty wooden pews. The large open space echoed with her footsteps as she walked toward a small metal cross attached to the center of the back wall, framed by timbers angled in curved lines alongside it, meeting in a shadowy apex high above. A raised platform held a hospital bed, light streaming down from an unseen source, painting her brother's face in a golden hue.

He's only sleeping, Cheryl thought, as she walked over. His body robust, shoulders and arms lined with sinewy muscle. A chiseled face, lean and tan, his teeth white between parted lips. His eyes open, a vibrant ice blue, with a smile on his face as she leaned in and kissed his cheek, his skin warm against her lips.

"Hello, Chipmunk."

"Hello, Wall-Rat." She reached out, circling his chest with her arm as she nestled her head against him, listening to the steady throb of his heart. The slow rise and fall of his chest comforted her, draining away her worries, easing her incessant fear of missing out on something she could never fully define, knowing there was more to be done, to be uncovered or discovered, before she could let go of her search for a solution.

His voice rumbled in her ear. "Tell me what you learned today."

"Nothing." She paused; her voice muffled by the flannel shirt he was wearing. One she'd brought to him in the nursing home to keep him warm. Borrowed

from him when she was a child. Used as a nightgown, the scent of his sweat comforting her at night. Then she looked up, her lips forming into a wide smile. "And everything."

"You're a contradiction. Still."

"And you're not really here. Are you?"

"True."

Cheryl leaned back, making room for him to sit up, his hand touching the side of her head. His strong fingers working through her thick hair, bound up in a careless braid. "But then, who of us really is? Here, I mean. With any semblance of being identified as to a defined location because—"

"Because we're on a spinning ball of fire and ice, hurtling around the sun, which is itself moving through the solar system. Part of the Milky Way, with nothing fixed in place."

He smiled. "That's right, Chipmunk."

Cheryl beamed, her eyes filling with tears. "That's why you climb—trying to find the balance between stone and air. Between gravity's harsh reality and the moment when we—"

"Learn to fly." He lowered his arm, lying down again, his eyes closing.

Cheryl leaned over, placing her lips against his ear. "I am become bird. Partner to the air. Stranger to the ground. I soar." She stood up and started to walk away, stopping when a stranger's voice called out to her.

"You can't, you know. Fly. Still unaware. Still so naive. The ground will always be there, waiting to pull you down."

Cheryl slowly turned around. The man in the bed was now JD. Wide awake, his eyes dark, looking at her with a disdainful smile on his face, appraising her as she stood frozen in place, watching as he sat up. When he spoke, his voice was a snake's hiss. "You need to wake the fuck up."

"You're not here. This is only a dream." Cheryl listened to her words. Pitiful denials, forced from between a clenched jaw.

JD smiled, his grin lopsided. Then his expression hardened, lips thinning, his face etched with lines drawn from painful memories, along with thin scars caused by edged metal. "It's all nonsense. Drivel, spewed from those who've never faced the hard truths that life presents." He leaned to one side, resting on an elbow, reaching up and rubbing his face. He shook his head, then coughed. "But your time is coming, just like your brother's found him. A long fall to a hard place." He looked at her. "And you're not ready. Not by half."

"Who are you?" Cheryl could hear the words in her mind, uncertain if she'd said them aloud.

"No one. And everyone. No better than most—nor worse than some."

"I'm dreaming. I can wake up."

"You've been asleep your entire life. Just like all the rest. Living your lives planned out, without regard to what's waiting for you. Out there." JD pointed to a window. The sky had darkened, black clouds gathering, a rumble of thunder buffeting the thin panes of glass. "The real world. Eager to claim everything you have to offer in return."

Cheryl opened her mouth to respond, wanting to deny his words. A flash of lightning scored the ground outside. A clap of thunder shook the building, dust sleeting down around her as JD came over, grabbing her by the upper arm, his fingers digging into her flesh as he leaned in, staring into her fear stretched eyes, his breath ice cold on her face. "You need—to wake—the fuck up!"

Cheryl sat up, her heart pounding, breath catching in her throat, chest pounding. She could still feel JD's fingers squeezing her arms and reached up to rub away the phantom pain, trying to make sense of what had just happened. To understand the forced narrative. To try and rationalize the dream into reality, knowing there had to be a connection. Then she heard a noise from the corridor outside her room: a metal clicking sound that quickly died away.

She went over and opened her door, moving down the hallway toward the lab, seeing an enormous shadow bent over in front of the server bank, leaning to one side, picking something up from the floor. Cheryl knew it must be Isaac, returning to check on the latest data crunch. She opened her mouth to call out to him, then hesitated, seeing a small box in his hand, attached by a thin cable to a port on the side of the main server stuffed with a mass of neural output readings recorded over several hundred sessions with JD wearing the Tee Cee.

Cheryl went back to her room, closing the door, leaving a slit wide enough to see through as she stood there, trembling, trying to think of a legitimate reason for the large man's actions and coming up empty. Shock narrowed her vision as her legs began to fold, almost spilling her to the floor. She gathered herself, closed the door and crawled back into bed, her mind racing, knowing JD had given her fair warning. That forces beyond her understanding were conspiring against her, having compromised Isaac. Realizing, as her mind came fully back into balance, that JD reaching out to her in her dream meant he was not beyond reach.

Major Kelly's office was just as inviting as the last time Cheryl had been there. The walls still mostly bare, with the same handful of photographs lined up in a row opposite the small oak desk where Jean sat in his chair, back ramrod straight, thick hands clasped in front of him.

Cheryl hesitated, waiting for Jean's nod before moving to the chair across from him. She leaned back, nervous as she tried to measure his mood. "Is there a problem?" Her voice was low, sensing a shift in the man's demeanor. Formal, more so than normal, his eyes fixed on hers, his lips compressed in thin lines.

"There has been a change. In oversight roles." Jean pressed his thumbs together, their tips white from the pressure. "You'll continue the project— but will no longer be reporting to me."

"Are you—retiring?"

"No. Two more years before I'll be wanting to call it quits." Jean hesitated, then leaned back, shaking his head slightly. "There has been a—" He shrugged, his wide shoulders pocketing the front of his uniform. "Reallo- cation of project over-sight responsibilities. A shift in budgetary support. We, meaning the military, will continue to provide you with full security support. Nothing changes on that end. But you'll now be reporting to a corporate entity." Jean let a corner of his upper lip raise, reflecting a glimmer of a rare smile. "I understand there will also be a sizable increase in funding." He gave Cheryl a considered stare. "Congratulations, Doctor Atkinson. You've raised some highly influential eyebrows, due to the reports of your recent success."

Cheryl pursed her lips, her eyebrows narrowing as she ran through a list of reasons for the sudden change. "I'm not sure I'd describe it a success. More like stumbling around in a windowless room, with my eyes closed, arms outstretched, finding a piece of a puzzle here, another one there." She cocked her head, looking at Jean, trying to discern if he was disappointed or relieved. "Been able to fit them together—more by luck than design."

Jean allowed a full smile to crease his weathered cheeks. "I've earned a few medals myself, following the same scenario. Handed out dozens more to men under my command, who completed their missions by doing the same thing." He shrugged. "Breakthroughs often come on the backs of people willing to lead the way through unknown terrain, refusing to wait for orders from those whose heads are shoved up—" Jean paused. "Whose minds are closed."

Cheryl grinned. "I've been lucky."

"We both know that's not true." Jean leaned back, lifting one hand, using it to cup his thick chin. "You strike me as more of an—intelligent and persistent force of nature. Unrestrained by the norms of conventional wisdom."

"Or just stubborn and pushy, always stepping way outside the boundaries of conventional science."

Jean let out a long sigh. "Whichever way you want to say it—I'm afraid our professional relationship has ended. You'll submit your next report to—" He narrowed his eyes, glancing at a sheet of paper on his desk. "A Ms. Coleman." Cheryl didn't flinch, though her posture stiffened for a moment before she forced a curt nod. Jean leaned forward, a curious look on his face. "Do you know her?"

Cheryl's relaxed, having expected some form of outreach from the group backing her project. "As a matter of fact, I do."

Jean studied her reaction, his eyes narrowed in thought. "You don't appear surprised—by this change of oversight responsibilities."

Cheryl crossed her arms. "It was predictable. One of many scenarios I've run through these past few months. With project control, or oversight, being pulled from the military. From you."

Jean got to his feet and held out his hand, waiting for her to stand up and grasp it, noting the strength of her grip. "I hope you continue to have success with the patient. Your work promises to be of great help to those who've served their country and suffered greatly from doing so." He paused, giving her an appraising look. "Goodbye, Doctor Atkinson."

She let go of his hand. "Please, Major—call me Cheryl." She looked around the office. "I hope to still see you around. Maybe we can get a cup of coffee sometime."

Jean nodded. "I'd like that, Doctor Atkinson." He moved to the door, holding it for her as she stepped through. Then he paused, lowering his voice. "Now that you're not reporting to me, if we do get an opportunity to grab a cup of coffee, you can call me by my first name. Its Jean." He waited a moment, looking her directly in the eyes, then reached out and shook her hand. "I wish you continued good luck—Cheryl."

Once Cheryl cleared the military side of the complex and made her way into a bathroom, she unfolded the slip of paper pressed into her palm by the major. It bore an address and time, written in a condensed line of letters and numbers. Her hand shook as she read it, knowing there was more to the change described than could be safely shared in the confines of the military facility. The promise of a more forthcoming explanation to be made once she could reach the nameless destination.

The restaurant was over-flowing with a line of people standing outside the double-doors, the parking lot filled, leaving Cheryl sitting in a long line of cars waiting to find a space. A tall, broad-shouldered man approached, bypassing several vehicles in front of hers, circling a large finger, wanting her to lower her window.

"You the Doc?" His booming voice held more than a trace of a southern accent.

"Excuse me?" Cheryl gripped the steering wheel of her car.

"The smart-ass chick Dancer keeps going on about."

Cheryl relaxed, aware the man was talking about Jean. She flashed a grin. "I suppose I am."

"You are—or you ain't." The man looked in at her, a serious look on his wide face, a thin scar running across one cheek.

Cheryl nodded. "I are."

He smiled, then opened her car door. "I'll take care of your car, ma'am. You go ahead in. Dancer's sitting in back. Under the big-ass fish."

Cheryl moved toward the end of the line, another solid-framed man standing near the crowded entrance. He looked up, hearing a piercing whistle, then reached out, brushing aside a knot of men and their dates without effort: a twin to the ebony-skinned man in the parking lot, with a much lighter skin-tone. "Make room, guys. Dancer's date is here."

Cheryl ducked into a sliver of open space beneath the man's heavily muscled arm and chest as he cleared a path. She clutched her purse in front of her, his arm around her shoulders, guiding her across a densely packed dance floor where couples were moving to music produced several generations ago. He finally delivered her to a small booth located beneath a large blue marlin, Jean watching with a grin as she slipped in across from him.

"Glad you could make it."

Cheryl placed her purse on the table. "Glad you invited me." She glanced at the crowd of boisterous people, several of them engaged in heated back-and-forth discussions concerning the relative merits of various branches of the military. "I think."

Jean shrugged, his hand in the air signaling to someone behind the bar. "The night is young, and we have a decent group of bouncers on hand. What's your poison?"

Cheryl noted the dark ale sitting in front of him. "One of those'll be fine."

Jean looked at her, his light-colored eyes on hers. "It's strong. A local brew. Has a proper bite to it."

Cheryl flashed a grin, her cheeks dimpling on either side of her full lips. "I've been known to bite back—on occasion."

Jean held up two fingers, one of a handful of bartenders working the bar flashing him a smile. Then he returned to an open appraisal of Cheryl, leaning back in a relaxed posture, his face slightly flushed, not bothering to hide his interest in her. "You remind me of a young officer I worked with, a few years back. Great field instincts. No one better at maneuvering through enemy terrain."

"Is he one of the men outside, waiting for me to arrive?"

Jean's eyes lowered, staring at the thick mug of ale. "No. He was killed. A great loss to his men. To his family. And to me." He looked up, his expression open. "Too willing, at times, to lead from the front."

Cheryl shifted in her seat, trying to find an angle that allowed her to see Jean's face and the floor of the large restaurant at the same time. "Isn't that where leaders *should* be?"

"No. Not at all." Jean reached over and touched the back of her hand with a finger, pressing lightly. "It's important for a commander to understand where he, or she, needs to be in oder to direct their people. Their prime responsibility—to try and outmaneuver an opposing force. Dying heroically in combat is—" He hesitated, a shadow slipping across his face. "The same as failing your men. Something done only when there's nothing left you *can* do." He pulled his hand back.

Cheryl nodded. "Point taken." Their server leaned in, placing two mugs of ale on the table. She lifted hers, taking a large swallow, savoring the heavy flavor.

The music drifted between mid to late seventies, with a handful of ballads mixed with a few protest songs and an occasional instrumental, played by the house-band to a mostly middle-aged audience, everyone enjoying the retro-atmosphere. There were a few younger men in attendance, their hair cut short, arms bulging from short-sleeved shirts, some of them having over-imbibed. Escorted to tables in the back or led outside to cool off. Waitstaff were kept busy, maneuvering their way between dancers, delivering enormous platters of food to tables and booths, along with plentiful helpings of liquid fare.

Cheryl watched as a steady flow of patrons arrived, ate, then left, partaking of the relaxed atmosphere before moving on to other nocturnal activities. She nursed a second ale, holding the glass between her hands, eyeing Jean as he finished laying out the reason behind slipping her the note. When he was done, he leaned back, hands on the table, taking a moment to finish his second helping of ale. "So, based on what I've been told, or been able to find out—that's what's behind the shift in project control."

Cheryl nodded, then reached out, selecting another fish nugget; lightly battered in a seasoned crust. "As I told you before—a predictable reaction on their part, based on my early, slightly positive results. An eventuality I've prepared for. Planned for."

Jean shrugged. "It seems I over-estimated a need for concern on my part."

Cheryl smiled. "I appreciate you looking out for the project, Jean." She took another fish nugget, telling herself it was the final one. "I've dealt with real and potential ramifications of the research I've been doing since—" She tilted her head, playing with her napkin. "Well, forever." Then she popped the chunk of fish into her mouth, chewing slowly, savoring the mixed flavors, washing it down with the last of her ale. "It's no different from any other technological advancement, starting out as simple tools before becoming weapons. The sharpened rock leading to the club, arrow, and missile. Chiseled words leading to the printing press to world-wide dissemination of propaganda online, for and against those in power. Pagers, meant to provide a means of silent communication for people in business meetings, turned into personal messaging, leading to distracted driving, mindlessly walking straight into traffic, and emotional abuse, resulting in tens of thousands of injuries and deaths. Not the original intent of the inventors, but predictable enough if someone had stopped to sit back and consider the possibilities. Positive *and* negative."

"And you see a measure of negativity in what it is you've been able to accomplish?" Jean raised his hand to signal for another round of drinks. Lowering one finger as Cheryl shook her head.

She shrugged, squeezing a lemon wedge into a glass of water, the ice mostly melted. "Tell me Jean—do you like your job?"

"Yes. I do." He paused. "Why?"

"What about the person sitting in a cubicle, pulling and pushing data from one server to another? Or answering calls from frustrated customers, looking for tech support? Or having to make calls, trying to sell things to people, no one wants or needs?" Cheryl shook her head. "Can you even imagine what that's like for them, day in, day out. With nothing tangible to wrap their hands around at the end of a mind-numbing week. Or month. Or—God forbid, years? Can you imagine answering the same way if you were in their position?"

"No." Jean shrugged. "Not compared with what I do now, overseeing a group of professionals dedicated to serving their country, supportive of each other." He leaned forward, his eyes fixed on hers. "And yes—for all those serving overseas, exposed to daily interaction with an unseen enemy, hiding behind friendly smiles, words of welcome, or having to ignore shouts of condemnation from those they're over there to protect. Losing friends to sudden violence. Having to make split-second decisions, leading to hours of agonizing over the results. Innocents killed, or friends left exposed to enemy fire. Hesitating to shoot—or shooting without taking an extra moment to properly identify the threat. Frightened young people, drained by the endless toll. Nothing, as you just put it, to wrap their hands around at the end of a day, a week, or a tour, ending without tangible results. Only the faces of those maimed or killed—on both sides."

Cheryl nodded, taking a moment to reflect on his pain. "And if I could make them whole? Would you want that for them?"

Jean stared at her, a muscular server slipping another glass into place, retreating without a word. "You need to ask? Isn't that the purpose of what you're trying to accomplish?"

She nodded. "It is. The *positive* side of its potential, helping to soften traumatic memories. Numb the pain of memories until the mind can heal. Until the person can accept what happened to them, or what they caused to happen." Cheryl leaned forward. "But there's another side to it. Another application going beyond traumatic event repressive therapy. One promising to be a boon to corporate entities. A solution provided to a different type of victim, if you will, leaving employees stuck in an endless loop of circular momentum, living the same day, repeatedly, with smiles on their faces, their emotions adjusted, encouraging—"

Jean interrupted; his face pale. "To make them happy. Or more to the point, satisfied with their lot in life. Using your creation, the Tee-Cee, to reset their expectations, improve their performance, or simply maintain it. Treating them like they're—" He swallowed, his expression troubled. "Machines."

"Exactly." Cheryl took a sip of water, watching as Jean shook his head, trying to process the information. "It's one of hundreds of eventualities I've spent years considering while moving ahead, proving the process has merit."

"But if what you say is true— "Jean held up one hand. "I mean, I know it is. No question about that. But if using it to return people to their roles as workers or soldiers, without altering the causation event." His eyes gleamed with anger. "That makes it sound—malevolent."

"Or profitable—when viewed from a corporate mindset."

Jean looked away, his jaw clenched, hands compressed into fists. "They'll do it, too. No doubt about it. Those bastards will use it. Keep feeding men back into the grinder, until they're used up, missing pieces of themselves or relegated to the discard pile, if they're lucky." He sighed. "They'd be better off dead."

Cheryl leaned forward. "That's why we need to understand the consequences, on *both* sides of this. In how it's going to be managed. Controlled. The potential too great to be denied those standing to benefit. Too dangerous, if used against individuals to adjust their behaviors, alter their memories, changing their world view."

"Creating a corporate, or worse—a national cult."

"Starting off with children. Encouraged to take relaxation breaks to reduce disruptive behavior patterns while in the classroom."

"Avoiding the need for taking medications. For ADD or ADHD."

Cheryl held out her hand, palm up, motioning with her fingertips, encouraging Jean to continue with the thought. He hesitated, opened his mouth to speak, then stopped, his eyes widening. "*Fuck!* That's who's behind this. Big Pharma! The corporations moving into position, using their influence to control the outcome." He stared at Cheryl. "To control you."

She smiled, nonplussed by his remark. He shook his head, staring at her, eyes narrowed as he considered her closely. "You—have a plan. To counter them."

"I've had a plan for over twenty years, ever since I started down this road. Not that I'll be able to prevail. Too high a tide rolling in and not a tall enough throne to keep my feet dry."

Jean raised an eyebrow. "A reference to—King Canute?"

"Was that his name?" Jean nodded, causing Cheryl to grin. "I sucked at history. Just remember reading about a guy who thought he was powerful enough to stop a rising tide."

Jean shook his head. "It was only a comment he made to teach his followers that no man, however powerful, can turn back the forces of nature. Only a divine God. But your overall point stands: change is inevitable, same as with the tide."

"And I'm doing what I can to control it. For as long as possible, hoping I can convince enough people of influence to put limits in place. To forestall some of the more negative applications." She paused. "Knowing that, like the king guy, I'm doomed to fail."

"Or you'll succeed, showing them that man would do well to remember the lesson, leaving any major alterations to nature—or God."

Cheryl raised her hand and waved it in a circle, signaling for another round. "Like that'll ever happen. Besides, we *need* to make alterations to humanity before letting people leave this place." She noted a look of confusion on Jean's face. "The earth." Then she smiled. "I mean—it's one thing to let the monkeys run the zoo down here. Another whole level of crazy, sending them out to try and run the universe."

CHAPTER TWENTY-FOUR

MOVIE SET, L.A. BASIN

Twain and Miranda's Story

The backdrop of the set was a long row of tenement buildings, false faces poised in sunlight, with over one hundred people working away, preparing for a late-night shoot. Dozens of serious-faced men along with a handful of women were setting up for a multiple car chase, to be followed by a series of crashes and predictable shoot-out, with the usual mix of exploding gas tanks and flaming wreckage creating visual effects. The scene was being rehearsed by a small army of stunt men and safety officers, covering every detail while a representative of the production company stood elbow to elbow with their insurance rep, wearing his hand out, signing his way through a thick stack of documentation.

Twain held Miranda's hand, guiding her past a spider's web of cabling tied to a large control board, a wide variety of pyrotechnics being tied into the firing circuits. They ducked between light crews working side by side with the set coordinators, along with a host of camera crews setting up for filming from alternate angles. Multiple scenes to be shot, then cut into the final edit months from now, long after actors, producers, director, stunties, and other support people had drifted away to other projects.

Miranda leaned against Twain. "It's kind of like being back overseas —with all the commotion. Preparation of gear. Tactics being gone through." She squeezed his hand. "Are you okay?"

Twain nodded, looking around for Dawg, stopping when he remembered James had him well in hand, both back in his trailer, one of them rehearsing his lines. The other working on breaking into a large bone, seeking the marrow filling the interior. "Yeah. I'm good." He looked at Miranda and forced a thin smile. "I'm frosty in the desert sun. Got my water. Got my gun. Ready to go and have some fun!"

Miranda frowned. "Glad we're not still over there." Twain held out his arm, moving her back as a series of transports crawled up alongside them, loaded down with cars and trucks, both new and old, delivered for the action sequence. Hundreds of thousands of dollars' worth of metal and glass cages to be turned into props, once set in place, and wired up. Their moment of fame, brief. Flames and twisted destruction waiting for them at the end of the shoot. Sacrificed for a few seconds of celluloid film before being hauled away to a crusher, turned into cubes of metal.

Miranda shivered as a flashback slipped past her mind's eye: aluminum caskets waiting to be loaded into the gaping maw of a large transport plane, two lines of serious-faced men in uniforms providing a solemn attendance.

"Are *you* okay?" Twain felt a shudder pass through Miranda, her shoulder pressed against his. He stepped back, pulling her around. "We can head back, if you—"

"No. I'm fine. Just excited, seeing all the chaos. Amazing how much time, effort and money goes into doing this. All for a few seconds of the—shooting?" She angled her head, squinting, the sun on her face. "Is that right?"

"Close enough." Twain moved her to one side, seeking a clear path through a field of colored flags. A high-pitched voice cut through the buzz of activities, a heavy-set man with a clipboard approaching, waving his hand as if being attacked by bees. One of a dozen assistants to the director, he rushed up, face beet red after his waddling-jog. "Phil wanted me to ask you to go over some changes he wants to make. He's in number seven, where the interior shots are being set up." He hesitated. "Your friend can come along too." The man's eyes drew together in a sparse nest of thinly plucked brows. "Though any changes he makes will play *havoc* with the *schedule*."

Twain grinned, noting the man's use of an English pronunciation for the last word. He nodded, watching as the disgruntled assistant spun away, scurrying back across the busy lot without stopping. Miranda started forward, turning around when Twain refused to move.

"What is it?"

Twain looked at her, his expression serious. "Thank you. For agreeing to come here with me. It's been—helpful. Seriously."

Miranda stepped closer. "No need. You were there for my mother. I'm here for you now."

"Only because of that? Because of Janice?"

She shook her head, her honey-blond hair in a thick braid, swinging over her shoulder. "You know me better than that." She leaned in and kissed him, then pulled back. "I'm here because of *Dawg*. He needs someone to take care of him while you're doing your acting thing."

"You make it sound—dirty."

Miranda grinned, her hazel-green eyes lighting up. "Now *that's* an entirely *different* type of filmmaking." She angled her head. "But I'm game, if you are."

Twain reached out, collecting her into his arms, holding her for a moment before letting go and nudging her into movement, guiding her as she stepped over and around carefully placed lines of tiny yellow flags, marking squibs that would be used to mimic the raking impact of automatic gunfire.

"It's trite. Almost condescending." Phil twisted his head, looking to one side, eyeing Twain. "Not natural to the character. Or to you."

"Okay." Twain shrugged, looking at the script he was holding.

"Really, Twain? That's all you have to say?" Phil sighed, tossing the script onto the table. "They'll have to do a rewrite—but there's not enough time for that. Besides, they'll probably *fuck* it up. Again." He looked at Miranda, who was standing by a small window watching the two of them going through the script for the climactic scene. "Sorry. Forgot there's a lady present." Phil paused. "My apologies."

Miranda mimicked Twain's nonchalant shrug, arms crossed beneath her breasts. She frowned. "Do you have any tissues?"

"Excuse me?" Phil cocked his head, not seeing the smile breaking out on Twain's face.

"For all the blood—dripping from my delicate ears."

Phil straightened up, confused. "Your—" Then he grinned. "Oh—I get it. Good one." He bowed his head slightly. "I like you. You're quick."

Twain spoke up. "She's a real pro, and a lot tougher than she looks." Twain noted the raised eyebrows on the director's face. "A professional *editor*, Phil. With a great big shiny office. Works for one of the larger New York media houses."

"Of course." There was a pause while Phil gave Miranda a considered look. "Are you here doing a story? If so, then my people failed to let me know. Or get approval."

"Not a story on you." Miranda pointed at Twain. "On him. About a man who professes to detest the fame and lifestyle of an actor yet keeps placing himself in front of the camera lens. The unblinking eye, capturing lies made into truth. Gore, nothing more than a sticky prop, swept away by the hand of time, along with historical facts. Reality twisted, re-assorted by false prophets, then stored away for future generations to view. Left to acclaim this is the world as it was, told true."

Phil stared, his mouth agape. "Who—wrote that?"

"I did. Just now."

Twain leaned over, his head near Phil's ear. "She's a real wise-ass but has a heart of gold."

Phil ignored him, holding out the script "Would you mind looking at these lines? I'll pay you whatever you want—and give you a writer's credit for any changes you suggest."

Miranda came over and took the pages. "I'd settle for being introduced to the female lead. I've always wanted to meet a *real* movie star." She smiled at Twain. He grinned, then went over and leaned against the windowsill, looking out at the activities centered around the nighttime shoot, knowing Phil was in capable hands.

Dawg looked up, the bone between his paws well gnawed, the marrow still intact. He rose, then stopped, trying to pick up the bone, unwilling to leave it behind. James watched him from the small kitchen table in the trailer, then turned toward the door as it opened, Twain and Miranda came through, back from their visit to the set. He raised an eyebrow. "We good to go?"

"More changes. Again." Twain tossed the revised script on the table. "For you too."

"For the love of a mean woman." James picked up the script, flipping through it, stopping when he came to several new pages. A few words had been crossed out, others added, bunched into the margins, connected in with narrow lines. He nodded. "Better. Much better. The flow works." He looked at Miranda. "You did this—I can tell."

"How'd you know?" Twain sat down, looking at James. The other man shrugged. "By her handwriting, you ignoramus. It's the same as on the grocery list she put together for the caterer."

Miranda grinned. "I did. Got offered a full-time job, too. But turned it down. Gonna stick with covering reality. It pays less and hurts a hell of a lot more, so what's not to love?"

Both men nodded, Twain pulling a second copy of the script out, going through his new lines. Miranda snapped her fingers, beckoning Dawg over. She clipped him into his harness, having to work it around the bone firmly clamped in his mouth. Then she opened the door, following him as he leapt down, her voice trailing away as it closed behind her. "Let's take you for a walk. Find somewhere you can bury that disgusting thing!"

The sun was down. Twain, Miranda, and James were sitting in a row of chairs on a small rise safely back from the action, overlooking a half-mile stretch of asphalt road running between the building facades. Twain sighed, totally relaxed, finished with his part of the film, Phil thanking Miranda for her help after he and his female co-star performed their revised lines with realistic emotions. They'd shot the scene in one take, the rest of the on-call cast and crew giving them a well-deserved round of applause. Now that the work of acting had ended, Twain smiled, happy to be a spectator, waiting for the fireworks to begin.

A small entourage of people came up the rise, stopping in front of him. One of them, a stocky man with wide shoulders, sighed, then spat out a handful of words. "We are *com-fucking-pletely* screwed."

"And why is that?" Twain grinned, knowing the stunt coordinator was about to ask him to step in, having heard a rumor of trouble on the set from James. "Don't tell me Barry's on the sauce again? What did he do this time? Take a run at one of the producer's wives? Or maybe—a daughter?"

The stunt director turned his head and spat a stream of tobacco juice on the ground. "He broke his damn foot jumping out a second-floor window. So, yeah. Most likely one or the other. Or both!"

"Good driver, though. One of the best."

"Second best. To you." The man paused, giving Twain a questioning look. "You willing to take the ride?"

Twain lowered his head, feeling Miranda stiffening in her seat beside him, her leg pressed against his. "Was watching the run-through earlier today when you were setting it up. How long until go time?"

"Just over an hour. Enough to do one drive through. You good with that?"

Twain nodded, knowing he was going to have to explain his decision to Miranda. And to James, a founding member of the stay-the-fuck-in-your-lane club. "I'm good. Give me a few to get ready. Be down shortly."

"Look me in the eye and tell me there's no risk." Miranda stood in front of Twain, her arms crossed, face set in a concerned look.

Twain hesitated, then nodded. "There's some risk." He saw her eyes widen. "The potential of something going wrong is always there when things are happening in real time. But we're professionals and know how to prepare for it." He put his hands on her shoulders. "It's no different from any other line of work, with a certain measure of risk assumed in putting yourself out there in the world. Same as you and I were doing—a few years ago."

"*Were* doing, Twain. Not anymore."

"True."

Miranda looked over at James. "You maybe want to chime in here? Offer something to—I don't know, try and talk your friend out of doing this?"

James nodded, then stepped forward, standing beside Miranda. "You're right. There's substantial risk and he shouldn't try and gloss over that." James paused. "But he's right too. The guy who gave him his first chance is in a bind. The entire shoot in danger of being canceled."

Miranda glared at James, then looked over at Twain. "And if you get hurt? What happens then?"

Twain shrugged. "It goes in the can, until the film gets released. People move on with their lives."

"Fuck you." Miranda spun around and headed into the shadows, Dawg at her side. The sun had slipped below the horizon, stars beginning to populate the sky. There was no wind. No sound of traffic. Nothing that would interrupt the silence between the three of them in the hour before the mayhem would begin.

CHAPTER TWENTY-FIVE

RIVER-SIDE CABIN, MID-COAST MAINE

Calvin and Jemma's Story

The cabin windows reflected a blue sky with puffy white clouds. The glass, dark faced, hid the interior until Jemma pressed her forehead against the pane, her breath fogging the view, the dry air quickly wiping it away. "You remembered the key, right?"

Calvin chuckled. "It's not locked." He turned his head, watching as Dawg raced around the corner of the small building, a blur of a red squirrel leading him to the nearest tree.

Jemma twisted her head around, staring. "You're kidding!"

Calvin shrugged, the pack on his back mimicking the motion. "Why would I do that? No one ever comes here. It's a long walk in, and there's nothing of any value inside. Stove's too heavy to lug out. And you'd need a chainsaw to clear a path through the trees blown down across the old roadbed."

Jemma moved to the rear of the small wooden structure, having to shoo Dawg away as he came bounding over, a satisfied look on his face. She opened a door made of thick slabs of hemlock, then stepped inside and stopped, sighing at the view through the wall to wall stretch of glass windows. "It's—*breathtaking!*" A wide expanse of dark-blue river ran past outcrops of ledges, scattered along the curled edges of a large cove. Stands of immense pine trees framed the opening around the cabin, connected by thick clumps of juniper brush surrounding pockets of yellow, sunburnt grass and deep-green moss. The interior walls were adorned with an assortment of framed photos of men with fishing poles and strings of fish, along with paintings of waterfowl and two shoulder mounts: thick-necked bucks placed on opposite walls, as if ready to do battle over the right to mate with a fertile doe.

"You like it?" Calvin stepped inside and slipped his arm around Jemma's waist, fingers cupping her body. Possessive. Protective.

Jemma slipped her fingers over his, encouraging the pressure. "It's incredible! Absolute—perfection."

Calvin kissed the back of her neck, then looked over her shoulder through the windows, watching as several boats slipped into view, running the wide expanse of river water to the sea, a half-mile along. "Until it's raining. Forty degrees outside. The river running brown. Icy spray stinging your face, gnawing away at any exposed skin."

Jemma twisted around, looking him in his eyes. "That sounds even more perfect." Rising to her toes, she kissed him, then leaned forward, forcing Calvin to release her hips to keep his balance. He met her tongue with his own, mirroring her movements as she began unbuttoning his shirt, slipping hers from her shoulders, tossing it to one side. His hands cupped her body, his cheek pressed against hers, breathing in the scent of her hair as he kissed her throat.

The cabin swirled around them as they sank to the floor, losing themselves in the feeling of their joining, her body beneath his, the wooden floor rough against his palms and knees, unnoticed. As was the loud barking of Dawg and the piercing shriek of an osprey guarding its nest, coming from just outside the cabin door.

"You heard me." Jemma fastened her bra, then spun it around, working it up over her breasts. "An air-bee-and-bee."

"A what?" Calvin, distracted by Jemma's movements, missed most of what she'd just said. Jemma sighed, loudly, buttoning up her shirt. "A rental property. For people to stay at. You can make some big bucks, believe me."

Calvin shrugged, still putting on his clothes. "No one's gonna want to pay money to stay here. It's a hunting camp. Not some hotel."

"They will, Calvin." Jemma spun around, pointing through the large windows. "Because of that. The effing view! It's worth a whole butt load of money once you put this place back into working order."

Calvin frowned, looking around the interior. "It's not *out* of order. This is exactly how it's *always* been."

"You'll need to add a refrigerator. And some lights. Oh, and running water. With a bathroom. Then—"

"It *already* has water. A hand pump, right outside the door. And there's an outhouse just past—"

"And new furniture. And an outside fire pit. And a fireplace, for when it's raining. Some nice curtains. And a new floor. And hardwood cabinets with a granite counter. And a *soapstone sink!*"

Calvin came over and took Jemma into his arms. "Stop. Okay? We just got here and you're already out the door, halfway back to the main road. Let's just enjoy it the way it is, without needing to turn it into something else."

Jemma opened her mouth to respond, then stopped herself, the look in Calvin's eyes letting her know he was hard up against the limit of his ability to adjust to her frequent outbursts of creative intensity. She nodded. "Okay. You're right. We've got enough on our plates as it is—for now."

Dawg came rushing in, sliding to a stop, nose pressed to the floor for a moment before coming over and bumping into Calvin's leg. His tongue hung from one side of his mouth, teeth gleaming in the indirect light streaming through the glass. Calvin reached down, rubbing him between his ears. "Who won the standoff? You or the bird?" Dawg licked his hand, then went over to Jemma, nosing her fingers for the treat she'd just pulled from her pocket.

⌇

The solar panels were in place, the cabling tied into a large converter and battery bank, ready for a local electrician to make the final connection into the local grid. They'd poured a new foundation with concrete holding tanks, curing while they waited for the organic waste-to-energy system to arrive: the specifications for its construction followed by a local contractor, intrigued by the concept.

"Animal shit. Turned into power."

Calvin nodded. "Along with organic waste. Food scraps. Leftovers collected from stores and restaurants. And manure. So, yes—there's some shit involved."

"Becoming power?" The man scratched his head. "Enough to run what—a few lights and a television?" He grinned. "Guess that makes sense, seeing how much crap they're putting across the airwaves, nowadays."

They had one major project left to complete: a combined livestock barn and generator house, enclosed in a post and beam structure Jemma had designed, along with Calvin's help. Her grandfather, Jameson, had driven himself up to go over the drawings, working with the two of them over a long holiday weekend, trying to blend Jemma's innovative ideas into what was possible, using lumber, pegs, and sweat. He was standing outside, watching Calvin as he drove in several wooden stakes.

"It's something. I'll give her that." Jemma's grandfather muttered beneath his breath, holding the drawing up, measuring it with his eyes against the spot Calvin had marked out. "More difficult to build than it needs to be—but doable."

Calvin came over and dropped a small maul on the ground. "The *aesthetics* are nice. It'll fit in nicely with the line of trees running alongside the brook. Shouldn't overwhelm the land.

Jameson squinted, shaking his head. "Yeah. Well, I guess it makes sense in you seeing it that way. Not wanting to piss her off, and all." The old man, pushing the end of a seventh decade, hawked up a gob of phlegm and turned his head, spitting. Then he folded the paper back up and tucked it into his pocket. He eyed Calvin, with a grin on his face. "Otherwise, might put a damper on your—nocturnal activities."

Calvin shrugged, hands on his hips, noting Jemma's approach. "That might have something to do with it, I suppose. But you must admit, it's an excellent blend of structural integrity, with non-traditional design elements. And reasonable enough in cost."

"Uh, huh."

Jameson turned around, his face beaming as he watched his granddaughter walk up. He greeted her with a hug. "It's an *impressive* design! Going to fit in nicely with the trees and waterway. An interesting blend of traditional and—*innovative* ideas." He gave Jemma a big hug. "I'm proud of the work you're doing up here."

She gave him a peck on his bearded cheek. "Thanks, Poppa. At least *someone* gets what I'm going for." She turned and stuck her tongue out at Calvin, who shrugged, a smile on his face as he leaned over and picked up the maul.

Calvin woke up, listening as his aunt's house seemed to be holding its breath, filled wall to wall with absolute silence, the bedside nightlight off. Another power outage, he thought, lying on his back with Jemma's hip angled against his side. He turned his head and checked the corner of the bedroom. Dawg had abandoned the room, looking for a cool spot, the weather having turned unseasonably warm, with hardwood trees barely in bud. He listened to the soft sigh of Jemma's breathing coming from his side of the bed. She'd made it a habit of late to chase him in her sleep. Seeking continuous contact with his body as he kept edging away, becoming over-heated. He was tempted to get up and slip in on the opposite side, waiting for the thud when she ended up on the floor.

A call of nature whispered in his ear, compelling him to rise and walk down the narrow hallway to the small bathroom. He moved with caution, uncertain where the dark bodied dog might be, not wanting to disturb him. The path proved clear, a quarter moon slipping a shaft of silver light through the tattered edge of a thin curtain shading the window of the front door. He opened it, the cooler air outside bringing a measure of relief.

Mist rose from the sloped ground, Calvin searching for deer that might have gathered in the small field, coming up empty. He moved down the steps and walked over to the edge of the lawn to take care of business. As he stood there, his instincts whispered in his ear, a sensation of being watched coming over him. He looked toward the road, but there wasn't any sign of a vehicle, or anyone else.

He finished up, then turned to head back inside, stopping when a voice called out to him, one low in tone and familiar. A shadow formed on the edge of the grass, separating itself from a puddle of darkness lying beneath the limbs of an ancient oak. He felt compelled to move toward it, as if he were floating, every movement effortless. Dreaming, he thought, wondering if he'd just wet the bed. He shook his head, trying to wake up, watching as the shadow resolved into an outline of a rangy-framed man, a line of white teeth in a crooked grin beneath two pools of dark. Becoming eyes. Open, revealing a slight gleam of reflected moonlight.

Calvin stared. "You're not here. You're dead. This is just a dream."

"Go ahead and tell yourself that, cousin. It doesn't much matter to me." The shadow came closer. Carl, his face still young, no longer a close match to his own, though with the same husky voice and lean body. He grinned. "I feel different, cousin. Can feel it—all the way down in my dusty bones." A raspy laugh followed. "Whatever you and your lady were smoking earlier—it's still working."

"You should go. I couldn't help you then. Can't help you now."

"What happened that night, Cal, well—that was all on me. Made my choice and paid the price for it. You made to pay as well, because of me. Something you're still doing. Been doing ever since." Calvin opened his mouth to reply. Carl cut him off. "Don't waste your breath." The shade of his cousin, or ghost, or whatever it was stared over at him. "Shit hand dealt you. Everyone eager to assign you the blame. And you—willing to play the martyr. Feeling guilty, carrying around the burden of my sins." The shade of his cousin looked at Calvin with sad eyes. "So stupid, Cal, doing that. I was dead. Gone. Through no fault of your own."

"Past is the past, Carl. Better to leave it alone—"

Carl raised his voice and started to sing, guitar music falling like rain from out of the late-night air. "The past is the past. Nothing good ever lasts. Like treasures let slip through your hands. Time moves along. Dusk turning to dawn. Like old friends and childhood plans. All gone to shadows as memory fades. Though we still bear the scars from the mistakes we've made. All of them earned, in the journey we've taken. Lovers left behind, though never forsaken."

The words were a tumble of bass notes, grinding their way through the hush of misty air. Calvin looked down, staring at where the ground should be. Unable to see it. No longer feeling it. "You always had a way of doing that, cousin. Spitting out strings of words, with me listening while you made promises to girls, offering to take them to far-off places. Gonna go set the world on fire." Calvin softened his voice. "Funny how it worked out, in the end. With you drowning in a beaver bog. The water cold—and dark."

The world spun in a blurred circle, nausea rising from Calvin's stomach, his balance lost. He fell, past the ground, beyond night and day. Tumbling in endless head over heel motions. A thick limb reaching out, smacking his face, stinging. Pain yanking him back. The bedroom wall behind him, head pressed back against it. His arms thrust out. Jemma's face a shade of pale white, her eyes wide in fear. Hand poised to slap him again. "I'm, okay." He reached up, gripping her wrist. "It's passed—whatever it was."

Jemma reached out with her free hand, touching Calvin's face, searching his eyes. "You couldn't hear me. Or *Dawg*, who was barking away, letting me know you were in trouble. I was so scared! You were trying to say something. Your eyes were closed. Something about drowning."

"Just having a dream, Jem. A bad one, but only a dream." He released her wrist, then took both of her hands in his. "It felt real. Like I was falling." He shook his head, willing himself to be okay to reassure her and Dawg, whose feet were resting on the side of the bed, whining, his muzzle poking against his side, seeking his touch. "I'm good." He slid out of bed and gave Dawg a quick rub of his neck and back, settling him down. "I'll be right back."

He stopped when he got to the bathroom door at the end of the hallway, looking out through the glass window of the front door, light slowly building as dawn approached. Then he went in and used the toilet, careful to avoid looking into the mirror. When he got back to the bedroom, Jemma was sitting up. She tapped the side of the bed, inviting him to sit down beside her.

"What do you think it means?" She leaned in, touching Calvin on his shoulder, her fingers brushing against the edge of the large scar on his left shoulder. The surface was smooth, lighter in tone, revealed in the dim light of the bedroom. Calvin shrugged, his shoulders rising and falling, the damaged area moving beneath her hand. "I don't think it means anything. It was only a dream, Jem. That's all."

She pressed her head on his chest. "It was more than that, Cal. You were moaning. Grinding your teeth—like you were in pain. When I tried to wake you up, you just stared straight ahead. For over a minute. And it really freaked me out!" She moved in front of him, her knees between his legs, looking him in the eyes. Taking his hands in hers, she lowered her voice. "It was a vision, Cal—not a dream. And it—"

Calvin smiled, shaking his head. "It was just a dream, Jem. People have them all the time. Good ones. Bad ones. Dreams like this one, too."

"Has it ever happened to you before?"

"Sure. I'm no different from anyone else. I've had all kinds, good and bad."

Calvin watched as Jemma tightened her lips, recognized the look, knowing she was like Dawg with a fresh bone. That she would keep gnawing away until she got to the marrow inside.

"Let it go, Jem."

"You know that ain't happening."

"Yeah." Calvin sighed, reaching up, rubbing his eyes. "I know."

Jemma yawned, then angled her head, eyes partly closed, a sleepy look on her face. "Was I in any of them?"

"Any of them, what?"

"Your *dreams*, dumb-ass."

Calvin jumped at the chance to change the subject of Carl's visitation. Nothing like it having happened to him before. Not one moment of midnight reflection, recalling the conversation they'd been having, or any other memories from the ride home that night. Enough reminders of it happening each day with people glancing up as he drove by, hesitating a second before nodding their heads. Or growing quiet whenever he entered the store, church, town office, or fire department. Talking a bit too loud while making false-smile greetings, before heading off to chores needing attending to whenever he showed up. Along with a handful of others who barely nodded, walking past him as if acknowledging a ghost.

"Yup. You've been in a few."

"And?"

"I said yes." Calvin rocked to one side as her fist struck him on his right shoulder. "You've been in *most* of them. Okay?"

"Which ones?"

"Which ones, what?"

"Do I need to get one of Dawg's bones and hit you over the head with it?" Jemma noted a flicker of interest from Dawg, still sitting by the side of the bed. "Which ones, Calvin?"

"All the good ones." He paused. "And a few of the bad."

"Share one with me. Maybe it'll reveal something about what led to your vision. About what it means."

"It wasn't a—" Calvin paused, giving up trying to deny what he knew to be the truth, still shaken by what had taken place. "Okay. Let's get this out of the way so we'll be able to get on with the rest of the day." He glanced out the window. "Which is gonna start in another hour or so."

Jemma smiled, wriggling her hips, settling in. "So—tell me about one of the good ones."

Calvin considered her request, looking at her with an appraising gaze. She had on a thin tee shirt, revealing the curve of her breasts. The rest of her bare, hands in her lap, providing a pretense of modesty. His body stirred as he reached for her, needing to thrust the vision of Carl from his mind. He held her face between his hand, staring into her dark eyes. "I'd rather *show* you what we were doing. In one of the *bad* ones."

CHAPTER TWENTY-SIX

COMPANY HOUSE, MARYLAND

Jared and Teresa's Story

The music coaxed Jared into a relaxed state, his eyes drooping as he listened to the words of a song from one of dozens of music channels available with the entertainment package that came with the house. The singer, selected at random based on his previous listening experience, had a deep, rough-edged voice with notes of a hard life sprinkled between hopeful choruses. The song pulled him to similar times in his own life, tears welling up from beneath his eyelids, an ache in his heart. Dawg lifted his head, then shifted position, tossing his large body into Jared's lap, ears pricked up, seeking his attention.

Teresa came out of the bedroom, having changed into a casual, yet expensive outfit, keeping her promise to go with him on a walk into the hills surrounding the homes in the small valley. She looked down, eying her new sneakers, specifically designed for hiking. They had thick soles, with an open weave fabric. Tan, with blue piping running along the top edges and up the sides, matched by a pair of color-coordinated socks, the tops carefully folded over, just above the laces, tied in perfectly formed bows. Teresa glanced into the living room, wondering if Jared would notice how nice she looked. Not that it mattered, she thought, knowing he missed little of importance, able to read her mood, adjusting his own to compensate. A trait of his that had drawn her closer to him every time they were together. Closer than she'd allowed herself to get to anyone in a long time.

She went over and pulled a bottle of water from the refrigerator, shutting the door with a nudge of her hip, her eyes narrowed in thought as she considered the future, knowing their relationship was ripening, the pressure for her to move in growing stronger, each day. The idea was tempting, Teresa knowing it would be easier if Jared would stop gazing at her with a look of adoration in his eyes. It unsettled her, the weight of his assumption she was perfect. Too great a burden, in knowing how far from that she was.

She stopped by the end of the couch and looked down at him. His eyes were closed, tears on his cheeks. Dawg's head was in his lap, looking up at her with amber eyes as Jared gently stroked his thick neck. When the song ended and moved to one with a livelier beat, it roused both man and beast. Jared stood up, wiped his cheeks, then reached out, taking Teresa in his arms, holding her close without speaking. Without any attempt made to explain his tears.

"There were two of them. Right here." Jared pointed to twin sets of deer tracks pressed into the dirt on the edge of the trail. "They were nibbling the buds from the tree."

"How do you know?" Teresa knelt, the large-brimmed hat she had on casting a wide shadow, hands on her knees, staring down at the impressions left behind by the sharp-hooved animals. She turned her head, looking up at Jared, having to reach out to keep her balance as Dawg came loping up from behind, nudging her as he slipped by on the narrow path.

"I learned from the best trackers in the world. Do you remember me telling you that I spent a couple of weeks with them, after—" He paused. "Anyway—I learned bush craft. How to start fires with next to nothing.

Find water holes. Learned where to locate temporary camps, when scouting the park for signs of large animals. Or poachers."

"Did you see any? Poachers, I mean."

"No. They were—" He paused again. "*Aggressively* pursued after my father died. Made to face—bush justice." He hesitated, waiting to see if she would pursue the subject, letting out a sigh of relief when she stood up and wiped her hands on the side of his faded jeans. He smiled, having to duck his head back because of the enormous hat she was wearing, dwarfing her narrow face. "Are you sure you brought a big enough *sombrero?*"

"*Hey!* It's a *Kaminski* design. A Loma, borrowed from a client." Teresa grinned. "I don't want to burn, and it's wide enough to protect my shoulders and arms. Besides—*I* think it's cute." She paused, looking around, happy to be out in the fresh air. "Where to next?"

Jared suspected it was a forced show of enthusiasm, hiking and other outdoor activities, not Teresa's cup of tea, wine, or any other libation. "I guess we can head back, take a shower, and get dressed. I'm planning to take you out for a nice lunch, seeing that you made dinner last night, and then cooked breakfast, too."

"My secret plan worked." Teresa came over, angled her head back, the brim of her large hat shadowing his face. She stretched up, rising to the toes of her barely used hiking shoes and kissed him, her slim hands circling his neck, pulling him in close, lips parting, inviting him to do the same, letting him know she had another plan in mind.

Jared stopped in the doorway of his bedroom, having come in from a rambunctious session of tossing a ball with Dawg. Reward for his having being patient while he and Teresa enjoyed a late afternoon nap followed by an early dinner, lunch having been removed from the schedule in favor of satisfying other appetites. Jared watched as Teresa rubbed lotion on her skin, causing it to glow in the light from the bedside lamp. "Dawgs settled down for the night, tuckered out from all the activity earlier today." Jared smiled. "He likes it when you stay over. Gets more exercise. More *treats*, too."

Teresa leaned forward, squeezing her shoulders together, making her breasts appear larger than normal. "I have some treats for you, too. That is—if you're not all tuckered out." Jared grinned, shedding his clothes, joining her on the bed

It was quiet. The bedroom was layered in shadows, a small nightlight doing it best to provide enough light to avoid Dawg, Jared having let him into the room after their nocturnal activities had come to an end. The shepherd lay on a dog bed in one corner, asleep, gently snoring away.

Teresa reached over and took Jared's hand, squeezing softly, letting him know she was awake. When she got one in return, she rolled onto her side, placed her hand on his chest, lightly running her fingers through the soft layer of hair. "You were crying—earlier today. When I came out from getting changed."

Jared remained silent, his breathing relaxed, mind beginning a slow slide into sleep. He pulled himself back, his voice soft. "It was the song. One I'd never heard before. Caught me off guard, I guess. Got me thinking about something—" He shrugged. "It doesn't matter."

"About what?" Teresa sat up, her body still tingling from her orgasm. Energized, as she always was after sex. "Jared?"

"Yes?" He opened his eyes, then slid up, leaning back against the headboard, hand over his mouth, covering the beginning of a yawn. "It was something about an—opportunity. Not missing out on it. Didn't really hear the words at first. Was more caught up in the rasp of his voice, and the way he was playing the guitar. Wasn't really paying attention to the lyrics. At first."

"It's all *one* thing, you *Philistine*. You can't separate the canvas and the frame from the paint. Or separate out the different layers and pattern of brushstrokes. It's an ensemble." Teresa paused, leaning in, seeing that his eyes were closed. "Jared. Wake up."

"I'm tired. And it's late."

"*You* wound me up. I would have been satisfied without you—paying so much attention to my needs."

Jared raised the edges of his lips, reflecting a sleepy smile. "Are you—complaining?"

"No." Teresa slid over, snuggling against him. "Just explaining. So, wake up and talk to me."

Jared nodded, another yawn slipping out. Then he told Teresa about a moment in his past when he'd missed out on what might have turned into a close relationship. With the daughter of a foreign diplomat. A beautiful Nigerian girl with jet black hair and ebony skin. Having missed out on an opportunity to join her and her family for a two-week retreat to their home, choosing to please his mother instead, leaving on another of her biannual field excavations. The girl having been sent away to a private school in Europe when he returned.

"So *that's* what triggered you thinking about the choice you made, or rather, didn't make. Never letting your parents—letting your mother know how you felt."

"I suppose so."

Teresa pressed her body against his. "No. You know so. Your tears were proof of that." She eyed him closely. "You're not exactly an outwardly emotional kind of guy. You didn't shed a tear during the movie tonight, while I was sobbing away like a baby."

"It was too predictable. The plot—"

Teresa sighed. "*You're* too predictable. You Luddite."

Jared grinned, his hand stroking her upper arm as they cuddled. "Not even close. The word you want is misanthrope."

"And you're a mister know-it-all." Teresa felt Jared starting to mount a defense and turned her face up, kissing him until he gave in.

"I concede the point, lovely lady." He sighed. "You win. Again."

She looked at him. "Why so formal?"

"I don't know." Jerad forced a smile. "Are we done?"

"I—suppose so." Teresa reached out, taking his hand. "Thank you, for being patient with me."

"Okay." He gave her hand a quick squeeze, then let go and slipped down in the bed, reaching for the covers.

Teresa frowned, her lips in a pout. "That's it? Okay?"

Jerad sighed, then sat up, his face set in a look of exasperation. "Is this when I'm supposed to go through the motions of asking you to move in—again? Hoping you'll finally wake up and see it as an opportunity missed? One *you'll* end up regretting later on?"

Teresa looked down, her hands clasped tightly together. "Maybe." Her voice thinned to a whisper. "I don't know."

Jerad leaned over, kissing her on her forehead. "Well, it's not a problem. Not for me. I told you how I feel. Nothing's going to change that. So, once again—no pressure."

"Might be easier—if there were." Teresa looked up. "Maybe if you got really pissed at me, for being such a—"

"Luddite?"

"Don't tease me." She looked at him, her eyes gleaming. Jared reached out, touching the side of her face. "I'm sorry. Hey—it's okay."

Teresa pulled away, then reached up and wiped her eyes. "I've wanted to say yes, a dozen times or more. The moment arriving and me—hesitating. Missing the—missing the opportunity." Her voice broke. "I'm so screwed up, Jared. You have no idea how much. You really don't know anything about me. I've made so many—"

Jared leaned in, stopping her with a kiss. "Enough. For now. Okay?"

Teresa nodded, then wiped her eyes. She slipped beneath the covers, waiting for Jared to join her. As she rested her head on his chest, she listened to the throb of his heart, her fingers gently rubbing the scar on his shoulder, knowing how much pain he'd suffered in his life through no fault of his own.

She knew most of her pain had been self-inflicted by a pattern of bad choices learned from childhood on. Determined not to screw it up this time. To avoid damaging the only man she'd ever met who was sensitive and strong enough to help her find her way to the damaged child, hiding somewhere in the shadows.

She waited until Jared's breathing eased to a raspy slip of air, lying just below the threshold of a snore. Then she lifted her head, placing her lips near his ear, her words barely a whisper. "I love you, Jared. And will be here with you. Soon. I promise." Then she settled back in, closing her eyes, a sense of relief washing through her as she drifted off to sleep. Unaware when Jared lifted his free arm and gently wiped away the tears on his cheeks.

JD

Before

The day of their wedding was glorious, though the weather was overcast, with shoreline waves roughened by Pacific swells, and rain squalls threatening in the distance. Far enough away to avoid the simple ceremony. The only attendees her parents, along with his mentor, an older man, standing up as his best man. No one else present except the minister, representing her faith. She wore a plain white dress, a small bouquet of locally sourced wildflowers held in her hands while an inexpensive cd player did its best to force music through its small speakers, failing badly. Of no matter to the two of them as they stood together, face to face.

He gazed at her, tears streaming down his wind-kissed cheeks, listening as she shared her love for him in a husky voice, reading from a paper that trembled in her hand. He recited his words to her, his voice quivering as he stumbled his way through words insufficient to express how he felt. His voice breaking, unable to finish, his friend taking the tear-stained paper and reading the rest while he watched her through his tears. Drinking in the look on her face, in her eyes. The image of her, hair done up in a simple twist of a braid, fastened in place by a faded blue ribbon, head tilted to one side, one eyebrow cocked, stirring him. Her fingernails cut short, no make-up, only a lopsided smile on her perfectly imperfect face. Losing vision of her behind a blurred curtain of joyful tears, openly expressed. Happier, then he'd ever been in his entire life.

CHAPTER TWENTY-SEVEN

LAB, RESEARCH FACILITY, MARYLAND

Cheryl

"We need—to talk." Cheryl looked at Isaac, then pointed at his chair. She waited as he lowered his body into it, the frame squeaking in protest beneath his weight. "It's about what's been going on the past few days. With the project. Where we are regarding the *next* phase."

Isaac stared back, hands clasped in his lap, remaining silent, leaving Cheryl to make the next move. Surprised when she leaned forward, her voice low.

"How's your mother doing?"

Isaac stared back. "She's—okay. All settled into her unit at the new facility, without *too* much complaining." He paused. "Thank you for asking."

Cheryl smiled. "Not at all. It's important that supervisors know how their employees are doing. How their family is doing. Or it should be, realizing the effect stress has on people's professional lives. Affecting their mental state. And physical state, too." She paused, giving Isaac a considered look. "Altering how one copes with the other stresses in life we have to deal with. Personal relationships, both in and out of the workplace, along with any—financial issues."

Isaac leaned back and crossed his arms. "I assume you're at the point of asking me why I did it."

Cheryl nodded, sitting down on the edge of her desk. "I'm going to need to know, Isaac. To understand, clearly, what it is I'm facing—before deciding how to move ahead."

He stared at her, a blush starting to color his pale skin. "Without me."

Cheryl leaned back. "It's a strong possibility."

Isaac shook his head. "You don't really have a choice. You already know what happened. What I've done in failing you." He lowered his eyes and stared at his fingers, his thumbs working in small circles, face gone fully red as he recalled the moment of his betrayal when the small Amerasian woman running the project from behind a wall of military security and corporate oversight had approached him in the hallway as he was leaving work, a few days before.

"The drive is pre-programmed, enabling it to pull data directly from the server. All you need to do is insert the end of the cable into any spare port and wait for the red light to stop flashing. Once it turns green, remove it. It won't take more than a minute. You can deliver it to me in the cafeteria in two days, at noon." Mari paused, then reached out and touched Isaac on his upper arm. "It's a basic security measure, designed to protect her research from falling into the wrong hands."

Isaac stared at the woman, eying her black hair, cut short, framing wide cheekbones beneath a set of almond shaped brown eyes. "Then why not provide it directly to her?"

Mari let a thin smile slip across her lips. "Doctor Atkinson would never accept there's any need, believing her customized program isn't susceptible to hacking attempts, or attack by viruses, or any other type of interference." She paused, trying to judge how desperate the large man might be, knowing to the penny how deep in debt he was, trying to keep his mother in a second-rate, full-service senior center. "We need you to do this, Isaac. You'll receive a—sizable compensation package. More than enough to enable your mother to stay where she is, for as long as it takes until—" Mari paused. "Along with all your other debts, settled in full."

Isaac stared at the small device. "With no trace left behind—no potential for discovery?"

"None. I promise. We have the best people available behind this, and their work is beyond anything the good doctor can detect. All you have to do is plug this in." Mari offered the drive; a block of dense plastic with a thin cable attached. When he reached out, she dropped it into his hand, smiling as his thick, oversized fingers closed around it.

Isaac lowered his head, his voice subdued. "You have my resignation, effective—"

Cheryl shook her head. "No, Isaac. You'll be staying on. I'll be using you to use them. The same way they were planning to do to with me, but in reverse. Allowing you to accrue enough funds to provide for your mother's future and yours." She stopped, a serious look crossing her face. "That way, once the project ends, you'll have something to fall back on."

Isaac frowned. "And they'll end up with your source code, able to cut you out. That's what they were after, despite what they told me."

Cheryl shook her head. "You really think I hadn't planned on this happening? The possibility of them coming to you, and you agreeing to do this?" She widened her smile.

Isaac looked at her, his face showing his confusion. "I—betrayed you."

She leaned forward. "You found an answer to your problem. It's one of the reasons why I kept you on. Because of your financial situation. Knowing they'd come to you as the obvious choice. And you did something you could easily have believed was for the reason stated, without doing me any direct harm in the process."

"You know better than that! I knew there was more to this then what I was told." Isaac shrugged, silent for a moment. He looked at Cheryl with a sad expression, seeing himself through her eyes. "And if I'd refused her. If I'd come and let you know?"

"I would have told you to reconsider. And you would have continued to be an integral part of everything I'm going to be doing next."

"And I blew it."

"Yes, Isaac." Cheryl gave him a solemn look. "You did."

It was early in the evening. A large rectangular building, its open interior cloaked in shadows along the sides, revealed an angled wall at one end in a wash of bright light. Three people stood at its base, two of them in tight-fitting clothes with thin-soled shoes on their feet. The other one, wearing casual attire and street shoes.

The wall was forty feet tall, its contoured face covered in an array of small, colorful protuberances formed in oddly shaped knobs, in dozens of sizes and shapes. An arrangement of triangular wedges and oblong holds, along with thick linear slabs fastened to the wall in random placements, simulating holds and ledges. Two thin strands of dull red rope hung in parallel lines from a pulley mounted to the metal joists overhead.

One of the ends was in the hands of a small, wiry man, the other one tied into a climbing harness, attached around Cheryl's firm waist and upper thighs. She stood at the base of the tallest section of wall, staring up with an intense gaze, her fingers white with chalk, flexing slowly as she planned each move she'd need to make. Then she began to climb.

"She moves like a—dancer." Jean stood beside the owner of the building, whose curly dark hair was running to silver along the sides of his head. The other man nodded, feeding the rope through his hands, leaving enough slack for Cheryl to move freely as she scaled the wall.

He glanced up at Jean, having to tilt his head to do so. "She's a freaking spider monkey! No fear, other than of failing to make it to the top. Pisses me off, watching her, knowing I'll never be able to match her, move for move. Not that I don't try, ending up having to buy the first round—every *damn* time!"

Jean continued to stare, shaking his head from side to side. "I've done some climbing myself, but nothing like this. Simple ascents. More muscle needed than mind."

The slim man glanced over, noting Jean's forearm, the edge of a tattoo showing beneath his rolled-up sleeves, his forearms strung with sinewy muscle. "Guessing they weren't recreational climbs, like hers."

Jean nodded, then gasped as he watched Cheryl leap from one hold to another, her body swinging to the side as she caught an edge of a hold with her hand, rolling into a tight ball of toned flesh, sticking a landing on a wide shelf. Then she leaned back, stopping to shake out one arm at a time as she stared up at the remaining holds.

"Another of her patented moves." The owner of the rock-gym muttered under his breath, his hands gathering in the slack he'd just given her so she could make her move. "She's going to make it. I can tell."

Cheryl eyed the final stretch of wall, a vertical stretch of simulated rock, with only three holds. Two of them, an unusual design. Fastened a full six and a half feet above the ledge, narrow in diameter, jutting out several inches. Neither one high enough to allow her to reach the top of the wall, though her friend had fastened one last hold a few feet higher, centered between them, just large enough to grab with both hands.

She clenched her lips, deliberating for a few moments, then grinned as an innovative approach blossomed in her mind, one she would never dare try in the real world. She leaned back, looking down at Jean and her friend, smiling, shaking her arms to help recover their strength, waiting until her heart settled into a rhythmic pulse, matching the relaxed pace of her breathing as she ran through the moves, picturing them in her mind. Then she nodded, knowing what she needed to do to overcome the impossible challenge, a warm glow flowing through her as she looked up, already tasting the bitter cold taste of the ale the man on the other end of the rope would soon be paying for.

Jean shook his head, in awe, watching Cheryl as she began her move, wondering how she intended to attempt what seemed to him to be an impossible challenge. One he knew had to fail, his mind unable to accept the reality of what he was seeing play out: an inverted handstand, Cheryl facing away from the wall, each of her feet stretched to full extension, toes finding a hooked purchase across the tops of the two, oddly shaped holds.

Then, with a curl of her abdomen, she thrust her arms up, between her thighs, seeming to pull herself up an invisible rope, her fingers finding their way to the middle hold, grasping it, using it to thrust her body up in one continuous motion. Her feet rotating on their holds, helping her leap up, catching the top of the wall, pulling herself into a standing position with ease.

She turned around, her face framed in the light from an overhead fixture, beaming in smug satisfaction. Then she closed her eyes, leaping out, tension in the rope catching her as she fell forward, arms spread, lowered slowly to the floor.

"I see now how you keep so trim." Jean helped Cheryl out of her harness, her fingers shaking from the effects of the climb. Her adrenalin was surging, her taut body quivering as she waited for him to release her. "Sane—it helps to keep me sane." She leaned against him, one arm surrounding his shoulders as he let the harness fall to the floor, a vibration of released energy running through her entire body.

"That was—amazing." Jean looked at her, his eyes wide with awe.

Cheryl grinned. "Nothing half-a-hundred Cirque du Soleil performers don't pull off, dozens of times a week. I learned most of my signature moves from watching them." She leaned back, releasing her embrace of his wide shoulders. "I'm steady now. Do you want to give it a go?"

"No." Jean shook his head. "Not at all. Have my own way to stay sane. And it's a hell of a lot easier on the body—that's for sure."

Cheryl gazed at him, her body still trembling slightly, burning through the last of her adrenalin. "Like what?"

Jean angled his head, then smiled. "I'll have to show you. In daylight—when you have a few hours to kill."

The air was bracing; wind biting hard as a small sailboat surged against an incoming tide, dancing along the edges of a sharp-edged chop. Waves slapped against its wooden hull, spray coating the polished deck with running beads of moisture. The cockpit provided a measure of protection from the stiff breeze for Cheryl, Jean bearing the brunt of it as he scanned the sea ahead.

"I love it! This is so freaking cool!" Cheryl shouted as the wind rose in a sudden gust, whipping her words away. She gasped, clutching Jean's arm as he angled the rudder, easing the list of the boat until the gust swirled away. "Is it safe to be out here?" Cheryl craned her neck, looking around the large bay. "I don't see any other boats."

"Lubbers—afraid of a minor blow like this." Jean slipped the bow in between two dark-bodied rollers, the wind slapping the jib sail into place, helping pull the hull through a heavy rush of saltwater. "We're fine. Unless we tip over. Then it's every man for himself!"

"Hey! Where does that leave me? I'm a girl."

Jean grinned as he looked at her, Cheryl wearing a faded sailor's cap, her damp hair gathered in tight curls framing her face, beads of water freckling her wind-reddened cheeks. "Yes." Jean reached out, brushing the hair out of her eyes. "You most definitely are."

The marina shower pulsed clouds of heated air, a wide stall encompassing Jean's thick, muscular body as he worked a bar of unscented soap through the hair on his chest, raising a sea of foam. The small marina had shut down services a few weeks ago, Jean's small sloop the last one tied to a pier, waiting to be hauled. It was safely snuggled up in its watery berth, the sails put away and gear stowed as a heavy rain squall had finally chased them from the bay.

Jean shivered, still feeling the cold, the brisk air having added to the chill of the cloudy day. He'd been amazed by how easily Cheryl had matched his every move while on the water, then helped him secure the boat, insisting on doing so, her hands trembling, fingers white with cold as she clung to his arm on the walk back in from the finger pier. He'd escorted her to the laundry facility, then led her to a hallway where the showers were located.

"There's a changing area in the woman's section. With private showers. I'll get you a robe. You can toss your clothes in a dryer, so they'll be ready for you when you're finished up."

"You seem to have a free hand around here." Cheryl looked at Jean, her hands still thawing out. "You're not the owner, are you?"

"No." Jean shrugged. "But I am an invested partner, along with a host of other people."

Cheryl gave him a quiet look. "Are you going to take a shower?"

Jean hesitated a moment, studying her, a moment of uncertainty passing before he let it go. "Definitely. Not gonna have you watching me shivering away like a leaf."

As Jean started to rinse off, his skin red from the steaming water, he closed his eyes against the force of the spray: hot showers a guilty pleasure ever since he was a new enlistee serving a yearlong deployment in South Korea. He'd been stationed high in the mountains on the DMZ, his platoon tasked with making day long patrols in freezing weather, the bone-chilling misery borne in stoic silence, knowing heated water and food would be waiting when they returned. The poor bastards on the other side of the lines had a much harder time of it, according to the occasional defector, showing up emaciated, frostbitten, and diseased.

Jean sighed, finally starting to feel warm again, gasping in surprise when a hand touched his upper back. It was cold, causing him to spin around. Cheryl stood in the opening, her robe parted, her body revealed in taut curves and toned flesh.

"The hot water—it isn't coming out. In the women's shower."

Jean turned away, his voice tight with embarrassment. "They're working on some of the plumbing today. Jason told me it was fixed. I should have checked. I'm sorry." He resisted the urge to cover his lower body, aware she had appeared to be unbothered by his fleeting appraisal of her exposed flesh. Having noted her making one of her own, in return.

"Are you up for sharing yours?"

Jean stepped aside, letting the stream of hot water find Cheryl's lower legs. "Of course. Least I can do, considering it's my fault you got so cold. Never should have gone out today." He stared as Cheryl tossed her robe toward a hook on the wall, missing, smiling at Jean as she stepped forward into the spray. "Would you mind soaping my back?" Jean looked at the bar in his hand, considering the ramifications, tossing caution to the wind as he reached out and started rubbing it on her back. Cheryl slipped around, taking his face in her hands. "Kiss me." Jean leaned forward, feeling her body pressing against his, losing himself to the feel of her n his arms, and the heated water, raining down.

CHAPTER TWENTY-EIGHT

LAB, RESEARCH FACILITY, MARYLAND

JD

Now

He could sense the pressure of outside interest, increasing in intensity. An externally sourced determination to sift through his memories, trying to release the bitter from the sweet. The intention was not in question, no threat proposed, yet. But the motivation behind it remained unknown, causing him to remain cautious. To withdraw. A wounded lion to its lair, watching the entrance for any sign of the hunter's approach, knowing one was out there, somewhere.

He angled his thoughts in an alternate direction, shifting the narrative while continuing to project the various storylines designed to protect his true self from being returned to the actual world. One he knew existed, could hear in the faint hum of machinery, vibration of voices. Feel in the brush of fingers against his face, firm hands lifting his body. The scent of deodorant, artificial spice or floral. A hint of perfume and moisturizer when one of them leaned in to check a connection or change the close-fitting hat placed on his scalp. More aware of her than the other, a man with as gentle a touch, layered atop fingers of steel. Like his own had been. Once. Several lifetimes ago.

"Shifting away from the actor—right on schedule." Isaac reset the monitor, widening the display angle, bringing the center of the image into focus. The edges of the monitor showed a fog of gray. "When are you going to get the rest of the scene filled in?"

"I'm *working* on it." Cheryl's voice was tense with effort. "Not that *easy*. Every time he heads off on another path, I need to tweak the programming, reconfigure the data dump, deciding what goes where." She cursed under her breath, a line of sweat beading her forehead as she jabbed at two different keyboards at the same time. "Deciding if it's contemporaneous to the story-line he's putting out—or something else. Something *new*."

"Like what?" Isaac shook his head, still amazed at Cheryl's ability to do multiple things at the same time.

Cheryl straightened up, rubbing her lower back as she checked her monitor, slaved to readouts showing a series of numbers and symbols moving too quickly for the eye to focus on. She let the image flow, trusting her years of experience with the programming to judge the accuracy of the data being pulled from JD's active mind and fertile imagination. "I don't know—not *exactly*. But he's in there, somewhere. Made up of pieces scattered everywhere. Hiding in plain sight." She sighed, hands on her hips, a stray curl dangling across one cheek. "Just don't have a grasp on what he's avoiding or who he is. Not yet."

"I like 'em all." Isaac stood up, heading to a refrigerator, and pulling out a soda. He held it up, looking at Cheryl, who shook her head. Then he sat back down, taking a sip, gazing over at her. "You?"

"I hate every one of them! They keep getting in the darned way. Or to rephrase that, I'm tired of having to guess who the real JD is."

Isaac grinned. "What about the dog? You don't have a problem with him, right? He's way too cool, and concurrent to every storyline. Maybe there's something you could do to isolate on him. Seeing how—"

Cheryl raised a hand, cutting him off. She slipped into her chair and began opening files, her fingers moving in a blur, tip of her tongue squeezed between her teeth. She took a deep dive inside her tri-helix based programming software, making wholesale changes on the fly. An action that filled Isaac with extreme distress, his instincts shouting at her to save before you change. Then test. Then save again.

JD slid away from the projected scene, understanding some of what was being done to try and uncover his identity. Desparate to avoid the attempt, knowing it would lead to an ocean of incomprehensible agony washing over him. Determined to prevent it, conjuring up a lightning quick response to an image of the shepherd being insinuated into one of his projections. He concentrated, creating an interference pattern, focusing on a collage of fictional memories pulled from people he'd met. Careful to avoid details that could lead her to him, with no last names, or place names, other than indistinct references, knowing the rules of his own game, played for however long he'd been adrift in limbo. He steeled himself mentally, then turned away, hiding in the shadows, avoiding the light.

"*Damn* it!" Cheryl slammed the desk, causing Isaac to react in shock at her curse, almost spilling his drink. "He's *running* again. Something I just did is causing him to head for the hills."

"That's good, though. Right?" Isaac grinned in response to the icy stare aimed his way, used to Cheryl's rapid mood swings, knowing how mercurial she could be. "Because of cause and effect. *You*, triggering a reaction by what you were just doing, what you were just focusing in on."

"The dog." Cheryl flashed him a smile. "You're *right!*" She leaned in and started punching keys; a printout of the last few minutes of data spitting out from a printer. Grabbing a highlighter from her desk, she started marking sections of the feed. "*Thank* you, Isaac. You've no idea how much I count on you being able to see things so clearly."

"A blind squirrel—with lots of acorns on the forest floor. I'm bound to stumble across one now and then."

Cheryl stared at the printout, the highlighter clenched between her teeth, mumbling from the corner of her mouth. "That's not true, and you know it."

Isaac shrugged. "It's truer than you want to admit."

Cheryl ignored his comment, her eyes narrowed in concentration as she turned her full attention to reprogramming a segment of her unique code. Isaac leaned back, eyeing the clock, wondering if he should tell her about his ongoing effort to identify the people in the multiple storylines that JD was presenting. Violating protocol: her protocol. He looked over, checking on her progress. Cheryl felt his gaze and glanced at him, a quizzical look on her face. "What is it? Did you think of something else?"

Isaac looked away, a wash of red tinting his pale cheeks. Cheryl angled her head to one side, her look of confusion morphing into one of sudden comprehension. "You've been up to something. I can *tell*. Sitting there, slouched like the side of a mountain on the verge of an avalanche. *What* have you done?"

Isaac sighed. "I've been looking where I shouldn't have."

"Where?" Cheryl raised her hand. "I don't want to know, not if you're about to be caught with your hand in the cookie jar."

"No worries, Boss Lady." Isaac hesitated a moment. "Not on *that* account, at least. It's just that—" He paused until Cheryl opened her mouth to respond. "I ran JD's image through the MIL-DAT system. A blind search, to see if there was a match. Visual results only, so there'd be no dipping into his records, if there *were* any. Did it with all the people in his storylines, checking them against Federal NGI and DMV records. Again, only for visual image hits, proving they're real—and not imagined."

Cheryl turned her attention back to the printout, her jaw clenched as she scanned through it, making a few more notations before sighing loudly, folding up the printout and sending it through a high-end shredder, like she did with all her notes. Then she leaned back, shaking her head, looking over at Isaac. "Why would you *do* that?"

"No good reason, I guess." Isaac lowered his head. He could hear the tone of exasperation in Cheryl's voice, reminding him of his mother's, causing him to feel as if he were about to get a scolding. Again. His mother's angry commentary a constant buzz in his ears from his earliest memories on. Grating, high pitched, and harsh edged at the best of times. Filled with dangerous vibrations of underlying rage at others. Cursing him, blaming him for everything bad that had ever happened to her. For ruining her body, his painful birth more than she could deal with. Abandoned by his father, wanting nothing to do with either of them. Then years of depression: a slow, torturous childhood endured with a constant barrage of barbed comments tossed his way each time she felt the weight of her despair. Life not having provided her the bounty she felt owed.

"That's not an answer I can work with, Isaac. I'm going to need more in case I'm drawn into having to deal with any ramifications."

Isaac stood up, his face frozen in an expression of neutrality. Fixed, as if he'd withdrawn inside himself and was no longer there. Cheryl watched as he walked away, heading toward the dormitory, leaving her with a look of confusion on her face, her hands clenched as if trying to find something to hold on to.

Isaac sat in the spare bedroom, shared with Cheryl when she was away overnight, brooding, having learned early on in life to retreat, keeping his feelings safely locked away from the surface of his face. Careful not to clench his huge hands, knowing it would disturb his mother. Knowing it might disturb the children in his classroom and frighten the teachers who looked at him with widened eyes, uncertain what they should do with the boy, half again the size of the other students. Taught to keep his feelings locked within a vault, protecting others from potential harm. Protecting himself from being turned into the very thing he was always being accused of.

"You're a monster! You've *always* been a *monster!* Tearing me apart. No concern for me or what I went through! A *fucking* monster! Do you hear me, *monster?*" His mother shouted, her face fixed in a permanent sneer, eyes withdrawn into her head behind a thick layer of fat. Her mouth open, a breathless scream coming out, phlegm striking him in his face. Her breath, a noxious mix of onions and sausage from a favorite meal, cooked and served by the son she despised, hated beyond all measure of the word, yet clung to, as no one else could stand her venality, her abrasiveness, and her simmering emotions converted to frequent outbursts of derisive observations.

Isaac looked down at the tiled floor, the memories echoing in his ears. He knew, as if JD were sitting beside him and able to talk, the two of them would share a truth in common. One binding them closer together than the large shepherd, connected in with each of the couples in JD's projections. Both clinging to the same vault, built of diversion and deflection. Using the same tools to prevent additional hurt from leaking in, or memories of unbearable pain to leak out. Each of them wanting to deny emotional exposure, their anguish safely buried deep within.

A soft knock on the dormitory door let him know Cheryl was outside, wanting to help. Caught within her own personal dilemma of having lost a big brother who'd been an innocent victim of fate. Now faced with an unknown man, having suffered a similar injury, left in the same place. And now having to deal with what *he'd* done to her, another burden added to the mix. He fixed a false smile to his lips then stood up, opening the door.

"I'm fine, Cheryl. Just needed a moment of personal reflection."

"It's okay, Isaac. Really. I'm certain you were careful, with no blowback pending. So—all good from my end. Okay?"

Isaac let a genuine smile find his face, his emotions in balance again, knowing how fortunate he was to be working with her. "I'll go help JD back to his room. Make sure he's tucked in for the night. You go ahead and grab some dinner. Go out, get some fresh air. I'm good, really."

"Okay." Cheryl gave him a look of concern. "Can I bring you back anything?"

Isaac shook his head. "No. But *thank* you." He followed Cheryl with his eyes as she walked away, whispering beneath his breath. "Maybe my *youth*, unstained by a mother's hate." He had just seen himself reflected in her eyes: a child, trapped in a man's body.

His grandfather, the only one who'd ever treated him for who he was, and not as he appeared to be. Telling him stories while they worked, side by side. Teaching him all he knew of being a man. About work, life, and death. His last lesson, taught from the ground, hands clutching his shirt, eyes staring up into a cloudless sky. Ending his life with a gentle smile on his ancient face, released from the feelings of joy and pain that came from being alive.

CHAPTER TWENTY-NINE

OFFICE, RESEARCH FACILITY, MARYLAND

Mari

The office door sighed shut behind her, Mari waiting a beat until a slim man sitting behind an unadorned desk lifted a finger: a signal she should sit down. Mari gathered herself and stepped forward, moving with a confidence she didn't feel, slipping into place, her hands centered in her lap. Then she waited as he finished reading the last page of her report, submitted to a uniformed courier the previous day.

The thin-framed, middle-aged man finally slid the document to one side, his hands folded on top of the table, light-colored eyes cold, unblinking. No underlying warmth in them, or his expression. His thin lips pressed together in two taut lines.

"Do you know what you are, Ms. Coleman?" The man's name was Luther, his thin voice tinged by a foreign flavor that did nothing to dispel the subtle notes of his disdain. Mari continued to wait, without daring a response, sensing this was to be a one-sided conversation: the invitation to meet left on her desk that morning, unsigned, with a room number and time. The lettering perfectly formed in exquisite calligraphy, well outside normal protocols requiring all written communications within the interior office space of the secretive facility to be pre-approved, registered, and delivered by security personnel, waiting for signatures by all parties involved.

It was an invitation Mari had opened with trembling hands, fearing it meant her termination, based on the unsolicited suggestions she'd included in her monthly report, daring to express her doubts regarding the recent approach to gaining access to the doctor's work. One she regretted having taken part in.

"You are a cog, Ms. Coleman." Luther raised one eyebrow. "Do you agree?"

"Yes. I'm a cog." Mari centered her Chi, focused on maintaining a slow heartbeat, her breathing steady, projecting perfect stillness.

The man waved a single finger at the report, dismissing her obvious attempt to let his comment pass without visible reaction. "You have over-stepped your authority. Or more to the point—you have no authority. Your personal opinions—" He paused, a sigh fluttering through the still air of his small office. "Have no value. Do you agree?"

Mari nodded slowly, keeping her eyes focused on his. "No. I do not."

He blinked, twice. A glimmer of surprise rising to the surface of his face before being swallowed whole, as if a small mouse wrapped in the coils of an enormous snake, leaving Mari wondering if she'd just taken an unrecoverable stance. "You would suggest your opinion has merit?" He paused, folding his fingers together, his nails polished to a delicate sheen, reflecting the harsh fluorescent light from the overhead fixture. The effect enhanced by the interior walls of the office, painted a clinical white, as if an operating room, her brain on full display. Her thoughts exposed. His hand holding a scalpel, considering where and how deeply he should cut. "I have been trying to understand the logic behind your decision to submit your—thoughts. Enlighten me."

"Doctor Atkinson is not who you think she is. I've spent time with—"

"We know of your interactions and have allowed them to continue, despite our concerns as to cross-contamination of your other duties."

Mari lowered her eyes in deference, falling back on reflexes learned from parental scolding's concerning her lack of dedication to schoolwork. Of her over-dedication to relationships with other students, particularly boys. She was happy to allow the strange little man the high ground while making an orderly retreat in her mind, content to survive to fight another day. Surprised by the sound of her voice, her will shoving words from between her clenched lips. "Your assessment of the possibility of cross-contamination is valid. One I considered before proceeding, decided it was an acceptable risk when measured against the potential reward."

"You believe your personal involvement with the doctor has created trust?"

"I do." Mari hesitated, then decided to plow ahead. "Doctor Atkinson, Cheryl—is more than she appears to—"

"The woman is a gear. Nothing more. One of many in a machine assembled long before you or—Doctor Atkinson were born." Luther waited a full three seconds, then lifted a forefinger, pointing at Mari, looking for a response.

Mari cleared her throat, then leaned back, relaxing into the uncomfortable seat, knowing her opinion, clearly stated in the report, had brought her to the attention of the odd man's superiors. Errors revealed, exactly as she'd noted. A significant opportunity now in the offing if those in power behind the scenes would admit to them. "I concede your point. However, Doctor Atkinson is *more* than a gear. Or, if you prefer to stay with the analogy, amend it to include one with a unique modification, added to the drivetrain of your machine. Constructed to operate in three dimensions, shifting rotational speed and torque in every direction simultaneously."

The finger lowered, bringing her to a sudden halt, Luther reaching for the report. "A gear, Ms. Coleman, is a gear. No matter how intricate its function. We will not belabor the point." He touched one page partway down. "You made a claim, a few weeks ago, that Doctor Atkinson uses an unusual program to help refine imagery from the stream of data being collected from the subject's brain." He paused, waiting to see if Mari would dare interrupt, continuing when she remained silent. "That she could determine, in real-time, between varying data sets simultaneously, working to define which one might be the actual subject."

Mari lowered, then raised her eyelids. Luther studied her for a moment before dropping the report on the desk. "I will concede the point as to her being a specific type of helical gear, if you explain why we are to assign a greater value to this woman's current project than progress to date warrants. We have her program. Our people have confirmed that it works, providing a superior capability for assessing large, disparate data bases. Greater than what we require for our current needs."

"You've opened the gates—with *no* idea of what you're allowing in."

Luther stared back, a lingering moment of silence filling the void between them. "I confess to a lack of understanding, based primarily on your lack of clarity."

"The siege of Troy. Big-ass wooden horse left just outside the main gate. Leading to the saying you should beware gifts from the Greeks."

The beginnings of a smile lifted one corner of Luther's lips, quashed immediately. "Thought the saying was to never look a gift horse in its mouth."

"Are you making a—joke?" Mari crossed her arms on her chest, gaining confidence.

"I most definitely am not. My point stands. We are the ones in control. The project will run its course. Our group will provide our governmental partners with what we promised, then move forward with the next step." Luther nodded toward the door, dismissing her. Mari stood up, walked over, then hesitated and turned around.

Luther nodded. "Yes?"

"I believe you're making a mistake."

"We're done here, Ms. Coleman. Good day."

Mari turned to leave, the strange little man's whisper thin voice slipping across the room, finding her ear. "I will, however, make a minor concession about what I said earlier. You are not a cog. You are a gear. Name it whatever type you wish."

She nodded, then stepped through the opening. Luther called out, teasing her with another question. "Do you know what I am, Ms. Coleman?"

Mari spun around, her eyes flashing in frustration. "The hand on the wheel of the *fucking* machine, I would imagine."

"No." Luther let his face go expressionless, his eyes without emotion. "I am but a rustling of a small leaf in the ear of one of those backing this effort. Nothing more. Nothing less. Not a gear. Not even a cog. Only a voice in the wind."

Mari stared at him. "People throughout history have done a lot, using only a voice. To the good of humanity—and *bad*." She left the office, the door pulled shut behind her, determined to ignore any further comments. None followed, the hallway quiet as her legs threatened to give out. She forced herself to make it to the nearest restroom where she emptied the bile built up in her stomach while tears of shame streamed down her wide cheeks.

CHAPTER THIRTY

SEAFOOD RESTAURANT, MARYLAND

Cheryl

"Followed? Really?" Cheryl angled her head, a look of disbelief on her face. Jean shrugged, tossing a handful of photos on the table of the booth perched under the large blue marlin. She picked them up, thumbing through them one by one, stopping to go back and look at several of the close-up shots. Her hands trembled as she placed them on the table while Jean signaling for drinks. The only other person in the large dining hall came over, one of the large men who'd met Cheryl the first time she'd been to the restaurant, lugging a bottle of tequila in one hand, two shot glasses in the other.

"Limes are out back." Their heavily muscled server sat the bottle and two glasses down. "You want me to grab some?" Jean waved him away. "It's okay, Skinny. You and Jason can take off. I'll lock up." The large man moved away, nimble on his feet. Jean called out, his voice chasing him down as he reached the main door. "Thank you. Thank Jason too. I appreciate the extra work you've been putting in."

Cheryl shook her head, barely noticing the exchange as she watched Jean pour two shots, sliding one of the narrow glasses over to her. Her eyes narrowed as she picked it up, staring at the yellow gold liquid before tossing it down. "Why would anyone want to follow *me?*"

Jean shrugged, his voice low. "Most likely the group that took over control—"

Cheryl widened her expression, fixing Jean with a hard look. "And why did you have someone *watching* me?"

Jean leaned back. "I asked a couple of friends to lend a hand because I thought it was *necessary*, based on who it is that's—"

"But *not* because you know something. Only a *hunch*. An *idea*. One you thought gave you the right to invade my privacy without *asking* first. And now you show me these—" She picked up the photos, tossing them at him, hitting him in the chest, watching as they fell into his lap.

Jean gathered up the photos, his voice rising. "It *was* necessary and still *is* necessary. Whether you like it or not, you're still in the *damn* cross-hairs." He softened his tone. "I don't mean to sound like that. You're not in any danger. I just had a feeling something was going on. Felt eyes on my back ever since we went to that rock-wall place. And later, out at the marina, Jason spotted someone there when he was working on the plumbing. A guy hanging around outside, looking out of place. He decided to follow him. Saw he was following us, then following *you*, after I dropped you off at your car. That's all there was or *is* to it, so far. I wanted you to know. Wasn't trying to scare you."

Cheryl reached over and put her hand on his. "It's okay, Jean. I understand. I'm not angry or frightened, believe me. It's just that I'm no threat to anyone working behind the scenes, other than being a pain in their butts whenever they come sniffing around, poking their noses into my space."

"I tried getting that stopped. Was countermanded by—" Jean hesitated. "Sorry. That's a need-to-know basis." He stared at the backs of his hand, eyeing the thick ranger ring on his right hand. "They suggested I play ball. Continue to run facility security, or they'd replace me with someone who would."

Cheryl held out her empty glass, giving Jean a nod. "They have you by the short and curlies, don't they?"

Jean stared at her, then refilled her glass, shaking his head. "Where did *that* bit of wisdom come from?"

Cheryl lowered her eyes, looking at the shot glass. "My brother used to say that, when he was having to put up with some wanna be climber, figuring that, if he was paying for a guide, he ought to be the one leading the way."

"Your brother sounds like someone I'd like to meet. Does he live around here?"

"No." Cheryl looked away, watching through one of the large plate-glass windows as two cars pulled out of the parking lot. "He doesn't live—any-where." Cheryl downed her second shot, wiping her mouth with the back of her hand as she slammed the glass down on the table, her hand over the top, preventing Jean from refilling it. "He died over twenty years ago. Result of a climbing accident. Was in a coma for three years before he—passed."

Jean tilted the bottle of tequila, refilling his own glass and raising it. "Sorry to hear that. To your brother, then. May we *both* avoid being grabbed by our short and curlies, without permission."

"Do you think I'm in any danger?" Cheryl head was lying on Jean's chest, the afternoon sun slanting through a narrow window in the small sloop's cabin. They were in the forward berth: the cramped space barely large enough for one. The two of them had managed to work it out, their lovemaking constrained by the low overhead, their pleasure somehow enhanced because of the limited movement allowed.

Jean ran his fingers through Cheryl's hair, noting it was longer since they'd started their relationship. Still undefined, the two of them happily enjoying each other's company whenever they had an opportunity. "No. You're good. They'll end up with everything in the end, with you getting the credit. And them ending up with the lion's share of the money, once the government contracts kick in." Cheryl was quiet. Jean waited, aware of the change in her mood. He closed his fingers in her hair, gently coaxing her head to one side, staring into her eyes. "What have you done?"

"Nothing. Not *really*. I just took a few—precautions. That's all."

"What precautions?"

"Let go of my *effing* hair, and I'll tell you."

The sun was all but down, its rays painting the pier in a rose-colored blush, the large bay quiet beneath a blanket of warm air; a late season warm front having passed through from the south. Jean tossed a small pebble into the water, watching as it sank into the depths. "Risky, doing that." He looked at Cheryl, sitting beside him, her body leaning against his. "What happens when they find out?"

"They'll never know—not until it's *too* late. Long after they've invested a hundred billion dollars or so into—"

"You mean *millions*."

Cheryl reached out, taking his hand, bringing it to her lips, kissing his knuckles. "*Billions*, Jean. With a big fat capital *B*. At a *minimum*, with them financing hundreds of thousands of Tee-Cee centers, all around the globe."

"Okay. I guess. But there'll only be so many people needing—"

"We covered this before, Jean. There are going to be multiple levels of individual and societal ramifications based on the potential use of this technology. It's going to affect *everyone*, eventually."

"I know. I mean—I remember what you said. It just seems to be—" Jean paused.

"What?" Cheryl looked at him, her face only a few inches away from his.

"I thought you were describing a *worst-case* scenario, like some kind of mental plague, spreading out of control." He twisted his hand, holding hers, squeezing firmly, knowing how strong she was, not worried about hurting her. "Do you honestly believe our government would allow that to happen? Allow it to be used on people who don't need it, or want it?"

Cheryl shrugged. "My brother always said you should plan for the worst, while hoping for the best. Knowing the needle on the scale finds a balance somewhere in between. Eventually."

Jean lowered his eyes and voice, whispering. "Hope in one hand, shit in the other. See which fills up first." Then he looked up, studying her face, gazing into her eyes, as if seeing her for the first time. "What did you do to ensure they won't be able to—" He pursed his lips. "Do their worst?"

Cheryl smiled. "Do you really want me to tell you? Isn't it enough to know I've had a plan in place to protect my solution, from the very beginning?"

"And if something, God forbid, were to happen to you? What then?"

"I built in a fail-safe. A dead-man's switch if you will. If I don't enter a code at a defined point in the future, using a backdoor channel I designed, it all shuts down. The programming fields collapse. Game over, until they engineer an alternative solution, which will eventually happen. Though too late to recover the money they've already spent. But I'll be able to slow them down, causing the public to distrust the system, allowing for governmental oversight of the entire program. Not that it'll matter in the end." She looked out at the horizon, the sky changing over to a deep golden hue. "The future is always there, waiting for us to find it. To lay claim to it, with tools we can only imagine of today."

Jean shook his head. "You're *that* sure of yourself? That your three-dimensional code isn't susceptible to counter-programming?" Jean watched as Cheryl grinned, a confident look on her face. He sighed, shaking his head. "And what if you aren't able to do it? If you're not around to enter the code. If you're incapacitated or—" He stopped, his face going pale.

"Dead?" Cheryl saw a flicker of pain cross Jean's face. "Then *you'll* have to do it." She raised her hand, stopping him before he could respond. "I already set it up. Everything you need to do, spelled out in a letter in a safe deposit box. Along with a special code. I'll give you the spare key once you agree to be my back-up."

"How will I know when or whether to send it? To keep everything running, or bring it crashing to a halt?"

Cheryl looked Jean straight in the eye. "You told me a leader has to know when to hold back and direct his forces—until realizing it's time to say the hell with it and lead the charge."

CHAPTER THIRTY-ONE

LAB, RESEARCH FACILITY, MARYLAND

JD

Something new was happening. A more directed attempt to seek him out, to try and pry apart the curtains on the stage and peer behind them, eyeing the backdrops in place, readied for the next scene. JD kept to the darkest shadows, biding his time, waiting, knowing someone had come to his side of the mirror, no longer satisfied with seeing his reflections. Seeking the hidden hand, pulling the strings.

Cheryl relaxed into the surge of information sleeting through her mind, the Tee-Cee cap supplying direct exposure to the images, sounds, scents, and sense of what was being projected by JD's creative mind. She'd set a timer in the program, designed to limit her depth and resolution of exposure to the informational exchange. A step taken with rational regard to potential risk, despite a firm belief in her capability to withstand any unforeseen effects.

The scene she was part of was familiar: a glade of grass surrounded by tall oak trees, their trunks covered in gnarled lines of gray bark. Leaves on their limbs provided pools of shade redolent with a scent of damp soil, a recent rain having scrubbed the air. The rap of a hammer echoed in the background, set against the whine of a saw blade. The scent of wood dust hung in the air, filtered through a spiderweb of bushes.

Cheryl was at the farm with Calvin, Jemma, and Dawg. She looked down, noting there was no sign of her body, having programmed herself in as an observer to the scene and not a participant. JD was still in control of everything she would see and hear, with full fidelity. Her emotions filtered to a safe limit, as if feeling them through a thick glove, provided a degree of mental separation in case JD took umbrage at her having trespassed into his private world, Cheryl uncertain what, if anything he could do, if so. The timer, set in minutes on her side of the veil, a bit of an unknown element here, where time might stretch into hours, or be compressed into a handful of seconds, dependent on the creator's whim.

Calvin turned his head to one side, firing the nail gun, stitching the last wall stud to the footer. One of the side walls was already finished, standing in place, braced by two angled boards. The frame of the barn was finished, waiting for the next section of exterior framing to be tied in, forming one corner of the building, holding it together. Squaring the building as his uncle always said, teaching him the way of the world, one sweaty lesson and a handful of calluses at a time.

Jemma came over, helping him lift the next section of wall upright, walking it into place, Bones, she thought as Calvin fired the pneumatic gun, made of wood, to be covered with a thick skin of plywood, then a thin layer of white fabric. Different methods, Calvin had told her with a grin. Not like the old ways, used for hundreds of years with modern materials having nudged v-notch boards and tar paper to one side.

"It's looking *real* now. Not just lines drawn on paper. Going together a lot easier than I thought it would." Jemma straightened up, taking a moment to stretch out her lower back, her dungarees hanging loose, the short, cut-off shirt she had on revealing patches of tanned skin, exposed as she twisted her shoulders back and forth. "Where's Dawg got off to?"

"Haven't seen him. Chasing squirrels, I imagine. He'll be back by lunch-time, scrounging for food."

"Speaking of, I ordered pizza from the Center. Didn't want to stop to make lunch. Bev said he'd bring it by on his way in from town."

Calvin shrugged, then pulled the trigger: shooting another nail through the footer. "Like *that* won't put a dent in our progress. You know he'll want to stay and chat us up."

Jemma gave him a dirty look. "He helped get me started down this road. Only fair he gets to see how far along we are."

Cheryl slipped across the opening of a long, winding field jutting downhill in a rolling finger of green. She drifted past groves of fruit trees and freshly turned soil, ready for planting. Continuing her journey, she moved along to its southernmost exposure to a thick forest nudged up against an old stone wall where an ancient line had been drawn, defining the line between wild and ordered. A boundary crossed at will by deer, rabbits, fox, and racoons, seeking food. She listened for the sound of barking, wondering if the shepherd would be able to sense her presence, staring in confusion or fear, a low growl of warning issued, unsettled by something he could not see or scent, yet knew was there. But there was no echo of his deep throated voice in her imaginary ear.

"You're not welcome here." The whisper came from behind, causing Cheryl to spin around, surprised at the sudden jolt of panic worming its way through her chest. The voice grew stronger. "You should go."

"I only came to see if—"

"You should go. *Now!*" The voice resonated in her imaginary inner ear.

"I will—when I can."

"Will it so. And *leave!*"

"I set a timer. There's no one there to pull me out."

"The other one. With the high-pitched voice."

"Not there."

There was a slight pause, the voice returning. "Then you've made a mistake. Do not make it again."

Cheryl sensed JD fading away. "Wait. I want to ask you one question." There was a moment of silence, leading her to believe the interaction was over. "One question. Please?"

"I owe you nothing. Have asked nothing from you, or any of the others offering me solace, pity, hoping to elicit a reaction." The whisper hardened. "To save me, without understanding why I am where I am. Why I choose to stay. Here." Another long pause ensued. "Have I answered your question?"

"Yes, regarding *where* you are. But I want to talk to you about *why*."

"Enough. You will leave as soon as you're able to." An icy wind swirled around the branches of the trees, Cheryl shivering despite standing in bright sunlight. "Do not come back."

She felt the cold air slip away as if through an unseen door, quickly opened then closed. Her imaginary skin prickled as the hair rose on her arms and neck. She shivered again, despite the warmth in the air, drifting back to the scene of construction, watching in envy as the couple continued to work together in a playful mood as they went about the building of a promising future.

"You did *what?*" Isaac gave Cheryl a hard stare. "Without any safeguards in place?"

"I had myself on a timer. There was no—"

"I don't give a *fuck* about that. You violated *every* protocol put in place. By *you!*" Isaac paused, his expression angry, light-colored eyes fixed on hers, head shaking from side to side. "Without letting me know."

"I should have waited." Cheryl looked up, knowing she'd hurt Isaac. That he was right to be upset. To be angry. Something she'd never seen with him before. "It was a risk, but one I—"

"It was a horrible decision. One I would have talked you out of. Prevented, if I'd had to." Isaac shrugged, his anger gone. "Which is why you did it." He sighed in exasperation. "Just wish you'd let me know about this—" He pointed to the second Tee-Cee, hanging from an arm of the chair that JD was resting in. "Being available. We could have worked up a plan. One with gradual exposure, proper safeguards in place, data reads analyzed to determine interference patterns and—" He paused, shaking his head again. "Everything else." He gave her a solemn look, a trace of fear in his eyes, realizing what could have happened to her. "Instead, we got you. *Queen* of the world, with no regard for what you might have done to yourself. Or to him." Isaac pointed at JD.

Cheryl shrugged. "I can assure you—JD's fine. And in complete control. Could sense his presence there, even with the filter I had in place." She shrugged, ready to move on. "I sequestered the data feeds, so nothing went into the main server. No need to report what happened."

"And what about the video feed?" Isaac pointed at the cameras. He saw Cheryl smile and sighed, shaking his head. "Don't tell me you *hacked* the effing security system?"

I had to. I—"

I said *don't* tell me. I don't want to know. Plausible deniability, for when they come in and take you away in handcuffs. Or a white coat, with the arms tied in back."

Cheryl waited, knowing Isaac was coming around to the new normal, his concern for her well-being driven by his brotherly feeling toward her, despite having resigned himself to the fact she would move on from him when the project ended.

Isaac relaxed his lips, his head angled to one side as he looked at Cheryl. "How was it—being inside JD's mind and not just seeing it from out here?"

Cheryl grinned. "It was amazing! The clarity *incredible*. Although I'm sure it was as much my doing as his, my own imagination used to fill in details around the edges." She stopped, taking in a deep breath, then slowly releasing it. "But it was the *energy* that stunned me. Of the people. Like I could feel everything they were feeling. They were so—real." She sighed again, then shook her head. "It was easy to move through the scenery. Floating, with no need to walk. Just look and go wherever I wanted to."

"Which grouping?"

"Calvin and Jemma, just past the last data feed. The new building well along, same as with the other scenarios, events moving on between each observance."

Isaac reached up and cupped his chin. "We could try keeping him wired in for a day or so. Get a series of more complete data streams."

"We'd be seeing them one at a time, due to the way he's jumping in and out, the gaps still there." She paused, biting her lower lip.

Isaac noticed, his expression narrowing. "What is it?"

Cheryl looked away, chewing her lip. "Something happened—while I was in there moving around."

"Could they see you? React to you, or interact with—"

"No." She raised a hand, cutting him off. "There was no *physical* presence. No bodily image. But I *was* seen."

Isaac closed his mouth, considering what Cheryl said. Then he looked up. "JD. He found you." He saw a shadow of concern in Cheryl's eyes. "Bet he wasn't pleased. I know *I* wouldn't be if a stranger came poking around in my life. Or lives."

"Not pleased is a *definite* understatement. He told me to leave and never return. Knew what I—what *we've* been doing. Doesn't seem in favor of our trying to bring him out of whatever—" She pointed at JD and the chair. "It is he's doing in there. Hiding away, wandering in and out of multiple storylines."

"Reliving his life, in pieces being told, here and there." Isaac raised his eyebrows, staring at JD, who was looking up at the ceiling, his eyes blinking every few seconds.

"It would seem so. Which leaves us *where?* Do we release him to his creations, giving him what he wants? Or do we keep trying to work out who he is. Help to soften whatever trauma he's suffered, physical and mental, like we started out to do." Cheryl crossed her arms, leaning against the edge of her desk. "I mean—we have the experience needed and the tools. But do we have the right?"

Isaac stared at JD. "That's *your* call to make. Not mine."

"Ours, Isaac. Still. Nothing's changed on that end. You've always seen him as an individual, been his advocate. You know him better than I do." Cheryl looked at the bank of servers. "I'm prejudiced, committed to rescuing him, seeing his comatose state as a cause to fight against. Looking at him and seeing my brother. While you—"

"Have a more dispassionate view of things."

Cheryl nodded, clenching her hands, looking away. Isaac stepped over and touched her on the shoulder. "I'm sorry, Cheryl—for letting you down. Sorry for what happened to your brother." He leaned in, easing her around until he could look into her eyes, seeing the tears on her cheeks. "But I'm *not* sorry for what his injury, his death caused you to become. Someone driven since childhood to where you are today, on the verge of making a significant breakthrough in the treatment of these types of disorders. Of every kind of mental disorder."

Cheryl wiped her eyes. 'That doesn't help me decide what's best for him." She looked at JD.

"Then maybe you should do what you've always done. Charge ahead, trusting you're making the right move, again. Remembering all the times you've thrown caution to the wind and made the next leap. Leading to this—" He pointed at the chair. "A tool that will help hundreds of thousands of people. Help people like your brother. To help him." He moved her over to JD, taking her hand and placing it on his shoulder. "So, make up our minds. Whatever you decide, I'll back you—no matter what."

Cheryl's eyes overflowed, tears on her cheeks. She wiped them away, sniffing, forcing a smile. Then she leaned down and stared at JD, looking into his eyes. Dark brown. No reaction in them or on his face. "I'm not going anywhere, buddy. I'm gonna wring out every one of your projections, squeezing every drop of data from each of them, using it to find out who you really are. Then I'm coming in and bringing you back into the—" She hesitated. "Into the *effing* world."

The church was quiet. No bed on the raised platform, this time, dim light filling the interior with a shadowed background. A solitary figure sat in the front row of pews, shoulders slumped. Black hair, hanging just over the collar. JD stared straight ahead, not turning to look when Cheryl scuffed her feet as she moved along the aisle.

She sat down beside him. "Is this my dream—or yours?"

"It's not a dream. More of a half-way house where people like me wait while being prodded by people like you."

"Kinda like trauma therapy." Cheryl grinned, relaxing into the flow of conversation. "Or an AA meeting."

"Cute." JD paused; his voice soft when he continued. "You're definitely more interesting than the others. Though definitely a giant pain in my ass."

Cheryl looked down. She had on a pair of jeans and a flannel shirt. Her hair was hanging over her shoulders in twin braids, her hands, folded in her lap, belonged to a much younger version of herself. "Your call, I take it—the image from my childhood. No doubt pulled from my memories, during our meeting at the farm the other day."

"True. And as for the reflection of youth, time is irrelevant from my position, holding no meaning."

"Yet your body still ages. Back there, on the other side." Cheryl waved a hand at the front doors, watching as they swung open, the horizon a dark line beneath a silver-gray sky.

"Yes. And when it ends, I end. All of it ends." JD turned and looked at her. "As it will for you, eventually." He smiled. "Even as a child, you carried yourself with the same determination. Just easier to put up with, the younger version of you. Easier to forgive you being such an—intrusive little bitch." He raised one hand. "No offense intended."

"None taken. And you're still an unknown entity to me, without a past for me to dig my claws into. No boyish figure to inspect, deciding whether I'd like the

way you were, when a child." Cheryl shrugged. "You certainly turned into a bit of a prick, as an adult." She shifted in the pew, crossing her legs. "And it appears you're still the one in control—for now."

"True. Here, and for now." JD's voice trailed off as he shifted his feet, clad in sneakers, white with daubs of brown mud on the toes. He had on a pair of faded jeans and a new dress shirt. Cheryl noted the strange combination and filed it away. "Did you bring me here so I can ask a few questions, or are you planning to lecture me again?"

"Some of both, I suppose. Haven't really given it much thought." JD leaned back, raising one leg, folding it over the other one, one hand clasped around his knee, holding it in place. His other hand scratched his chin, a day's growth of beard showing in a black fuzz between his thin fingers. His hair was longer now, bound in a ponytail, his skin tanned to a dark brown, teeth white and perfectly straight. A slight hint of hazel-wood cologne wafted over, drawing Cheryl's attention. Familiar. One her father and brother would wear when going out.

She decided to take the initiative, leaning into the next conversational thrust. "I appreciate you bringing me here. Had hoped you'd reach out again. That's why I've been leaving you alone for the past few days. And I know—time isn't an issue here. Just thought I'd let you be."

"For a while."

"Yes." Cheryl looked at him. "I haven't given up on trying to help you find a way back."

"Which is why you are here."

Silence filled the void between them, interrupted by a faint creak of wood settling as the sun slipped over the edge of the faux horizon. When Cheryl opened her mouth to speak, JD raised his hand, fingers spread, palm up. "Do you know how many memories you can hold in your hand?" He waited while she shook her head. "All of them. And none." He turned his head, a sad smile on his face. "Every smile, laughter. Each tear on cheek. All the moments shared, places seen, food, music, and words enjoyed. All of those, always there, ready to float to the surface to experience over and again. But—" He looked into the shadows above the cross. "The memories of the touch of a hand, the feeling of warmth from the delicate press of skin to skin. Of a sharp elbow in the side of your ribs while lying in bed. Cold feet, on the back of your legs. Exploring touches, made during the night after an exchange of heated words, wanting to reconnect." JD sighed, his breath fluttering the walls of the imaginary church. "Those memories are like the wings of a dying butterfly, fading by the moment. Impossible to recall in full. Creating unimaginable loss. A vacant abyss, where someone once stood beside you, sharing the same space at the same time. Gone, to yesterday's call."

Cheryl reached out, compelled to touch him, holding back. "Which is why you're living three lives, now. Striving to reclaim what you had. To put yourself back in the same space you shared before—"

JD leaned away, his eyes finding hers. "And where are you in this effort? Aren't you trying to do the same thing, wanting to recover what you lost when your brother died? If not able to do it for yourself, then determined to do it for others."

Cheryl bore his stare for as long as she could, then broke away, her eyes looking up at the dull gleam of the cross. "Are you saying I won't succeed? Because I've already helped—"

JD's image thinned, his voice becoming a drifting whisper. "You won't fail, Cheryl. Because you'll never stop. That's why I'm going to resist you for as long as possible. To prevent your succeeding with me, at least. I don't really give a damn about anyone else. About their lives, their memories, or their traumas. Not theirs or Robert's, which I can feel as if it happened to me. Your memories, now mine."

His face was a cloud of dust, a mask of gray. "Don't give a flying fuck about their loss of self, or their inability to find their way back. None of it, Cheryl. Chipmunk. Doctor. Don't care about them or you. Not in the least."

The soft slip of re-filtered air replaced the echo of JD's whisper in her ears. Cheryl stared at the ceiling, the brass cross replaced with an intersection of white metal frames, supporting ceiling tiles. She sifted through the conversation, wondering how much of what had been shared was a dream, vision, intuition, or residual effect from having connected in with JD. The bonding felt real, stronger now since she'd made the crossing to his side of the veil between them. She could feel it whenever she looked at him, knowing he was aware behind his staring eyes and vacant expression. Knowing he was preparing his defenses, biding his time. More capable than she was in controlling the three worlds he'd carefully designed. Worlds he could slip in and out of, avoiding memories of whatever horrible event had chased him there.

Cheryl took a deep breath, holding it for as long as she could before letting it out. "I'm coming for you. For you, and all the others. I will not fail. Not this time. Never again." Her promise was joined to a series of images: the bones of her unique code. She knew she needed to tear it apart and start over again, tweaking the tri-helix spiral's construction, swapping new symbols in and out, then running the program against itself, seeking another breakthrough. Something JD would not see coming. Something the corporate entity, waiting in the shadows to wrest everything away from her, could not conceive as possible. Her code as unique as if formed of her own DNA.

She closed her eyes, a smile on her face as she fell asleep to the sound of water running through a narrow canyon. To the sound of her brother's slow breathing as he trailed behind, letting her lead the way.

CHAPTER THIRTY-TWO

GEORGETOWN UNIVERSITY, MARYLAND

Cheryl

"Good to see you again, Ms. Coleman." Cheryl gave Mari a wide smile as she finished putting her notes away, the auditorium emptying out. "I was *hoping* you'd return. Your *insightful* observations a highlight, each time we've spoken."

"I've been busy—with a lot going on. Finally able to show up." Mari paused, sensing a change in the other woman's approach. "Another *excellent* performance."

Cheryl raised an eyebrow. "Interesting choice of words."

"Not how I meant it to sound. Not *exactly*. But it *is* a type of performance in how you conduct your class. Like—"

"There's no need to explain, Mari. I was only teasing you." Cheryl waited for the other woman to nod. "I'd like to invite you for a drink—at a place nearby that a friend of mine owns. It's near the water, with great seafood. *My* treat." Cheryl lowered her voice. "I've got something interesting to tell you about, having to do with my work."

"Okay." Mari forced another smile, her senses sending out alarm bells. "I should really—"

Cheryl interrupted. "You're wondering—why me? Right?" Mari nodded, taken unaware by the gesture of friendship, her instincts urging her to step back and make a more thorough assessment of the situation. Cheryl reached out, touching her on her upper arm. "The last time we had coffee you mentioned a few things that got me thinking. I responded at the time without full consideration of what you'd said, thinking I understood the angle you were taking." She paused, then grinned. "A *fault* of mine, listening with my mouth at times. My father said I was vaccinated with a phonograph needle." Cheryl noted the puzzled look in the younger woman's eyes. "It's a *thin* needle, used for playing records. *Vinyl* ones. Like in the old-timey days."

"Yes. Of course." Mari forced a tentative smile. "You threw me for a moment."

"So? Are you in?" Cheryl waited, backpack slung over her shoulder, ready to leave.

Mari took a deep breath, then nodded, clutching her purse to her chest. "I—am. And thank you for the invitation. But I *insist* on paying. I just got a big raise for the work I've been doing."

The parking lot was less then half-full, a Wednesday evening with a heavy overcast, threatening rain. A large bouncer, a man Cheryl knew as Jerry, stood at the door, holding it open as the two women approached. One of the other bouncers reached out, catching Cheryl's keys as she tossed them his way. He smiled back: a wolf whistle cutting through the air as the two women entered the restaurant.

"Valet service. Nice touch, even if it was a bit sexist." Mari studied the interior, noticing the spartan decorations of the long dining and dance floor, framed by a mahogany topped bar running halfway along the opposite wall. "Definitely not in line with what I was expecting."

Cheryl reached out, taking Mari by the arm, pointing her toward the section of booths in back, "The focus here is on the *food*, which is beyond excellent. Decent enough table service and, unfortunately for you, some of that *old-timey* music—from back in the day."

Mari nodded, then froze, spotting the large blue marlin poised over a small booth. "Is that *real?* The fish, I mean?"

"Big Blue?" Cheryl nodded. "Yeah. One of owners caught it, then mounted it."

"Not before it was *dead*, I hope." Mari noted Cheryl's weak smile at the poor joke, her guide taking her by the hand, pulled her along.

"I'll show you around. I know the guy who—" Cheryl pointed at the fish with her free hand. "Caught *that* beauty. It's hanging over his private table."

"Meaning—*yours* too, I take it—if I'm not presuming too much." Mari smiled, softening the observation.

"You're right. It is, given the nature of our relationship. Drink?"

Mari nodded, holding her purse in one hand, her instincts chattering in the background, telling her to turn around and run away. "*Absolutely!*"

They spent a few minutes talking about the weather while looking at a menu, waiting for their drinks to arrive. Then Cheryl leaned forward, elbows resting on the table, face cupped between her hands. "You mentioned how busy you've been. At work. Nascent Industries, correct?"

Mari hesitated a moment before answering. "Yes." The two of them looked up, one of the large-bodied men behind the bar bringing over their drinks. Cheryl picked up her glass and held it out, waiting for Mari to do the same.

"Cheers."

Mari hesitated. "No toast? Isn't that—bad luck?"

Cheryl shook her head, savoring the tart-flavor of the margarita, made with a bottle of top-shelf tequila from Jean's private stock. "Not at all. Lucks built on the back of thoughtful effort and paying close attention to one's surroundings. I'd wager we're both diligent in the work we do. Careful to pay attention to *where* we are and type of people we're associating with." Cheryl paused. "Don't you agree?"

A silent nod of her head was Mari's only reply, knowing Cheryl had baited her trap with the promise of inside information, and that she'd walked into it. The smiling woman sitting across from her was in control of the conversation. Self-assured, like the unusual little man in the secured section of the facility, though Cheryl was warm and inviting, with a playful smile on her lips. Her light-colored eyes bright with anticipation, as if looking forward to a lively game of give and take. Made even more unnerving because of her carefree attitude, Mari aware the stakes were incredibly high for them both.

Their server returned, delivering a large basket of seasoned fish nuggets. Mari stared at them, trying to estimate the calories, while Cheryl reached over and placed several in her plate, using a set of tongs.

"The house specialty, freshly caught and dipped in a *unique* seasoning. They're *loaded* with calories, though."

"They look great." Mari, her appetite gone, forced herself to reach out with a fork, stopping when Cheryl interrupted.

"My assistant, Isaac. I understand you know him."

Mari forced herself to continue, spearing one of the smaller pieces, lifting it to her lips, blowing on it gently before trying it. "You're right." She chewed, then swallowed, returning Cheryl's quiet stare. "The seasoning is unique, just like you said it would be." She popped the rest into her mouth, washing it down with a healthy sip of her drink, mixed on the heavy side. "As to your assistant, Isaac—yes, I know him. We met a few weeks ago when I approached him with a request. From someone higher up the corporate ladder."

"Along with an offer. A very *generous* one."

"That he *refused* to consider. Refused to even discuss it, about to walk away when I—" Mari firmed up her expression. "Mentioned his mother."

Cheryl shrugged, popping another morsel of fish into her mouth, eyes closed as she chewed it, then swallowed, sighing as she reached for her glass. "I appreciate your being honest with me. A difficult position for you, squeezed between pressure to advance your career and what must be a deeply ingrained *cultural more*, dictating adherence to a rigid code of honor." Cheryl took a healthy sip of her drink. "I assume that to be true. Your parents, especially your father, being rather old school about that sort of thing. Neh?"

Mari lowered her eyes, understanding she would need to put everything on the table. Knowing she needed to trust what her instincts were telling her: that this woman, unlike anyone she'd ever met before, was equal parts predator, mentor, and guardian lioness of her invention. Bound up within a childlike approach to life, one she was displaying in full, sitting on the other side of the table, chewing on another fish nugget, a wide smile on her face. Her eyes lit up in anticipation, open to whatever came next.

Jean entered the restaurant, surprised at having found Cheryl's car in one of the reserved parking spaces beside his own. He saw her sitting in their booth, a woman with her, sitting with her back to him as he walked over. Cheryl looked up, spotting him, a smile spreading across her face.

"Hello, Jean. This is my good friend and associate, Mari. Mari Coleman." Cheryl noted a quick exchange of glances between the two of them. Mari spoke up. "Major Kelly and I know each other. We met a few months ago in his office." Mari looked directly at Cheryl. "They assigned me as liaison on your project, responsible for handling the exchange of your progress reports to those I was reporting to—behind the scenes."

Jean looked at Cheryl with a confused look. She slid over, patting the seat beside her, inviting him to sit down. "You couldn't have known that Mari and I had already met." She turned and gave the other woman a quick grin. "Met her after one of my classes. Ended up inviting her to coffee so we could talk. Didn't know at the time she was there to scope out the territory, doing some fieldwork on me, trying to verify if what she'd read or been told was accurate."

Jean eyed Mari, who smiled back, her face slightly flushed, halfway through her second drink. He narrowed his eyes. "You were on a—recon mission."

"*Exactly!*" Cheryl beamed. The bartender came over, handing Jean a sweating glass of dark-bodied ale, stopping long enough to raise his bushy eyebrows, looking at the two women, leaving without a word as they shook their heads, refusing a third drink.

Mari leaned back, feeling pressure to comment when the other two turned their full attention to her. "So—now that we know we know each other, where does that leave us?"

Jean glanced at Cheryl, waiting for her to speak. She leaned forward, keeping her voice low. "With you showing us all your cards, working with me so I can thwart the powers that be for as long as I can. Knowing we'll lose the war, eventually, but winning as many battles as we can along the way." She lifted her glass, the others matching her, seconding her toast.

CHAPTER THIRTY-THREE

OFFICE, RESEARCH FACILITY, MARYLAND

Mari

There was a long pause: the small, unadorned office filled to the brim with silence. A hush of air slipped from vents in the ceiling, matching the sibilant tone of the man's whispery voice when he finally spoke.

"We have an issue."

Mari nodded, forcing herself to swallow a smug look. "With the code."

Two pale blue eyes, their expression as cold as shards of ice, fixed her with a stony stare. "Yes. With the code."

Mari leaned back in the chair, trying to make an accommodation to its intentionally uncomfortable design, intended to focus its occupant to pay close attention and respond with brevity. A succinct exchange of verbal information, encouraged. "Your people cannot *break* it."

"They inform me it is—unbreakable. Until they can bring more advanced techniques to bear."

"As was reported. In my notes." Mari reset her emotions, aware the other man's mood was troubled, but firmly in control. And dangerous. "At our *last* meeting."

"Yes."

Mari waited for a sign from the diminutive man to stay or go. None was forthcoming, so she shifted her hips, searching for a less uncomfortable position. "I've been in contact with her. With the doctor." The man remained silent, arms at his side, as if a poorly posed mannequin used to sell items devoid of appeal. "She has a list of demands." Mari paused. "Would you prefer them in print?"

A hand appeared above the surface of the desk, a single finger lifted, Mari taking it as a sign to proceed. "Control of the coding is to remain hers. There is a backdoor built into the junctions between the three data collection loops and the central programming core, which shift every few days allowing opportunity for updates, which alter the basic programming, rewriting itself. Almost as if it were a living—no, an *evolving* construct, constantly adapting itself to the data being collected. Processing it on the fly. Then shoving it on through to be acted on."

"An advanced form of AI." Luther maintained a posture of indifference. "Nothing groundbreaking in that. Not enough to bow to an attempt at extortion."

"Demands—not extortion." Mari didn't flinch, her breathing measured. "After all, *we're* the ones who stole it from *her*." When the pale man blinked, she continued. "As to the claim of it being nothing more than an innovative form of artificial intelligence, I would hazard a guess that it's proving to be beyond anything our current group of programmers are capable of mimicking, as if it *were* an advanced form of life, feasting on any attempt to attack it. Becoming stronger each time. Resisting every—"

The finger lowered, withdrawing beneath his palm like the tail of a snake, slithering back into a pile of rocks. "Let the doctor know we will consider her demands. Send them to me when you—"

Mari stood up, pulling a single sheet of folded paper from a pocket of her dark-colored dress pants. "She anticipated you would see it that way." Placing it on the desk, she turned to leave. His voice stopped her at the door, as she knew it would. She didn't bother looking back.

"You have become a more critical gear. Is that part of her plan—or your own?"

"Both." Mari let the door close behind her as she strode down the corridor, confident and unafraid.

"They'll react. They'll have to. It's wired into their *effing* DNA." Isaac frowned. "Funding pulled. Threats made to our—"

Cheryl shook her head, cutting him off. Mari had stopped by, filling her in on the results of her meeting with the nameless corporate entity, who Cheryl had jokingly nicknamed Barnabas Collins, based on his description: a reference the younger woman hadn't been able to place. Isaac, startled by Mari's unexpected appearance at the lab, had been tongue-tied, his face turning red, unable to meet Cheryl' gaze. Once Mari had left, Cheryl touched him on his arm, assuring him his former digression was no longer an issue.

"Your mother is where she needs to be. Where you need her to be. The funds are unrecoverable, I made certain of that. A financial friend of mine has them tucked away in one of the same dark shadows where the big boys hide theirs."

Isaac arced his eyebrows. "You have a lot of interesting friends."

"I've led a very interesting life."

Let's hope it continues as planned." Isaac gave her a sad smile. "I fear for you—when you get like this. Self-assured. Brandishing your ego as if a shield, while inside you're still the highly advanced child waving your hands in the air, weaving a magic spell to try and keep the monsters away."

Cheryl considered his words, knowing her decision to invite Mari onto the team had caused Isaac to feel conflicted: caught between his shame at having failed her trust, and concern for her, bordering on love. A feeling he was still struggling to define. "We're all children in the dark, Isaac, doing our best to find our way through." She paused. "I'm going back in." When she saw his eyes widen, she cut him off. "I'm going in, so I need you focused on helping me to convince—" She pointed at JD, reclining in his usual position, Tee-Cee on his head, data feeding into the server, then glanced at one of the wall-sized monitors, displaying a night-time scene filled with vehicles, people standing around them in tight circles, others lined up nearby, making slight adjustments to control boards. "To convince JD to let me guide him back. Whichever one he turns out to be."

The secured meeting room had a veneer of heavily curtained walls, with thick carpeting. The ceiling was covered in panels with scalloped openings, a spray of noise deadening material applied, reducing any chance of an echo, preventing use of recording devices positioned outside the walls. A large electric field generator was humming away in the center, eliminating use of cell phones or portable listening devices from within, everyone in attendance having been thoroughly searched, electronic devices collected in the lobby, ten floors down. The middle eight floors were empty, leaving the penthouse suite as the only usable space, where twelve men were sitting in a semi-circle around a large oak table. Luther stood to one side, ready to provide answers to questions asked. The rest of the men were busy reading through a thick report describing progress of the project to date.

"We are, apparently, at the mercy of this unusual woman because of an *unforeseen* issue. One we must deal with—for the time being." The speaker, a man in his early fifties, broad shouldered with a thick neck, wore a jovial expression, meeting the wave of hushed voices rising in dispute of his claim. The influential group of men not used to being at the mercy of others. He raised his hand, silencing them with a dismissive wave. "I've read through the latest report, submitted by our friend in the field—" He gave a perfunctory nod in Luther's direction, standing quietly off to the side. "And have scoured the original progress reports provided by Doctor Atkinson. I'm not open to listening to a rehash of statements of fact, only a vote on whether to accept her terms—or not." He fixed each of the eleven men with a stare, waiting for them to bow to his authority, allowing a smile to twitch the corners of his full lips as they leaned back, silent. "Luther, if you would—please relate the potential positive *and* negative results of any actions taken in regard to the demands Doctor Atkinson has put to paper and pen."

Luther nodded, then stepped forward, a sheaf of papers in his hand. He walked around the table, handing a copy to each of the men. He rejoined the heavy-set man, who nodded, encouraging him to speak. "I have insinuated one of my people into a role as our intermediary. They have—"

The large man interrupted. "A Miss Coleman. Working in project support."

Luther nodded. "Yes. Ms. Coleman has become critical to my efforts to secure information from the doctor—"

"Doctor Atkinson, with multiple PHD's in various disciplines." The large man nodded again, an indication Luther should continue.

"Securing information from Doctor Atkinson's project, through direct and indirect means."

The large man raised a finger, interrupting again. "I've recently received information *not* included in the report Luther handed out. And, from my private conversations with him, allowed under the agreement we all signed, I have various—options—needing our approval in oder to try and regain *full* control of the operational component, to include, but not be limited to—"

A man sitting at the far end of the table spoke up. "You're talking about the program we'll be using. *Her* program: this Doctor Atkinson. One unlike anything we've seen before. Is *that* the operational component you're referring to—Ed?"

"Yes, Thomas. And thank you—for helping to define the *crux* of our problem, as well as the need for this special session to discuss, as mentioned a moment ago, options currently under consideration, as well as providing everyone here an opportunity to offer their own suggestions. this being a—*democratic* form of group *autocracy*."

The men smirked, looking at each other. A few of them chuckled, while most of the others carefully assessed the mood of the room. Thomas leaned back, arms crossed, eyes fixed on the Ed, nominal chairperson responsible for leading the meeting, quietly measuring him with his eyes, his expression unreadable.

The discussions came to an end after a handful of people stood to make their individual points, the others quick to dismiss a few of the more pointed solutions being discussed to try to wrest the secret of the code's design from its creator. Thomas and Ed worked together, redirecting the others to an agreement to use less objectionable means of acquiring it.

"We concur then, to continuing to develop the various revenue streams, based on wide-scale adoption of this promising technology. Our stated goal: to secure control of the code within the parameters discussed and accepted, while the design and implementation teams are working on testing and making increased efforts to alter the base code for more—expansive uses in the near future."

A murmur of voices circled the table. Ed waited until they subsided, then leaning down, placing his large meaty hands on its surface, his voice firm. "By a show of hands, anyone voting to reject our plan of a more benign approach—make yourself known." No one moved. Ed tapped the table with a fist. "Gentlemen—we stand adjourned."

Luther sidled up to the chairperson, selected to the role for a duration of six months, his term now half-way through. He did not care for the man's disposition, especially now, a drink in his hand, words flowing as he regaled the others with his take on where things stood and where they would soon be heading.

"A moment, sir. If you will."

"It's Ed, Luther. Call me Ed. The meeting's over. We're just a bunch of over-paid, under-educated captains of industry standing around, swapping our best guesses of what happens next."

"With an eye on increasing *earnings* potential, of course." Thomas walked up with a bottle of off brand whiskey in hand, offering to refill

Ed's tumbler. Getting a nod, he tipped it, waiting for a second nod, then setting it down on a nearby counter, loaded with an array of fine foods.

"That's right, Thomas. Name of the game, securing our positions before the next tsunami of technological change comes sweeping over the horizon, carrying those of us who've prepared—to higher ground."

"And from there, we aim our sights at the highest ground of all." Thomas glanced up at the ceiling, then raised his glass, waiting for Ed to join him. The two men touched them together, eyes fixed on each other with discerning stares.

Luther coughed, just loud enough for Ed to hear. "Yes, Luther?" Ed noted the look on Luther's face: pensive, his lips drawn into a tight line. He motioned with his glass, letting the thin, quiet man know he should speak his mind.

"I'm concerned." Luther lowered his gaze. "As to the solution path discussed—and passed."

"How so?" Ed tilted his head, his light-colored eyes reflecting the soft lighting from overhead. "Do you mean towards the doctor? This Atkinson woman?" When Luther nodded, Ed shrugged, then took a sip of the cheap whiskey Thomas had poured. "She's safe enough for now. Nothing to worry about there."

Luther nodded again. "Yes. Of course. But I'm referring to the proposed use of the technology. It seems—beyond current capabilities, what some are suggesting. Looking to use it for *in situ* therapy, in the workplace and schoolroom environments. Reconfigured—"

Ed swung a ham-sized hand in a half-circle, taking in the group of men, controlling financial wealth in the billions. Some of them known to the world at large, the rest selecting an anonymous approach, hiding behind a wall of shell companies scattered throughout dozens of countries. All of them with direct interests in big pharma, eager to prepare the ground ahead for the leap to non-chemical therapy based on the efforts of one, uniquely talented woman. "We're but the *first* generation of those to follow, preparing people for a future they can't imagine to exist. Knowing we must adapt if we are to survive. Evolve, so we can thrive—out there." He lifted his arm, pointing straight up, Thomas nodding in agreement.

"And what of those who resist the—adjustments required in order to prepare them to function—out there?" Luther stepped back slightly, keeping a stoic look firmly in place.

Ed shrugged, eyeing the mid-grade whiskey in his glass, offered as a mild rebuke by Thomas, who knew he owned the top distillery in the world. He raised it, downing the rest of alcohol, wiping his lips with the back of his hand. "*Fuck 'em.* Every mother-loving one of 'em."

CHAPTER THIRTY-FOUR

SET, L.A. BASIN

Twain and Miranda's Story

"It's time." Twain let go of Miranda's hand and stood up. James joined him, his hand extended. "Good luck." Twain took it, looking around for Dawg, then remembered Miranda had left him in the trailer, not wanting any distractions when Twain left to suit up for the stunt sequence. Miranda looked at James. "Aren't you supposed to say *break a leg?*"

James turned his head and spit, Twain copying the action. "You *never* say that to stunties." Both men shook their heads. "It's bad luck."

Miranda shook her head, uncertain if they were joking. "I—didn't know." She looked at each of them, telling by their tight expressions they were serious. Twain reached out and touched her shoulder. "It's okay. We both spit on the ground at the same time, so I should be fine."

Miranda cleared her throat then hawked up a large glob of mucus, watching as it hit the edge of a gravel road. "Does that help?"

Twain grinned. "Absolutely." He let his smile fade away as he leaned in. "I'll see ya in an hour and we'll go grab a bite in the commissary." James cleared his throat, causing Twain to glance over. "And a drink." Then he spun around and ambled down the hill, his shoulders swaying as he stretched his arms, without looking back.

Cheryl hovered above the organized chaos, having jacked into JD's feed. She looked down at a sea of light trucks and people, moving with rehearsed determination, their eyes tight, lips set in focused lines as an amplified voice counted down the time before going hot. Cheryl slipped to a higher focal point, moving without effort to one side and back up the slope of a small hillside, recognizing the actor called James, and Miranda, Twain's close friend. She looked for the shepherd, surprised he was not there, logging the detail away for later review. A horn sounded. The voice booming, calling everyone to their marks. Stuntmen slipped into their vehicles. Pyro-technicians stood behind their boards, fingers poised. Actors, bunched in small knots, stayed safely out of the way. All except for one.

Twain clasped the wheel of a late model sedan: heavy-bodied, with an oversize engine purring away beneath a glossy black hood. He could feel the vibration in his feet and hands as he ran through the action sequences, mentally rehearsing the multiple collisions and skidding turns assigned to him. He was nervous, as he usually was before a stunt, though confident in his skills and those of the other drivers. He'd already filmed his green screen scenes, ready to be edited in to fill the seat of the car once it was ready for the big screen. His close-ups digitally stored away, to be cut into place long after the nighttime theatrics ended.

A hand slapped the hood of the car, signaling Twain it was one minute to go time. He closed his eyes, issuing the same prayer used before each of his missions while overseas. "Keep me in your hand, this day. A willing soldier, on patrol. And if it is my time to die, accept my soul—and see this weary body home." He lifted his dog tags, kissed them twice, then tucked them away. Another hard slap of hand to metal hood released his foot, punching the accelerator, tires spinning as he sped away.

Miranda, watching from the hillside, shivered, wrapping her arms around her chest. James noticed, taking off his jacket, using it to cover her shoulders. "Are you okay?"

"Yeah. I guess so. Just a chill." She looked at James. "Should I spit *again?*"

"Nah. That one you did earlier should be more than enough." He reached out, pointing to a black car swinging around a curve in the road, pursued by a large white van. "Here he comes."

Cheryl moved away from her viewpoint behind Twain's friends, sliding downhill, rising to a level above three cameras, poised above the roadway on gimbal mounts, each on a separate set of tracks, ready to move in tandem with the vehicles as they passed by. A rumble of engine noise washed through her, far stronger to her senses than if she'd been standing there in person. Or hovering, she thought, the vibrations felt in every atom of her non-existent body.

"Why—are you here?"

Cheryl didn't react or bother to turn around. The voice was coming from inside her head as JD attempted to unsettle her. Failing. She was used to ignoring minor distractions, trained to focus on what she was doing by her brother, tossing pinecones and small stones her way as she scaled a series of fifteen-foot ledges in their backyard, trying to make her fall. "I wanted to ask you something."

JD hardened his tone, increasing the volume of his words, adding a background hissing. "You're altering the timeline *here. Now.* You need to *leave!*"

Cheryl hesitated, then clenched her jaw. "Piss off."

"What?" The background noise faded away, Cheryl noting the surprise in JD's voice. She grinned. "You heard me. Hard not to, with you being in my head and all, right above my ears."

"You don't know—you have *no* idea what you're doing. What you're causing to happen!"

"Then *help* me. Fabricate a better place where we can have a face-to-face discussion. Help me to—"

"He's *fucked*, because of *you*. It's too late to avoid it." JD formed in front of her, a dark cloud, arms reaching out, fingers squeezing her shoulders. Painful, a shock of realization running through Cheryl, sensing how real this world had become to JD. His hands spun her around, shaking her until her imaginary teeth rattled in her skull. "This is *all* on you! You *caused* this. Open your *eyes!* Watch what you've done. To *him!* To *them!*"

Cheryl blinked, disoriented, finding herself behind the wheel of a large car, the hands in front of her twisting to one side, then the other, the car forced to slew from side to side, bouncing off parked vehicles, sending a motorcycle crashing into one, the driver somersaulting through the air, disappearing from her view. Cheryl's head snapped to one side from the force of the collision, her vision blurring. A loud curse slipping from her lips. His lips, she corrected, knowing it was Twain's vision she was sharing as she felt the sharp tug on his body, another crashing impact coming from the side, forcing the vehicle into a grinding slide along a line of old cars.

Twain checked his time, realized he was a half-second ahead of the next explosion, easing off the gas pedal as the next stunt came up in five—four—three—two—one. A jolt from below slammed the chassis of the car as a charge sent it into a flip, careening over a knot of scurrying pedestrians who appeared to be running for their lives. Another knot of people were lined up directly ahead, upside down, spinning right-side up as the car continued to roll over, landing on all four tires, then plowing straight ahead.

Twain blinked his eyes to clear his vision, waiting for one of the stunties, dressed as a woman, to scurry aside. An unrehearsed moment occurring when his heel wedged in a crack in the faux sidewalk. Twain twisted the wheel, sliding the front of the vehicle to one side, ducking his head as it sliced through and then along a brick-veneer façade, clipping the supports as it went into a skid, the entire structure falling away from the stuntman and the street, landing in a huge pile on the roof of the car, crumpling the hood, Twain driven down and to the side, ending up with his head jammed onto the center console.

Cheryl tugged herself free from Twain's body, clawing at the air, trying to find purchase as her fingers passed through layers of metal and bricks without meeting resistance. She willed herself to rise above the chaos of emergency vehicles screaming in along with a small army of extras, rushing to toss debris aside, trying to get to the man still trapped inside the battered automobile.

Miranda clapped her hands, amazed at the realism of the chase scene: Twain maneuvering his car between several chase vehicles with hesitant reactions, making it look as if he were on the edge of losing control. Then the vehicle he was in swerved, penetrating one of the false fronts of the buildings lining the street. Miranda clenched her hands, nervous and excited at what she was seeing, then glanced over at James, wanting to ask if it was over. His eyes were staring straight ahead as he rose to his feet, shouting for the other spectators to join him. To go and help free their friend. Miranda watched as they raced away, frozen in place, eyes widened in shock, feeling as if someone had ripped her heart and lungs away, unable to breathe. Her mind numbed by what was happening directly in front of her.

Isaac removed Cheryl's Tee-Cee, hanging it on a support arm. He took her upper arm, helping her sit up, her face white with shock, body trembling, eyes unable to find a single point of focus. He held out a bottle of water, watching with concern as her hand rose, pushing it away. "I—screwed up." She shook her head, trying to force herself out from a mixed fog of adrenaline and guilt. "I—screwed *everything* up."

Isaac pulled a chair over and sat down, taking Cheryl's hand, concerned at what might have happened to her mind from the effects of reconnecting into JD's projection, leading to a potential for serious repercussions. "You didn't screw up, Cheryl. The data feed was—off the chart. A completely new series of—" Isaac stopped, remembering the clarity of the scene. "I'm not sure how to describe it, but it *definitely* isn't like anything we've seen before."

Cheryl reached up, wiping away tears of frustration. "I *killed* him."

Who?" Isaac squeezed her hand. "JD's still here. Kicking and breathing. Well—still breathing, at any rate."

"Twain. The actor. He's dead. Because of me. Because of my having interfered."

"Are you serious? He *can't* be dead, Cheryl. He was *never* alive. Only a projection by JD, using him to hide behind."

"JD has the right to his illusions, to do whatever he wants. I *don't*."

"Don't have the right to do what? To help him—force him if you have to in helping him find his way back?" Isaac took her hands, assisting her as she stood up, supporting her weight as she stumbled over to her chair. Her voice was low, tired, drained of energy. "Check the data stream. I marked it—at the beginning when the spikes started showing. Run it back and tell me what you see."

Cheryl felt a wave of nausea tugging at her stomach, the residual effect of motion sickness from being inside the vehicle. Being inside Twain, she thought, a flush of shame coloring her skin. She glanced at a small wastebasket under the desk, then swallowed, deciding she'd manage. Her fingers worked over the keyboard, pressing a series of worn keys, pulling up the file Isaac had stored a copy of, duplicating the recent projection.

Cheryl watched as a sequence of symbols spun in a tri-helix spiral of linked data points, almost able to see the images in the raw data. Isaac reached out, pointing to a large monitor, directing her attention to the scene she'd been fully immersed in. A gray shadow hovered in the background, drifting above the ground while the camera crews and pyro teams moved in a synchronized dance, following the speeding vehicles with rail-smooth motion as walls of dust and debris from bursting squibs ran in between exploding charges, tossing vehicles into the air.

"That's me." Cheryl squinted. "I—think."

"No." Isaac shook his head. "It's not. You'd already moved into the lead car at this point. I watched you do it, using a monitor sequenced to your specific feedback channel, kept separate from his." Isaac pointed at JD, still lying in his chair, the cap in place, his eyes darting back and forth under his eyelids, the movements mirroring what was happening in his mind.

"He—" Cheryl looked at JD. "*Let* it happen. No—he *made* it happen."

"What happen?"

"A woman. Or rather, a stuntman, dressed up as one, carrying a lifelike doll." Cheryl rubbed her eyes, then the sides of her head, a headache sliding from one side of her frontal lobe to the other. "He *wanted* it to happen. Didn't matter whether I was there or not. It wouldn't have made any difference." She twisted in the chair, staring over at JD. "You're a real piece of work, *buddy!* Almost had me convinced." She looked up as Isaac hovered over her, his eyes filled with concern. "Thank you, Isaac." She saw him blush, knowing he was uncomfortable with praise, her recovery from the traumatic event starting to take place, an emotional jolt to her psyche, experienced from a first-person perspective, so to speak. "You've helped me in ways I haven't *begun* to give you credit for."

"Except when I—didn't." Isaac stepped back, hands at his side, eyes on hers. "Nothing's really changed, since—"

Cheryl flashed a sad smile. "No. It hasn't. But I wouldn't be where I am without you. So, until we get this son-of-a-*bitch* hauled out of his *effing* fantasy world—"

"Language, Boss Lady. And it's worlds, plural." Isaac reached out, touching Cheryl on her shoulder.

She nodded. "True. So, until we wedge him free, we *keep* at it. Together. Trying to come up with some way to track him back to his lair, then smoke him out."

CHAPTER THIRTY-FIVE

BEACH, MID-COAST MAINE

Calvin and Jemma's Story

The roar of a fierce gale brought a heavy surge of waves crashing ashore, each trying to outdo the other. A spray of ice pellets whipped across rippling sand, slapping against fluttering clothing, stinging exposed skin.

Calvin and Jemma crouched against the lee side of an enormous length of a driftwood tree, their bodies curled in alongside the bone-white trunk, bleached from years of sun and salt spray. The roots at one end looked like the talons of a giant bird of prey, the twisted fingers of wood sifting sand from the air, blown by a strong, late-winter storm. Dawg, hunkered down near their feet, looked miserable: the sleet of fine particles of ice and dirt having driven him to cover, stinging his eyes when he'd tried to chase a large gull drifting low over the frothy surf-line, looking for an easy meal.

"It's a *blowin' four shore*." Jemma did her best to mimic a thick down-east accent, failing badly, her voice breaking into laughter as Calvin turned and stared at her. She grinned, regretting it as particles of dirt found her lips, wiping them away. Then she looked up, her eyes bright with tears of joy, loving the feel of nature in its full glory. "It's—it's some *wicked awe-sum!*"

Jemma got closer that time to the local dialect, picked up from townsfolk stopping by to check out the recent additions to the farm and store. Some of the younger ones eagerly signing up for job opportunities, now that both buildings were nearing completion. The months had wound their way from cool and damp to dry and cold, to *effing* freezing cold, then rounding the corner to damp and cool again. A late nor'easter had arrived, pounding the coast, a lure to those willing to visit the long, white sand beach and face the worst nature had to show. No one else had dared the tempest today, the two of them alone. Summer travelers having left months ago, safely tucked away in southern climes.

Calvin, trying to hide a smile, failed, his hand held up to block out the wash of fine white sand. "Yeah. I could say the same for your accent. In case no one's told you lately, it really does blow."

Jemma wiped her nose, in constant drip from the cold air, squinting, her eyes all but closed against the salty sting of the spray. "Speaking of which—" She slid over, her hand working at the zipper of Calvin's wind-proof nylon pants, worn over a pair of thermal hiking shorts.

He stared at her. "You're kidding. *Really?* Out here where—"

"There's no one within a country mile of this place. Stop being a baby and spread your legs." Calvin complied: the wind a scraping knife on his exposed skin, soon replaced with the heated blade of Jemma's tongue.

Calvin's old truck rattled into the parking lot of the gas station and small store located halfway up the neck road, leading to the city. The store was still open, though few people had dared to venture out, staying close to home in case of a power outage from falling trees. Ready to spring into action, starting generators, a staple for most of the homes sharing the narrow jut of rocky land poking a finger of granite into the eye of deep ocean waters.

"Well—are you coming, or not?" Calvin looked at Dawg, curled up in the passenger seat, licking his paws, working the sand out from between the pads. He'd dropped Jemma off at the farm so she could check on the roast she'd starting cooking earlier. Sent right back out into the storm to get a few items needed for the pies she was planning to cook later. Dawg glanced at Calvin, then dropped his head, sighing, unwilling to exit the warm interior of the vehicle. "Okay then. No treat for you." Dawg's ears pricked forward as he looked over at Calvin. Then he returned to cleaning his paws, preferring the heated embrace of the cab.

"They say it's hitting close to *forty*, out there." The heavy-set elderly woman behind the counter gave Calvin a wide smile. Her eyes, a light gray, matched the color of her hair. Silver, cut short and curly. "Where's *Dawg?*" She started ringing up the goods he'd selected. "Got a special treat for him—like always."

"He's among the missing." Calvin looked outside, checking the truck. "We were down at the beach earlier. He had all he wanted of it. Lying out in the truck, staying warm. Turning into a real *pussy-cat* lately."

"Jemma's home cooking probably has something to do with that, I imagine." She glanced at Calvin's waistline, without comment. He shrugged, handing her a twenty and a ten. "Most likely. She's busy putting up an order of pies for the church supper, tomorrow night." He took the dollar bills she handed back and stuffed them into a donation jar, along with the loose change, followed by a twenty: the picture of the little girl compelling. A local child in need of specialized treatment for burns suffered in a local house fire.

"People say her place is shaping up nice. Gonna be something once it's finished. Lots of organic produce to sell. Fresh fruit, meat, baked goods and the like."

"That's her plan—other than the meat. She's still trying to work her head around slaughtering any of her pets, as she calls them."

"Imagine you're helping her with that, along with anything else she needs handled. Right?"

Calvin picked up the groceries, the lights flickering then coming back on. "I am. Like I've been doing for *others* in town. Lending a hand where I can. Tossing in an idea here and there. But it's *her* thing, not mine."

"Heard you was tossing in more than just ideas." The woman's smile was infectious. Calving shrugged, turning for the door. Her voice stopped him. "It's good, Cal. Real good, you with someone like her in your life. We all feel that way. Especially today, seeing how it's— well, you know. It being the day and all."

Calvin nodded again, then leaned forward, pushing the door open against a stiff wall of wind.

"Why is *he* so mopey?" Jemma motioned with her chin at Dawg, her hands working on rolling out crust for a long line of pie plates, sitting on the counter. She would soon be filling them with a thick mixture of wild grown and cultivated berries, collected from her own and a dozen local gardens during the previous summer and fall. Calvin looked at Dawg, the shepherd with its head between its outstretched paws, lying on the new kitchen floor in a heap of furry sadness, his eyes following every move Jemma made.

"He wouldn't get out of the truck. At the store. So, he didn't get a treat."

"Ellen didn't give you one, for him?"

"He wouldn't go in. I told him what his choices were, but I don't think he believed me. He will the next time."

Jemma gave him a disappointed look. "Calvin—you could have given—"

"I could have. But I *didn't*." Calvin's tone suggested an end to his side of the discussion. Jemma closed her mouth, focused on rolling out her crusts. A few minutes later, Calvin came back into the kitchen after changing out of his clothes. He came over to the counter and placed his hands on Jemma's hips, enjoying the flex of her body as she finished rolling out the last batch of top crusts.

Dawg was wagging his tail, crunching his way through a small pile of snacks. Calvin let it go, knowing Jemma had as much claim to the shepherd as he did. More, if you counted the hours spent with Dawg's head in her lap, snoring away while she read a book, one hand rubbing between his ears, the other slowly turning the pages.

"Roast smells good." He touched her neck with the tip of his nose. "You do *too*. Like fresh air and sea salt."

"I already took a shower. So, it's lavender, with a hint of lilacs. A new scent, one Shannon worked up. I'm trying it out for her."

Calvin sniffed her head, working his nose into the braid hanging down her back. "I was talking about your hair."

"Oh. Yeah. I didn't bother with that. Get to it later, after I get the pies topped off and in the oven."

Calvin was quiet for a moment, then stepped back so Jemma could move to the other side of a large, butcher block table: one he'd purchased for her, designed for cutting up quarters of beef. Turned into a pastry table, for now. "Sorry. For before."

"Not a problem." Jemma glanced up, busy pouring a thick mixture into each pie dish. "I could tell something was bothering you, when we were approaching the beach."

"It's the day. Or rather—tonight is."

Jemma stopped, putting the large bowl down. "I completely forgot." She came over and leaned her head against his shoulder, wiping a drop of sweat from the end of her nose against his shirt. "I'm sorry. I should have figured it out."

"Ellen—she told me how lucky I am to have someone like you in my life. Told me everyone feels the same way."

Jemma started filling the pie crusts again, her head down. "Didn't think they cared all that much for me. Being a newcomer, changing things around here the way I have. She's barely had anything to say to me when I've been in there. None of them do. Always polite and smiling, but never going beyond that."

"You weren't born here. That's all there is to it. And you don't go to church, though you support it, donating baked goods for their monthly suppers. But they probably figure you're just doing that to help advertise your store."

"Is that what *you* think I'm doing?" Jemma spun around, her tone rising to a level consistent with the wind howling against the eaves. Calvin reached up, his hands cupping her face.

"You know me better than that." He leaned in and kissed the end of her nose. Another drop of sweat hanging there, salty, and sweet. "This is the first year in a whole basket-full I'm even half-way to feeling okay. *That's* what she was pointing out. As to how they see *you?* Well—that's on you to change their viewpoint—if you've a mind to."

"How? I mean, none of them, including you, are all that open to strangers showing up, smiling, talking a mile a minute, trying to fit in."

"Then don't." Calvin stepped back, leaning against the wall.

"And do what—just show up? How will that change—"

"That's right, Jemma. Just *show* up. For no special reason. Be there because you *want* to be there. Help them set up for church suppers. Go to events at the school or fire-station. Listen to people when they gossip, swapping stories of their kids or grandkids. Of their aches, pains, worries and such."

"How would *that* make any difference?"

"It worked with *me*. You just keep showing up, waiting for someone to ask about you. How you're doing. What you've been up to."

"Bev told me the same thing before he passed. Like *he* used to do—showing up and seeing if he could help. Told me to ease into living here. Warned me about making my offer to you. Said you weren't a man to be pressured." Jemma reached up, wiping tears from her eyes.

"Bev was—a *rare* treasure. Became part of the town the minute he arrived, able to see it for what it was. His paintings: filled with small houses, traps and boats in the yard, woodpiles stacked. All spread out, overlooking the water like flower gardens, each one blending itself, side by side, with the next. Captured that in his paintings, before his shoulders gave out."

"Okay."

Calvin stepped forward, taking her in his arms, giving her a smile. "And *no* more treats for Dawg. For today. Okay?" When she nodded, he gave her a hug, then left without another word, heading into the living room to work on a special design element for the store.

A heavy fog crept in, reclaiming the land. Burying it in a blanket of thick, damp air. The ground lay bare of snow, stained by dead grass, and fall leaves in various colors, dripping with moisture.

Calvin was standing outside, unsure why he was there. He knew it was because of the date and the hour. He wondered if headlights would appear, his cousin begging him to go to the station, to celebrate his birthday. When he reached down to pet Dawg, there was no sign of him. Then he tried to move away, unable to, his body stiff, stomach contracting as if punched. Calvin sighed, aware of what was coming. He wasn't afraid, only questioning how long he'd have to bear it.

"Do you know what a weed is, Cal?" His cousin's voice croaked from behind him, like a raven in the early morning hours, announcing itself to a waking world. "I'll tell ya." Carl stepped forward, his body a dark shadow, less dense than before. Angular and familiar. "It's something out of place, standing out among all the rest. The same whether it's on a lawn or in a garden. A weed is proof that no matter how much you try to conquer nature, it thumbs its nose at ya. Making you sit up and take notice. Compelling those who see it as a weed to do something about it."

"Guess that bucket of wisdom should make some sort of sense to me. But it doesn't." Calvin knew it was another dream. Or a nightmare, depending on which way the wind would end up blowing. "Is there a point to—"

"I always have a point to make, Cal, with the spreading of my knowledge. Especially the kind I'm gonna be laying on you." The shadow became fully shaped, stepping out of the near edge of fog. Tall, walking with a slight limp. Face outlined by false light, with no moon out or house lights lit. "You know the difference between a weed and a rose?"

"Can't wait to find out—cousin."

"A rose among weeds ain't no different from a weed in roses. Each an aberration. although you'll never find the first one 'cause a rose doesn't have what it takes to grow in weeds. But a weed, well that's another story. It's vilified, eradicated time and time again. Poisoned, plucked, and penalized for daring to trespass beyond well-defined limits. And because of that, despite the hand of man being placed against it from long before any of us were drawing breath, it continues to exist. To thrive. Strengthened by the constant weeding out of the weakest ones, lost to abuse. The survivors, lying in wait, biding their time, the tiniest part of themselves lurking in the soil. Lunging back into growth the minute you turn your back."

"Like you, now. The prodigal weed, returned."

The shadow dissolved, leaving his cousin in its place. Carl walked up, stopping a few feet away, hands in his pockets, rocking slightly as if listening to music only he could hear. "No. I'm definitely gone. And I'm not coming back, that's for sure. Not as me, at any rate. But I can still find you. Drawn to you whenever you open the door." He paused long enough to let Calvin try to work through the meaning. "It's you, Cal. You're the weed, like all the others. And I was the damn rose. Here, then gone in a blink of an eye. While you persevered, bearing up under unfair assault. Taking the blame for what I did. Protecting me, at a high cost to yourself. Coming back stronger for the experience. True to your roots if you will." He paused again, his voice breaking into a sequence of notes, toe tapping the ground, another song gestating in the air.

Calvin cut him off. "Enough, cousin. Is there some message you want to share with me? Something of value about today or tomorrow? Talking about the past doesn't help none. So, if that's all you got to—"

"There is a world of hurt heading your way, Cal. A world of hurt that you don't deserve but will once again have to bear up under. And I just wanted to let you know—there's not a damn thing either of us can do to avoid it."

Calvin stared up at the living room ceiling while Jemma stood on a ladder, wielding a paintbrush while he supported her, holding onto her hips, admiring the way her body moved beneath his fingers, felt through the overalls she had on. Drops of paint speckled the front of his old work shirt and the backs of his hands and face, hitting him whenever he looked up, trying to see how much longer it would take for Jemma to finish daubing away.

He mumbled a reference to Michelangelo and the Sistine Chapel, Jemma responding with a swipe of her hand, leaving a line of paint on top of his hat. The session ended in messy laughter and shrieks, the two of them in a tangle of limbs on the plastic-covered floor. Their clothes came off with reckless abandon, bodies covered in the water-based paint. Easily washed off in a shared shower once they'd completed their own unique style of body painting.

As Calvin toweled off, he recalled his cousin's words, wondering how he would deal with losing Jemma, if the dream had been a premonition. The thought brought an ache to his chest, and he reached for her, pulling her close, wrapping his arm around her chest, face buried in her unbound hair, eyes staring through the moisture fogged window, looking into the distance.

CHAPTER THIRTY-SIX

COMPANY HOUSE, MARYLAND

Jared and Teresa

"Two of them. One for me. One for you." Jared's face beamed in the mid-morning light, his hands holding onto a pair of new, dark-blue, off-road bicycles, with color coordinated helmets hanging from the handlebars. "Instead of walking. It'll make it easier to get further in to where the springs are." He looked at Teresa, waiting for her to express her gratitude at his thoughtful gift.

She tilted her head, confusion puckering her lips, eyes narrowed, arms hanging at her side. "Bicycles? Springs?"

"The ones I told you about, running down into small pools. With tiny waterfalls—in the hills." Jared's face lost its smile. "We can use—" He moved his hands back and forth, the bikes gleaming in the sun, their colors reflecting a multitude of blue-black shadings. "These. Get up there. Without having to walk." He stopped, the look on Teresa's face letting him know he'd missed the mark, again.

Teresa stepped forward and touched his arm. "I appreciate you *doing* this, Jared. Another surprise—like the diamond earrings, which I *loved*." She paused, looking at the bicycles. "Just out of sequence—and *way* too early."

"Same as with these."

"No." Teresa shook her head. "The timing's okay. I mean—we're a couple now. Two months since I moved in, so no issue with you trying to surprise me with material things. But this gift is—well, it doesn't really work for me. I've never learned to ride one of those." Jared opened his mouth, Teresa cutting him off. "And I don't intend to start now. Okay?"

He nodded, a false smile on his face as he looked away. Teresa knew she'd disappointed him. Dawg sensed it too, coming over and leaning against Jared's leg, looking up, trying to coax a rub, failing. Jared worked the two bikes in a small circle, heading them back inside the garage, leaning them against the wall. Dawg followed, nosing his hand, getting a quick scratch between his ears for the effort.

Teresa knew she would have to come up with something to lift Jared's spirits: a weakness in him, his emotional strength not as strong as her own. His only weakness, exposed to her occasionally over the past few weeks, spending more and more time in each other's company. She reached out, taking him by his hand, leading him back inside the house as the garage door slowly closed behind them.

Teresa looked up from the fashion magazine she was leafing through, having watched Jared pacing around the house for the past hour, going outside to toss the ball for Dawg then coming back in, sitting down, trying to satisfy his need for activity by watching one of his sport teams play one of their sporting events. She'd done her best to relax him, enjoying his trembling response to her administrations, thinking it might induce him into a more relaxed state. But Jared had recovered quickly and was now on the verge of fraying the last of her remaining nerves.

"Jared." Her direct tone pulled his attention away from the sea of colored grass he was staring at, his team about to win or lose, based on his recent grunts of displeasure, leading her to think it was the latter. "You need to go. Either that—or I do." She placed the magazine on the coffee table, then reached over and shoved him. "Go play with your new toy. You know you wanna. Please?"

Jared sighed, picking up the remote and shutting off the television.

"Okay. Guess it wouldn't hurt to give it a test ride. Then take it back in for any adjustments needed." He heard Dawg coming on the run, nosing through the pet-door leading in from the fenced-in backyard. The shepherd came over, sitting in front of him with an expectant look in his eyes. Jared smiled. "You're getting way too smart for your own good. Too bad you don't have these." He held up his hands, rotating his thumbs, then headed toward the garage, Dawg close behind.

The ride had been fantastic, the trails firmly packed by recent rain, providing effortless movement high into the hills. The air was clear, a cold front having pushed through, dragging moisture away leaving behind a clear view of the gated community below, outlined in sharp detail with people moving about on the sidewalks as vehicles slipped between groups of trees. No one in a hurry with a long holiday weekend ahead.

A rabbit flashed across the path: a blur of brown, gone before Jared's eyes could fully register it. One of several using the path to move from place to place, their tracks in the dirt, alongside those of deer and house cats. Along with an occasional dog track, though none were as large as Dawg's.

Jared squeezed the brake handle for the rear tire, a slight squeal warning anyone following too close behind he was slowing down. Not that there was any possibility of a collision today: no one else using the winding trail put in for hiking or biking. The ride up to the secluded pools had been clear of any traffic, by foot or tire, the sandy edges unblemished by footprints, pristine until Dawg lay down in the shallows, using the cool water to help lower his body temperatures. The long-legged animal had made the most of the opportunity during the three-mile run in from the access gate, sprinting ahead, then doubling back, covering twice the distance.

It had been a matter of an hour-long ride for Jared, having to make several stops to reset the chain, adjust the seat angle and height, along with finding the right fit of his helmet. He frowned, having been gone longer than anticipated, wondering if Teresa would notice, looking up from her lapful of magazines, eyeing the clock and wondering where he was. He eased the brake, allowing gravity to pull him down the decreasing angle of slope, slipping through the gate, turning onto the roadway, its smooth asphalt surface glimmering with an oily sheen in the angled rays of late afternoon sun.

"Would you mind?" A soft voice with a southern accent called to him from the right side of the road. A tall, medium framed woman with blond hair waved her hand, standing in a driveway beside a large cardboard box. "I need a hand moving this inside. In case it rains."

Jared pedaled over and slipped from the bike, letting it lean against a neatly trimmed hedge. He approached the woman, who was standing in front of a large, attached garage, its door open, revealing an orderly scene with everything in its place on walls and storage shelves. He nodded, knowing a few more minutes of delay wouldn't matter. "No problem. I can move it inside for you. More than happy to do it."

Jared leaned down, stopping her as she bent over to help, her shirt opening, exposing the top of her ample breasts. "That's okay. I can slide it over. Just give me a second." He gave the large box a shove, moving it with no problem. Then he leaned down and put his shoulder into it, keeping it going, aiming for one side of the two-bay garage. "How's this?"

"Perfect! It will simply thrill my husband, knowing it's inside. Like I said, in case it rains. He's away for a couple of days and was worried about it showing up while he was gone. Kept going on and on about how they'd fucked, I mean, screwed him over, delivering it while he was gone."

"Not a problem now." Jared paused, looking over to check on Dawg, seeing him sitting by the bicycle. "If there's nothing else, I'll be going."

She smiled, her lips overly plump, eyes heavily made up. "Can I get you something to drink? It's the least I can do with you taking time to help me out like this. Interrupting your ride with your doggy, and all."

Jared shook his head, pointing at the over-sized water bottle strapped to the frame of the bike. "Still have plenty of water left. So, I'll be getting back to it." She thanked him again as he pedaled away, a slow wave of his hand in reply.

Jared lay in bed, listening to the soft stir of breathing as Teresa slept, her nose slightly stuffed from a recent increase of pollen in the air, affecting her allergies. He thought about what it must have been like for her, growing up without having learned to ride a bike. Along with her lack of interest in outdoor activities, other than a laughing game of throw the ball for Dawg, then run away as he brought it back. The shepherd bumping into the backs of her legs with his shoulder, spilling her to the ground, then lying across her body while she shrieked at him to let her up, casually dropping the wet ball onto her chest.

Jared knew Teresa was not a child of nature, not that it was an issue for him. Her knowledge and interest in art of any kind provided hours of lively discussion about creative mediums, along with her appetite for scientific, supernatural texts and novels, mirroring that of his own. Their conversations would often center on concepts of life, and what happens afterwards. Delving, occasionally, into quantum physics or the origin of consciousness. Both topics leading them off on long, rambling discussions, with equal measures of give and take, spurring sudden flashes of insight rising to the surface, along with a few heartfelt arguments requiring liberal applications of make-up sex, helping to soothe hurt feelings.

He sighed, unable to sleep, something lurking in the back of his mind, recalling an exchange made months earlier, right before Teresa revealed her feelings for him. When she said he didn't know her, didn't know the mistakes she'd made. She'd been ready to reveal them, until he'd interrupted her, not wanting anything to alter their relationship, new as it was. As he lay beside her now, he wondered what she might have said, and if he'd made a mistake in not letting her tell him.

Dawg came over to the side of the bed, his nose reaching up, touching Jared in his side. Not looking for water, or to be let outside. Just checking in, sensing when there was a need for reassurance. Jared reached over the side of the bed, rubbing the shepherd's thickly muscled neck. He turned his head and whispered. "You—are another miracle in my life. Delivered by the hand of fate. Sent to help me find my way through a dark and troubled world." The same words had been said to him, years ago, a soft voice in the dark from a girl lying beside him, her ebony hair and skin unseen in the shadows. Slipping from his bed, leaving words behind for him to hold onto, offered to the one who'd been her first, as she had been his. Two lonely children, clinging to a moment of shared intimacy before the tide of his life had changed, rising in a tsunami of howling beasts and bright flames, ripping them apart. He rolled onto his side, cupping Teresa's hip, pulling her against him, promising himself it would never happen again.

JD

Before

There was no place he looked where he couldn't see possibilities. Everything revealed. Every word, at his fingertips. Writing effortlessly, again. Mentally clear, because of her. Wherever he turned his gaze, he saw people laughing, relaxed, easing into their day in perfect synchronicity with cast and crew. Because she was there, behind every great idea flowing from the other writers and him. He could feel her energy shining down from every overhead light, every rain bar. From the tip of every camera crane. There, everywhere. His assistant came running up, telling him she was there, on set. In his office.

She stood in the doorway, refusing to sit, looking at him as he sat on the edge of an enormous desk, hands on its surface as he leaned back, eyes staring at the floor of his office. "Are you—certain?"

"Yes."

"When?"

"Planted—or being sprung?"

"Both. I mean, I thought you were, you know—being safe. That you weren't ready—"

"Last month, at my parent's house. In my old bed, with me wearing my cheerleader outfit. The one you just had to see me in, saying it wouldn't fit. Well—it did. And now I'm gonna get fat. Real fat." She looked at him, arms hanging at her side. "Then we'll see how much you love me."

"So—seven months, then. Until."

She smirked, though her eyes revealed her tension. "There's the college math background kicking in. Yeah. Right in the middle of effing summer. In effing L.A."

"I'll take you home. It'll be cooler there. You mother will—"

"No. I'll stay here—wherever you want me to be. Not expecting any special treatment." She looked at him, his face gone blank. "What?"

He shook his head. "I don't know—don't know how I'm going to manage it.

I mean, I might not have enough left over." He looked at her, his face screwed up in a troubled look. "What if I run out? What if I can't make enough of it?"

She narrowed her eyes. "It?"

"Yeah. I mean, I've already given you so much. Everything you could ask for. And now—this." He pointed at her belly, ignoring the pained look on her face. "Something's gonna have to give." He came over and knelt before her, pressing his head against her stomach, his arms circling her hips, pulling her in. "Our child. Our sweet little child. How am I supposed to find enough love for you both? I've already given all I have to you." He looked up, his eyes filled with tears. "Every single drop of it."

She cried, her hand on the back of his neck, belly gently bumping his head. Her tears fell, mixing with those on his cheeks as he looked up at her. She answered him, her voice soft. "Then we'll just have to make more of it. More love. As much as possible in the time we have left until the little—until the little bugger pops its head out and says enough."

CHAPTER THIRTY-SEVEN

HOSPITAL, L.A

Twain And Miranda's Story

The beeping of the heart monitor drove Miranda crazy. She glanced at it, wishing she knew how to turn off the sound, not needing a piece of metal, glass, and electronics to tell her how her man, his head heavily bandaged, was doing. She knew Twain was still there, his hand squeezing hers, flexing every few minutes, tight enough to cause pain. Proof to her he was fighting to get back, despite the old, cold-hearted nurse insisting it was only nerve impulses firing in his damaged brain, signaling his hand. Remnant sequences, she said, stemming from the last thing he'd been doing, just before the accident.

James was sitting in a chair tilted back in the corner of the private room, his head resting against the wall, cowboy boots stretched out in front, hat tilted forward over his eyes. He appeared to be asleep, but Miranda knew he was awake, aware of where she was and how she was feeling. Ready to coax her away to a small bed set up along the back wall when she was ready to give in again and get another hour or so of troubled sleep, over twenty-eight hours having passed since they'd pulled Twain from the wreck.

The host of machines surrounding the head of the bed produced a steady background of white noise, the clicking sounds and throbbing of a red sensor matching Twain's breathing and heartbeat, loud in Miranda's tired ears. A hissing sound came from one of the tiny speakers, sounding like the escaping vapor from the heavily damaged cars radiator as a crowd of people gathered around with torn fingernails and bloody hands pulling debris off the collapsed body of the vehicle. She closed her eyes, head bowed, the memory sharp-edged.

Voices called out, drowning out the steady clicking of the turn signal. Miranda stood a few feet away, held back by Phil, his arm around her shoulders, his hand against her upper chest, his fingers cut, blood starting to clot, getting on her clothing. Miranda was in shock, recognizing the signs, having been in similar situations many times. The thud of a façade shook the ground as a demolition team removed it as a threat to the safety of the people gathered around the pile of crushed metal and bricks. The wavering screams of sirens penetrated the air, hurting her ears as their vibrations cycling through her skull. Miranda was aware Twain was seriously injured, overhearing medics discussing his vital signs. Again, too familiar, understanding the decay of his internal systems, beginning to fail, unable to keep him attached to body and soul. To himself. Not a fight to be won by hopes and prayers, but by will and a determination to hold onto everything he could. To come back to her.

She listened to Phil's words of encouragement, knowing them for the lies they were, though she welcomed his prayers and those of several others, whispering words of support to her as they passed by. Miranda dismissed them, gently, knowing it was as much luck as skill that would end up tilting the odds in Twain's favor, along with his willingness to fight back.

The rescue consumed everyone's attention on the set. Bricks tossed to those who turned and tossed them to others. The body of the car was exposed, roof first, crushed in. Doors cleared next, driver's side first. Tools were brought to bear: jaws of life Miranda thought as she watched them prying open the cage of metal around Twain's unresponsive body. The EMTs lifted him out, carrying him to the nearest ambulance, then driving away with a roar of engines, sirens wailing.

Phil was saying something to her, hard to follow, Miranda listening to a howling in the distance: a continuous and heart-breaking sound from Dawg, voicing his distress. Echoing from the hill where their trailer was placed, raising the hair on her neck and arms. She stumbled away, a scene of destruction from her past flashing before her eyes: mounds of scattered cinder blocks and clay veneer, remnants of a building crumbled in place from a momentary flash of blinding light. A young man wearing a vest concealing blocks of plastique having yelled his final words before disappearing in a cloud of energy that flattened an entire school, a community brough to its knees, spilling a whimpering wash of carnage across a wide street between shattered walls. A mewling cry from those who could still breathe. Silent stares from eyes of those left looking into a void, where the living could not follow.

Phil caught up to her, taking her by the arm. James following close behind, limping slightly, his face streaked with dust. "They got him out. He's alive." Phil pulled Miranda around. "I'll take care of Dawg. I've got a car ready to take you and James to the hospital. Okay?" He leaned in, shaking Miranda's arm. "You were over there—overseas. I know. Twain mentioned it. But this isn't like that. *Look at me!* This is an *accident.* No one trying to get people hurt. *Hey! Look* at me."

Miranda trembled, tears washing down her cheeks. "I'm—I'm okay. I'm good. And you're bleeding. You should let me get some—"

"I'll be fine." Phil released her. "We all will, because of what he did. Because he—" He stopped, his face revealing his pain, and guilt.

Miranda touched him on his shoulder. "It's not your fault, Phil. It's not."

Phil nodded, taking a deep breath, coughing, his lips red from inhaling the dust from the bricks. Then he looked at her. "You've got to go." He paused, shaking his head. "I told you about taking care of Dawg, right?"

Miranda nodded, then turned and headed toward the car, the driver holding the door open. James was right behind her, his hand on her back.

"He's strong. Looks like he's been through something like this before." The head nurse had returned, her shift about to start, coming through the door of Twain's private room and chasing a small army of nurses away whose shifts had ended. She cleared them from the doorway, scolding them, telling them to go home. Miranda came over and stood beside her, looking down at Twain, holding a cup of coffee brought by the older woman who was starting to win her over, despite what she'd said the night before.

"Thank you. For the coffee." Miranda lifted the cup, taking a sip, the flavor bold, strong, and delicious. James stared at her, smiling when she handed it to him. He took a long swallow, sighing with pleasure then handed it back. "Guess I'll head down and see how good the grub is. You want anything?"

Miranda shook her head. The nurse nodded at James. "Go to the coffee bar and ask for Roger. Tell him the gray-haired bitch said to give you the special blend." James grinned, bowing his head. Then he grabbed his hat by the brim and placed it on his head as he left, having to part a new crowd of young nurses, hovering in the hallway outside the door.

"Some positive signs starting to show. His vitals are—good." The nurse took Twain's hand, holding it. Then she leaned down and whispered in his ear. There was a slight response, the tendons in Twain's wrist contracting, then relaxing. "He's still in here." She looked over at Miranda. "Like you were saying—last night."

Miranda noted the comment with a nod, her eyes spilling with tears, hand shaking. The nurse came over and took the cup. "I'd cry myself, if I weren't such a hard-hearted woman." She pulled Miranda over to a chair, helping her to sit down, handing her a box of tissues. Then she picked up a clipboard, turning to leave.

Miranda wiped her eyes, looking up at the head nurse. "What—what did you say to him?"

The nurse turned around, smiling. "I told him he was lucky. Lucky to have such a nice piece of ass to come back to. You know how it is with men—they're all the same."

Miranda stood up, going over and leaning down, carefully placing her head on Twain's chest, ear pressed just firm enough to hear his heart over the sound of the damn beeping, determined to do whatever it took to hold onto her man.

CHAPTER THIRTY-EIGHT

AUNT'S HOUSE, MID-COAST MAINE

Calvin and Jemma's Story

Calvin stared at the piece, deciding it was done. Not perfect, the dark lines of solder running thicker in some places than in others. He convinced himself it added to the handmade effect as he held the stained-glass window up to the morning light, admiring the play of light through the thick, textured pieces of glass. It was early morning and he'd spent the night at his aunt's house, working late to finish it up: the window meant to be an anniversary present, marking the first time he and Jemma had been together, physically, deciding that was when their relationship had become more than co-workers. Now having become much more than friends.

Calvin had formed the scene from dozens of pieces, creating a summer sunrise, captured in a multitude of soft pastel colors. He frowned, considering as he slowly rotating the window. Or a sunset, he mused, taking a moment to look at Dawg, the shepherds head tilted to one side, wondering when they were going to leave. "What do *you* think, Dawg?"

The shepherd woofed, finishing with a soft whine, eager to be released to run to the truck: an intrusive red squirrel back at the farm needing his attention, having dared to venture too close to the farmhouse, poking its small nose and beady eyes where they didn't belong. Calvin shrugged, then used a large black contractor's bag to wrap the present, wondering if he should try to find some ribbon or a left-over bow, tucked away in the eaves of his aunt's attic.

There were a few left over from when he'd cleared out the attic years ago, telling his aunt it was a fire hazard. Priceless memories: his aunt's soft reply. An accommodation reached with hours spent combing through each bag and box pulled from the sun-heated eaves, his aunt shedding tears now and then, holding an old card or faded drawing in her shaking hands, relating a story of how much it meant to her. Leaving Calvin to return most of the tinder dry items to new shelves in the middle of the attic floor, less susceptible to spontaneous combustion. The hours spent with his aunt that day had been safely locked away in his own memories, pulled out from time to time, reflecting on the love she'd shared with him, as close to him as his mother who'd passed away when he was seventeen. Brought in to live with his aunt a year before she'd lost her own son, Carl. Tending to him while recuperating from the same accident, under her continuous care. Everyone else in the family orbit falling away, with sullen looks and stiff faced attitudes whenever he came around.

Calvin carried the window over to the backseat of his battered truck, nestling it in place behind the passenger seat, using a collection of tools, ropes, and assorted work clothes to wedge it in place. Then he opened the passenger door, letting Dawg leap inside. He paused for a moment then closed in Dawg's face, telling him he'd be right back, heading inside to find a ribbon and a bow.

Jemma stood back, eyeing an empty window frame centering a view down the length of the field, feeling the warmth of the rising sun on her face, the light streaming through, painting the interior of the store in a soft, golden hue. She'd been ready to order a new thermal window with built in blinds to buffer the direct sunlight, but Calvin had hemmed and hawed, convincing her to hold off. She'd finally agreed, expecting him to show up with a single-pane window pulled from the broken-backed storage shed at his aunt's house, wanting to save her money, a claim used now and then to try and get his way.

Jemma didn't mind, knowing it was Calvin's attempt to stake a claim to what they were doing to bring the old farmstead into the twenty-first century, wherever possible. She turned around, hearing a crunch of gravel out front, the original surface of the parking area left alone: no solid pavement allowed anywhere on the property. Calvin telling her the granular bed of soil would let water slip through, carried away by the slope, prefiltered by a thick bed of natural gravel beneath the ground as it slipped toward a salt-water marsh a mile away.

Jemma stepped outside, a wide smile on her face, open and inviting, fading away as she watched a huge silver pickup truck rolling to a tire scrunching stop.

"I wanted to apologize. That's all." Tom stood in front of Jemma, hands on his hips. "You never gave me a chance to—"

"To do what? Explain you sticking your cock in someone you knew was my friend? Or assuming, the last time you were here, you'd be spending the night?"

"Look, Jem—we've both made mistakes. That's just the way it is. No one's perfect. Not me or you."

"You're wrong, Tom. You're perfect just the way you are. A perfect asshat!" Jemma held up her hand, forefinger to tip of thumb, thrusting it toward the man standing in the driveway. "So, take yourself out of here, before I call the cops."

Calvin pulled his truck into the edge of the parking area, parking beside Jemma's, halfway on the grass. He recognized the other truck parked there as Toms, the two of them stopping the animated discussion they were having, fixing their attention on him. He lifted his hand, waving, then reached over to open the passenger side door, hesitating, seeing the look of apprehension on Tom's face. "You wait here a second. Let me go and get the lay of the land." He chucked Dawg on the shoulder. "That red squirrel will still be there, and I'm giving you one more day to teach him to stay clear, then I'm popping him with the air rifle." Calvin exited the truck, leaving the present in back, determined to greet Tom halfway, just like before.

Calvin finished securing the new window in place, a perfect fit. He knew it wasn't energy efficient, the dozens of single panes of glass conducive to thermal transfer. But the effect was everything he'd hoped for. He set the straight claw hammer he'd been using down on the far end of the store counter, used to make a few adjustments to the boxed-out section of the opening before putting the screws in. Calvin grinned, listening to Jemma and Tom arguing out in the new building housing the methane powered generator, recently arrived, and mounted on a concrete platform, conduits already in place for the power feeds and fuel lines.

"Why, Jem? To what end?" Tom shook his head, a sad smile on his face. "Pouring all this money in, with no hope of recovering it when you decide to sell."

"I'm not selling, Tom. *Ever.* This is my place. *My* plan."

He looked at her, his voice soft-edged. "Are you sure about that?"

Jemma struggled to stay in control, feeling the tingle of emotions rising in her chest, ready to match him, angry word for angry word when he finally lost it, as she knew he would. One of many reasons she'd left home, deciding to head north. "You'd better be talking about my Granddad."

Tom shook his head. "You're a lot of things, some good—some bad. But you've never been naïve." He stepped closer. "Great set-up here, with all the bells and more than a few whistles too." He reached out, placing one hand on top of the generator, rubbing the glossy shine of the paint. "Everything a man could want." He smirked. "What's not to like? Nice piece of land. New buildings. Along with a sweet piece of—"

"Coffee, anyone?" Calvin came through the two large doors of the new barn, opened, letting the light in. He was holding a large carafe in one hand, a wooden tray with two cups, and a container of light cream in the other. "Fresh ground. Dark roast."

Tom smiled, turning to help Calvin with the tray. Jemma stood still, an army of angry words backed up in her throat, waiting to release them in Tom's direction, forced to hold back with Calvin standing in the line of fire.

"I shouldn't rile her up like that." Tom sipped the coffee, his eyebrows rising as the flavor hit his tongue. "Jesus, Cal—this is some *good* shit."

Calvin nodded, waiting for Tom to finish getting his thoughts out, knowing from before that if left alone to do so, the large man would eventually work his way around to seeing all sides of an issue. It reminded him of his cousin, despite the differences between the two of them. Carl capable of making rash decisions with the talent to turn those mistakes into musical lessons, resonating with his many admirers. Himself, always known around town as Carl's cousin. Never Cal, or Calvin. A relationship he hadn't minded at the time. Better than the way people greeted him after the accident, referred to by his own name, with curt tones and dismissive attitudes. Blamed by most for cutting short the life of one of their own, with talent and opportunity to make a name for himself, reflecting on the entire community.

Tom shook his head. "It's just that—we're so much alike. Both hardheaded. Her, more than me, most times. But you know that already, with the two of you getting together and all."

Calvin held his words, letting his hidden thoughts roll their eyes, marking how wrong the other man was. He knew the day would find its way around to the silver truck pulling away in a spin of gravel, leaving him to listen, nodding his head, while Jemma vented her spleen: poisonous emotions having built up during the hours in between.

Jemma stared at Calvin, who looked back at her without speaking, both locked in a moment where words could not fill the void between them. Jemma broke first, taking a stab at Calvin's off-handed suggestion. "So, you're saying I should just shut up and listen to him. Let him talk, without calling him on his shit. Let him say anything, even when he's saying the most full-of-shit things about—about everything. You. Me. Us. The farm—"

Calvin shrugged. "Why does it matter, Jemma? I mean—in the end he's gone." He paused, turning to look at the empty parking lot, Tom off on a food run, telling him the girl at the center store had given him a sign she would welcome his attention should he decide to stop by on his way out of town. "Besides, he's not as bad as you're always making him out to be. He runs a bit outside the norm, but at least he's consistent."

Jemma stared, her mouth open, then shook her head, her face getting red. "Don't you *dare* defend him! Not to me. I mean it, Cal. That's the *last* thing I need right now." She lowered her head, arms crossed on her chest. "I can't believe you—"

"I'm not defending him. I'm trying to protect you, from feeding into—"

"I'm not needing you to do that. I'm a big girl. Can take care of myself! And there's no danger of me ever, I repeat *ever* letting that a-hole back into any semblance of what my life is like now!"

"I'm not looking to protect you from *him*."

Jemma pulled back. Her eyes narrowed in anger; brow furrowed in confusion. A volatile mix, one Calvin had weathered a time or two in the months they'd been together. He glanced around, wondering what had happened to Dawg. The perfect foil to her rapidly approaching boil. Coming along in a slow amble, nudging Jemma, insisting she pay attention to him, diverting her attention long enough for her emotions to settle. A muted barking let him know it wouldn't happen now, Dawg chasing his tiny archrival, who was leading him on a merry chase along the edge of the backyard.

"So, you're saying *I'm* the one who's wrong? That I'm causing all this— this *crap* to happen whenever he's here?"

"Not what I'm saying, Jemma. Not at all. But you're the one letting it get to you. Taking it way more seriously than you need to. While he—while Tom thrives on the chaos he creates, using it to fuel him, emotionally.

Which sucks for everyone around him. But it's who he is, for whatever reason it is. I just know you're better than that. More—"

"*Fuck* you." Jemma came over and leaned into his face. "You don't have any right to judge me. Hiding in your cave, ducking your head, avoiding responding to the things people say about—have said about you. For years. Undeserved. Unwarranted. Un-*fucking*-fair." Tears sprung from her eyes. "I love you, Calvin. Nothing will ever change that. Nothing. But don't tell me what I am or what I'm not capable of." She reached out, poking him in the chest, emphasizing her words. "That's my prerogative, not yours. Or my father's. Or even my Granddad's. Only *mine*." Then she spun around, going outside, heading to the far end of the field.

Calvin shook his head, knowing he needed to let her cool off. He retrieved the coffee tray and mugs, going inside to make their lunch.

Jemma was standing alongside an old stone wall, head angled down, staring at the ground. Hearing a noise, she looked up, seeing Calvin coming toward her carrying a picnic basket, Dawg in the lead. She reached out, taking his hand as he came up. "Sorry. I know you were just trying to help. And you're right, I do that. Not with you—but with Tom. And my father, too. Both cut from the same material. Thick slabs of stone, for all the thinking they put into things. Relationships, being one of a hundred examples." Jemma looked away.

"Not a problem. I'm good."

"But it *should* be, Calvin." Jemma shrugged, her voice low. "If only so you could let me know how much of a bitch—" He didn't let her finish, dropping the basket to the ground, and taking her in his arms, kissing her. Long enough that she had no choice but to respond, her hands slipping up, cupping his neck, pulling him in until he pulled back, breaking her embrace to catch his breath.

Dawg swung his nose between the two of them and the basket, its top popped open, revealing a collection of food and handful of treats. A clear sign to him it was time for his pack-mates to eat.

The silver truck was back in the parking area, Tom nowhere in sight. Jemma and Calvin skirted the generator building, angling toward the store. As soon as they stepped inside, Jemma gasped, the interior of the wood-paneled room resplendent in a rainbow of colors, tinted by the stained-glass window Calvin had installed when he arrived. "When did you—?"

"This morning, before bringing out the coffee. Before—well—all the rest."

"Oh, Calvin—it's beautiful!" Jemma walked over, tracing the uneven lines of solder, rubbing her fingertips on the thick, textured pieces of glass. "You made this. For our store."

"For you." Calvin came over and leaned his chin on top of her shoulder. "That's why I was having you hold off on ordering a window. Thought it would be good to add some color."

Jemma spun around and gave him a hug, her cheek pressed to his chest. "I don't know why you put up with me. I can get so—"

"Human. Real. Someone with feelings, who's not afraid to show them?"

"Bitchy. Moody. Unreasonable, and unfair."

"Potato. *Potahto.* All I know is—" He kissed the top of her head, breathing in the scent of her hair. "We're a perfect match."

Jemma leaned her head back, then stretched up, whispering in his ear. "I love you, Calvin."

A cough came from the doorway leading into the main house, utilized as a dining area. Tom was standing there, a piece of pie in his hand, crumbs of crust and small berries falling to the tile floor as he took another bite. "Soon as you two get out of the way, I'll be heading out."

Calvin stepped back, releasing Jemma as he sat the picnic basket on the counter, then headed inside to get a mop to clean the floor. Jemma stared at Tom as he brushed by, angry again, amazed at how quickly it had returned. She closed her eyes, taking a deep breath and letting it out. Dawg, sitting in the store's corner, watched her, cautious, but on alert, as if sensing the coming storm.

Tom held the last of the pie in one hand, giving Jemma a quiet look. "Looks like you two are getting serious. Got here too late, I guess, to open your eyes."

"My eyes *are* open, Tom. And you're right, we are serious. And you want to know why?"

Tom dropped the pie on the floor, then stepped on it with the heel of his boot, grinding it into a section of the recently sanded original wooden flooring, staining it blue. "Can't wait to find out, Jem. Please—enlighten me."

Jemma forced herself to ignore the stained floor, hands clenched at her side. "Because he's a real man. Knows how to treat people with kindness and respect. Women, men, and animals too." She looked for Dawg, but he'd disappeared. "Always willing to listen. Letting everybody get their say—without interrupting. Something you're incapable of, your ego getting in the way, even when you're trying to be half-way decent, tripping you up because it so big."

"Sounds like you're talking about this." Tom grabbed himself, leering, his eyes bright, face turning red. "You two deserve each other. You, still playing the role of fucking martyr, like no one's ever been screwed around on before. And he's no different than me, Jem. Just hasn't had to put up with your bullshit long enough to—"

"Careful, Tom." Jemma was standing in front of the new window, her silhouette framed by the light, washing over her in soft colors.

"Oh. Okay." Tom raised his hands, backing away. "Jem's rules, just like always. Nothing's changed. You're still the same—" Tom hesitated, unsure what his next move should be.

Jemma leaned forward, placing her palms on the counter. She kept her voice low, her words measured, letting go of her anger. "I feel sorry for you, Tom. I really do. Able to see, for the first time the hurt little boy you've always been. No one understanding how frightened you are—afraid someone will see that in you. Calvin's right, you're not a bad guy. You're not stupid. You're just a sad little boy, trying to act like a man."

Tom straightened up, a tic in his cheek making it jump. His eyes glazed over, hands clenching, arms trembling. "*Fuck you*, Jem. Fuck you and your *plans*. And your back-woods boyfriend and his piece of *shit* dog!" He spun around, heading to the door: a large woven basket hitting him in the back of his head, triggering an immediate response. He spun around, his hand closing on the handle of a hammer lying on the far end of the counter. He threw it at the stained-glass window, Jemma reaching up, diverting it with her hand.

Calvin stepped through the door from the house with a dish towel and bottle of cleanser in his hand, catching the straight end of the hammer claws in the side of his head, dropping him to the floor. His body hit, the hammer still embedded, driven further in as he landed, hands outstretched, fingers twitching as lightning coursed through his mind. His vision fading, the last thing he saw: Jemma reaching for him, her eyes filled with a look of horror.

JD

Before

She touched her belly, responding to the press of a small fist. Felt, but still not seen. The first brush of butterfly wings having started a month ago. The faintest whisper of what was to come. That first touch turning in to an exploratory poke, increasing each week into what had become an all-out assault as a new life struggled to remain in control of their increasingly compressive environment, demanding more room. While its father busied himself in fulfilling his commitment, banking up as much love as possible before the blessed event, still a handful of months away.

The filming of his latest creative effort was well along, his mentor having signed on as co-director and godfather to their child, the latter title holding the most meaning to the older man, his aged face beaming whenever he saw her on set, rushing to take her by her elbow, escorting her around, asking a host of questions as to her health, emotions, and any new developments having to do with the baby.

Her husband the same way, looking over at her during every break, his eyes full of hope, wanting a daughter. With her promising him she'd do everything possible to deliver a healthy child, no matter the sex. A slight moment of alarm in his eyes when she teasingly suggested it might be twins, leaving her having to admit the truth as he dragged her toward the bedroom, determined to produce even more love.

The naming process had settled into a game of give and take. His mother's name discarded out of hand, with no consideration allowed, refusing any such attachment to the 'project' as he was calling it. Her own mother's middle name slipped in ahead of her cousin's, a suggestion met with nods from the members of her family, halfway across the country. Approved with warm smiles by a circle of close friends, scattered throughout the greater L.A. basin.

She sighed, remembering what they had gained over the past two years, their lives becoming a dream well earned. Paid for with sweat, tears, and the gut-wrenching pain of withdrawal. Nourished with will, commitment, creative energy, and love. All of himself now offered her. More than she felt she deserved. Doing all she could to return the same.

CHAPTER THIRTY-NINE

SEAFOOD RESTAURANT, MARYLAND

Cheryl

Cheryl sat beside Jean, sharing their booth with Mari: the four of them at the restaurant with Isaac sitting in a chair at the end of the booth, his enormous body too large for the table. It was an overcast day, the dining area shadowed, sunlight unable to penetrate through the wall of windows, their curtains lowered with the doors closed. Opening was still two hours away: a handful of staff busy in the kitchen preparing food, restocking the bar, leaving the small group to tend to themselves with Jean bringing over a tray of drinks.

Mari, invited to attend by a note slipped into her hand by Jean, knew the officer had become an integral part of the doctor's plan to stymie the wide release of her technology until scientific councils and governmental agencies could put controls in place, limiting its use. Mari aware it would eventually get out into the world at large, despite Cheryl's best efforts. Their best efforts now, she added, with Isaac made part of the team. All of them willing participants, understanding the depth and reach of each other's capabilities, and their willingness as a group to see the fruitless plan through.

Jean removed the empty glasses from the first round of drinks, bringing a large dish of fish nuggets and bowls back to the booth, along with glasses of water for the others, and another mug of ale for himself. Cheryl waited until he sat back down then leaned forward. "There may be consequences, professionally *and* personally—for you both." Cheryl eyed Mari and Isaac, waiting for them to acknowledge her comment with a nod of their heads. "Consequences that will require you to actively subvert my efforts. To do your best to derail my life's work."

"Again." Isaac spoke, his voice subdued, words directed at Jean, gauging how the man felt about his betrayal, despite the assurances Cheryl had given him. She leaned in, sensing his unease.

"Jean understands, Isaac. And knows I'd already factored what happened into my equations, long before the project started. All possibilities considered *and* covered, including your actions and Mari's." She looked around the table. "Every possible scenario considered—and planned for."

"Other than the possibilities of your *own* missteps." Isaac fixed Cheryl with a solemn stare. "I'm amazed at the width and incredible depth of your ego. Well-hidden, when out in public. But when you're in the lab, focusing in on the meat of an issue and trying to force the results to go your way—it's something, watching you wrestle with it." He lowered his eyes, looking at his fingers, avoiding her stare. "I wonder, Cheryl, whether you've taken *all* possibilities into account, in not allowing anyone to look over your shoulder, making an equally dispassionate assessment of your potential to—*fuck* things up."

Cheryl looked at Isaac without reacting, her fingers trembling slightly as she reached for her water, with Jean and Mari taking notice. "What makes you think I'm having to wrestle with a solution? Or that I'm unaware of the—*size* of my ego? I admit I *have* one, like everyone else sitting at this table. Mine not all *that* different."

Isaac shook his head. "I could almost believe you're serious. That you actually see yourself that way."

Cheryl clenched her lips, turning to look down the length of the hall. "Someone else told me the same thing—a long time ago."

Cheryl took a deep breath, letting it out, staring at Robert while she held on to the limb of the tree. Her forearms were burning, causing her to lose count of how long she'd been hanging there. Determined not to let go. To continue defying gravity's relentless pull while Robert watched, shaking his head, a sad look on his face as he held a stopwatch in his hand.

"I met this man, a while back—living in the area doing odd jobs. One of the original recreational climbers, opening a host of new routes—long before advanced climbing equipment and techniques came along. He took me under his wing, teaching me things that couldn't be learned in magazines or books, written by neophytes with enough money to buy their way to the top of walls. Paying guides to haul them up routes hammered in place by people with far less skill. *Punks*—like me."

Robert leaned back against the trunk of the tree, crossing his arms on his chest, checking his kid sister's time. "He told me it was always there, waiting for every one of us." He paused, looking up into the limbs of the tree. "The abyss. Ready to pull people from wherever they were, climbing or not, all the way to the hard end of a long fall." He paused, seeing Cheryl's face, her lips pressed tight, tears in her eyes, refusing to let go. "And then there's the wall, waiting to shrug off the weak or the careless." Robert felt a sense of warmth run through him, measuring Cheryl's will against his own, proud of her stubborn spirit. "Along with those with skill, but *blind* to their limitations. Unable to see themselves for who they *really* are, where their capabilities end. He told me I was as daring as any of them—the new wave of climbers. With more skill and far greater will. Even more than his own."

"It is. You're—my brother. Best—climber in—the *world!*" Cheryl's voice, thinned by exhaustion, was a strained whisper, her fingers beginning to slip, her shoulders and forearms on fire.

"I'll never know. Never got the chance to climb with him."

Cheryl fell from the limb, hitting the ground, her legs folding, absorbing the shock. She rolled to one side, lying there, unable to move: shoulders, arms, and hands throbbing in pain. "So, you never got to find out. To go up there with him and find out who was better."

"I *could* have gone. Should have, but never did."

Cheryl turned her head, looking up at her brother: the question in her eyes unasked. Robert shrugged. "I did *consider* it, dozens of times. Thought about trying one of the maidenhead routes he'd scouted out. To claim it for myself."

"To be the first."

"It would have been wrong—him not being there to help guide me."

Cheryl frowned, shaking her head, lying on her back while she shook out her arms and wrists, encouraging the blood to return. "Because he didn't want you to be first. Right?"

"No. Because he fell off a ladder, helping paint a barn. Broke his back. They lugged him away and stuck him in a home, where I watched him wither away, dying a few weeks later."

Cheryl closed her eyes, imagining the horror of not being able to climb. Her brother came over and helped her to lean up, gently massaging the blood back into her upper arms and shoulders. "And the lesson taught?" His voice was soft, his fingers firm, kneading her muscles, causing pain that Cheryl ignored as she considered his question. She angled her head back, the feeling in her hands returning in pins and needles. "Tell me."

"Will is a tool—*and* a weapon. A small dose can help you work out when to push on or pull back. Using too much of it, going beyond your limitations—you can die." He snapped his fingers near his sister's ear, causing her to jump. "Just like *that*. The same goes with ego."

"But—"

Robert cut her off. "No buts, Chipmunk. There's no other way to say it, or to see it. Gravity and the wall—they don't care. They never will. You need to care about yourself and your partner, when climbing where few dare go. Knowing how to thread the line between too much and too little. Whether it's will, ego, strength—or fear."

"I shouldn't have held on so long." Cheryl scrunched up her face, a spasm of pain coursing through her shoulders as Robert worked to loosen her tendons. "Risking damage to myself. Then no more climbing until I heal." She sighed. "I *still* have a lot to learn." Robert didn't answer, silent, gently brushing his fingers through the curled mop of her tangled hair. She pulled away, turning around, and looking up at him. "I *promise*, Robbie. I promise to learn as *much* as I can, so I can go with you. To the *top* of all of them. You and I, together. I swear it. I'll find the balance. I will. You'll see."

He brother nodded. "I'm sure you will, *mop* head. Just hope I'm still around when you do. It might take a while, knowing how stubborn you can be."

Isaac waited, along with the others to see what Cheryl's reaction would be, with Jean giving him a long, searching look until she finally responded. "Your point is—valid. And I'll need to let *all* of you help me with the long-term planning. To try and decide what and how much to share with the enemy camp." She gave each one of the team a short nod. "But *I'm* the one in charge, with final say on what we end up doing. Okay?"

"I *like* the idea of us being double agents." Mari slid over, closer to Isaac, feeling connected to him. "Working against the one's looking to take control, letting them know about the system's weaknesses, planting false flags." She looked at Cheryl, who'd ordered a margarita, sipping it while working her way through a small helping of fish nuggets. "Ones you'll be deliberately programming in. Allowing them to break it, reprogram it the way *they* want, then using it in a host of applications."

Cheryl leaned back in the booth, amazed by Mari's insight. "Yes, with them using tools still in development. Today. By bright young minds working with enough computational power to ensure they'll find a way to untwist the strings of my code. Forcing them to spend more time and money, delaying them as long as possible while they chase unicorns. Until they finally find what they *think* they're after. Holding them off long enough for the authorities to have a say in how to use the technology. To prevent, or at least *limit* the potential for its misuse."

They dedicated the rest of their meeting to drinking, eating, and further discussions on how to protect the secrecy of their subversive attempt to resist the corporate stooges who were looking to create a world where people could be manipulated into staying in their assigned lanes. Satisfied to live and work as thinking, organic robots.

After the other two left, Jean looked at Cheryl and sighed "That was *not* a pretty picture." He shook his head. "I mean—you can't let all you've worked for be used to provide *that* outcome. People led around by their noses, like cattle, eager to leap into railroad cars, to be carted off to the slaughterhouse."

"Bet the guy who invented trains never imagined them being used like that. Guess I just have a more—sinister imagination."

Jean shook his head. "I haven't known you very long, but I call *bullshit*." He kept his voice low, leaning in. "You've got *something* cooked up. I can tell. Been on the pointy end of a *fuck-stick* often enough to tell when something's off in the local environment. And I'm smelling an ambush." He paused, giving Cheryl a hard stare. "Just trying to figure out who's being lured into the kill zone. Them—or us."

"I like the sound of that." Cheryl, noting Jean's confusion, leaned against him, taking his hand in hers and squeezing it. "The *us* part. And I promise you—it's not going to be end up biting us in the butt." She reached out with her free hand and pulled the paper umbrella from her drink, spinning it around, staring at it. "I'm going to allow them to extend their line of approach. Establish a few hundred thousand forward bases. Let them build up mountains of my innovative munitions before forcing them to have to swap out from the—those guns they were using back—"

"Rifles."

"Yeah. Rifles. Like the old ones they were using in the war—the one in the jungle, before they changed over to the newer ones. The ones the toy company was making."

"Your mean the old, reliable M-14's. Swapped out for M-16's, with major design flaws in the beginning. And the—toy company—who never made the *rifles*, only fabricated a few of the components. Like the plastic grips."

"It doesn't change the point I'm trying to make." Cheryl pulled away slightly, looking up at Jean, a smug look in her eyes. "I want them to think they have me well in hand. Have control of my code and my program. *That's* the real prize. The other, the Tee-Cee, easy enough to replicate. But my code—that's unique."

"And eventually, as you said, *breakable*. Right?" Jean looked at the woman he knew was as unique as her invention. Knowing he couldn't imagine not having her in his life. He waited for her to answer him, a sense of unease in his voice as she shook her head. "What have you *done?*"

Cheryl shrugged. "Nothing. *Yet.*" Jean held his breath, staring until he had to exhale, as if discovering an IED beside a trail, wondering when it would explode. "I'm just giving them what they're looking for: a way to assert control in a process that will reinvent the way the world runs." Cheryl bit her lower lip, waiting to see if Jean would buy her story. "That's all."

"And what happens then? After they get the—get the bases built and the ammunition all swapped over?"

"It all goes—" Cheryl raised her hands in the air, fingers spread open. "*Kablooie.*"

CHAPTER FORTY

PRIVATE YACHT, NEWPORT, RHODE ISLAND

Luther

"Have a drink, Luther. It's not *poison*, though enough of it *will* kill you."
Ed motioned for Luther to pour himself a margarita from a sweat-lined
pitcher sitting in the center of the table, surrounded by wide-rimmed
glasses, already salted, along with a small dish of sliced limes. The two of
them were sitting on a large yacht, tied up alongside a long pier.

"Your reference to poison and death is noted." Luther gave Ed a small
nod. "I'm fine with water."

Ed sighed, scratching his belly, leaning back in a padded chaise lounge,
enjoying the sun. "You're a single-minded man, Luther. A single-minded
man." He glanced at Luther, the thin man sitting in the shade. "It suits you,
and the job you're paid to do. Though not nearly enough in compensation
based on what we stand to gain. Most of it coming from your advice and
efforts made, helping us to succeed." Ed paused. "*If* all goes as planned."

Luther shrugged, allowing the slight revelation of his inner-most feelings. "There is always that caveat in any endeavor, with failure being the
wisest of teachers, which will not happen with *this* opportunity."

Ed pursed his lips, resting the glass in his hand atop his ample abdomen, staining the silk shirt he was wearing. He leaned back, looking up
at the sun, his eyeglasses reflecting its image. "I never quite know how to

take your meaning, Luther. Often left having to pull your sentences apart, then put them back together again, trying to see if there's more there than meets the ear."

Ed took a sip of his drink, enjoying the mixed flavors: the tequila a custom product, unavailable to the public. Not that he gave a damn about exclusivity, the purchase of several dozen cases made because he understood the complexity of the distillation process, having seen it for himself firsthand. With his fingers stained by the soil where the agave plants grew. Working with the field hands, wearing the same garb, sweat running down his face and on his back as he spent a long day in the fields, side by side with them as they collected the key ingredient. "I've decided to increase your salary, as well as that of this Coleman woman."

Luther nodded. "It's Mari. With an I. From her mother's lineage. Asian."

"Mari—with an I." Ed studied Luther's face. "I stand corrected, again. A recent habit of late, my being corrected by you. Not sure I like what it means. Either you're getting smarter or I'm getting—"

"You shoulder a great responsibility, while I am but a funnel of— informed data. In support of your, or rather, of the *group's* cause."

"A rare equivocation on your part." Ed stared at Luther, then took another sip of his drink, the glass sweating as the ice melted.

Luther nodded. "This is a rare time in human history."

Ed leaned forward, holding out his cup, watching as Luther placed several cubes into it with a set of tongs, then carefully refilled it. A new wedge of lime offered and accepted. "Indeed, it is, my friend." He paused, taking a sip. "Is that an accurate term, for how you see our relationship?"

"It is accurate for what you are to me. However, I would suggest someone in your position steer clear of those who profess to be your friend whenever possible. Especially those with—equally large egos."

"You mean Thomas—with his big brass Texas sized cojones?" Ed laughed, his drink slopping over, further staining his shirt, its light-red fabric turning the color of blood.

Mari studied the thin piece of paper the thin man handed her, hand-written in squid ink on rice paper, designed as a onetime transfer of critical information.

"I assume you know what to do with it, once you've memorized the contents." Luther nodded at the list he'd provided her, containing names and dates of the meetings he'd attended and the names of the people who'd been there. A trove of information, serving as evidence to the negative of when certain well-known figures had gone missing from the view of those following their every move. Markets known to rise or fall based on a speculative review of each one's facial expressions, tone of words, and posture. He watched the younger woman's eyes widen as she reached the section detailing the transfer of monies into her account: their release pending, based on what she was expected to provide at their next meeting.

Mari scanned the list, allowing the data to scroll through her mental vision as if credits at the end of an epic movie. She had an eidetic memory, a genetic gift from her grandfather on her father's side. Her hands were trembling, the increase in money tripling her income, aware the man on the other side of the desk was taking careful note. He seemed almost reptilian, his stoic demeanor and staring eyes watching her as if he were able to taste the air, able to sample the scent of her breath, her sweat, her every thought. She nodded sharply, the data transfer complete, then wadded the paper into a compressed ball and placed it in her mouth, her saliva instantly turning it into a slimy pulp.

Luther reached over, handing Mari a cup of lukewarm tea, gratefully accepted, hastily swallowed to clear her throat. He watched as she stared into it, knowing she was looking at the Asian symbols he'd selected for her, represented two words: white and tiger. A nod to the light coloration of her skin and her potential for actions taken from the shadows. "We have an understanding."

Mari nodded, projecting a calmness she did not feel. "Of a sort, yes."

Luther stared at her, the corners of his thin lips moving up a fraction of a millimeter, threatening to crack into a smile. "It will become clearer, as we work together, what needs to be done—and when." Mari stood, giving the still unnamed man a small nod before turning around and leaving the small room, knowing the meeting was at an end and that he would not stop her as she left, with a whisper-thin question, gently tossed her way.

Luther stood up and retrieved the cup: a valuable piece crafted by an ancient artisan. Collected during his stay in the far east, seven years of his life spent studying with master practitioners of Taoism, learning secrets from those standing at the end of a line stretching back through dozens of generations. He'd given himself over to all they asked and offered in return, able to recognize when they were holding back, protecting knowledge forbidden to outsiders. Telling in its absence, their shadowed expressions hiding unspoken truths, ones he'd carefully sifted for from thousands of characters in hundreds of texts, revealing secrets measured by the shape and size of their influence on negative space.

Luther hummed a simple tune as he rinsed the thin-walled cup, using spring water delivered from a temple located high in the mountains of China. Packaged by a friend living in a small village nearby, put into wax sealed ceramic containers, placed inside a handmade wooden crate, moved across the ocean and a continent by air, at extravagant cost. An indulgence he allowed himself: the ritual of the tea ceremony admired for its simplistic, exacting motions. He sighed, returning for a moment to the last time anyone had seen him for who he was, and not for how he looked.

CHAPTER FORTY-ONE

HOSPITAL, L.A.

Twain and Miranda's Story

"I told you—I'd be okay." Twain's voice was a husk of its former self, his attempt to smile failing as a grimace of pain cycled through his head. Miranda touched his lower right arm, one of the few spots unmarked by the crash and frenzied attempt to pull him from the crushed cage of the vehicle, engine hissing, with gas leaking, the chance of fire imminent.

"Lie still and let your body heal—you idiot."

"You're crying. Again."

Miranda smiled, wiping her eyes. "Allergies from all the pollution. You can have your L.A. smog. I'll stick with New York's."

"Or maybe—somewhere in between." Twain's voice was stronger, his words clear as he adjusted to the limited flexibility of his tightly bound chest, having suffered several broken ribs, added to the menu board hanging from the foot of his bed, with a long list of his other injuries.

Miranda leaned in, touching her nose to his, her eyes widening in a pretense of surprise. "Are you suggesting I quit my job and move in with some famous Hollywood actor? To live in sin. In my mother's house?"

"As a matter of fact—I am."

"Okay." Miranda straightened up. "I've got nothing *better* to do. Sitting around here all day, waiting for you to get back to work. Might as well get *something* out of it." She paused, considering. "Is Arizona a common property state? You know, fifty-fifty, leaving me with half of whatever you're worth?" Twain slid his hand out from under the top sheet covering his chest, his middle finger extended.

James put his arm around Miranda's shoulders, her face gone white with shock, the doctor giving her a moment to accept the news. Dawg, allowed in to visit Twain, was sitting beside the bed, muzzle pressed against his side. He lifted his head and looked over, sensing her distress.

"The tumor is—well, it's treatable, as to relieving the outward symptoms. But it's going to prove difficult, if not impossible to remove."

"Did the accident—" Miranda stopped, her voice cracking, struggling to steel her emotions, having seen more than a few close friends and professional acquaintances lose their lives while covering conflicts overseas.

"Cause it? No. Not as far as the tumor goes. But the scan of his head did reveal it, so that's something. Gives you time to—"

James shook his head, giving the younger man a sharp look as he touched Miranda on her shoulder. "Come on. We'll go outside and let this sink in before we wake him up." He started to usher Miranda through the door, but she pulled away, shaking her head, drying her eyes as she went over to Twain. She reached down, rubbing Dawg's ears, letting him know it was time to go out and use the grass facilities. James snapped his fingers, calling him away.

Miranda took Twain's hand, his breathing labored, eyes closed, eyelids moving as he dreamed. His color had faded, as pale as the plastic bags feeding vital fluids into his body, other more colorful liquids draining away, leaving him balanced somewhere in the middle as he waged a battle to survive. One she knew he would lose, eventually. She watched him, waiting for him to wake up so she could let him know where he stood, thinking about the trip they'd been considering as soon as he recovered from the accident. A hike into a place called Havasu Falls, a journey that had been on her bucket list for years, now added to his, Twain had told her he loved the idea of them doing it together, hand in hand. The same way they'd been spending their time looking at pictures and videos online. Miranda gazed down at him, wondering if the local tribal authorities would allow her to make the trek, while carrying an urn beneath her arm.

Cheryl watched the monitor, the scene unfolding in real-time, her heart going out to the woman, although she knew she didn't exist. A fragment of the three stories being played out by JD's creative mind, the question of whether she'd ever existed, still to be answered. Cheryl was tempted to slip the spare Tee-Cee on and see if JD would show up, willing to answer her if asked the question. She decided to wait, a plan in development that Isaac had suggested, designed to use the full potential of her unique programming tool to shake things up in the imaginary world of JD's damaged mind.

CHAPTER FORTY-TWO

LAB, REASEARCH FACILITY, MARYLAND

Cheryl

"He's putting them out of commission. Leaving them in comas, in hospital beds." Isaac eyed Cheryl, waiting for her to comment. "Another point in common—between *two* of the three projections. So far."

"It seems that way. And makes sense too, the head wounds matching up along with the scarring on JD's left shoulder." Cheryl glanced at her improved program running on her laptop, busily digesting a new set of commands aimed at enhancing the identification of specific points of commonality hiding in the petabytes of data stored on her servers. A task impossible to resolve in a workable time frame with current search programs, including her original version, which the corporate entity had in hand. Her latest version, two days spent in rewriting it, was proving to be up to the task. "Other than with Jared—so far."

She stood up, using her hands to ease the stiffness in her lower back: an hour spent at the Rockery earlier in the day having helped to clear her mind, though it was leaving its mark now. "It seems our friend is looking to pull back, willing to sacrifice the externalized versions of himself, trying to protect the insular one. The *real* one. Helping us zero in on the obvious choice."

Isaac headed to the refrigerator, bringing back two sodas. He sat down, opening one, taking a long swallow, covering a burp with one hand. "Jared. Not the one *I* was betting on." He saw Cheryl staring at him. "What? Like *you* don't have a favorite?" He offered her the other soda, knowing she'd refuse it.

"I *do*. But we can't be certain it's *any* of them. I'm mean—I'm starting to think they're not—" Cheryl pointed at the door of room number one. "Really *him*. More like defensive mechanisms, designed to prevent his having to face the memory of whatever happened." She looked at Isaac, who was shaking his head. "You don't agree?"

"No. Not without evidence for or against it. Besides, if I was trying to hide something from you—" He clenched his lips, staring at the floor.

Cheryl looked at him. "It's still *us*, Isaac, working through this together. Maybe you should let go of what—"

"It's not *that*, Cheryl. I just had an idea—about his personal motivation." Isaac leaned back, his arms crossed, the can of soda held between his fingers. "I mean, I've never really cared one way or another who he—who JD is. Just another challenge to be dealt with. More difficult than the others we've worked with to uncover, with no defined starting point to work back to. But, as to having some burning desire to solve whatever his problem is, then no. It's only a job, nothing more. If he wanted to be left alone, I was fine with that. Just needed him to give up his name, so we can wrap this up and move on."

Cheryl nodded, her lips tight with regret, knowing Isaac was voicing a contrarian view of what he really felt. "Like that guy in the story. The children's story—about some girl with a wooden wheel who was trying to guess who he was."

"A spinning wheel. And his name was Rumpelstiltskin."

"That's the one." Cheryl softened her tone, staring at him. "And I know you're not serious. You *can't* be serious, seeing the way you are with him— have been with JD since the very first day."

"Do you, Cheryl? Do you really think you see me? That you *know* me?"

"I—thought I did."

"Think again, boss. Might do your ego good, having to stop and question your assumptions." Isaac raised his hand, palm out. "I'm sorry. Didn't mean it to come out like that. It's just that you seem to have lost your dispassionate viewpoint about this project. Obvious enough to me, at least, in how you're continually placing demands on him, unlike the others we've helped." He nodded toward JD's room. "You seem to have let it become personal, as if you're trying to sublimate your feelings—because of what happened to your brother."

The room in the nursing home was a cavern, dimly lit, with heavy curtains drawn across the only window. Cheryl stood in the doorway of her brother's room, hands on her hips, frowning as she noted the shadowed interior. She strode over to the window and yanked back the thick layers of sound-deadening fabric, shoving the heavy pane of glass to one side. Air flowed in, causing the door of his room to swing shut, sealing with a muffled thud

Cheryl looked over to see if her brother would react to the increase in light or the noise, but his face remained still, eyes closed, like he'd been ever since the accident, over a year ago. It was the same look he'd worn when they wheeled him out of the recovery room in the hospital: a team of doctors doing what they could to repair the damage from the rock that struck him down. A fluke accident, the ranger said, the angular stone barely rating a second look when stumbled over while hiking. Of little consequence, with little result beyond a bruised toe or dirty hands braced against a face-plant in the trail. But deadly as a bolt of lightning when under the tug of gravity, dropping toward the ground below, meeting an uncovered skull left momentarily unprotected, a constant threat when climbing in mountains, more so in some places than others.

"Time to wake up, sleepyhead. Daylight's burning. Got places to be, walls to climb, so rise and shine!" Cheryl busied herself adjusting Robert's pillow, propping him up so sunlight could reach his face. Easier now, his weight having dropped off during the months of his silent non-recovery, his head long healed, mind yet to return, at least far enough to let others know he was still there. But she knew he was in there, able to sense him listening to her, reading her emotions as easily as she could read his. No one able to convince her otherwise. Not anymore. The people working in the facility having finally bowed to her adamant insistence Robert was going to be fine, in time. That everyone needed to be patient and keep prodding him with words and actions, letting him know he was still part of the world. Of the local environment. Of his family, with the two of them spending hours together, every day.

"Our Lady of bright sunlight and fresh air is returned, I see." The door was half-open, a young minister from the local Congregational church leaning in. "How is your brother Robert doing today?"

"He's still being a stubborn donkey-*butt!*" Cheryl grinned at the minister: a patient man with a humorous side, always willing to drop by for a visit when she was unable to get there due to a school project or doctor's appointment.

"An—elegant description. I applaud your efforts at reducing your proclivity toward the use of coarse language." He paused, then started to explain what proclivity meant, stopping when the young girl made a face, letting him know she was aware of the words meaning. He moved onto another subject of potential concern. "How are *you* doing? All caught up on your schoolwork?"

Cheryl nodded, her hands busy combing her brother's hair, in need of a trim, but clean, her thrice weekly washings keeping it gleaming and neat, with his face shaved on the same schedule, her ability to perform both tasks accepted as normal by the facility employees, looking on her efforts with warm smiles, aware she brought positive energy with her into all the other patient's rooms, making sure to circulate between them during her frequent visits, checking in on each resident. Coming in before and after school, with entire days spent there on weekends and holidays. Patients and staff had bowed to her unwavering will and dedication, directed at keeping a rock-solid connection with her older sibling, though the minister noticed the silence filling the void between Cheryl and her parents as the family unit slowly dissolved away. He closed the door, a look of concern on his face as he walked away.

"There is a need to discuss the—*difficult* realities before us." The doctor looked at both of Cheryl's parents, waiting until they nodded, silently accepting his judgment as to their son's care. "The damage is permanent. Recovery—beyond reach. I would recommend continued treatment, as little of that as is possible in his case, if there were any chance of a return to consciousness."

"He's still here!" Cheryl was sitting on the side of Robert's bed, holding his hand, squeezing it as hard as she could, hoping to cause enough pain to wake him up, proving the man in the white coat was a liar: that her brother would sit up, opening his eyes, calling her Chipmunk as he reached out and tousled her hair, cut short like his.

Her mother started over, stopping when Cheryl pinned her with a glare. "This is all *your* fault!" She looked at her father, his hands hovering at his sides, unable to meet her eyes. Little more to her than ghosts, standing in the shadows of her world, less alive than Robert. "You two have *no* right—"

The minister came over and placed his hand on her shoulder. "They do have the right, Cheryl. By blood and by law." He knelt, taking her hand. "Robert was strong. I know he—"

"You don't *know* him! You never *knew* him."

"Through your stories of him, I do. And based on everything you've told me, the things you've shared with me, held between us in a sacred pact, that if he could reach out right now and speak to you, what would he ask of you? From you?" The minister pointed at where her parents stood, having retreated to the far wall, unable to meet her accusatory stare. "What would he ask from them?" He leaned in, his voice low. "We can want something to be true—can wish for it with all our heart—but in your brother's case there's no compelling reason to keep him here when a far better place is waiting for him. For us all, one day. His day now."

Cheryl allowed him to coax her to her feet and encourage a final kiss, a last goodbye. Then he eased her toward the door where two men in suits were standing, paperwork in their hands, waiting for signatures. With a sudden yank away from the minister's grasp, Cheryl threw herself across the room, hands reaching for her brother's face. She slapped him, twisting his hair, trying to shock him back to her side of reality. The doctor and minister grabbed her hands, stopping her, an orderly rushing in to help the minister carry her from the room, the door closed behind as her wails of abject misery echoed along the hall.

The small rectory was an island of silence. Empty, other than the young girl and minister, with his arm draped around her shoulders, tears in both of their eyes, in need of mutual comforting. The door sighed open, one of the orderlies who'd help bring Cheryl there looking in, nodding, retreating with a sad look on his face.

The minister whispered. "Your brother has passed. I'm so—"

"No. He's not gone. I can still feel him."

"In spirit, yes. That part of him will remain with—"

"No. He's *still* here. I can feel him." Cheryl placed her hand on her chest. "Here. Not in one of those idiotic versions of some kinda afterlife."

"You mean—you don't accept he is with our Lord. Correct?"

"No." Cheryl shook her head, looking up at the minister with a solemn expression on her young face. "My brother taught me about the actual world, not some two-thousand-year-old superstition. Taught me how to read the energy in trees, animals, and rocks. People too—when they're not being pigheaded and closed off to it. The real world that *never* dies. Energy just being made into energy, circulating around, changing form, but still here. Still—" She looked around the small room, her voice dropping to a whisper. "Everywhere." Then she reached out, touching the minister on the back of his hand. "You can't feel it, can't you?" He shook his head, staring at the cross on the wall, trying to follow what she was saying. Cheryl sighed. "Then I feel sorry for you. I really do. But I respect all you've done, getting them to let me come here all the time. Convincing the insurance guys in their suits to look the other way. Getting me a job as a volunteer, so I had the right to be here."

The minister gazed at her, admiring how bright Cheryl was, earnest in what she believed, knowing that one day she'd awaken to the truth as he knew it to be. "Thank you, Cheryl, for saying that. It's always been my pleasure, the time we've spent together." He paused, reaching up to wipe away new tears. "I will miss both you and our talks. Now that—" He paused. "I assume you'll be spending more time with your parents now, letting them help you to heal. To help you move on with your life. Your *own* life."

Cheryl looked directly into his eyes, her face fixed in a cold stare. "My parents, if you'll excuse the expression—can go straight to hell."

The minister twisted in the pew, eyes wide in shock. "You—you can't mean that, Cheryl. I *know* you don't believe that! Your parents made the most difficult decision anyone can have to make in choosing to end a loved one's life, no matter the promise of his being in a better place, or wherever you want to name it. Wherever you think it is." He reached over, taking her hand. "They've just lost their child to a terrible accident, through no fault of their own—or his."

Cheryl looked at the small cross attached to the wall behind the pulpit, a serene look on her face as she gave him a gentle pat on the back of his hand. "That's where you're wrong. They haven't lost a child." Cheryl stood up and went over to the door. Then she turned around, the light in the hallway casting a shadow that reached all the way to the minister's feet. "They murdered my brother. They just murdered us both."

CHAPTER FORTY-THREE

TEA SHOP, WASHINGTON D.C.

Luther

Luther entered a room inside the narrow entrance of a non-descript building, without a sign on the outside detailing the services to be performed or items sold. The owner, an elderly man of Asian heritage, thin with a serious expression, offered a deep bow showing respect, perfectly executed then returned by Luther, albeit at less of an angle, establishing his position as a person of higher social status. With the greeting completed, both men nodded, satisfied with face given and received. Then the diminutive man led Luther to a door closed off to the public, hidden behind an angled section of wood paneling with nondescript frame.

Luther stepped inside, pulling the heavy door shut behind him with a quick tug, sealing the edges against any possibility of sound leaking through. He stood with clasped hands, noting the room's impressive simplicity, the interior a mix of light and dark faced hardwood strips, placed with an eye to matching the intricate grain of one against the next, creating a whole. The room was in balance. In perfect harmony. Large, hand-crafted tiles covered the floor, carefully located to create a stir of faint images with the design of one bleeding into the next. A small wooden table, sitting low to the floor was fashioned from thick slabs of ebony-faced wood, resting on top of four carved legs with dragons' feet, symbol of the day's meeting agenda. The other participant had already arrived, seated at one side of the table, his thick legs crossed, business suit unbuttoned, allowing an ample belly to spill out between his chubby thighs.

Luther folded his hands together, bowing, executing a perfect ninety-degree inclination, holding it, his eyes fixed on a point just below the other man's, made to wait a beat longer than manners required, released by a perfunctory nod. He straightened up then settled into position opposite the representative from the People's Republic of China, his feet clad in stockings, hand-woven from ecru colored strands of natural fibers, his street shoes left outside the sealed door, alongside those of his host.

"I am honored by your agreeing to meet." Luther did not ask the identity of the man, their meeting arranged via a series of calls and three visits made to the Chinese Embassy, each one leading further into the obsequious labyrinth, passing through interviews with a small army of political gatekeepers. His overly polite escorts had quietly peeled away, replaced by equally polite officials with a series of penetrating questions answered in a deferential tone, leading to an arrangement for a final interview, taking place now. Here. A single piece of folded rice paper pressed into his palm by a passing stranger on a crowded bus, with a number to call, politely advised he place it from a public phone in a library, or museum.

The overweight man had swollen cheeks and thin slits for eyes. When he spoke, his voice was a wheeze of breathy effort. "You have satisfied those who direct people like you to my attention. Now, if you would be so kind—satisfy me."

Luther hesitated, tempted to tell the man to apologize for his rudeness. His curt words in Mandarin meant to intimidate. "With permission, I have words unwritten—and written, to share with you."

"You may speak." The man shrugged. "Then I will let you know as to acceptance of the other."

Luther took a deep breath, letting it out slowly, composing his thoughts before revealing information he knew would change the course of the civilized world.

Ed listened to the humming of the carrier wave, designed to protect against interception of verbal transmissions when dealing with information of vital importance. Luther's voice was whisper-thin, as always, but clear. "We have moved to the next step."

"When will *I* become involved?"

"The moment I hear from them. The wait for their response, a dark bird flying in a moonless sky. Arriving without warning. Unannounced."

Ed sighed. "The question was *when*, Luther."

"Within three days. Long enough for them to check with their scientists, vetting the concept, though unaware of the special code required to carry it off. There would have been no reference included in the package you asked me to deliver. Correct?"

"Of course not." A moment of silence followed, Ed's voice soft when he replied. "I'm not as stupid as I'm sometimes required to act."

Luther waited a moment, aware of having overstepped. "Of course not. Sir."

"I'm not pissed, Luther. Your assistance is vital, as always. And, as I've been telling you since we first met—call me Ed."

"Yes. Sir. I'll be certain to remember that." Luther waited, another long sigh slipping through the encoding/decoding program on the other end of the call.

"Again, as always, excellent work, Luther. Another deposit has just been made into your account."

"Thank you, sir. And, as I've told you before—completely unnecessary." Luther smiled, having anticipated Ed's offer.

"This preliminary outreach is to be kept—off the books for now. I'll share it with the group at the right time. Early days, my friend. Still early days."

"Of course." Luther paused. "I understand—Ed."

The call ended, with Luther left staring at the phone for a moment before hanging up. The elderly head librarian gave him a nod and warm smile, letting him know, again, how much she appreciated his generous contribution to their reading initiative for low-income children. Luther crossed to the twin glass doors, about to step through when she called out to him.

"I hope you're able to find your phone. I hate when mine goes missing. Usually ends up under my car seat, or in the cushions of my couch. You should check there."

Luther turned around and smiled. "I will do that. And thank *you* again, for the use of the office phone."

CHAPTER FORTY-FOUR

SAILBOAT, MARYLAND

Cheryl

The tide was slack, the small sailboat rocking gently at anchor inside a small cove: poked into a sandy shoreline curling around a snarl of driftwood and thick brush, preventing easy access to a remote island. One rarely visited, Cheryl and Jean spending a weekend away, holding hands while they explored small tidal pools. The evenings were spent cuddling on the foredeck, looking up at the stars, sipping wine while dining on pre-packaged home-cooked meals, until other appetites pulled them below. They were down there now, tucked into the narrow berth, using hands and lips to explore each other's body: the confined space quickly heating up.

Once the boat settled back into a slow rocking motion encouraged by an incoming tidal swell, Cheryl reached over, covering Jean's chest with the top of a linen sheet. The cabin air had cooled, a soft breeze slipping through an overhead hatch that revealed an abundance of stars, twinkling in the cool early springtime air. Jean murmured something, halfway asleep, then rolled onto his side, facing her, his body warm against her skin, running at a higher temperature than her own. Cheryl settled in, the sheet and blanket tugged around her shoulders, closing her eyes as she listened to the sound of waves washing along the shore.

Jean's voice coaxed her awake, a whisper in her ear, his voice soft. "It must've been hard—having to face that, young as you were. Although someone's age has little to do with measuring the pain of losing someone you love. Loss is loss, no matter how old you are when it finds you."

Cheryl turned onto her side, facing him, enough light coming through to let her see his eyes. "You mean losing my brother, right?" She reached up, touching the side of his face, feeling his hand on her upper thigh, gently running back and forth along the toned curves of her body. She'd shared her memories of the day her brother had died, reliving them while on deck, with Jean's arm around her shoulders, the bottle of wine beside them, watching as the sun slipped over the top of the small island.

"Yes." Jean reached up, caressing her hair, the slight dampness of the sea air having tightened her curls. "I wish I could have met him. Sounds like someone I would have enjoyed spending time with. Getting to know."

Cheryl smiled. "You do know him—in a way. I mean, he had a lot to do with how I turned out. A great deal, considering what it is I'm doing now. What I've been doing since I was a kid." She slid back, running her fingers over Jean's chest, feeling the muscles beneath his skin, loving his body, his masculinity framed with a full set of emotions. "I've always felt like he's *still* here, guiding me. Keeping a close watch."

"I hope he knows when to keep his eyes shut." Jean flinched as Cheryl tugged the hair on his chest. He waited a few moments before starting again. "I lost people, close to me as brothers. Closer, in a lot of ways. Some of them—" Jean hesitated, Cheryl finding his hand and squeezing it, waiting for him to continue. "Under *difficult* circumstances. Too many of them. Each leaving a—" He swallowed, his jaw clenched, eyes bright with pain. "Leaving a void—that's still there." He blinked, then looked at Cheryl, tears on his cheeks. "We were but children, playing a game. Barely aware of the risks." He grew silent. The cabin creaking slightly as the tide turned. "Until we were men, counting the cost. Carrying the loss with us until our own dance in the sun comes to an end."

Cheryl pulled herself into his embrace, with a gentle probe of tongue, tasting the salt from both of their tears, combined. Cheryl lowered her head, kissing his upper chest, listening to the sound of his heart while riding the slow rise and fall of his chest, her eyes growing heavy as she thought about the type of life he'd led. Far different from her own, but sharing the same need to respond emotionally, without limitations. His own, dampened by the reticence strong men were cursed with, unwilling or unable to expose their pain to the light of conversation with those they loved.

Cheryl sighed. "I'd never shared what happened—in the rectory. What I said to the minister. Never told that to anyone, not even my cousin. And she's as close to me as any sister could be." She pulled her head back, seeing that Jean was looking up at the overhead, less than a foot and a half above their heads, his eyes closed. She knew how tired he was from the long day of exploration and their recent bout of amorous activity. Lowering her head, she settled back in, drifting off, hand in his. The gentle lapping of water against the hull lulling her to sleep.

Cheryl was dreaming of her childhood home, tucked into the foothills of New Hampshire. She was standing outside, beneath a layer of stars. The air cold, fogging her breath.

"Hey, Chipmunk."

Cheryl twisted around, looking up toward a small hill behind the house, trying to see where he was, having recognized Robert's voice. "I can't *see* you."

"Because you're looking with your *eyes* and not your mind. Idiot."

"Don't—don't call me that!"

"Why not? You're behaving like one. Not eating. Not talking to mom. Being a real—I don't even know where to begin. Thought I taught you better, teaching you to not waste time or opportunities. Not when there are mountains needing to be climbed. New routes to be bagged."

"With you! I wanted to do all that with *you!* Not alone. Not by myself!"

"I'm not going anywhere. Still here. Still beside you—every step of the way."

"You know what I mean. With you *here*. Alive. The two of us—a team." Cheryl paused. "Again."

"So—narrow." Her brother's voice grew serious in tone.

"Excuse me?"

"Your viewpoint. Like looking through binoculars, the wrong way around."

"I only did that the *first* time! And I was only a child, barely old enough to go with you."

"Still."

Cheryl sighed, her arms crossed, feeling the cold of the air, the coat she was wearing too large by several sizes. It was her brother's, still holding the scent of his body. His sweat. Along with a smear of blood along one shoulder where they'd used it to keep him warm while bringing him out of the woods. "I'm not narrow minded. I hate when you say that!"

"Then explain your plan." The voice circled her thoughts, coming from straight ahead. "You're not eating. Not engaging with others. Not even with the minister, who's been here several times to see you."

"To quote me the same old nonsense." Cheryl paused, looking down. "Nothing new there."

"It's one of many angles, all of them heading to the same point. You could learn a thing or two about—"

"I have. I've read all the books. About everything having to do with—" Cheryl hesitated, not wanting to use the word.

Robert chuckled. "With death? And what happens next?" He swung around beside her, his voice in her right ear. "Reading is *not* understanding. Getting out in the world and talking to people, asking questions, walking where they've walked—that's how you learn." He paused. "And as I've been watching how you're dealing with things in the real world—I have to tell you, sis, that you're acting like an—"

"Idiot. I know." Cheryl hesitated, her voice lowering as she continued. "And so were you, by that same measure, in taking your helmet off." There was a moment of silence, long enough for Cheryl to think she'd caused her brother to abandon her.

"Do you remember when I came back, having finally made it up the Hawksbill?"

"Yes. You were still walking a few feet off the ground with your chest all puffed out. So proud of yourself. I was proud of you too, but mad I didn't get to be the first to climb it with you."

"I never told you, or anyone else, not even Tommy. Never said how I skyed the last part. Up and over the tip of the beak. No one able to figure a way to do it—until me."

"How did you—do it?"

"Unclipped from the rope. Had a trace line with me. Tied it to a carabiner and tossed it up over the top of the wall, so it would be there when I made it up. Then I fastened the other end to my pack, and the end of the rope, so I could pull them up behind me."

"You—free-climbed it?"

"Yeah. I did. Got up to where the crack petered out, just to the side of the bulge. Then—I leaped."

"But—how did you know? I mean, how did you know there'd be a hold?"

"I didn't, but figured one had to be there, waiting for me to grab on and finish the climb. Bagging the bitch."

Cheryl considered the move Robert had just described, wondering if she would have dared try it. His voice drew her back.

"Your own Hawksbill moment is coming. And it's gonna require a leap of—well, whatever you want to call it. Faith, instinct—or just blind luck. But it'll be yours to make. Or not."

"When?"

"Someday. But only if you're still in the game. Chipmunk."

"I want to see you! Why are you hiding?"

"Close your eyes. I'm right there, on top of the wall. On top of the

Hawksbill where I took you that day. The two of us climbing up the backside trail, then me letting you dangle your legs and arms out over the edge so you could feel the warm air rising."

"Holding my belt—so I wouldn't fall."

"Like I always said I would. Having your back, Chipmunk—every step of the way."

Robert's voice faded away, the dream coming to an end, recalled from what seemed a lifetime ago, and feeling as if it had been yesterday. Cheryl sighing, remembering waking up outside, curled up in her brother's coat, a light coming on over the back door of the house as it opened. Harry the hound loping up to lick her face and hands as she tried to hold him off. Her mother standing in the doorway, staring out, face drawn, looking weathered in the yellow light. Cheryl rising to her feet, running down the hill, giving her mother a hug, clinging to her. Unable to forgive, but finally able to understand. Looking up, speaking for the first time in days. "I'm hungry." Her mother smiling, reaching for her hand, leading her inside.

CHAPTER FORTY-FIVE

PENTHOUSE SUITE, WASHINGTON D.C.

Luther

The man he'd come to visit wasn't there to meet Luther as he exited the penthouse elevator. He didn't hesitate, moving ahead along a narrow hallway that opened into a large, sunken living room. A leather couch placed along one side was framed by large windows letting in a wash of light. Thomas was sitting on one end, leaning back, holding a tumbler with an inch of amber liquid in it.

"You arrive bearing good news, I hope. Your sudden request for a visit coming at a troublesome time for me, schedule-wise." Thomas pointed to a chair opposite the couch, his eyebrows raised when Luther ignored him, refusing to sit.

"It's my back." Luther tilted his head, acknowledging the man's offer. "Acting up."

"Of course." Thomas looked at the short, thin man, standing in a stiff pose. "I won't bother offering you a drink, knowing you do not imbibe." Thomas held up his glass. "Understand you're more of a—tea man, according to Ed. He mentioned you'd been by to see him." He paused. "Recently. On his boat."

Luther nodded, his hands folded together in front of him. "Yes. Going over the items he's putting together—" Luther looked at Thomas, receiving a nod, letting him know he should continue. "Items for next month's meeting of the—social club." Luther saw a smile come into full bloom on Thomas's face, the man enjoying the use of the cover name Ed had suggested to the others. Not that anyone would dare reveal to someone outside the secretive group the true nature of their association.

"Agreed. Meeting in private is warranted, but let's not kid ourselves, Luther. Ed couldn't put an agenda together if his life *depended* on it. He doesn't have the patience. Too busy pushing his—well, let's just leave it at that. After all, I know you answer to him and are loyal—to a fault." Thomas raised his hand as Luther opened his mouth. "Not that there's anything *untoward* going on." He paused, holding up his glass, admiring the play of light through the dark bodied, amber liquid. "Hell—I'm up for the position myself, in a couple of months."

"Four." Luther lowered his gaze, studying the floor, noting the lines in the surface of the marble tiles.

Thomas frowned. "Yes. Of course. Then you'll be reporting to *me*, helping put my agenda together." Luther waited, looking up, a neutral look on his face betraying neither interest nor concern, knowing Thomas was about to make a proposal.

"Tell me, Luther—what do you know about a Russian?"

Luther hesitated long enough to allow Thomas to think the question had surprised him. "He's—been making some very—pointed inquiries, pertaining to our project."

"To Ed, correct?"

"Of course."

"But not through you?"

"No." Luther allowed his expression to narrow, feigning a measure of indignation at the insinuation. The Russian in question had reached out to him through an intermediary, several weeks earlier, asking about the best approach to use with Ed.

Thomas moved his glass from side to side, the liquid swirling against the edges of the thick glass. "Wouldn't matter, either way. I imagine they all know what we're up to. Russians, Europeans, Aussies, along with everyone else. Even the *damn* Chinese, with someone in our little group having let something slip, somewhere along the line."

Luther noted a slight narrowing of Thomas's eyes. "Once the agenda's completed, the social club will put production and delivery mechanisms into place. The list of properties we've identified for acquisition are already being purchased as we speak, for the initial set of—wellness centers. Building permits already requested and submitted, with bribes paid so construction can begin immediately. As the group discussed. At your last meeting."

"You mean *our* last meeting." Thomas gave Luther a perfunctory nod. "You're an integral member of the team, Luther, whether you care to admit it or not."

"At *your* meeting, sir, with the group. I am but a minor piece of the project. A useful tool—nothing more."

Thomas sighed, then tilted his glass, finishing it, keeping his eyes locked on Luther's, measuring the honesty of his modest remark. He knew Ed had hired the quiet man with shaven head to manage the disparate demands brought to the fore every month by those of the group with pressing engagements that required them to be elsewhere. A firm response needed from time to time with Luther constantly having to remind each of them of the forfeiture clause in the contracts they'd signed. Their original investment of several billion dollars lost if they failed to uphold their sworn agreement to attend when summoned. An agreement signed in red ink drawn from their own flesh, each man knowing the consequences of failing to live up to the requirement for utmost secrecy.

"I wonder, Luther, speaking hypothetically of course—that if I put you in contact with a—let's say a friend of a friend. Someone interested in joining our efforts to—I don't know, maybe bring whatever the hell it is we're looking to do with all this shit—to bring it to another level. While everyone else is focused on rolling it out across the entire *fucking* world. Do you think Ed would be amenable to a private meeting to discuss something like that? Between the two of us—as equals?"

"I am not in a position—"

"Yes, or no, Luther. It's a simple question. Just nod or shake your head."

Luther started to shrug, then stopped as he saw a flush of anger on the other man's face. "A meeting, yes. I think it's—a possibility. But not an agreement."

A long moment of cold silence filled the expansive room. Luther waited to see how his future would play out, balanced between the two most powerful men in the world, each holding reins tied to dozens of governments in their hands. Thomas finally smiled, reaching to refill his glass. "Glad we had this brief chat. Let's keep it between ourselves for the moment. I'll be sure and run the idea by Ed in a few days. No need to burden yourself with setting that up. You can go." Thomas made the dismissal with no outward emotion shown, having completed his probe. Luther was aware he would never be anything other than a pawn in either man's eyes. A sacrificial piece, his usefulness acknowledged, while his thoughts or feelings were of little or no concern.

He bowed his head, then turned and walked away, pleased his predictions were coming to pass. He knew he was several moves ahead of the game being played between the two men, along with other powerful and ambitious men on the other side of the world, moving into position, ready to pull the gameboard out from under all the other players in the game, in one fell swoop.

CHAPTER FORTY-SIX

DIVE SHOP, MARYLAND

Jean

"She *can't* find out." Jean gave Jason and the large, thick bodied man standing beside him, named Skinny, a firm look. Jason glanced up at his partner, then back over at Jean, sitting on the corner of a beat-up desk. He grinned, his teeth forming a perfect line: gift from his Uncle Sam, replaced when he'd lost most of his original set during a rough sea landing. Skinny by his side, helping him to haul a Navy Seal team off a remote beach while under heavy fire. "Because she'll get *pissed!* At *you.*"

"No." Jean shook his head. "*That* I can deal with." He gave Jason a steady look, draining the smile from the young man's face. "It's because she'll do *everything* possible to shake you off her tail. *That's* what I'm worried about. And don't kid yourselves—she can *do* it." The dive shop at the marina was closed for the season: a few ex-service types stopping in now and then to service their gear while swapping stories. Taking on an occasional job posted on a dingy bulletin board, most having to do with recovery of property lost overboard. Hard-edged men, with hearts of gold, killing time for the most part. A better vocation than the killing of men, something they all agreed with when the talk turned to darker periods in their lives.

"I have two more teams going—in hot-swap coverage, round the clock. With decent enough skill sets for over-sight duties." Jean gave them both a firm stare. "Limited—in handling any *hard* work that might need doing."

"Nothing wet though. Right?" Skinny spoke up, his voice a growl, a thick scar lining the side of his throat, result of a knife thrust that would have ended him if not for a last second tackle by Jason, knocking his assailant down then firing a round into his head. The two of them standing back-to-back, dealing with an ambush in a narrow alley, far from home.

"No. Nothing like that expected. Just want you to stay alert—and *be* prepared."

"Because you're in love—" Jason stopped, the rest of his words frozen in his throat by the icy look in his former leader's eyes. "Got you five by five, boss man." He waited a beat, unable to resist another jibe. "We'll treat her as just another nice *ass-et* then. Staying *a-breast* of—" Skinny grabbed the smaller man's arm and yanked him toward the door, returning the favor owed, saving him from a burst of unfriendly fire.

Cheryl rattled away, her hands moving as she talked, emphasizing her words. She was filling Mari in on a host of options under consideration, readying an all-out assault on JD's kingdom, wanting to strike before he could finish closing the loops, restricting her ability to uncover who he was.

"Are you getting *all* this?" She rounded on Mari, who kept glancing over her shoulder. "What's going *on* with you?"

"I don't know. I just feel—funny. That's all. Like I have an itch on my back. One I can't quite reach." Mari raised a hand, stopping Cheryl as she started to move her hand over. "Not a *real* one. But something else. Like I'm being—"

"Watched." Cheryl's expression darkened as she whispered a curse under her breath. "It's Jean's doing. He's being overly-protective."

"Wise man." Mari nodded. "And a reasonable precaution, considering how exposed you are."

Cheryl looked around, trying to identify the culprits, having a pretty good idea who they were, unable to spot the two, oddly matched men in the crowd of office workers gathered in front of glass-faced buildings, enjoying a few minutes of sunshine. A large percentage of them were women, scattered between islands of men on their phones, all of them clad in their corporate uniforms made of expensive cloth, with perfectly coiffed hair, and tense postures.

Cheryl didn't see the two men she was looking for. "I'm *not* exposed. Not in any *real* meaning of the word. A target of interest, yes—because I'm putting myself out there, with *intent*. Something that *lug-headed* marine doesn't like to admit is crucial to what needs to happen next."

Mari shrugged. "Okay. You're not exposed. But the position you've put yourself in, holding all the ace cards—*all* of them—" She leaned back, staring at Cheryl. "Is a definite threat to people who won't be willing to take it lying down."

"I'm no threat to them, *yet*. Still a long way from *that* becoming an issue." Cheryl saw the look of disbelief on Mari's face. "What?"

"You're a threat simply because you have power. The type of people on the other side of this are not used to anyone else having control over any piece of whatever project they're involved with. Let alone the most critical part of something as revolutionary as *this*." Mari leaned forward, staring directly into Cheryl's eyes. "You put yourself in their cross-hairs when you allowed Isaac to share the code. And before you get started in on your argument—I *know* it was my doing, setting that up. But you *knew* it was going to happen, or at least you knew it was a *strong* probability—and did nothing to prevent it. Correct?"

"You're right." Cheryl frowned, looking away, watching the comings and goings of the people passing by the outside patio of the health-food restaurant where they were having lunch. When she looked back over, she saw a satisfied look on Mari's flawless face. "Stop grinning. It's not funny."

"It's a little funny, my forcing you to admit I'm right."

Cheryl shrugged, picking up her menu, looking for the most expensive choice. "What do I care? *You're* the one buying lunch."

A small, elderly Asian woman pushing a baby stroller came to a stop, the two people she'd been following having moved beyond her viewpoint. Her mission had been carried out: the information gathered of no interest to her, satisfied at having followed the instructions sent to her on a code-locked phone, received in a package with no return address. One she'd destroyed as soon as she'd punched in a unique code and deciphered the scrambled text, knowing her employer would send a new one the next day.

She reached into the stroller, touching the infant, his chubby cheeks lifting at the corners as he smiled. Her other hand removed the camera attached to the sunshade, tiny in design. Holding hundreds of images on the small chip inside, to be dropped into the next available mailbox using a pre-addressed envelope destined for a PO box in a small town, an hour's drive away.

"You marked her, right?" Jason whispered into a wireless microphone programmed to a military radio band well outside normal communication boundaries. Impossible to intercept, according to the manufacturer supplying it to the military. Jason frowned, remembering the seal team on the beach, their position revealed despite use of the same technology.

"Yup. Middle-aged amah, shoving the buggy."

"Stroller, you dumb ape."

"Fucking *dump truck*, for all I care." Skinny turned his head and spit, a large brown splat of tobacco juice painting the granite steps of the building he was standing in front of. Jason heard him over the receiver in his ear and shook his head, watching from a distance as his partner leaned against a stone column, hand to his face, pretending to yawn.

"That's *nice*. Real classy move."

"My middle name. Classy." Skinny coughed as some of the juice ran down the back of his throat. Jason grinned, moving away from the open area where he'd taken up surveillance, tucking a small digital camera away in his pocket as he slipped into a crowd of tourists.

CHAPTER FORTY-SEVEN

HOSPITAL, MAINE

Jemma

Jemma's phone vibrated, startling her as she started to drift off. She reached out, knocking it from a small bed-side table, trying to dampen the sound with her foot as it hit the floor beside Calvin's hospital bed. She picked it up, muffling a yawn with one hand, exhausted, having spent the previous afternoon and night in a lonely vigil at the local city hospital.

Jemma checked her phone, seeing it was another message from one of the group of women she'd met at the church supper. Checking in to see if she was okay and if Calvin was any better. She looked at him, still unconscious, wishing he'd open his eyes: a lopsided smile spreading across his face as he sat up, swinging his legs over the side of the bed, wanting to get out of there and go home. To their home, as if the events of the previous day had never happened.

She winced: the image of him collapsed on the floor of the store, still vivid in her mind's eye. A waking nightmare, with her locked in shock, unable to accept it was real. Waiting, trying to come to grips with what had happened as the agonizing wail from an ambulance grew louder. Unable to draw a full breath, staring at a pool of blood as it soaked into the unfinished floor of the store.

Tom ignored Jemma's screams of anguish as she tried to push him away. He ripped off his shirt, placing it against the side of Calvin's head, wadding it up and stemming the flow of blood where the straight claws of the hammer had been forced out by the jarring impact of his head hitting the floor. He tied it around Calvin's head, using the sleeves to hold it in place, all the while letting Jemma know, repeating the words in a calm voice, that she needed to call for help. She finally recovered sense enough to hear him, her hands shaking as she dialed the rescue number, her words falling into sobs as she tried to give them the address, unable to continue with Tom taking the phone from her hand, letting the emergency response team know where they were and what had just occurred.

The ambulance arrived a few minutes later, followed by a contingent of pickup trucks with flashing light bars fastened to their tops: the local fire department and militia, as Calvin had called them when Jemma asked why there were so many odd-looking emergency vehicles parked in the driveways of homes scattered throughout the small town. They lined both sides of the paved roadway running past the small country store, serious faced drivers and their passengers milling around, helpless to do anything else as EMTs carried a stretcher in, strapping Calvin to it, then carrying him outside. A small army of men rushed over to help as soon as they cleared the door, held back by a contingent of local and county police, called in to help control the scene. The unofficial caravan of vehicles made illegal U-turns, following the ambulance as it pulled away, heading to a large hospital in the city, a half-hour away.

A County Sheriff was inside, interviewing Tom. Jemma still in shock, her hands trembling, wondering if she'd just killed Calvin. Breaking down, sobbing, formed into a puddle of tanned flesh, jeans, and flannel shirt, sitting on the floor, staring at a pool of Calvin's blood.

"*I'm* responsible. I lost my cool. Threw the hammer, trying to break the window. The colored glass one. Hit him—Calvin—hit him in the head as he was coming out." Tom stood alongside the counter, bare-chested, the sheriff taking notes, muttering under his breath. "Accident, it sounds like."

"No." Tom shook his head. "I knew when I picked it up—the hammer, knew what I was doing. It's *my* fault. *My* responsibility. No one else."

The older man stopped writing, eyeing Jemma, who'd finally stopped crying. Still sitting on the floor, arms wrapped around her knees, silently rocking back and forth.

Tom looked at the sheriff. "She should take something." He picked up a small bottle of pills the EMT's had left, a town police officer having brought them inside the house. "I'll need to go and get her a glass of water."

"Thoughtful of you." The middle-aged man looked at Tom. "Not the actions of someone with a bad temper *or* intentions." He continued writing. "Like I said—an accident, pending any further information." Then he nodded, releasing Tom, watching as he stopped and squeezed Jemma's shoulder before heading inside the attached house.

"I caused it. Not him." Jemma stood up, her hands on the end of the counter, face set in a determined look, her eyes red, but free of tears. "Tom was only trying to break the window, like he said. That one." Jemma pointed at the stained glass, angled rays of light shining through in a wash of colors, painting the floor of the store, close to where the pool of blood had begun to congeal. Smeared by Tom's knees as he'd slowed the bleeding. "I reached out, trying to stop it. The hammer. Reached up to grab it—or deflect it. I don't really remember. I just wanted to keep him—Tom, from breaking it, knowing he'd regret it as soon as it was over. The fight. My fault—not his."

The sheriff stared at her arm. "You're hurt." He reached out and took her forearm, gently turning it toward the light. There was an angled cut on her wrist, showing little blood, most having dried up and fallen off. "From the claws of the hammer, most likely." He let go. "As I said—an accident. Bad luck for—" He paused.

"Calvin." Tom was back, a glass in his hand. He lowered his head, his cheeks red with shame as he handed it to Jemma, along with two of the pills. Mild sedatives to ease her grief. She gently pushed his hand away, drinking the water, back in control.

"You said you hit him." The sheriff looked down at his notes. "Hit Tom." He glanced at Jemma who nodded, staring at the floor.

"With the first thing I touched. I don't remember what it was. I was just so—so *angry*. Out of control." Jemma looked up. "*My* fault. *All* of what happened. My—" She looked up as a local police officer came in. He came over and reached out, touching Jemma on her arm.

"They called. He's there, heading into surgery as soon as they get some scans done, making sure he's stabilized. EMT's said for you to head in when you can. No hurry. They'll have him under for a bit." He glanced at Tom, then the sheriff. "I can run you in—if you want. Okay, Jemma?" She looked at the sheriff who nodded, closing his notebook, sticking his pen in the spiral winding. Then he glanced at the corner of the store, noticing something out of place. "Grab that for me, Elbert. Lying right over there." The police officer went over and leaned down, picked up the picnic basket, turning it in his hands, finding the handle then holding it out. "It's a basket. Looks to be homemade."

The sheriff held up his hand, a signal for the other man to stop talking. He sighed, shaking his head. "A foolish accident—nothing more."

Jemma stared at her phone, then checked to see if there was a message from Tom, who'd volunteered to stay at the house until Dawg returned: the large shepherd having disappeared before Calvin's injury occurred. Nothing seen of him since. There was still no message, though dozens of people had left voice mails. All of them offering condolences on the mishap, as it was being called. Asking if there was anything she needed.

Jemma forced herself to put together a short account of Calvin's condition, then sent it as a group message to everyone who'd reached out, asking them to forward it to anyone else in the local area, wanting to know how he was doing. Tears filled her eyes as she recalled Calvin telling her that people in the small town bought you at your own price, whether for any work that needed doing, or in building relationships. That you got back what you put out, long as you were genuine. False smiles quickly returned to the sender, unopened.

Jemma closed her phone and leaned back, listening to the steady whir of machinery monitoring Calvin's heart rate, blood pressure and other vital statistics. A drain in the side of the bandages covering his head slowly dripped clear fluid into a line leading to a small bag tucked away on the other side of the bed, marking the passage of time as Jemma closed her eyes.

A shadow filled the doorway, pulling Jemma's attention away from the magazine she was trying to read, given to her by the nurse: a fashion magazine with a picture of a beautiful woman on the cover. Someone famous, she thought, noting the perfect skin and makeup, feeling as far removed from that world as the model would be sitting behind the wheel of an old tractor. Or nailing studs between a header and footer, propping a new wall into place. She teared up again, amazed there were any left, having shed a bucket full over the past twenty-four hours. Jemma looked up, a tired smile on her lips. "Hi, Tom."

He came over, hesitated a moment, then reached out, unsure where to put his hand. Jemma reached up and took it, squeezing gently, then letting go. He saw the tears in her eyes. "Bad news?"

"No. Too early to tell. No real change expected for a day or so, until the swelling goes down." Jemma dropped the magazine on the floor, then stood up, moving to the head of the bed, checking the numbers on the small screens. "They'll be sending him south, later today or tomorrow morning. To have more tests done. Get a better scan of his brain before they do anything else. At least they—got the bleeding stopped."

"One of your neighbors came by. Offered to hang out and wait for your dog to show up. Still not back, the food I left out—untouched." Tom watched as Jemma nodded without comment. "I'm sorry. For everything I—"

Jemma cut him off, holding up her hand, waving it. Tom stepped back, turning to leave. She waited until he was at the door. "Did they clear you to go?"

Tom stopped, without turning around. "Yes. Your statement sealed the deal. Thank you." He stood in the doorway, back to Jemma. "You could have hung me out to dry, deservedly so. I owe you more than I can ever repay. For all the shit I've put you through. For hurting you. Again."

"It was never you, Tom. Or me. It was *us* that didn't work, for all the nasty accusations tossed back and forth. Both of us too stubborn, I guess, to just give up and walk away."

"*You* managed to do it. And then I *fucked* it up, coming here and interfering."

"Just let it go, Tom. And try to move on—like I did."

Jemma waited until the door swung shut, closing with a metallic click, her eyes drifting to see if there would be a reaction from Calvin. None showed on his face, pale beneath the thick wrap of bandages, a day's worth of stubble on his cheeks.

She turned and looked out the window, watching as three children played a game of tag in a small, tree-lined space, nestled between two wings of the hospital grounds. A couple sat on a nearby bench, leaning in, having an intense discussion while sitting just a little too far apart from each other. Most likely divorced, Jemma thought, each of them locking in on something of little consequence, gnawing away at each other as if it were the most important thing in their lives. She sighed, shaking her head, wanting to go down and tell them to stop. To tell them how quickly life could turn on you, leaving a wound that might never heal.

CHAPTER FORTY-EIGHT

LAB, MILITARY FACILITY

Cheryl

"Jared's next—the last man standing." Cheryl leaned back, adjusting the Tee-Cee, her feet in the stirrups, newly fastened to the chair, preparing to go back into JD's world. "Time to see if we can *alter* the sequence. Stir things up a bit."

Isaac shook his head, unhappy with Cheryl's plan. "Seems to me we've— that *you've* already done that, interfering the first time. And then *again*."

"Nothing bad happened—not from the first attempt."

"Other than *pissing* him off. Enough to tell he was *not* a happy camper."

"I know, Isaac. Been through it a dozen times with you already. But if I don't do this *now* we might miss our chance."

"*His* chance, you mean. To stay hidden away. From *you*."

Cheryl leaned back, ignoring Isaac's pouty-lipped attitude. "Just get me in there—and monitor the *damn* data streams."

Jared eased his bike through the gate at the head of the hiking trail, bending it into a tight curve, his lower leg brushing against the bristled edge of a recently trimmed hedge. He felt the tug of the small branches through the thin fabric of the riding pants he was wearing, stretching down past his calves. Their claim to reduce wind-drag was of no real importance to him, focused on building endurance, not speed.

It was coming onto early evening, the sky overcast, threatening rain. He'd picked Teresa up after work, having to wait outside while she dealt with a hesitant buyer, leaving just enough light for him to get to the pools in the hills, then get back home before full dark. He was looking forward to a hot shower and dinner. Or supper, as Teresa insisted on calling it, one of many accommodations made to their living together. Each one eagerly accepted; his life centered on a path bringing him a level of joy he'd never felt before.

Jared heard a loud panting from behind as he started up the first rise. He cursed under his breath, knowing it was Dawg, having made his escape from the garage. Most likely when Teresa opened the door to put the recyclables out, wanting to do her fair share of the chores now she was living there fulltime. Jared relaxed, knowing the die was cast. Besides, he thought, the large shepherd could use the run, his weight having increased of late, despite Teresa's insistence the extra treats she was giving him had nothing to do with it.

The pools beckoned, barely able to reflect a darkening sky, the sun having sunk below the horizon. Jared had been forced to stop and adjust the bike's chain, slipping off just as he'd arrived at the turnaround point. He'd been able to get it repaired, having to hold a small flashlight between his teeth, with Dawg coming over and nosing his hand, trying to help. A muttered curse chased him a few feet away, head down, watching his every move. Jared finished the repair then headed back, fifteen minutes behind his self-imposed schedule. "Come on, numb-nut!" Then he winced, half-expecting to hear a reprimand from Teresa, chiding him for using the derogatory word.

"It's *crass*, that's why. And inaccurate. When you say that it only proves who the real—" Teresa paused.

"Yes?"

"Who the real *cretin* is."

Jared grinned. "You must have bought yourself a thesaurus." Teresa responded with a hand gesture, showing him where he ranked in her life. Jared glad to see he'd made number one, again. He shook his head as he came over and kissed her. "And *I'm* the crass one."

The path was difficult to see, a slightly lighter shade of dark in a wandering line of shadows cast by bushes growing alongside the trail. His progress was slowed out of necessity, Dawg loping ahead, stopping now and then to lift his nose in the air, catching an occasional stray scent, eliciting a muttered curse from Jared feeling uneasy as he tracked the steady approach of a storm, thunder rumbling in the distance, along with flashes of lightning.

"Just keep moving, you—sorry excuse for a *pothole*. Before I crash into you and break my damn neck." Dawg paused again, forcing Jared to squeeze both brake handles, the dual squeals causing the shepherd to leap ahead, then look back in confusion.

Jared finally reached the end of the trail, slipping through the gate and swinging to the right, passing the house where he'd helped the woman a few weeks earlier. She was standing outside, smoking, a slow wave of her hand letting him know she'd seen him and Dawg, the shepherd looking back at him, wondering if he could go say hello. Running over when released with a nod, the woman bending down, calling to him, her voice soft. "Who's a *beautiful* boy? You are. Such a *beautiful* big boy." Jared checked his watch, hoping she'd take the hint, darkness approaching with a vengeance.

She stood up. "I'd like to thank you, again, for helping me out the other day."

"Not a problem." Jared hesitated, trying to remember if she'd given him her name.

"I'm Victoria. But everyone calls me Vicky." She held out her hand and Jared shook it. "I'm Jared. Sorry—for not having introduced myself before."

"You were busy. Had your hands full moving that heavy box—all by yourself." She came over, closing the distance. "I *still* owe you a drink, as I recall."

"I'll have to take a rain-check. I'm late getting back and there aren't any lights on the bike. It's an off-road model. So—"

"Of course. No need to apologize. You go on ahead, both you and—?"

"He's named Dawg. With an AW in the middle."

"Cute name. I like it." She bent down and gave Dawg a scratch between his ears. Jared nodded then waved as he pedaled away, the shepherd swinging around to the front of the bike, head held high, tail wagging.

A short, thickly built man came out of the house, his neck as big around as one of his thighs, his dark eyes glaring. "Who the *fuck* was that?"

His wife shrugged. "Just some guy on a bike, coming off the trail. And his dog.

"You know him?"

"He's been by from time to time. One time with a lady friend, but she hasn't been with him recently. Not that I've noticed. I think he lives near here. Don't really know much about him."

"He the guy helped move the shit I ordered?"

"He is." The woman looked over. "And a *good* thing, too. The rain would have ruined the box. Would have ruined whatever was in it. You, away all the time, not being here to take care of things. Leaving it up to me to—"

"Shut the *fuck up!* Go inside and make me something to eat." He turned toward the garage.

"Where are you going?"

"None of your *fucking* business, Miss Friendly, smiling at every swinging dick that comes sniffing around. Get back in the house and start dinner." He pulled out a key fob, punching his thumb on a button, opening the garage door. "And put a sweater on. You're nearly busting out of that top."

Teresa looked at the clock on the dining room wall, then reached for her cellphone, not able to find it, left behind somewhere in the house. She walked down the hallway to the front door, opened it and looked out. Again. A look of concern started to grow in her eyes, with Jared a full half-hour later than promised. Dinner in the oven, staying warm. Wine breathing. Music in the background, including several songs from the singer he liked, a CD available, ordered from a postal address in Maine as a surprise for Jared, in celebration of their fourth full month of living together.

Teresa sighed, wondering if she should go look for him, to see if he needed help. She went into the bedroom, looking for her phone, unable to find it. Then she grabbed the house key, locking the door behind her as she headed down the driveway.

Jared tapped the face of his phone, mounted to his handlebar. He tried calling Teresa again, to let her know he was on his way back. There was no answer, her voice mail picking up, so he ended the call, irked by her lack of response, having left a message when he'd reached the pools, knowing the issue with the chain would delay him and not wanting her to worry.

Teresa's habit of leaving her phone behind in the car, bathroom, or any of several other places bothered him, more than a few of his phone calls or texts going unanswered, a hit-or-miss issue at times, especially when he needed to reach her. When he'd let her know how irritating it was, she'd shrugged her shoulders, telling him she didn't have the same attachment to her phone as most people, including him. That there were other priorities in *her* life. Jared had offered a logical rebuttal, telling her it might have more to do with her choice of a soft ringtone, his offer to change it for her met with a deafening silence.

Jared sighed, then pulled up a song from his phone, one he'd first heard the day he and Teresa had gone on their one and only hike. So far, he thought as the music started playing in his wireless earphones, convinced he'd be able to convince her to go again, one of these days. Dawg, a dozen paces ahead, looked back over his shoulder, checking on Jared who smiled. "Lead on—you big, *beautiful, beautiful* boy!"

The headlights of the thick-set man's car caught a reflection from something near the side of the road, just ahead. He squinted, his vision blurred from several large drinks consumed at the house, bothered by the glare of streetlights lining the private road. He reached for his driving glasses, but couldn't find them, left behind when he'd started the car, pulling away before his wife could close the garage door, trying to stop him.

Teresa wondered what she would do when Jared finally showed up, realizing he'd walk his bike back to the house with her, knowing he'd refuse to ride ahead. A flash of lightning split the sky, thunder following close behind. She hesitated, about to turn around when she caught sight of Dawg loping into view, tongue hanging out, appearing to be smiling.

Jared noted the lights approaching from behind, the small mirrors mounted above the handlebars reflecting headlights approaching on high beam. He eased over to the side, leaving plenty of room for the vehicle to slide past. A roar of its engine, heard over the music in his ears let him know it was speeding up to do so. He lifted his hand from the left handlebar and waved, letting the driver know it was safe to pass.

The man floored the accelerator, the large engine pulling the heavy bodied car forward, intending to scare the bicyclist in the funny-looking clothing, letting him know to stay the fuck away from his wife. He blinked several times, having a hard time making him out, another car coming into view, its headlights a blaze of white, combining with the streetlights, causing him to lose sight of the bike. A thump from the right-front fender let him know he'd just made a serious error in judgment, choosing to speed away as if nothing had happened. He jammed his foot down on the gas pedal, narrowly avoiding a pedestrian, her hands raised in a meaningless attempt at warding him away, his front bumper just missing her.

Teresa fell back, her heart in her throat, shoulders hitting the ground. She'd heard the muffled sound of a collision, thinking it must have been Dawg, his reflective collar invisible to the car coming from behind. Then she looked for Jared, an icy hand reaching down her throat, squeezing her heart, causing her to get up and break into a run, her eyes widening in fear, desperately searching the edge of the roadway for any sign of movement.

Cheryl found herself immersed in the scene, watching as it unfolded before her eyes. Her view was from above and to one side, with the tableau of dog, bike, and car spread out before her. A director's view, she whispered to herself, with actors moving from mark to mark, delivering rehearsed lines with varied inflection, depending on the script and leeway given them to improvise.

"You have delivered this cruel outcome—again. Interfering where you *do* not belong."

Cheryl turned around. "There you are. Right on cue." JD swung around in front of her, wearing the same face as the JD lying in the chair beside her in the lab. The same JD who'd come to her in her dreams and told her to wake the fuck up. An angry man, one she would pull from his false world by his ears, hair, or balls in order to bring him out.

"You seem upset." JD's words dripped with condescension. "You were hoping to save him. To try and save them all."

Cheryl shrugged, her false body clad in the clothes she was wearing in the lab. "Not at all. None of this, despite the excellent presentation you've put together, is real. I know that. We *both* know that. Just another diversion, most of them pleasant enough. A bit more horrible of late, with you ending their stories the way you've chosen to do."

"You thought I was one of them. Didn't you?"

"At first." Cheryl nodded. "And you are—in a manner of speaking. Each of them representing something in common with you. My program having filled in the missing side of the cube, identifying points of concurrency. Exposing you—"

"Fuck off." JD frowned, hands on his hips, slowly shaking his head. "I'm *done* playing games with you. You can stay. I'm leaving." He turned away, waving one hand in dismissal.

"You can *try*."

JD spun back around. "What's *that* supposed to mean?"

"That here, in your own head, you've been untouchable. But back there, in the lab where *I* rule, you're trapped, strapped, and at *my* mercy. An arm's reach away. Close enough to reach over and do—this." Cheryl waved her arm nonchalantly, JD's head rocking back as if hit with a hammer. "And this." Cheryl reversed the motion, hitting JD on his scarred shoulder, his body flying away, thudding against a light pole, dropping to the street beside Teresa, who was kneeling, her thin shoulders shaking as her hands reached out to Jared, calling his name. Her lover lying on his back, eyes fixed and staring, chest not moving, the fender having knocked him beneath the tire of the car, crushing his life away.

"Can you *feel* me, JD?" Cheryl walked over and picked him up by his chin, the look of desperation in his eyes feeding her anger. "Have you *enjoyed* playing your games?" She let go. JD's body fell to the ground, held in place with Cheryl's foot on his neck. "You *knew* we were trying to help you—and refused to let us. Not because we're evil, but because you won't let go of *this*—this *fantasy* world. Afraid to come back and deal with whatever load of shit got dropped on you."

JD shrugged out from beneath Cheryl's foot. He got to his knees, then stood up, moving away. He stumbled, tripping over Teresa's legs, no reaction coming from her as he fell onto his knees. He looked at Cheryl, his eyes widening in awareness.

Cheryl smiled. "That's right, JD. She's *real*. And I'll keep you here, watching her grieve—every second of every hour of every day, made to feel *everything* she's feeling. Everything you've made happen to her. As real as what happened to *you*." Cheryl paused, her tone softening. "As real as the tragedy you suffered. Why you're here, hiding away, biding your time, waiting to die. Wanting the peace of oblivion."

JD raised his arm, hand outstretched, pointing at Cheryl with tears in his eyes. "Stop. Please. I—I never wanted this. *Any* of it. Never meant to—" He paused, his eyes narrowing. "They're not real. *None* of this is real. *You're* not—not *real.* You *can't* be. Not in *here!*" He reached up, pressing his fingers into Cheryl's lower arm, her skin flexing beneath his touch. "But you *are.*"

"I am. Both here *and* back there." Cheryl lowered her voice. "And so are *you.*" She touched him on his shoulder. "Take your time. When you're ready to do the work of climbing up out of your bottomless hole and facing your pain, l promise I'll guide you to a place where whoever it is you lost will be waiting to see you. To offer their support. To help you to heal."

JD nodded, then looked down at Teresa, who was cradling Jared's head in her lap. His chest moving again, eyes refocusing, gasping for breath as he rolled onto his side. Teresa staring as if seeing a ghost. JD stepped back, standing beside Cheryl, his voice firm. "I'll make it right. All of it. And let you know when I'm ready." He looked at her. "Ready to let you help me come back."

The lab was in shadows, lights dimmed by Isaac who was sitting in a chair beside Cheryl, holding her hand. She waited for him to release the straps from her legs and help her to sit up. His odd-colored eyes were full of questions, her conversation with JD on a loop within a loop, unavailable to Isaac over the live data stream.

"It's done." Cheryl's voice was shaking, drained from the emotional roller-coaster, her mind ringing with vibrations, fireworks popping off in front of her eyes as connections within her brain resonated with energistic feedback, despite the heavy filters she'd put in place.

"You were flailing, with your arm. You hit JD. Twice." Isaac paused, her words slowly registering. "Done? What's *that* mean? Were you—able to reach him?"

"It worked." Cheryl's lips were pinched in reaction to a wave of pain as a spasm ran through her frontal cortex. "Your plan. Adapting the calibration program to send him subliminal messaging, leading him to believe we could interface physically with him. From both sides of the mirror."

"Then why isn't he—" Isaac pointed at JD, who was staring up at the ceiling, eyes blinking, nothing changed. "Back?"

"Because he's staying behind. To fix it. To make everything good. Going to give everyone a happy-ever-after ending."

"Why? I mean—what's in it for him?"

Cheryl paused, trying to recenter her thoughts as they started to drift away. "I guess it's his way of preparing for—what comes next. Dealing with his *own* trauma, hoping we can help ease him through it." She rubbed the sides of her forehead, Isaac handing her pills and a glass of electrolytes, prepared for when she came out from under the Tee-Cee. She swallowed them, draining the glass as she washed the mild sedatives down. "I really don't know, Isaac. He told me he'd give us a signal when he's ready for us to walk him back out."

"What signal?" Isaac leaned forward, his hands clenched. "*When?*"

"Whatever he chooses. Whenever he decides." She sighed. "I don't think we'll have to wait too long. He's tired of hiding. Of carrying around the burden of whatever happened to him. Something worse—far worse than anything he's shown us. One he's ready to lay down."

"Then you've done it." Isaac gave Cheryl a quiet look. "Proven your technology works—under the *least* favorable conditions."

Cheryl nodded, her intense headache starting to fade, drained of every drop of emotional energy. She looked at Isaac, his eyes studying her, worried. A hint of a smile ticked up the corners of her lips as she answered him.

"Of course." She leaned back in the chair, head turned to one side, staring at JD, her voice barely above a faint whisper. "Was there ever any doubt?"

CHAPTER FORTY-NINE

YACHT, SAG HARBOUR

Luther

"That's splendid news, Luther. Great news—for us all. Never doubted it happening. Not with the doctor's background and reputation for overcoming all obstacles." Ed paused, holding his cup: a special blend of tea prepared by the man he considered as more than an assistant, having proven himself a trusted confidant. "She'd make an impressive addition to our—group, other than her being saddled with an overabundance of morality. And an excess of concern for the greater good of people, not seeing them for what they are: a restless mass, like those clumps of frog eggs. The ones with the little specks inside, surrounded by—" Ed paused, searching for the word. "*Goop*, I guess." He leaned forward, blowing on the cup, moving it from one hand to the next with no handle to hold on to. "You know what I mean?"

"Frogspawn." Luther sipped his tea, his cup held firmly, knowing the heat was not enough to cause blistering, only momentary pain. Endured by those who could see beyond self. Educated in the connection between nothing and everything, between pain and joy. Aware of the balance of the universe, the web of its ethereal energy spread from pillar to post.

Ed smirked, taking another sip of the unusually flavored tea. "Yeah, that sounds about right. What *most* folks are. Not all—but enough to keep things in order. Important—the balance between those born to lead and those content to follow. Something I know more than a little about, having an eye on the future like I do. About to redefine the social order. Having worked my ass off to get us out *there*. Get our asses off this *fucking rock*. Leaving all the—all the *frogspawn* behind."

Luther bowed his head and waited; aware one could only discover true balance when using the middle eye. Understanding the shifting of the smallest grain of sand could influence the collapse of entire mountain ranges.

"The tea—" Ed's voice cut through the still air of the office space below deck: the weather overcast, a rough chop on the water. "It has a—sweeter flavor than before. Though just as aromatic." The overweight man sighed, holding the cup below his nose, inhaling deeply, "Wish it was whiskey, but I'm appreciative of tradition. Even *yours*, or the one you *pretend* to follow, seeing you're not Asian."

Luther met his look with a submissive nod. "I appreciate you humoring my suggestion—in lieu of alcohol."

Ed smirked, taking another swallow of the tea. Larger this time, the thin walls of the cup having wicked some of the heat away, unaware of the sour lying just beneath the sweet. The balance of his ambitions about to be brought into alignment with the plans of those governing more than a billion and a half citizens. A mass of people with a unified, deeply ingrained view of their rightful place in the greater world.

After a few minutes Luther reached out, retrieving the precious cup from Ed's hand, the large man's fingers slowly relaxing, his eyes half-closed as his heart coasted to a gentle stop. His final breath slipping out in a sighing hiss. Luther carried the ancient cup over to a small sink, along with his own, placing them on a thick, handwoven mat. He used a bamboo handled brush to stir a carefully measured amount of temple-sourced spring water into each of them, the bristled ends of wild boar hair circling the symbols on their bottoms: the one in Ed's cup meaning blindness. Two symbols in his own: an open mind.

Luther hummed to himself as he finished packing everything away. The poison he'd administered would be untraceable within the hour, breaking down into organic components, impossible to distinguish from those in the man's own digestive system. An herbal remedy used to treat cases of extreme imbalance, exhibiting symptoms of dizziness, reduced vision, and a lack of mindfulness. Extremely effective when given in small doses. More so when liberally applied, based on the size of the patient and the result intended.

He stopped at a different library this time, with another donation made, allowed access to a private phone in the director's office. Another number dialed, answered on the first ring. "The Knight is off the board." Dead silence met his words, the person on the other end of the untraceable call hanging up without a word.

Luther watched as Thomas nodded his head, greeting the man approaching the table with a nod, waiting for him to sit down. He knew Thomas was irritated, and hungry: the time change from jetting across the Atlantic on a private plane having thrown his system out of balance. The new arrival took a moment to stop and survey the room, their table located on the second floor of an exclusive Chinese restaurant in an area of London known for preparing traditional cuisines from countries across the globe. It was midday, the interior uncrowded, the room they were in empty of other patrons.

A driver had picked Thomas and Luther up at Heathrow, delivering them to the establishment for an off the books meeting with a person seeking admittance to the innermost sanctum of the social group, a spot having recently opened. The head waiter, a diminutive, constantly smiling host of Asian heritage, had bowed in a polite greeting, explaining there was an issue with the plumbing, service limited to a few honored guests. He'd lead the two men to a table in the center of a private room, bowing to each of them again, perfectly executed. The sign of respect acknowledged by Luther, ignored by Thomas whose hands were trembling, needing another drink, despite having consumed several on the way in from the airport while riding in the back of a private car.

They were now a party of three: the last of their group a man whose roots were planted firmly in Russia, though he called London home. His name was Petrov, tall and wiry in build with a broad-shouldered frame: his eyes light blue and direct. They reminded Luther of a bird of prey, seeking the faintest movement in his local environment, fastening on each one with raptor-like attention. Thomas was the first to speak, having already ordered another drink, unhappy at the lack of hard liquor, having to settle for rice wine. Or *peasant piss*, as he kept called it, making a face each time he took a sip. "Peter, my friend. It's good to see you again."

Petrov nodded, not appearing to be bothered by the anglicizing of his given name. Thomas dove right in, ignoring Luther, who sat back, hands in his lap, silent. "We have suffered a loss. A *significant* loss, truth be told. One of my partners, and a close friend. His money, still pledged, important to our cause, though I must admit, I'll miss dealing with his—ambition."

Petrov raised an eyebrow. "Even now? His share still available after his—untimely death?" He leaned in, hands on the table, ignoring the glass of wine sitting in front of him. "His people, the ones who run his organization, they will surely want to pull back, questioning any further expenditures."

"Not to worry, my friend. *Your* buy-in is in process of review by the group. The monies are still needed, along with your influence with your government. Once a member has been approved, the funds are non-returnable—as you agreed to, upon submission of *your* application."

"Of course." The Russian looked at Luther, eyeing his simple clothing, considering him, by his quiet demeanor, as the more dangerous of the two. He glanced at the American, who seemed woefully unaware of his aide's capabilities and marked him as a foolish man. Or an idiot, Petrov thought to himself, knowing that made him dangerous as well, though for a completely different reason.

Thomas cleared his throat. "We've considered your list of site properties, and the outreach plan proposed to deal with your government. Extremely detailed and well thought out, meeting most of our selection criteria. An *excellent* beginning to our relationship." He reached for his glass to make a toast, then reconsidered, unable to stomach more of the weak rice wine. "Luther, if you will, please explain the recent breakthrough with our technology. I'm certain it will impress Peter. A bright and promising future in front of us—soon to be realized."

"Of course." Luther's face made a thin shift in expression, with no change to the solemn look in his eyes, noted by Petrov. "I have two handouts, printed on rice paper. You may deposit them in the wine when you've finished reading them. I will answer any questions as they arise." He handed each of the men a copy, then cleared his throat, filling them in on where things currently stood.

The quality of their meal more than made up for the lack of hard alcohol. The three of them shared a wide variety of authentic Chinese dishes. Luther managed a small bite here and there, his palette cleansed with a sip of lukewarm tea between each course. He artfully wielded a polished set of chopsticks, pulled from an inside pocket of his plain jacket, selecting choice morsels of roast duck, seared tuna, grilled beef, and perfectly seasoned noodles. The last course was an array of delicately shaped confectionery blossoms. Each one a perfect sculpture of golden, honey crusted leaves stuffed with a semi-sweet filling. Designed to melt in one's mouth, washed down with a special blend of rare tea leaves, steeped to perfection, releasing a soft floral bouquet into the air.

Petrov watched in awe as Luther rinsed his chopsticks, using them to pluck the blossoms from a carefully balanced stack, using deft movements. Not a single leaf made to crumble as he delivered one to each of their plates. "A—perfect presentation." Petrov nodded, acknowledging Luther's superior skill, understanding the countless of hours of practice required to perform the act. He reconsidered his earlier assessment, adding the word *exceedingly* in front of dangerous.

Thomas, oblivious to the exchange and display of skill, dove in, his hunger having returned. The lure of the sweets coaxed him to try the chopsticks left ignored during the meal. He failed, having to use a finger to balance the morsel until it reached his lips. Then he closed his eyes, sighing in contentment as it melted on his tongue. "Absolute heaven."

Petrov moved to copy him, stopping when he saw Luther's hand move slightly, side to side, going unnoticed by Thomas. The young Russian leaned back and rubbed his flat stomach. "Looks great, but there is no room left inside the inn. This is the proper expression?"

"Close enough—and too bad for you, my friend." Thomas raised his eyebrows slightly. "Would have expected more of an appetite from someone with your reputation for, shall we say, an *excess* of self-indulgence when it involves *women*."

"Haven't you heard, my American friend? It is a *new* day. Beginning of a new age. Our President, a man with high ambitions, calling on us to follow his excellent example of prudence and moderation in service to the State."

Thomas snorted, chewing loudly, before swallowing another of the elegant blossoms. "Sounds a lot like the *Chinese*. You should come spend some time in the States. Do you a world of good, seeing how *we* get things done."

"It might at that." Petrov eyed Luther, a thin smile on his lips. "I will consider your advice, my friend."

"Please, Peter. Call me Thomas. We're on a first name basis in our little club." Thomas looked at Luther and smiled, as if seeing him for the first time. "Isn't that right, Luther?"

Luther nodded, raising his hand to draw their server's attention. "Yes, Thomas. It certainly is."

Luther borrowed a cellphone from the manager of the restaurant and placed a call to a local number, waiting until someone answered. "The Rook is no longer on the board. The bishop is fully engaged." A thick slice of silence met Luther's words, the person on the other end of the untraceable call sucking in a deep breath, hesitating, as if about to comment, then hanging up.

CHAPTER FIFTY

SENATE OFFICE, WASHINGTON D.C.

Jean

A long-legged woman with a fashion model's body opened a solid wooden door, stepping aside as Jean moved past, closing it behind him. Jean stopped, waiting for an invitation to make his approach, nodding to a younger man sitting behind an enormous desk, elbow resting on its top, supporting his chin, an office phone clasped against one ear, his eyes closed. The metal placard on his door had identified him as Senator Cole Randall, from the Great State of Connecticut, who'd once served with Jean overseas.

Jean stood with his arms crossed, back braced, noting the younger man was still in great shape, with a chiseled face, his lean cheeks highlighted by the mid-afternoon sun, painting a wall of leather-bound books with a soft golden glow.

The Senator cupped his hand over the end of the phone. "Come on over, Major Kelley. Not looking to bite anyone—for the moment, at least." A thick carpet several paces wide all but swallowed the bass tones of the man's deep voice as Jean closed the distance, knowing the call was nearing the end, Cole's voice dropping into the typical uh-huh and you-don't-says, indicative of a fading interest in the topic being discussed.

Cole cursed under his breath, slamming the phone into its cradle: old school technology still having a place in the world of politics with cell phones discouraged, limited in their use. Phone records part of the traceability system mandated for official governmental business. "Fucking *supplicants*. Donating a thousand bucks here and there every few years, thinking you work directly for them."

"Don't you?" Jean smiled, softening the remark. The Senator was a younger version of himself, a highly decorated lieutenant who'd rotated out after three tours: several minor injuries and one serious one adding up to a lingering disability, forcing him into an early release. Leading to new opportunities, now a representative of an extremely wealthy and influential portion of the United States, a country he'd sworn to support and defend. Still the same man with high morals, nothing having changed in that area. And still single, avoiding the breaking of any marital vows, known about Washington as a healthy male, with a wandering eye.

"You called, sir. And I answered—or rather, my secretary did. What can I do for my former boss, Major Kelly?"

"It's Jean, now—Senator. I'm retired. A month ago."

"Easy to say. Hard to do—Jean." The Senator paused, then nodded. "And it's Cole, seeing we're alone."

Jean leaned back in a heavily built and thickly padded seat. "Need to share some things with you. Just the basics for now, though there're tons of data behind the words, available for you to be fully briefed on—*if* you decide to get involved."

"I'd expect nothing less from the man higher-higher was always calling the *'get-to-the-fucking-point'* guy."

Both men smiled at the use of one of Jean's former nicknames, conjured up by his fellow officers upon exiting his brief and straight to-the-point briefings. A title Jean knew about and quietly supported, having once read that brevity is the sole of wit. He figured it should apply to the numerous briefings he had to attend, with an abundance of half-wits droning on and on, most of them intelligence officers, going overboard to prove they deserved the name.

"There is a clear, and *soon* to be present threat to the United States, and all who live within its borders. Including the world at large, not that we can do anything about that. Not from here. At least—not today."

Cole shifted forward in his seat, his legs pulled back, squaring his shoulders behind the nameplate on his desk. He took a deep breath, letting it out slowly as the weight of the two oaths he'd made to serve and defend his country and the constitution landed on his wide shoulders. "Tell me—whatever you can."

"He wants to meet you. That's *all* I know." Jean tossed a wet towel at the bathtub in the hotel room where he and Cheryl were staying, missing badly, watching it splat against the side, falling back onto the tile floor. He went over and picked it up, dropping it in, able to hit the target on his second pass.

"Just *him?*"

"Far as I know."

Cheryl stepped back into the bathroom, her head wrapped in a towel, hair still wet. Another one tied around her waist. "You didn't bother asking—*did* you?"

Jean glanced over, staring at her breasts as she frowned. "No. I didn't." Cheryl sighed, then turned and walked away. Jean stepped out of the bathroom and walked over to the window of their room, watching as Cheryl stood in front of a closet, fanning her fingers through several outfits, trying to decide which one to put on. "But I *trust* him. Always have. There were many times when I placed my life, and those of my men in his hands."

Cheryl pulled a black dress from the closet, holding it up, covering her exposed breasts. "How's this?"

"Like the *no towel* look better."

"Stop it." She narrowed her eyes, turning slightly, staring into a full-length mirror, watching how the fabric moved. "Hope he's not like *you*, all macho and muscle." She paused, her lips crooked, considering. "His smile looks nice. He's a handsome man. And *single.*"

Jean came over and reached out, spinning her around, pulling her in against him, her arm holding the dress out to one side. "You looked him up?"

"Of course. Getting to know the lay of the land, like your Chinese guy suggested. The one who wrote the little book."

"Sun Tzu."

"Sure. That guy."

"I'm telling you—Cole's *not* the enemy."

"Isn't he though?" Cheryl stared at Jean. "You think this government gives a raccoon's butt about personal freedom? A few of them might. Maybe. Your friend being one of the good guys. But how many others are going to feel the *same* way, facing reelection and needing donations to stay in their seats?"

"Enough of them will stand up for what's right. Hopefully." Jean frowned as he listened to the sound of his words, knowing they sounded hollow.

Cheryl reached up, letting the dress fall to the floor, having decided against it, wanting to take their conversation in a different direction. She circled Jean's neck with her hands, the towel around her waist released with a shrug of her hips. "I *love* that about you—believing that people will do the right thing." He leaned in to kiss her, stopping when she tilted her head to the side, continuing to speak. "Like believing in Santa Claus, unicorns, and the tooth fairy. For all I know you still believe in the guys who started this whole thing, a long time ago." She let him kiss her, felt him starting to respond, then pulled away. "It reminds me of the song—the one where the woman asks where have all the cowboys gone."

Jean undid the towel on her head, tossing it aside, winding his fingers into her wet curls, pulling her close.

Jean made the introductions, then stepped away as Cheryl and Cole began discussing her project and results to date. He stood ready, if needed, to explain some of the finer points to Cole, able to speak the same language. Practiced at separating the simple from the complex, reducing endless reports on expected battlefield deployments by his superiors into a series of *if this happens* here, *then forget about everything else and get as many troops and bullets* here, *as fast as possible, with air support assets sent from* here.

Cole waved his hand, releasing Jean from his observation post, encouraging him to avoid letting the door hit him in the ass on his way out.

Cheryl found Jean in the Senate cafeteria, two senior members of the Intelligence Committee having recognized him, backing him into a corner to exchange stories from their past service, a handful of close-call events being shared. She held back, watching as he excused himself, heading into the bathroom while she stepped back out into the corridor and waited. Jean found her there, touching her on the shoulder as he walked by, encouraging her to follow him outside, where he took her by the hand, knowing his behavior might have confused her. He opened his mouth to explain, Cheryl stopping him before he could say a word.

"I figured it out, Jean. Recognized one of them from TV. Better not to be introduced and have to answer any questions of why I'm here with you."

Jean nodded, looking at her, a grin on his face. "So, you're not pissed?" Cheryl shook her head, her eyes shifting slightly, looking down the granite steps, as if having lost something. Jean stepped in, lowering his voice. "How did the meeting—"

Cheryl shook her head, starting down the steps, holding Jean's hand, walking away along a wide sidewalk until they were clear of the Capitol building. She led him into a small café with a wide assortment of baked goods, the aroma of strong coffee percolating from within. She sat down at a corner table, facing the door. "He *gets* it. *All* of it. I swear I saw him age twenty years in the hour we spent together." Cheryl paused. "I *scared* him, Jean, and I assume he's seen some terrible things in his time. With you. Over there." She fixed him with a knowing stare.

Jean nodded, taking her hand, squeezing slightly then letting go, holding up two fingers, pointing at the coffee mugs behind the counter, the server nodding. "Then he believed you—accepted the information you delivered?"

"Yeah. Cole seems like a bright guy. Saw ahead of where I was going, more than a few times, before I even got to the core issues. Jumped in and began painting the outlines. I just had to fill in a few spots, here and there."

"Cole was, and still *is* one of the best. Would have made General, until—"

"Showed me his scar. Proud of it, too. Like it was a badge of—" Cheryl stopped, staring at Jean. "Of *courage*. I just *got* that. Like the book they made us read in grade school. Which I didn't want to, of course, resisting anything someone told me I *had* to do. Especially when it involved things happening in the past. Never any interest in looking in the rear-view mirror."

"We can learn a lot from looking back." Jean gave her a discerning look. "About mistakes we've made, trying to prevent making them again." He paused. "Just like you can learn a lot about someone—from looking at a scar—on their upper thigh."

"Don't worry, Jean—no one could *see* us. We were in his private study. Besides, he's got chicken legs—not like *yours*. Especially since you started working out at the Rock."

Jean knew Cheryl had missed his point and decided to let it go, for now. He placed a side-conversation with Cole on his personal agenda for their next meeting. "Did he mention next steps?"

Their coffee arrived, Jean waving the cream away, both liking their caffeine with no extra adornment. Cheryl held her mug between her hands, a slight shiver working through her, wondering if it was from the air conditioning or a residual effect due to the conversation with the Senator. Not that it mattered, the serious faced man left mulling over his options, letting her know he'd be in touch, through Jean. Two old war buddies exchanging a call, allowing their conversation to be kept off the official call logs.

"He looked scared, Jean. Or maybe—I don't know. Worried. Hard to tell, my not knowing him like you do."

"The two emotions often go hand in hand once you poke your head over the ridgeline and see what's waiting for you on the other side." Jean reached out, touching his mug to hers, taking a drink, enjoying the strong brew.

CHAPTER FIFTY-ONE

MARINA, MARYLAND

Jean

Jason tossed a surveillance report on top of a battered desk used to hold diving equipment in need of servicing or repair. Its surface was covered in deep gouges and stains, appearing to have survived an all-out assault by someone wielding a dull chainsaw. Jean picked up the folder, thumbed through it, stopping now and then to ask a question, then continuing to read. Skinny left the office, letting the door slam behind him, unwilling to stand around.

"Thorough. Nicely done. Between this—" Jean touched the report. "And what the other teams got—it's pretty damn clear what we're up against."

"Teams?" Jason tilted his head. "Thought you'd gone back to rotating just two. Us and the other guys."

Jean shrugged. "Got some extra help. An old friend put me in touch with some guys—who know some guys. Got eyes and ears on two of the operatives. Another friend of mine's digging through his contacts, looking for—"

"*Jesus*, Dancer, how many *effing* friends do you have? I've known you for a while now, and one thing's for certain—you ain't *that* friendly."

Jean grinned. "Okay. Make that *acquaintances* then, or whatever you want to name 'em, long as they can get the intel I need. And as it stands right now—it's not looking good for our side of things."

"*Shit.*" Jason sat down in a battered chair, leaning back, hands behind his neck. "Your lady friend. Your *only* lady friend, if you know what's good for you—is she in any danger?"

"No." Jean paused. "But she's of interest to a few groups, and that could be good or bad, depending on how we play this. On how they choose to react."

"They, meaning our foreign friends on the other end of a very deep hole. Right?"

Jean didn't answer, his eyes focused on a point somewhere far away, remembering seasoned veterans talking about walking frozen terrain, looking for places to maneuver around or dive into. Deep ravines, keeping troops out of the sight line of enemy guns. Turned into traps, set up to lure men into tossing themselves down, believing they were out of the fight, for a few minutes at least, their backs exposed to machine guns dug in weeks before, waiting for the day to arrive when death would stalk the land, changing it into a killing ground.

He shook his head. "Yeah. Tough group to go up against. Was stationed up where it happened, for a bit. Kid of eighteen. Had read all the books, poured through SLA Marshall's writing, with the after-action reports. Up on the Dee-Em-Vee, going out on patrol, imagining what it must have been like for both sides during the conflict. Different way of fighting then. Different weapons. Different times."

"But the soldiers are still the same." Jason frowned. "Including women, now. Out in front, facing the same shit."

Jean lowered his gaze, staring at Jason who stared back. "Yeah. We're still putting it all out there, like everyone else. On *both* sides."

Skinny came barging back in, stopping in the doorway, head brushing the top of the frame, shoulders against the sides. "You done playing with your peckers yet? I'm starving *and* thirsty. Got to be to work in an hour, so—drop your cocks and grab your socks, recruits. Got a *war* to fight, and it ain't happening on an empty stomach!"

"How far—do I take this?" Cole looked at the surveillance report Jean handed him. "Do you want me to go through channels, putting in a request for a response from their embassy?"

"No. She said to let it go." Jean shook his head, a frown on his face. "Said it wasn't an issue—for her."

"What's *that* supposed to mean?"

Jean shrugged. "Fuck if *I* know."

"Christ, Jean—you're sleeping with her, right?" Cole noted Jean's nod. "Why not have her explain it to you, in between—well, I suppose it's not *in-between*, what with you being old."

Jean ignored the dig. "*You've* met her. Not like she's gonna tell us *everything* she's got going on. She's not exactly—an open book, especially when it comes to her long-range plans."

"Okay. For *now*. But I'm not in the business of operating with blinders on." Cole held up his hand, stopping Jean before he could begin. "Not supposed to be in this kind of business at *all*, even though I'm forced into it at times. Blind luck, whenever something works out as planned. No different here than it ever was over there. Same—muddied results."

"Blood's the same color, though."

Cole sighed, glancing at the report. "Thanks, I guess, for keeping me in the loop. Not that it does me any good." He paused. "I've been nosing this around with some people I know. Sitting in oversight positions on research groups, already looking into this type of tech."

"Any feedback you care to share?"

"Interest in the concept—yes. But as to the technology needed to accomplish it—no. Nothing tangible. Only vague rumors of some unknown group trying to bring something like this to the public. Someday. But not even close to being able to. At least—not yet."

"Still early days, Cole. But I swear I heard the rumble of artillery outside my window last night."

CHAPTER FIFTY-TWO

REDEMPTION

Final Chapters

Miranda and Twain

Twain leaned his hand on Miranda's shoulder, using it to help him get down the last stretch of an angled path, leading to peyote-blue waters in the canyon below. It was early spring, the air clear, wrung dry of moisture with morning still a few minutes away. He felt cool, nearing the end of a long, two-day hike into Havasu Falls. The two of them had shared the trail with a dozen like-minded people, coupled up like them. Sitting around at night, sharing stories of where they were from, jobs they'd set aside long enough to make the sabbatical to a place held in their imaginations. Excited on discovering they were in the presence of a real movie-star, Miranda having revealed Twain's secret identity while he was out answering a call of nature.

They were the last of the group to arrive at the pools, their new friends up to their waists in the flow of water, most with tears in their eyes as if newly baptized. All of them moved by the natural beauty of the canyon, its energy spiraling between red-white sandstone walls, reflecting from an azure-blue sky overhead. Others were climbing to ledges so they could dive in, everyone's voices kept low, doing their best to respect the sanctity of the spiritual location belonging to the native group holding ancestral claim.

"It's more beautiful than I dreamed of." Miranda shook her head, feeling as if she'd arrived home, with her aching feet having trod this same piece of ground, her eyes having seen the same flow of water in a previous life. She turned and looked at Twain, her eyes overflowing with tears. "And to think I was going to come here by myself. With you—in an urn."

Twain angled his head to one side, his smile lop-sided, a signature pose used to great advantage in two films, just released. He spread his arms, inviting her in, wrapping her in a bear hug, eliciting envious looks from several women and a few of the men standing nearby. "Would have been quicker, what with me slowing ya down—my balance still off."

Miranda placed her forehead on his chest, moving her head from side to side. "Would have been impossible." She looked up, her eyes searching his, as if to verify he was there, and that this wasn't a dream. "We're here, right? For true?"

Twain nodded. "Yeah. We are."

Jemma and Calvin

Calvin reached out, touching Jemma's swollen belly. Again. Amazed at how compact it was. A round bump, like half a basketball placed under her shirt. She placed her hand on the back of his, holding it there, knowing their baby could feel it. People moved past the two of them, smiling as they exited the farm store, nodding at her, holding a variety of goods in bags. Two young girls stood behind the register of the crowded store, helping to bag groceries, offering to lug them out to customer's cars.

"We should probably move this moment inside." Jemma took Calvin's hand and headed inside the farmhouse, bypassing the kitchen where a dozen pies sat on a wide, granite topped island, cooling off. "Been a good day. Again. Thanks to you."

"To us." Calvin pulled her through the living room, heading into their bedroom at the end of a hall.

"Yeah. *Us.* I like the sound of that." Jemma gave him a coy smile, tilting her head. "I have something for you."

Calvin shook his head, reaching for her. "I have something for *you*, too."

Jemma took his forearm, using it to support herself as she kneeled. Then she looked up, seeing the expectant look in Calvin's eyes. "Not *that*, you idiot!" She shook her head. "This." She pulled a ring out of her pocket: a thin silver band with a small gemstone embedded. Blue, the color of his eyes.

Calvin looked down, confused as Jemma reached up and took his left hand. She slid the ring onto his finger. "Will you, Calvin, the man I love beyond all others, who has helped me find my home here. To not only find it but build it *together*. Will you do me the honor of becoming my husband, for me to love, to grow old with, to honor and—to try my best to—" She paused, tears streaming down her cheeks. "To *listen* to. And maybe try to obey."

Calvin folded his legs, joining her on the floor. He took her face between his hands, gazing into her eyes. His own, as full of tears. "I thought you'd never ask." Then he leaned in, kissing her.

Teresa and Jared

Jared brought in the last load of Teresa's things, placing another box filled with her shoes on the bedroom floor. He straightened up, watching as she hung her dresses in the closet, using most of the hangers. She'd already put some of her shoes away, lined up in neat rows along the bottom. Her other things had filled most of the drawers in his bureau. He smiled, feeling her energy flowing through the bedroom. Throughout the entire house. Swirling within his heart, open to her, completely. He went over and pulled a large package from behind the headboard of their bed, placing it on the bedspread, waiting for her to turn around and find it. When she did, her eyes narrowed, looking at him with a questioning look.

"What—have you done?"

"Doing it." He smiled at her. "Right now."

"You didn't—" Teresa's lower lip trembled, tears in her eyes as she stared at the rectangular shape.

"Did."

"No. They said they wouldn't let it go."

"They did."

"Really?" Jemma began to tremble, her hand clenched.

"Really." Jared took her hands, squeezing them softly. "It's *ours*."

"It is?" Teresa shook her head, unable to believe it. "Completing the collection?"

"Yes." Jared paused. "Found these, too. Guess I forgot to return them." He held up a small velvet box. "Seem to remember you liking them. They looked great—when you had them on that night."

"You—kept them? All this time?" Teresa raised her hands, wiping her cheeks.

Jared took her hand, closing her fingers around the earrings. "I did. Had to take back your bicycle—to cover some of the cost. Sorry. I know how much it meant to you, sitting out in the garage, waiting to be ridden."

Teresa broke into a breathless sob, shaking her head. "That's okay. I—I think I'll manage to survive not—"

"Psych. It's still out there. With customized training wheels on it, for when you're ready to learn how to ride. Then we'll—"

Teresa's lips found his, ending any further discussion. She tossed the jewelry box on the bed, pulling Jared down to the floor, feasting on his lips, his tongue. Lying on top of him, looking down, her tears painting his cheeks.

Cheryl reached up, wiping her eyes: the scenes JD was projecting, heart-warming, letting her know he was ready. All the loops closed, like he'd promised to do. First step to closing the one in his own life as well. She looked at Isaac, who stood beside JD, looking over at her with a quiet look on his face.

"Get the other Tee-Cee set up. It's time."

Isaac stared at the screen. "I—don't get it."

"Right there. In front of you. JD's letting me know to come find him. To help bring him out." She moved over to the second chair, removed her lab coat, and leaned back.

The immersion into JD's environment was complete. It was a scene familiar to Cheryl's eyes with ledges, pine trees, juniper bushes, and stands of birch trees. Misty shapes hovered in the background. Shadows, blending into the bottom of low-hanging clouds. Distant mountains, their tops hidden from view. A steep wall of gray-faced granite rose nearby, hugged along the base by a clinging tree line.

"Requiring—a leap of *faith*." Cheryl shouted the words, knowing he was there, somewhere. In the edge of trees, behind a rock, or atop a ledge.

"Not so large a move as that." JD's voice was a whisper from behind, causing her to spin around, the tone wistful, hovering between playful and sad. He looked at her, trying to smile. Failing.

"Not planning to go all out—and try and bring my brother back?"

"No. But I appreciate you sharing memories of him. Helped me understand why you've been so—"

"Pushy? Determined?" Cheryl grinned, her eyes crinkling at the corners.

JD shrugged. "A *pain*—in my ass."

Cheryl grinned. "Something my brother always called me. But then, you already knew that."

JD smiled, still carrying an unseen burden, his shoulders sagging. "Having a hard time with this, even though you've been clear on what you're offering in return. Helping me—" He looked away and stared into the distance, hands hanging at his side.

Cheryl moved over, feeling the ground beneath her feet, wearing a familiar pair of worn hiking boots, with scuff marks on the toes. Another gift from JD. "Went through it myself. Not that I know your personal circumstances, but more than willing to share mine." She stopped in front of him. "It pissed me off, my parents allowing that to happen. Pissed at myself too, for not having been there to prevent it."

"Your brother's death? Nothing you could—"

"No." Cheryl sighed. "Talking about *before*. When he got hurt."

"You're being up there with him wouldn't have changed anything. You're just angling your viewpoint, so it parallels my experience. To show me it's not all that different from anyone else's. Horrible things happen to good people, all the time. Impossible to avoid when it comes along. Just have to bear it as best you can." JD's voice dropped. "If you can."

"We can wait until another time—if you're not ready."

"No." He sighed, his thin shoulders rising and falling. "I'm good. Resigned to the fact that waiting won't change anything. So—let's go."

Cheryl reached out and took JD's hand, leading him to a different scene, one of her own. The woods and ledges dissolved to an ocean beach. A light surf sighed across wet sand as the tide turned, running away. Gulls called, their voices softened by a gentle breeze. Small boats churned the water further out, as if tractors plowing the surface, leaving white rows trailing behind in sun-dappled furrows. "I *love* this place. One you showed me, or showed to yourself, I guess. Isaac and I just voyeurs, sneaking peeks over the shoulders of your people." Cheryl grinned. "Frisky couple, especially on that stormy, winter day."

"It's in Maine, on the mid-coast region. Went there once. Stayed a couple of weeks."

"With someone special, right?"

"You're guessing. Again."

"Twain and Miranda. Calvin and Jemma. Jared and Teresa. Sensing a real trend there, JD."

He let go of her hand and stepped away, moving to where the water was rolling in, letting it wash over his feet. Bare now, his pants rolled up, toes covered in sand, hands jammed in his pockets. "She was—much more to me than any of those women. Or as much, I guess. Pieces of her in all of them. Pieces of myself in each of the men." He turned around. "Guess that makes me—vain."

"Or smart, trying to face whatever happened to you by spreading the pain between all of them, wanting to try and soften the blow."

"I'm going with vanity." JD hesitated. "She used to—" He stopped, looking back over his shoulder as if she might be there, coming along the grass-covered dunes.

Cheryl walked over, hands behind her back, feet bare, leaving deep impressions in the damp soil. "We can talk about this all day—or we can get you home again. Are you ready?"

JD didn't answer, hands pressed to his eyes, then he nodded. Cheryl raised her voice. "Isaac—pull the plug." She watched as JD opened his eyes and looked at her, hands lowered, a questioning look on his face. Cheryl leaning in and smiled, fingers fully extended. "Don't ask. The answer is—yes, it definitely will." Then she began folding down her fingers, one at a time.

"Will what?" JD narrowed his eyes, giving Cheryl a questioning look.

"Hurt like *hell*." Cheryl folded her thumb into her palm. "Sorry.

Cheryl opened her eyes. Her real eyes. She was lying in the chair, the Tee-Cee still fastened in place. Her projection had ended just as a pulse of energy went through the leads attached to JD's head. She stared at the ceiling, afraid to look over at JD, wondering if her latest strategy had worked: a concentrated feedback loop sending a wave of emotions through the Tee-Cee to help jar JD's consciousness into releasing him. A form of mental shock therapy, highly refined and, hopefully, of benefit to him. Some of her patients in the past wakening from their somnolent stupors with blinding headaches, though all were grateful with the results in the end.

Isaac leaned over, looking at her with a wide smile. "You did it. He's *back*."

Cheryl broke down in a series of silent sobs, her head twisting from side to side while Isaac released the straps binding her body in place, grasping her chin in one hand as he removed the headgear. He pressed her head back, gently wiping away her tears, gazing at her for a moment before going over to check on JD, whose voice was an endless wail of misery, his body twitching from the effect of the treatment.

Cheryl rolled onto her side and curled up in a ball, feeling as empty emotionally as when her brother had passed. Knowing she could have saved him. Now. Could have helped guide him back, leaning over the top of the wall he was at the bottom of, trying to claw his way to the top. Offering her hand, helping to pull him back into his life. Into her life as well.

It was morning. The lab was quiet, all the monitoring systems shut down. The only sound, a light rush of air moving through the ventilation system. Cheryl had her fingers on the handle of JD's room, hesitant to open it, afraid the day before had only been another dream. Then she heard Robert's voice whispering to her, coaxing her to make the leap. Taking a deep breath, she leaned forward, pushing the door open.

JD was sitting up, his legs swung over the side of the bed, holding his head, looking down as if deciding whether to get up or go back to sleep. He looked at Cheryl. "I'm—really here." His voice was pitifully weak, throat raw from the high-pitched screams he'd been producing when he first came back, the level of emotional feedback that had jolted him free, overwhelming his ability to manage the abuse caused by the amplified, false stimulation of reality.

"Yes. You are."

JD mumbled something, Cheryl unable to make it out, coming over and kneeling in front of him. "I couldn't hear you." She picked up a glass from his nightstand, handing him a syrupy drink designed to help ease the hoarseness in his throat, waiting as he swallowed it down. When he tried speaking again, his voice was barely a whisper, but clear enough for her to make out what he was saying.

"My name. David." He coughed, taking another swallow. "I'm David."

Tears welled up in Cheryl's eyes as she smiled. "It's nice to meet you. David." She waited, wondering when or if he'd take the next step, knowing he wouldn't care where he was, or the year. None of the inane questions poised in movies or books, irrelevant to what most patients waking up wanted to know. The location of their mother, verification of the number of their limbs, seeking an explanation for their body's physical deterioration.

"I know you." David closed his eyes, then opened them again, as if to verify he was truly awake. "Cheryl. It was in—the data you streamed when you came to find me." His voice was growing stronger, as if a pet bird testing its wings after being released from years of captivity. "Everything." He shook his head. "I know everything about you. Perhaps more than I should." He coughed several times, clearing his throat. "But it worked. You convinced me to—" His eyes found hers. "To make the leap. The same thing your brother said he did."

"Anything *you* care to share, to help balance the scale? Your age, last name, mother's maiden name? Social security number. Things like that?" Cheryl smiled, tears running down her cheeks, knowing he was fully back, his mind in one piece.

David rubbed his throat, then looked around the room. "No. Not right now. Still trying to—" He coughed. "Get my feet under me. Speaking of which—" He leaned forward, trying to stand. "I need to go to the bathroom."

"Of course." Cheryl stood up, helping him to his feet, taking his arm to steady him as he moved across the bedroom floor, his feet shuffling in the slippers she helped put on his feet, the soles smooth, pale, and soft. She led him to the restroom at the near end of the lab, waiting as he went in. Alone. For the first time. Isaac or herself always in attendance over the handful of months he'd been under their care.

She stood outside, shifting from one foot to the other, swaying slightly, humming an old tune her parents used to play. Her father, with a beat-up guitar in his hands, and her mother, in a handmade dress, flowers twisted in a wreath around her head. The two of them singing an endless song while she and Robert lay on the living room floor, waiting for the chorus, the two of them joining in with loud voices. "For the times—the times—*they are* a-*changing*."

CHAPTER FIFTY-THREE

OFFICE, MILITARY FACILITY

Mari

Luther could feel a rush of excitement run through him, the only sign of it, a slight gleam in his pale eyes. "An amazing accomplishment. No defined starting point to work from, with multiple personality disorders to search through."

Mari studied the man, his name unknown to her, sensing his elevated energy. "Projections, not disorders."

"The difference?" Luther gathered himself, back in control

Mari paused, wondering if this was another cryptic test. "A patient with multiple personality disorders is unaware they're not real. That only one of them is their original self." She paused, waiting until the man on the other side of the desk raised a finger, a signal for her to continue. "And our patient, JD, or rather David, he knew the—"

"Their patient, Ms. Coleman. Or, more accurately—the doctor's."

"Yes. Of course. *Her* patient, Doctor Atkinson's, he knew who he was all along. The projections were designed to protect himself from having his identity revealed. Not wanting to be connected back in." Mari frowned. "I mean—back into the real world."

"Requiring what must have involved a substantial transference of emotional energy."

Mari nodded. "Yes. From a single source, sent through each of the multiple projections. Cycling between them, creating a diverse assortment of feedback from all the characters, if you will. In each of the various settings."

"And which did you find to be the most compelling?"

Mari needed a moment to catch up, the normally taciturn man stunning her with his sudden interest. "I—don't know. Never stopped to—"

"A lie." Luther raised his hand at an angle. "Not intentional. Not directed at me, but yourself. What is the expression? From the English writer of note. To thine—"

"Own self be true." Mari let a thin smile crease the line of her lips. "Shakespeare. But you already knew that." A smile mirroring her own served as the man's response. Mari nodded her head. "If I had to choose—it would be Twain. The actor."

"Interesting."

"You had another one in mind as my choice?"

Luther raised an eyebrow. "The consultant. A role you would be most familiar with, based on your assigned responsibilities regarding the project."

"Twain. Definitely him." Mari waited for another question. None followed. The man shifted his finger, pointing at the door. Mari left, covering half the length of the long corridor before it occurred to her how strange it was, a man who'd never shared his name with her, asking which character she felt most drawn to, as if they were actual people. She let it go, focused on her plans to meet up with the members of the resistance group, eager to be introduced to the man behind the mirror.

"They're welcome to *every* line of code. The *entire* design. *All* of it." Cheryl looked from Mari, reflecting a stoic expression, to the three men sitting around the end of the booth. Isaac, frowning. David, with a bewildered look in his eyes, and Jean nodding, having listened to her explanation of what she was planning to do before they'd left her apartment.

"Why not?" Cheryl spun in a half-circle, checking the line of her cut-off jeans, taking a moment to admire her exposed calves, slim, with firm muscles and tendons lying just beneath lightly tanned skin. "We've proven it works, under impossible circumstances. And it's needed, now—more than ever before. They have the money to invest, and I'll get enough out of the buy-out to continue my research without having to apply for grants. Enough money to live on, travel, do whatever I—" She looked at Jean, smiling. "Or whatever *we* decide to do, without having to worry about a thing." She paused. "Disappear, if we want to, living off the grid, hiking, climbing, or whatever comes to mind."

Jean let the comment slide by, disturbed by her cavalier attitude. "You know they'll break it, eventually. Thwarting your plan to control what they'll end up doing with it, using the—"

"Yeah. Heard you, the first hundred or so times you've mentioned that." Cheryl flashed him a smile. "Thwart? Really? Where'd you dig *that* word up? From a comic book?" Jean didn't respond, his lips pressed tightly together. Cheryl stepped over and looked into his eyes. "You're such an old lady, going on and on about me not seeing the trees for the forest." She touched his face, the tip of her fingers tracing a web of fine scars on his cheek. "I've got it covered, Jean. I *do*. They haven't got a clue who it is they're dealing with."

"Do you?" Jean put his hands on her waist.

Cheryl lost her smile. "What's *that* supposed to mean?"

Jean opened his mouth to reply, then paused, shaking his head. "All I know is—you've raised a lot of interest in this by letting the cat out of the bag. Now the shoe is on the other foot, with you deciding to leap, before—"

Cheryl grinned. "You're trying to divert me." Jean moved his hands, placing them lower down, grasping her bottom, squeezing. "Is it *working?*" Her phone rang before Cheryl could answer him. She cradled it to her ear as she looked in the mirror again, considering if the low-cut top she had on revealed too much skin.

"We'll *be* there." There was a slight pause, Jean hearing music and people's laughter over the speaker. "In *ten* minutes." Cheryl squinted her eyes. "What was that? Tell her to order us the fish. *What* did she say? Tell her I *know* I have, but I'll be sweating it off tomorrow, on the wall. Besides, they're so good—okay. I'll let you go." Cheryl pulled the phone away from her ear, then put it back, listening for a moment before responding. "Fine. Tell her to order me one too. With vinaigrette on the side. I don't care *which* one. Her choice."

Jean waited for Cheryl to put the phone in the back pocket of her jeans. "Isaac, I presume."

"Yup. He's already there. With David. His first night out. And Mari, too." Cheryl hesitated. "He seems to do better spending time with her, now that he's passed through his—down days."

Jean nodded, crossing his arms on his chest. "Can't imagine what he's going through. Has been through."

"Gonna get a lot worse for him, and soon. Hoping tonight will trigger an opening with him hanging out, listening to the rest of us bantering and bickering with each other. David, smack-dab in the middle of it all." Cheryl fastened another button on her shirt, noting a slight nod of approval from Jean as she did so. "Kinda like putting him through shock therapy again, only this time—with fish nuggets and booze."

David looked over at Jean, feeling his eyes on him. He forced a smile and a nod, watching as the other man returned one of his own. "Something on my face?" David reached up, using a napkin to wipe his lips, having finished most of a basket full of fish, using liberal portions of house-made tartar sauce with each nugget.

"No. You just caught me out. Staring. Being rude." Jean turned, looking at Cheryl, her eyebrows raised, enough to let him know a discussion about his table manners was in the offing. "Sorry. I'm just trying to come to grips with him—with David sitting here, and not—"

Cheryl put a finger on Jean's lips, shushing him. "Just stop. Hole's deep enough already. Stop digging."

"It's fine." David slid another smile out of his dwindling reserve, using it to let Cheryl's friend know the furtive looks from the members of the group didn't bother him. "I'm still trying to come to grips with being here myself."

Cheryl reached out, touching the back of David's hand. "I can take you back, whenever you want to leave."

"I thought—" David looked at Mari, who was sitting beside him. Isaac's imposing girth at his usual spot in an office chair, outside the tight confines of the booth. "She, I mean Mari—I thought she was taking me back." Mari noticed him staring at her and smiled, trying to make out what he was saying, hand to her ear as a young couple passed by, voices raised, belting out the lyrics to a popular song written well before their time, being played, loudly, by the house band.

Cheryl, sitting across from David, leaned in. "She's leaving from here, heading straight home. So—*I'm* your ride for tonight."

David nodded, shifting in his seat, feeling constricted by the press of emotions welling up. He looked out at the people on the dance floor, wishing he were back on the other side of reality where he was in total control. The band leaned into the song they were playing, encouraged by the sizeable crowd's positive reaction, everyone singing along, their voices rattling the rafters. A fine layer of dust filtered down, stirred by the spinning whir of paddle fans. David stared up at them, his eyes glazing over, head slumping forward, feeling himself falling over the edge of a world he'd only recently awakened back into.

"Are you feeling any better?" Cheryl and Jean were standing on either side of David's bed. He was back in his own room. His new home, of a sort. "The sedative should help. It's mild. Just strong enough to dull around the edges a bit."

David slowly closed, then quickly opened his eyes, as if checking to make sure he was still there. His breathing was steady, body relaxed. A look of mild concern on his thin features that he might fall back into the waiting clutches of a false security, used to ward away the constant whispering coming from the wind-swirled surface of a vast ocean of pain, always there. Wanting, needing to try and conjure up some small measure of joy, enough to pull himself away from the looming abyss. He closed his eyes, losing himself to the numbing effects of the sedative.

"You'll be fine. It's barely more than a scratch." She held his hand. Her hair pulled back, light blond, with red highlights, tied with a blue strip of cloth. Eyes gleaming in the bright sunlight.

David frowned. "It's more than a scratch, Meg. It's bleeding. A lot!" He looked away, watching as a line of waves rolled in, raking the sloped edge of a white sand beach fronting a ledge-shouldered cove. He winced, the press of a napkin against the slice in his palm dissolving the last of his resolve as the sting of salt water forced into the shallow cut caused him to flinch. "Jesus, Meg! What the—"

"Stop being such a baby. It's almost stopped. Just give it a few more minutes. Use that million-dollar imagination of yours to go somewhere else. Same place you were, most of yesterday and this morning, fingers hovering over your keyboard, mumbling under your breath, pecking away at the keys like some crazed accountant trying to make the numbers agree."

"It's called working."

"Daydreaming, more like it. Lucky that people are willing to pay you to do it. Otherwise, you'd have to go out and get a real job."

David considered responding with another long-winded explanation of how wrong she was. Reminding her again of the pressure he was under, trying to come up with something new to pitch to studio heads, producers, and the rest. Trying to find a different take on the same worn-out story lines told since people first climbed down out of trees and sat around in circles, looking in each other's eyes, spinning tales across a glowing bed of coals, through curtains of dancing flames. Swirls of spark-filled smoke rising, pointing their gnarled fingers at the stars above.

"There. All set. See? No more blood. Just a—huge, gaping gash, splitting the flesh, exposing muscle, sinew and bone." Maggie grinned: her front teeth separated by a slight gap. Hardly noticeable. Easy to fix. His friends eager to recommend orthodontists, unaware of how enticing the slight imperfection was to him. His beautiful Meg, or Margaret, as her parents called her. On special occasions, allowed to call her Maggie Mae. With a guitar in his hands, serenading her with verses pulled from an old song. Ringlets of loose curls raining down her narrow shoulders. His eyes glistening with joy, loving the taste of his nickname for her, in the nasal-bass sound of his words. But never Peg, her grandmother's name. Earthmother to her New England clan, located a few dozen miles away from where they were sitting.

"Thank you, Maggie. My sweet Maggie Mae."

She tilted her head, considering him, her hazel-green eyes framed by skin toasted a light shade of tan. "And you without your guitar. Too bad—you might have gotten lucky."

David reached out, taking her head between his hands, his finger brushing the small scar on her cheek, left by a dog bite when she was a child. He leaned forward, kissed her gently, then pulled back. "I already did."

Morning broke around two cups of coffee, David and Cheryl sitting together in the facility's cafeteria. A large plate, filled to the brim with pancakes and links of sausage, sat in front of David, along with a glass of juice. He stared at the food, wishing for a shovel to help fill the hole in his body. Constantly hungry, needing the fuel to help recover his full strength. He stopped eating long enough to give Cheryl a smile. "You're not eating?"

She shook her head, sipping her coffee, the mug held between her hands, enjoying the warmth. "Going to be working out, later—once Isaac gets here to babysit you."

"I *could* go with you. Get some work in on a treadmill. Lift some weights."

"Not here. And not at a gym. There's a place I go called the Rockery, with climbing walls. Forty-foot section for the pros. Thirty, for novices, who'll be there in force today. Better than hot yoga." Cheryl looked at his plate. "Better on an empty stomach, too."

"Maybe next time, then." David shoveled another large helping of food into his mouth, chewing for a minute, using a large swig of juice to wash it down. "I'd love to watch you. Climb, that is. Seeing how I have—memories of you doing that. In here." He pointed at the side of his head, his hair longer now, almost down to his ears, a slight curl to it. Jet black, with a few strands of gray starting to show up.

"We can definitely arrange that, once you're up to it. Right after you take a run at doing some of the *other* things you need to focus on. Again—once you're up to it."

"Yeah. That's the elephant, always there, standing in the center of the room."

"Then maybe I should put the Tee-Cee on its head? Though I'll need to find a longer strap."

David lowered his eyes, staring at the plate of food, half-eaten. "I had a dream. Last night. About—her. A good one, from before the—" He pushed his plate away, his appetite gone. "I guess, I mean—that's a *good* sign. Right?"

Cheryl shrugged. "Probably. You're going to want to find someplace comfortable to start from, then work your way up to whatever happened. I can induce a mild, chemical coma. Try to keep everything under control. Could try coming in with you, helping to absorb—" She stopped as David shook his head.

"No. You risked your sanity, exposing yourself like you did without knowing the potential for damage." David looked at her. "Isaac explained everything you did. The risks you took." He lowered his head, then looked away, staring through the windows, watching people moving past them. Some in uniforms, others in street clothes. "I owe you—everything, for having done that. Even though I'll probably be cursing you to hell when I—"

"There's no hurry, David. We're breaking new ground here, without rules *or* procedures. Nothing in place to tell us what happens next."

"So, we're both going to wing it, then. Take a leap of faith—like we're climbing the Hawksbill."

Cheryl kept a flash of irritation from her face, a moment of resentment rising from David being in possession of an intimate portion of her childhood memories. "Yup."

"When? I mean, it's got to be a ton of money spent, me being here. Now that I'm on my feet again, I can't imagine them, or you thrilled to have me hanging around."

"You're here until *you're* ready to move on, David. To get back to the life you were living before your accident. Sucks, that it happened to you, I get that. But I ended up turning what happened to *me* into—well, something *positive*. Spending a butt load of time, energy, tears, and grant monies getting the solution developed to where it could help you. Which it can *still* do, David. Believe me. I'll be able to give you closure. I promise."

David looked up, fixing her with a stare. "Okay." Then he pulled the plate back over, using a fork to spear another sausage link, holding it up, looking at it. "What happens—after?"

"Weeks of physical and emotional therapy, while we get your personal details straightened out. Still waiting on the details, whatever you're willing to share of what happened. Whatever you remember or can recall. Then we'll get a final payoff figure from the accountants."

David pushed his plate away. "What makes you, or anyone else think I have enough money stashed away to pay for—to pay for everything you've provided. I mean, this place is *great!* Excellent food. The staff is nice. Accommodations a bit spartan for my taste, but clean." He stopped, seeing her grin. "*What?*"

"Numbers from the *other* way around, David. Not *from* you, but *to* you. A nice sum. Payment for your having been a participant, aware of it or not, in our project. We've already settled your outstanding medical bills. You owe nothing and have gained a *lot*. Physically and financially, from being an integral part of the success of the project. Against your will, but despite that, part of the solution path, proving it works under the most adverse circumstances." Cheryl paused, pursing her lips, giving him a considered stare. "As far as your *mental* state goes, there's still work needing to be done there. You know that better than anyone, with all the trauma you put your mirrored selves through, reflections of your own. And it's *still* there, waiting to bite you in the ass when you least expect it. Something I've always focused on first, in reaching out to, and then retrieving people who've been in your situation."

"Then why were you so—impatient with *me?*"

"Because you were not like any of the others, David. Making you special. And I owe you a lot, for having forced my hand. Pushing me and my solution into places I'd never imagined it could or would ever have to go."

"Does that mean I get a percentage of what they're *paying* you? Call it a—product improvement fee. Twenty percent seems like a fair number, to start with."

"I'll happily have that discussion when you're ready to leave." Cheryl reached across the table, hand out. "Deal?"

David shook it then sighed, pushing his chair back from the table. He watched as Cheryl reached out, snagging a sausage link from the small lake of syrup it was sitting in. She shoved it in her mouth, chewing with gusto, savoring the spiced flavor. "I'll pay for this later—but it's so *effing* good!"

CHAPTER FIFTY-FOUR

TEA SHOP, WASHINGTON D.C.

Luther

A second meeting with the Chinese cultural minister was well under way, Luther sitting cross-legged on the other side of the same wooden table, the squat representative of the Chinese government across from him, his ample buttocks crushing the life out of a silk-covered pillow, testament to his higher position of authority and desire to be as comfortable as possible.

Luther bowed, mentally vocalizing the Chinese word *shagua* in his mind, an obsequious smile locked in place on his lips. It meant fat-ass, if intended as an insult. Or addle-headed, if applied with a teasing inflection when speaking to a close friend. Luther understood the official was not a friend, as he listened with the patience of a dead man as the obese bureaucrat prattled his way through his many accomplishments to date, including his plan to obtain a copy of the American doctor's unique code, unlocking the full potential of her tri-helix based programming language. More valuable now, based on news of her recent success. The man finally found his way to the end of his self-aggrandizing flight of ego, taxiing to a breathless stop.

"Do you not agree?"

"I do." Luther bowed, stopping a degree short of his earlier bows, offered during their first meeting, the other man's eyes snapping open at the potential insult, holding steady, then allowing the obvious mistake. The obese official muttered something under his breath, Luther expecting it to have been an insult against his ethnicity as he continued. "The code is critical to your success. The means you suggest using to secure it—a potential cloud in what is *still* a clear sky. I am certain—"

"Cease your crude attempt to speak as if you are Chinese. Or Cantonese. Or any of a dozen other East Asian ethnicities. I am fluent in the caustic language of Western commercialism. Hawking their wares everywhere as if fisher-women selling their goods from the alleyways." The man leaned back, using the wall to brace his shoulders, another sign of the decadence, the corruption of the will of those raised in the modern age, born into positions of power within the highest levels of the people's government. Anathema in an earlier age, prevalent now, the lines between Sino-Russian brokers of influence having become far less distinct.

"You are making a mistake." Luther leaned forward, pushing back against the other man's will. "One with potential consequences to the plan."

"Our plan. *Mine* now. No longer yours."

Luther leaned back and bowed his head, to the exact angle demanded by tradition, hoping to mollify the official, wanting him to think the code delivered was the latest version. Aware it was still his plan, still on track. His own ego of little weight in the greater scheme, when measured against the potential gain to humanity, despite what the elephant sized pile of dung on the other side of the table had planned, his ass perched on a prized possession of the owner's wife. The cushion reluctantly offered by their dutiful host upon demand. "Of course. You are correct."

"A plan paid for, on the back of the people's efforts."

"Your plan. Yes. Although it may lead to—conflict. With those who will oppose your efforts, once they become aware—"

The official cut him off. "My people assure me this is of little—"

Luther returned the insult, interrupting, his voice stiffening. "When one approaches a *tiger*, it is wise to sit back and study it to learn its movements and moods. Not as if it were a dog on a leash, relying on the foolish advice of those who cannot see the difference."

The large man clenched his jaw, prepared to deal with Luther's rebuke, then he swallowed his words and opened his ears, reluctantly. He let out a long sigh, softening his rigid stance. "This woman—the doctor, she is the tiger in this *jiaoben* of yours?"

"She is, and well protected by a powerful wolf, with many pack-mates. Along with other friends in *high* places, exerting influence over those who sit—"

"A Senator. One of note. A former student of this *wolf* you refer to."

Luther nodded, impressed, and somewhat unsettled by the other man's knowledge of the players involved in the high-stakes game. "Under his command, once. Well above it, now. And you are correct—he is an important piece on the greater board."

The official shook his head. "You still see this as if a game, Luther." He noted the slight reaction to having used the smaller man's name. Then he leaned forward, wishing to cut through the veil of tradition and mind-numbing ceremony. "A new day has arrived, from a dawn started a generation ago. There are thousands of men like me, poised on the verge of taking our country, and the billion and a half people within its borders, forward, on a—" He smirked. "*Another* long march."

The man stopped again, considering his words, knowing how necessary the sacrifice of his ancestors had been. How important it was to grasp the opportunity in front of them now, to build on their efforts, today. "I will pass your concerns along to my advisors. We shall meet again, before making a final decision. Giving you time enough to prepare yourself against potential fall-out from those on *your* side." Then he nodded, ending the discussion.

Luther stood, rising to his feet with ease. The man looked up, then raised his hand, grunting as Luther grasped it, bracing his legs, helping the obese man to his knees, then to his feet. He held out a hand, having to steady the official for a moment while a wave of dizziness sloshed through him. Once his balance had returned, the man shrugged, speaking with a genial tone. "We must avoid failure at all costs, you and me. A delicate pastry to place in one's mouth, indeed. Requiring a practiced touch."

Luther refused to allow the shock he felt to reach his face, or eyes. "You are speaking of an approach made to the woman, seeking the key?"

"No, Luther my friend. I am speaking about potential for any fall-out between our two countries. There are no winners in a hot war. No profit to be gained. Best to encourage constant preparation for each side, requiring new weapon systems to replace old. American companies working behind the scenes, helping their competitors overseas while making false claims of theft of trade-secrets, constantly raising the stakes, leading to monies being invested in the purchase of newer technologies. The masses on both sides made to pay, happily so, enriching the few. Afraid of the—what is the word for an American child's nightmare creature?"

Luther kept his voice soft, realizing the other man was not a fool, blinded by years of entitlement and privilege. "The bogeyman."

"Yes. Just like the ones in their scary movies. Only *this* threat to the security of all sides is *real*, despite groups on both sides being blinded by the mountains of money to be made. We, my friend—must be diligent. Reassuring our people, placating them, enriching them—until we take control. Of *everything*."

CHAPTER FIFTY-FIVE

YOGA STUDIO, MARYLAND

Jean

Sweat poured from Jean's brow, his lips set in a compressed line, muscles and tendons stretched beyond any sane measure of discomfort. The pain in his legs, calves, and lower back was a slow burn. His body parts were united in protesting the request being made of them. An order now, his mind telling his inflexible body to *shut the fuck up* and *get with the program*. He angled his head, just enough to see Cheryl, hands flat on her yoga mat in the row in front, looking back at him through her spread legs, trying not to smile as she watched him struggling.

"No need to push it, hero. Italy didn't get built in a week. At least, I don't think it was."

Jean grimaced, returning as close to a smile in return as he could muster, his lungs full of air, trying to squeeze another inch of angle into his cramped posture. A soft voice with a southern drawl floated into his ears, the words coming from behind as a long-legged, willowy framed instructor who looked limber enough to tie herself in knots and still be able to outrun him, came up, placing her hand on his shoulders. "Let the air out of your lungs, Jean. It will help relieve the tension, allowing you to breathe *into* the stretch."

Jean straightened up, his face red from embarrassment and the strain of forcing his body beyond its normal limits. He took a deep breath, releasing it as he leaned over, his fingers pointing at the mat. Then he took another breath, letting it go, his body inching further down as he kept breathing into the stretch, imagining he was poised, at twenty-thousand feet, balanced on the open ramp of a transport aircraft. He and his team leaning forward, ready to perform a HALO jump. A moonless night beckoning. A dark and foreboding ground lying somewhere far below, painted in black, with no city lights in evidence. As peaceful a moment in his life as he'd ever known, leading to the men of his recon team calling him *Cool Hand Kelly*.

"That is much better, Jean." He could feel her hand on his shoulders, another touching the back of his upper thigh, encouraging his effort. "I can tell your mind is relaxed. Breathing is good. The body will follow wherever the heart leads it." Jean couldn't help himself, enjoying the compliment and the feel of her fingers. Then her voice tightened. "Cheryl—you need to loosen your hips. You are *much* too tense. Where is *your* head and heart?"

Jean angled his head, noting the look of anger flashing across his yoga partner's inverted face. He gave her a long, peaceful smile, then closed his eyes, enjoying the slow fall into the center of his body, continuing to plummet, the studio floor rising, smacking him in his side, Cheryl having reached out, shoving him over with her foot.

"I take it we're not coming back." Jean had been waiting outside, enjoying the late morning sun while Cheryl finished her advanced yoga class. She'd finally come through the single glass door of the small studio, giving him a firm look. "*I* am. *You're* not."

"I didn't mean to interrupt you getting to your Chi, Qi, or Pi. Whatever you call it. Was just trying to improve my flexibility."

"Yeah, well—you didn't help, that's for sure. Besides, Chi isn't something you hunt for, like prey. It's about finding your balance, within." She muttered something beneath her breath, Jean pretending not to notice.

"I'm sorry for showing you up like that in front of Sandra." Jean paused, smiling. "She seemed to take a shine to how *I* was doing, especially for a beginner."

"Are you *deliberately* trying to make me angry? Because if you are, you're doing one *hell* of a job." Cheryl gave him a half-smile, letting him know she would forgive him, eventually. "Why'd you want to come with me today? There had to be something better to do than—"

"I told you. Wanted to improve my flexibility. Get past brawn and biceps and start working on my lower body. Try and get it stretched out." He noted the corners of her mouth turning up. "Get your mind out of the gutter. Wasn't talking about doing it for *that*."

"Okay. I believe you." Cheryl used her towel to wipe her head, the weather staring to warm. "And just for the record, you're more than *up* to the task. No worries there." She reached out, taking his hand, squeezing it before letting go. "And as for your sudden interest in flexibility? Believe me, the moves depicted in the book I showed you aren't for beginners. It takes years—"

"For *climbing*. With *you*. Not on fake walls—but *real* ones. Trying to get in shape to go up the one you and your brother were always going to climb. The Hawkshead place."

"It's the Hawksbill." Cheryl stared at Jean, shaking her head, eyes starting to fill. "You really want to do that? To climb with me?"

Jean shook his head. "Crazy, right? Got no real skill, and *no* experience. Not like those people at the Rockery. Kids, older women, the blind kid. Most of them—well, they don't look to be in great shape, yet still go by me like I'm standing still. Left hanging onto holds like I'm standing at attention, waiting to be lashed for having fallen asleep on guard duty."

"They don't still do that, do they?"

"No. But the threat's always in play and no one wants to be first to find out if the old rules still apply."

Cheryl gave Jean a warm smile. "I appreciate you wanting to improve your skills, Jean. And yoga *definitely* is a move in the right direction."

"So—am I still banned from coming here with you?"

"No. Of *course* not. I just need to get you into your own class, one for beginners. Making sure it's not with Miss *Touchy-Feely* as your instructor."

Jean looked at the photos Cole handed him. "Know this guy. Saw him around the marina. No idea who the other one is. Looks like an Asian version of Santa Claus—without the beard."

"He's head of Chinese Cultural Affairs, which means he's Internal Security. Like our FBI, if you throw in the CIA, NSA, along with half a dozen *other* agencies, including the mafia, drug lords, and most of the heads of the larger corporations."

"Take it you're not exactly a fan of his."

Cole shrugged. "Not so much. Or any of the other groups, either, except for the FBI. *They're* still running true to center, keeping it between the lines for the most part. At least—as far as I *know*."

Jean eyed him. "Aren't you the one in charge of oversight? I mean, if anyone knows, it's you. Right?"

"You'd *think* so, but the chairmanship is temporary, only good as long as I'm sitting here." Cole looked over at the seat behind the imposing bulk of his desk. "Lots of asses, resting there over the years. Some, bigger than others. Mine's just one more." He shook his head. "I get information spooned out in regular doses, a few pages at a time, with limited details. Until I threaten someone, which opens the paper pipeline, flooding my office with a tsunami of mind-numbing reports and other shit to wade through. Draining away all my resources. Along with my time and attention, and that of my people, who need to focus on a host of other priorities."

"Like running for reelection, trying to keep your—ass in the seat."

"Yeah." Cole looked at Jean, his eyes revealing a weariness of spirit. One both men had seen and shared with others when coming in from a mission. Shoulders slumped from the weight of physical and emotional exhaustion, along with the aftereffects of hours of adrenalin burn, trying to keep their shit together long enough to change out of the tools of war, do the after-action talk through with the Intel guys. Then shower, shit, and collapse into racks. Grabbing a few hours of coma like sleep, until the images of what they'd seen, done, and been scarred by found them, again. Burned deep in brains grown numb to gentler memories of the world waiting for them back home.

Jean shrugged. "Different war zone. Same battles."

Cole nodded, tapping the first photo. "So, who's the weird-looking guy? Know him?"

"Don't know his name. He's associated with the group funding the project—the ones I told you about."

"The one that Cheryl's friend, Mary is working for."

Jean didn't hesitate, surprised at what Cole knew. "Mari. With an I. Yes."

"Why the linkage, between the two of them?" Cole leaned in, studying Jean's eyes as if searching for something. Jean shrugged, starting to stiffen up.

"How the hell would I know?"

Cole fixed him with a hard stare. "Take a guess. *Major.*"

Jean raised his eyebrows lightly, adjusting to the change in command structure, his protege in a position as nominal leader of all things military. "Okay. He's liaison to those supplying the money. Running the information gathering end of things, working with Mari. Where it all ends up going, I don't have a clue." He paused, raising one hand before Cole could say anything. "But I do have my suspicions. Or rather, Cheryl's. She's confident it's a multi-national group of billionaires, looking to lock up her solution for their own gain. To use it in ways that could alter how we live. How we think. How we—"

"Behave. I know. She told me the same thing. Do you *agree* with her assessment?"

"I do. And when the fuck did the two of you meet? And where?" He raised a hand. "Never mind. I don't want to know. I don't even care."

"Explain why that is, Major."

Jean hesitated, realizing he would have to admit what he'd known for some time. "I've heard everything Cheryl's had to say about this—solution path of hers. How it's capable of being twisted in a dozen directions or more. Bent to include every segment of society. A real game changer, with more money and power at stake than anything anyone's invented before, including gunpowder."

"Which, ironically, the *Chinese* came up with."

"And other countries stole, leading to the development of guns, cannons. To the beginning of modern warfare."

"With the shoe on the other foot, this time."

Jean nodded, rubbing the back of his thigh, sore from his morning yoga session. "She predicted that. Predicted *all* of this. Took appropriate measures, preparing for *every* eventuality."

"How *long*?" Cole's firm expression hadn't changed. "*What* measures?"

"From when she *first* came up with the idea, back when she started to develop her—unusual code. Her innovative program. Before creating the new technology."

"Jean. I *need* to know. And I'm asking as your friend. Today."

"Implying there could be a subpoena tomorrow?"

"How long? What measures?"

"Since she was a kid, Jean. Barely out of her teens. As to measures, I have no idea. Haven't asked. Don't want to know." He paused, giving Cole a hard look. "You'll have to ask her."

"Will I need to put in a formal request, to get her in front of me?"

Jean shook his head, laughing. "Do what you did *last* time. Meet with her again. I'm certain she'll be happy to fill you in. Give you all the details. Not that you'll have a clue what she's talking about. It's an entirely new language, this thing she's created."

"What makes it new?" Cole leaned forward again, his voice low, measured, probing.

Jean shrugged. "Because no one would *listen* to her. Just kept telling her to do things the way things have always been done. She was forced to play along, all the time building—" He stopped, his mind opening to a new reality.

"Building *what*, Jean?"

Jean looked down at the thick carpet, a smile on his lips, listening as Cole took a deep breath, preparing to insist on an answer. "She's created a *false* front, showing others what they *expect* to see. And she's also built another one. A *parallel* one—of her *own* creation. One where she makes all the rules, protecting us against a harsh reality that only *she* knows is coming."

"What reality?" Cole's voice was tight with frustration. Jean looked at him, smiling.

"One where humanity, as we know it, gets left behind. Like a useless appendage. Like an appendix. People who are unwilling or unable to make the changes necessary, left standing on the ground looking up, with nowhere else to go."

"How do you know she's right? That her vision of this is as clear as she thinks it is?"

"You talked with her. Heard what she had to say. What did you come away believing when she filled you in about all this?"

Cole shrugged. "Didn't. Have never spoken with her, other than the one time we met here, and at dinner—with you."

Jean tried to keep the look of confusion from his face, failing. "Then how did you know—"

"My people picked up some chatter. How—I can't reveal. But it involves what Cheryl's working on, been working on. We've talked with everyone who's ever known her, helped her develop what she's using. Know every-thing about—everything. Just needed to hear it from you."

"Prick."

"Comes with the job, Major." Cole hesitated. "She's playing a dangerous game. One that's bound to burn her fingers *if* she's lucky. Worse, if she's not. Or if we, you, and I—fail to protect her."

Jean lowered his eyes, staring at the thick rug in Cole's office. "Anything you need me to do. Anything. Just ask Cole."

"Does that include betraying her trust? Risking your relationship?"

Jean thought for a moment, the idea of it causing him to feel sick. He looked up. "Anything, Cole. Anything to save her—including that."

"You're quiet." Cheryl gave Jean an appraising stare. "Took the starch out of you, did he? Your new yoga instructor?"

"He wasn't able to make it in today. Some young woman took over. And yeah, she really kicked my Irish butt."

Cheryl eyed him, knowing he was teasing her. Maybe. Sensing there was something more behind his difficulty in meeting her eyes. "How's Cole doing? Anything new to report from his side of things?"

"Witch." Jean cursed under his breath.

"Excuse me?" Cheryl leaned back, her eyes narrowing as Jean lifted his hand, stopping her before she could start down the wrong path.

"You, reading my thoughts—like a witch. The one in the old movie with the girl and her dog. The one from the—"

Cheryl's eyes hardened. "I suggest you land on *north*."

"Was that the pretty one? Belinda?"

"Glinda."

"Oh, okay then. *Her*."

And?"

Jean sighed, having wanted to wait until tomorrow to fill her in, his body drained of energy, mind heavy with the realization, finally, of where everything was heading. As if he were the first person to rub two sticks together, creating a fire, thousands of years ago. Shocked when it worked, standing there, mouth agape, seeing into the future and wondering what would become of his discovery. The flame on the stick burning up to his fingers, causing him to throw the damn thing away, watching it land in dry leaves, starting a forest fire. "We need to talk."

CHAPTER FIFTY-SIX

LAB, MILITARY FACILITY

David

David reached up and touched the side of his head. He felt the slight impression left behind from the attack, his eyes wincing as he recalled the sound it had made: a crisp crunch as his attacker punched the end of a ball-peen hammer into his skull. Wielded by a large man, his face appearing from the shadows of a dimly lit, narrow alleyway. A bastion for lost souls camped out in mutual discomfort, lending emotional support to one another, sharing stories of loss, pain, addiction, or hard luck. People trying to find their way back into the light of lives left behind, unable to face the burden of their memories. Lost between the cracks of a world without resources enough to provide adequate care for lost children, tucked away inside adult bodies. Most wearing tattered scraps of military clothing, tattoos of their service to their country etched into their flesh, along with the scars of the wounds they'd suffered. Or those cast out from broken homes, trying to find sanctuary for their physically or chemically abused bodies.

David opened his eyes, staring into the darkness of his room, every particle of ambient light erased by a sheet rolled up and placed at the bottom of the door. He craved the ebony of night, wrapping it about himself like a thick blanket, sheltering him from the searing light of his own loss. Knowing, as he lay there, he hadn't earned the same right as the others to duck away. Didn't deserve use of the same excuses, having walked away from a life filled with vast promise and limitless opportunities. Away from friends: good people with earnest intent, offering an extended family in replacement of his own when his parents had died in a foggy crash on a back-country road.

Walking away from the man who'd stepped up, willing and able to be a father figure to him, becoming mentor, supporter, and godfather to a child in waiting. Dropping a set of house and multiple car keys into his outstretched hand, a next-door mansion left behind, emptied of the sound of life from two people, their voices in mixed harmony, singing songs to an unborn babe. Gone. In a snapping of fate's finger, causing a spark that burned away all his dreams, his happiness, his joy. Leaving an empty shell behind, shuffling through rooms bearing the touch of her creative hand. Of a nursery, bedroom, bathroom, and kitchen. Dishes left unwashed on the counter. Clothes scattered on an unmade bed. Ghosts, haunting him from every corner, everywhere he looked. Pictures, the people in them blurred behind a veil of tears, protecting him from the unbearable images of her beautiful face. Of the two of them, appearing as if strangers to his pain dulled mind, posed with an arm wrapped around her waist, thickened with impending birth. Unable to remove them from the canvas of the life they were painting together.

David recalled the night in the alley. The moment of his release, having woken to the noise of someone eating celery in the dead of night, listening to the steady crunch of teeth biting through the crisp stalk, coming closer. Footsteps, in a slow shuffle, accompanied by heavy breathing. A shadow looming over him, enormous hands lifting him from the ground, from the filthy sleeping bag beneath his too thin frame. Holding him up by his jacket, bunched in a large fist. The man's face easily recognized.

An ancient soldier, castaway from a forgotten war. Gray-haired, with deep-brown eyes, and a broad, scarred face. Dark eyes twisting in anguish, his deep voice shaking with emotions beyond his ability to express. Pain slashed into the lines of his ebony skin, felt in the trembling of his long, thick fingers clutching the front of his jacket, gazing at him, shaking his head, tears in his eyes.

He remembered feeling no fear. At peace, knowing the moment he'd been in search of was finally at hand: his escape from life, unable to open the door himself. He'd asked why, the question reacted to with a widening of the man's eyes, his tortured expression softening into a look of reverence, as if seeing an angel. When he spoke, his voice was a series of bass notes played on a battered instrument. "Because my friend—we are all God's children, each and every one of us. And he told me to send his children home."

David lay in his bed, wrapped in a cocoon of blankets, a pillow over his head, remembering how a warmth had flowed into him at that moment. A feeling of love, beyond any he'd known since—since the day he'd placed his head on Maggie's belly, knowing everything he'd ever needed, had ever longed for, was there, between his arms, beneath the press of his cheek. Nodding in the alleyway—tears in his eyes, smile on his lips, watching as a long, muscular arm drew back, followed by a blur of motion, the snapping sound of crisp celery in his ear.

He reached up, wiping away his tears, knowing it was time. Time to come fully back into his life. To begin the last leg of a journey begun two years earlier, recovering all the good he'd ever known: the love Maggie had returned to him with every glance, every reflection of his searching stares. Shaking his head, wondering how lucky he'd been to find her. To be found by her. Time to return to where he'd last seen her, last held her in his arms, last felt the taste of her on his lips. Home.

"You're *sure* about this?" Cheryl had rushed over to the lab, the call from Isaac catching her as she was heading out to meet with Cole. Their appointment canceled. David the priority. She finished strapping him into the chair. "I don't mind waiting."

"I do. It's time." David looked up at her, his eyes open. "Will it hurt? As much as the *last* time?"

"No. We don't need amplified emotional feedback for this. But as to your level of emotional pain, yeah, that's a given." She lowered the Tee-Cee into place, then went over and sat in the other chair. Isaac frowned as he secured her legs.

"Don't understand why you're insisting on dropping in with him. Never had to do it before."

"I know. But I need to be there to support him."

David leaned his head to one side. "You know I can hear you, right?"

Isaac looked over, giving David a smile. "Pipe down, *lab-rat*." He held the Tee-Cee above Cheryl's head, waiting as she lifted her arms, running her fingers through her thick hair, then placed it around her skull, fastening it in place.

Cheryl reached up, touching his arm, smiling. "Thank you, Isaac. For everything." She took a deep breath, holding it for a moment, releasing it slowly, then gave him a quick nod. "See you when we get back."

The sky was gray. Formed of a solid cover of flat-ironed clouds, as if someone had forgotten to add in texture. A charcoal drawing, hanging over a line of gray-faced buildings. Featureless, blank eyed widows staring back.

Cheryl observed from an outside viewpoint, hovering above several lines of vehicles traveling between strips of pavement separated by white lines, most of them moving with speed while staying in their lanes. One standing out, making an occasional dart to the left or right. She floated down, taking up a position inside the backseat, watching as David and his expectant wife exchanged words.

"Deep breaths. Breathe in, two-three-four. Out, two-three-four. In—"

"Shut the *fuck* up and *get* us there!" Maggie was huffing air in and out of her lungs as if suffering from emphysema and trying to blow out birthday candles on a dozen cakes. Their birthing book, and its suggested breathing techniques handed to her in case she needed to reference it, tossed through the car window as David pulled out of the driveway.

Color-coded tabs stuck to important pages, made it look like a porcupine. A scream of pain from another contraction had induced a firm request to lower the effing window, followed by the fluttering of pages as the book sailed away. Followed by another suggestion that he should, as his extremely pregnant and over-due bride put it, find the *god-damn* gas pedal, and *shove* it to the *effing* floor.

David did his best to comply with Maggie's request, then glanced over to see how she was doing, seeking visual confirmation of what his ears were reporting. Not good, not good at all, he said, having to refocus, the wheel slippery in his sweaty hands, lane markers difficult to follow, his eyes watering as he tried to remember the route they'd picked out while staring at road signs as if seeing them for the first time.

It was late morning, weekend traffic building in thickness. A decision needing to be made on taking an alternate route, one that would cut substantial time off their estimated arrival, at the expense of rough surfaced roads, slipping in between the crumbling edges of low-income housing and a wide drainage canal, marking the border of middle-income suburban sprawl. The exit ramp slid closer, David eyeing it as another scream inducing contraction began, glancing at the time on the radio's display. His job, his *only* job, to measure the time between and during each contraction. Vital *effing* information, the suggestion screamed his way from the passenger seat, adding that he should *pay-the-fuck* attention to his driving, the nose of the car edging to the right as the exit ramp led them away from the main road.

Once clear of the highway, David was forced to slow down, several potholes requiring him to swerve from one side of the road to the other. A white van coming along from behind laid on its horn, racing by, hitting the potholes, almost losing control. The passenger looking through the closed window, mouth open in soundless rage, middle finger raised.

David twisted the wheel, narrowly avoiding another hole, his spouse recording a negative rating about his driving, adding it to a long list of other shortcomings, beginning with his having created the very issue she was now dealing with. As if it were all his fault, having insisted she try on her old cheerleader outfit. An image he quickly scrubbed from his mind, focusing on getting them to the hospital as soon as possible, helping to bring a beautiful new and vibrant energy into the world, one they would nurture and guide. A perfect expression of their love for one another. Multiplied, many times over, the three of them bound by deep family ties.

"How much—oh *fuck. Another* one. How long—David?"

"Almost there!"

"How long?"

"Five minutes. It's just a few streets up—I think."

"The contraction, you *idiot!* How long?"

"Uh, two. And a half. Minutes. I don't know. Maybe shorter." The ensuing wail of abject misery was almost loud enough to clear the roadway ahead.

David jammed the brake pedal, twisting the wheel to one side to avoid the large, windowless white van, passing it on the left as it slowed to a stop, still in the travel lane. His foot heavy on the accelerator, he sped ahead, focused on the road in front of him, leaving timing of contractions to the nurses waiting somewhere up ahead and a few streets over. A loud ripping sound, the sharp-edged noises catching his ear, was familiar, causing him to glance in the rear-view mirror, noting the van was moving again, racing to overtake him. He wondered why it was coming on so fast, his own speed twice the posted speed limit. Four-way flashers were ticking off in half-second intervals as he slowed down, pulling into the next corner, the car bouncing over a broken section of pavement.

The van slammed into them, the heavier vehicle causing the lighter car to spin in a half-circle, forcing it into the only tree left standing in a ten-block radius. The back tires of the van skipped to the left, losing traction, causing a slow roll over, ending with a sliding crash into three parked cars.

David tried to open his eyes, only one able to comply, the other sealed shut, liquid dripping down the side of his face, splashing onto his shoulder. He turned his head, a bolt of pain numbing his vocal cords, driving a moan of shock-laden pain from his mouth, unable to call out to Maggie. His teeth clenched in agony as his one good eye widened in shock, seeing a piece of something gray driven into his upper left chest, pinning him to his seat. The car was tilted at an angle, rear wheels off the ground, nose compressed into the lower section of the front seats. A siren was wailing in the distance, the sound of it muted by shock.

David felt himself relaxing, his eye closing. Meg, silent beside him. Margaret, his Maggie Mae. A jolt of adrenalin shoved the shock away, both eyes forced open as his free hand rubbed a clot of blood away, his hearing coming back, the volume slowly building until the siren in the distance became an endless scream from his trapped wife. Her cries tearing him to pieces, his voice joining hers, venting his agony, knowing somehow, something horrible had just happened, turning their life upside down.

He reached over, his voice nearly gone, feeling for Meg, lying in the lower section of her seat, its back tilted down during the drive. Her body had slid ahead from the impact, filling the floor with a pool of blood-soaked clothing, her distended abdomen compressed between the edge of seat and crumpled dash. Her eyes were wide open, staring into his. "She's *gone!* Our baby. I felt her die."

"You don't—you don't *know* that Meg. You can't—know that."

She took his hand, her upper body unscathed, other than scratches from the imploding windshield and side window. Bits of glass covered the seat, the trunk of a dead tree within easy reach. David reached over with his free arm, touching her face. "She's going to be okay. You will be too. Both of you—will be okay. I'm—I'm a little fucked up right now—but I'm *still* here."

Meg's eyes were full of tears, her skin pale, every one of her freckles standing out. He started brushing pieces of glass from her hair as she closed her eyes, her raspy voice softly drifting away. "Just a scratch, right?" He found her hand, squeezing it, knowing he would never let her go. "Yeah. Just a scratch. Lucky." Night fell, taking him into its soft embrace, a smile on his face. The warm air of the ocean, stirring his hair. The cut on his hand, healing. A trail of sweet kisses dripping across his forehead, as gentle as a summer rain.

"Hey! Buddy! *Open* your *eyes!* Come back, *man! Look* over here!" David struggled to lift the weight holding his eyes closed. Something was pinning him in place, his strength ebbing away. He turned his head slightly, a sharp pain gnawing away somewhere in the side of his neck. An older man with beautiful brown eyes looked at him, mouth moving, no sound coming out. A pinch on his cheek bringing him back into the world. A sharp sting, overriding a steady throb in his skull.

"Gonna pry the door open. Try to get you out. Help is coming. You stay with me. Need to know you're still with me. Okay?" David nodded, feeling liquid sloshing in his ears, his voice sounding muffled. "Good. I'm—good."

David watched as the large man yanked the door open, following his eyes as they shifted down, seeing a thick branch penetrating through his shoulder. Listening to the dying wail of a firetruck as it roared into view, visible through the shattered windshield. Turning his head, he continued to follow the man with his eyes as he ran around the crushed front end of the car. Another man joined him, helping to pull the passenger door open, his face going white, leaning over, and getting sick.

The vibration in David's shoulder introduced him to a world of pain, one he barely had time to step into, let alone fully explore as agony overtook him in a whirl of vibrant energies, colorful and explosive, created by a burst of physical jolts, backed by the whine of something familiar. A saw, he decided, cutting through wood. His father bringing him to their new home, still under construction. The sound of hammering, much like the pounding in his head, timed to the beating of his heart. Then the whining stopped.

David turned his head, looking for Meg, his world spinning upside down. Falling away, a moment of time when he was floating, until landing with a thud. Voices fading in and out, someone playing with the volume control. Firm hands holding him in place. His own hand losing touch with hers. Needing to find her, to let her know everything was gonna be okay, just like in the song. His Maggie Mae, the light from a campfire coloring her face, her hair, her smile with the perfect gap. His beautiful, imperfect, perfect girl.

Voices broke through the fog. David's mind clearing enough to let sound through unimpeded. Men with tight jaws, shouting, swearing, their tone over-flowing with frustration. And fear.

"Hurry! There's gas all through here. We need foam. Where's the other unit? Get the damn jaws in place. Now!"

David was lying on a stretcher, someone holding down his arm, a needle in his hand. He looked away, watching a firefighter without a helmet leaning into the driver's seat, a thick piece of metal in his hands. He could see Meg, still held in place, the crumpled embrace of metal pinning her lower legs. She was reaching over, trying to help, delirious from loss of blood, an IV in her arm. Her face pale, eyes half-closed. The man turned, shouting at another man, prying apart the metal frame of the passenger side door with the mechanical jaws.

"Hurry!"

"Where's the fucking foam? Can't cut her out of here without it!"

"They're close, but the fuels under the floorboards. We got to get this done before—"

A low-pitched woof sounded, flames rising from beneath and within the space where Meg was pinned, the firefighter in the driver's seat rearing back, his hair on fire. A man reached in, pulling him clear of the burning fuel. Rolling to join him on the ground, his hands burnt, still burning, a spray of foam knocking them to the ground, covering both men and the front end of the car in white. The gas was still burning, flames eating into the seat from below. Spiraling up. Meg fully awake, her eyes widening in awareness of what was happening.

David rolled to one side, falling from the gurney, landing on his uninjured side, rising, stumbling forward, reaching for her, a piece of sawed-off wood protruding from his left shoulder, limiting his ability to touch her. He was screaming in terror, refusing what his eyes were seeing, his ears hearing, what his heart was desperately trying to deny. Her screams of terror blended with his own, forming a duet, both singing at the top of their lungs, until the stage lights went out, and the music stopped.

The room David awoke into was lit by a soft golden light, filtered through a thick fog that blanketed the view from a large window. A bed with various pieces of equipment on it centered one wall of the small room, monitoring a patient lying beneath a white blanket, hands on top of a sheet turned down, just above her chest. His heart lurched. Meg. His *Maggie!* Alive. Her cheeks flushed with a hint of rose-petal red, as if brushstrokes from an artist's brush, painting her in the full blush of perfect health.

David crossed the room, taking her hand, tears overflowing his eyes when she opened her own and smiled up at him, the slight gap in her teeth revealed. "You found me. You came. You always have, no matter the obstacles in your way." He was at a loss for words, his memory of what he'd seen still clear in his mind. The smell of burning fuel, plastic, and flesh, staining his nostrils. The scent of her perfume, her hair, her skin, rising to rinse it away. Alive, the nightmare ended. Next page in the script flipped. He opened his mouth, uttering two words, afraid he'd bring the world to a shuddering stop. "Our—child?"

Meg closed her eyes, stiffening in the bed, her shoulders arched, head pressed back into the pillows. Shaking. Her entire body trembling. Then she recovered. "Sophie. She's here. A perfect little angel. Do you want to meet her?"

David closed his eyes, afraid to open them. Afraid to look and see a charred corpse. The sound of a mewling cry forced his eyelids apart. An infant lay in his arms, swaddled in a white blanket with pink trim. A small face scrunched up in complaint, mouth open, tiny hands in tiny fists, with perfectly formed fingernails, so frail, scowling, as if angry at the world for having taken her from the comforting compress of her mother's womb. "She's *beautiful*. Absolutely *beautiful*."

"Sophie. Sophia. Just like you wanted. Like you said."

He leaned down, kissing both of his girls. Sophie, on her wrinkled forehead, just below the soft cap she had on. Meg, on her cheek, then her lips, as she turned into his. She gazed up at him as he rose, watching as he wiped his eyes. "Are you happy?"

"Yes." David's voice broke. "I am. As happy as I've ever been." He paused. "Thank you. For loving me. For giving me the chance, the opportunity to love you back. To love you both."

"For a little while." Maggie lost her smile. "She needs to go back."

"Of course. Back to the nursery."

"No, foolish man. Back. It's time." He stared, not understanding, his instincts rising, whispering something in his ear. Her voice beat him to it. "I brought her here so you could see her. Its why I'm *here*. So, you can say goodbye to us. We need to go back, David. Soon."

David collapsed, his knees giving way. He grabbed the side rail, holding on, the metal cold in his hands. "No! Stay here—with *me!*" His voice was a fractured plea for mercy as he searched her eyes, seeing the truth. Realizing the nightmare hadn't ended. That it was still there.

The room spun in a circle. David's body curled in a ball on the floor. Pain sleeted through him. From his damaged shoulder to his burned hands. Passing though him as if a cloud of rain, the air becoming still, hushed with anticipation. A woman stood at the window, looking out. Meg, his Maggie *again*. Arms wrapped around a firm abdomen. He would not allow himself to believe his eyes. Turned his head, the bed empty. No one there.

"She's gone."

He looked over at the other Meg. A false goddess, gazing at him with a sympathetic expression. "Gone?"

"Yes. Released from the false reality of a world that doesn't exist. Will never be as you wish it to be—only the way it is."

"You're not here. Just my imagination—trying to protect me."

"No. I'm real." The false Meg walked over and reached out. "I'm as real as *you*, in the flesh and blood. Here. Take my hand."

David hesitated, unable to deal with another blow, his emotions stretched beyond his ability to cope. "I—don't believe you."

"Take my hand, David. It's time for you to go back."

"Where?" He held back, refusing to touch her. "Why? I don't *want* to go. Bring *her* back! I can't *do* this. Not alone. Not without *her*."

The false Meg sniffed, dismissing his misery. "You certainly made a mess of things, leaving the way you did. Not bothering to lock the front door. Car in the driveway. Food, rotting in the kitchen. Without stopping to pack a bag. Just walking out the door and heading off. No plan. No destination. Just wanting to be somewhere else, become anyone else. Wallet shoved in your neighbor's mailbox, becoming an anonymous man, off to suffer your way through a harsh and uncaring world."

"Stop this. Or I *will!*" David stepped closer, his lips pressed against her ear, forcing himself to ignore her scent, dismiss the color of her incredible eyes. "Go away and *leave* me alone! You're an *impostor*. An outsider, with *no* idea what you're saying. Guesses, that's all—"

"You left the keys and deed to your house with your mentor, the man next door. Dropped into his hand, telling him it was all his. Leaving, with no idea if or when you'd be returning. Told him to keep it, tear it down. Told him how much you loved him. Respected him. How much he meant to you. To you and to me. Then you turned around and walked away, leaving him standing there, crying, heart-broken, having lost not only the man he considered a son, but a woman as close to him as if his own daughter. And a child. With him a godfather, left in waiting. Left mourning. In pain."

"You weren't *there*. You can see what's in my mind but can't understand what I was going through. Am still going through. Why I never—"

"The first man you met, for any appreciable span of time, was a consultant. Letting you stay in his mother's house after she'd passed away, watching over it while being remodeled. Learning how to do things from the contractor: a man with the patience of a saint and empathy for what you'd been through. Not told the details, but able to sense what you were carrying inside."

"You—*can't* know that. *Any* of it."

"Fuck you and your *pathetic* excuses, David. Your *pointless* denials. I know it all. Can feel it all, as if it happened to me. The guy you got a ride with, who claimed to be a hit man, out for revenge. Some story about—well, you know the scene. You wrote it for him later, when you let him crawl into your head and stay there. But that wasn't the plan then. You were still living in the actual world, struggling to come to grips with what had happened. Horrible, unimaginable, in the damage it did to you. I know. I felt it *too!* A loss so great, it'd be enough to make anyone insane. To go crazy with grief. Enough to want to off themselves. But you didn't do that, David. You were too strong. Too healthy. Because of my love for you. Knew I wouldn't want you moping your way to some sorry end."

David walked over to the window, looking out at the featureless horizon. Staring, able to see their faces. Each of them. All the people who'd helped him out along the way. False Maggie came over, standing beside him, her voice low. Soothing. "They found you, as if placed in your path for a reason. The veteran, regaling you with stories about the places he'd been, things he'd seen, had done."

"Leave me alone." David stepped back, hands dropping to his side. "Please? Just go away and leave me here."

She shook her head, reaching out for his hand. "No, David. You *agreed* to do this. We're here until I say so. I'm not leaving without—"

David lashed out, expecting his hand to pass through her, his palm meeting flesh and bone. Palm left stinging, leaving a mark on her face, her cheek red, the small scar showing white. Her beautiful eyes filling with tears. "I'm sorry. I—I'm so sorry, Meg."

"Do you believe me now? Could have avoided all that if you'd just taken my hand, like I asked." She reached up, rubbing her skin. "You're stronger than a week ago. Eating better will do that."

"You've been watching me."

"Of course. Just because I'm on *this* side of things doesn't mean I stopped caring about you. Where you were and what you were doing, or more to the point, *not* doing with your life."

"I'm—"

"If you're going to keep apologizing, don't bother. *Do* something, instead. Get back in the game. Back to your work. Get back to what you came here to do."

"I was going to. Eventually. Until—"

"Yeah. Until." Meg reached up, touching the side of his head. Her fingers pressing against a white circle of hair, the exact size of the business end of a hammer. "*That* had to hurt."

"It did. The sound it made, more disturbing than the pain."

"Trying to help your homeless friends. Failing, but trying to help one who meant the most to you. Paying a high price, in the end."

"I thought I'd gotten through to him." David paused, looking down. "Turned out I was wrong." He leaned back against the window. He sighed, turning to look at her. "Are you done scolding me?"

"Almost. You used the coma as a convenient way to escape the pain. Not from the head wound, but the one you were still suffering from losing me and Sophie. Hiding away, building a world you had complete control over where things happened the way you wanted them to. Writing your stories, three at a time. Compelling, to a point, thought they were only diversions. All of them. Which brings me to my point." Maggie paused, taking a deep breath, and letting it out. "Release me, David. Release your pain. Keep *all* the wonderful memories. *All* of them, both the good ones and bad from when we were together *and* apart. Never let go of those but toss the ones holding no weight. That add *no* value to your life, now. A life filled with promise. One you need to get back to."

David stared at the floor, the tiles shifting to sand. Walls dissolving, sun above, water in front, his feet bare. Back at the same beach. Meg gone. Cheryl looking at him, her eyes filled with empathy. He stepped over, taking her hand. "Thank you. For helping me through that. I'm sorry you had to—how much did you feel?"

"All of it."

David nodded, pulling her in, hugging her, feeling her body trembling. The look in her eyes telling him the price she'd paid, helping to guide him out. Again. He looked around, taking one last look from behind the mirror. Then he raised his voice. "Isaac—bring us out."

CHAPTER FIFTY-SEVEN

YOGA STUDIO, MARYLAND

Cheryl

The humidity hung from the sky as if a thick wet curtain pulled in place, trapping the city in a hot, steamy shower stall. Bodies dripped with moisture as the temperature refusing to budge, even at night. Staying *eighty-too-damn-hot*, Cheryl muttered as she hesitated in the doorway of the yoga studio, tempted to go in and take another cold shower. Sighing, she made her way over to her car, thinking of Jean and wondering how he was making out; his sailboat broken into during the previous night, though nothing of value was on board, other than an old handheld radio, unused flare-gun, and an ancient CD player.

Jean had called earlier, asking her to go with him, disappointed when she'd rejected his invitation out of hand. His boat. His problem. Cheryl aware she already had enough things on her plate, needing her attention. A nagging ache in her lower calf recently added to the list, causing a slight limp in her stride. Still there, despite a session of hot yoga, her self-proscribed course of treatment, followed by the shower she'd just taken. To be followed by another as soon as she got home. Then a glass of wine, sipped while listening to Jean fill her in on the results of his investigation at the marina.

Her car beeped at her, flashing its lights several times as if excited to see her. The thought led her to wonder about Dawg and what had become of him. David never once mentioning the large shepherd. Too late to ask him now, having left the facility a week ago. A new backpack in hand, along with a new wallet with a set of identification papers and a debit card connected to an account with a sizable amount of money in it. His hair had grown out, with a slight curl, hanging just below his ears.

"Am I allowed to ask where you're heading?" Cheryl watched as David finished packing. He gave her a warm, lopsided smile that tugged at her heart, having grown close to him from sharing so many of each other's memories.

"Always, Cheryl. Whatever you want to know. I'm an open book—to you."

"Okay. Where?"

Davd dropped his pack and spread his arms, hands outstretched, pointing in opposite directions, north and west. "Somewhere between here—and there."

Cheryl grinned, shaking her head. "Promise to drop me a postcard whenever you can. Letting me know if you find a place you think *I'd* like to visit. A quiet beach somewhere. Maybe up in Maine?" She knew some of his back story, not all, having spent hours talking late into the night while he finished rehabilitation and made a gradual adjustment to being around people again. Real people, engaging him in small talk, helping him integrate back into a form of normalcy while in the confines of the facility. There had been regular visits made to the restaurant, where the music and crowds were still an issue for him, at times. The effect softened by an occasional visit from Mari, she and David leaning against each other while sharing a meal, or dancing to a few of the slower songs being played.

David nodded, gave her one last smile, then leaned down and grabbed his pack, slinging it over his shoulder and walking away. Cheryl watched him go, tears flowing down her cheeks, knowing, without a doubt in her mind, she would never see him again. Part of the healing process. Having to be left behind, along with his Maggie Mae. No longer anchoring him to his past, the mooring ropes slipped free, allowing him to move on.

Cheryl was not crying now, the droplets on her cheeks a mix of sweat and beads of water wrung from the stifling humidity of the oppressive air. As she reached her car, Cheryl hesitated, aware she was being watched. She reached up, cupping a small silver locket in one hand: a recent purchase, worn around her neck for the past few weeks. A new acquisition, causing a look of concern on Jean's face when he'd found it on the bathroom counter after she'd come back from an evening meeting with Cole.

"Where did *this* come from?" Jean lifted the locket, staring at Cheryl. He half-smiled. "Did Cole give you this? You've been spending enough time with him."

Cheryl grinned, taking the piece of jewelry from him, letting it dangle from her fingers. "It's been *two* times, Jean. And no—it's not from Cole. I never accept gifts from men until the third date—then have wild, uninhibited sex with them on the fourth. The only exception—you. Luring me with your sailor's skill. And a *working* shower." She kissed him, then spun around, head tilted down. "Do up my dress."

Jean complied, starting at her waist, having trouble squeezing the small buttons into the equally small loops, his thick fingers poor tools for the job at hand. He frowned, thinking about how long it was going to take to reverse the process after having dinner with the senator in question, and another one of his various female friends.

Cheryl started the car, checking her mirrors as the air-conditioning struggled to cool down the interior. Then she shifted into gear and drove away. Jason kept to the shadows, watching as Cheryl exited the parking lot, the damp night air swallowing her taillights with a smoky haze, hovering just above the ground. Jason knew Skinny would pick up her tail, leaving him to stay behind. His plan was working to perfection, a heavy bodied, black sedan sliding from the far end of the yoga studio parking lot, following Cheryl's car as she drove away. He lifted his arm, placing the voice-activated comms unit near his lips. "Delivery—on the way. Number three on the menu." There were two clicks in reply, radio silence encouraged whenever possible.

A middle-aged woman of Chinese ethnicity muttered beneath her breath, silently urging the driver of the large car to be careful not to tip their hand, alerting the woman in the vehicle they were following. She was the senior agent for the head of cultural affairs, tasked with attaining the key to unlock the advanced program designed by the American scientist. Her superior, a pig of a man with a mocking demeanor had carefully explained the importance of doing so as soon as possible, deaf to her suggestion it could cause an international incident.

"The key to her code will be with her, at all times. Secreted in her clothing or hair, placed in something small, somewhere on her person. Possibly *inside* her body. You must be thorough in your search—though *no* harm is to come to her. Is that clear?"

The large, obese, and heavily sweating senior official of the Republic of China transfixed the senior agent with a glare, the agent bowing deeply, along with the other two members of her team, released to fulfill their assignment. To shadow the American woman until a suitable time and location presented itself for her abduction and subsequent search.

The senior agent resisted an impulse to utter a curse, angry at being treated as a pawn, aware the two men assigned to assist her would report the smallest hint of disobedience. She planted a false smile on her lips and leaned forward. "You heard our wise and most knowledgeable leader. The time draws near for us to take from this woman the seed needed to help our country grow more powerful, leading our people into a glorious future. Taking our rightful place as leaders of a new world order."

She gave each of the two men a warm smile, then hardened her expression, causing them to flinch, her reputation for violence well known. "So don't *fuck* this up!"

Jean scratched his head, eyeing the open companionway of the small sloop. He'd just used a ladder, having to climb into the cockpit, the boat pulled from the water and resting in the boatyard, supported by jacks. He searched for signs of physical damage or theft, none showing, everything exactly where it had been the last been he and Cheryl had been aboard, wanting a last night on the local waters before hauling the sloop.

He smiled, remembering how calm the water had been, the two of them sitting on the foredeck, their favorite spot, leaning back, looking up at the stars. They'd spent an hour holding each other's hand without speaking, Jean aware Cheryl was a thousand miles away, no longer there with him. Not bothered in the least by her frequent mental absences, realizing she'd find him again when she returned. And she had, thanking him with a kiss that offered a promise of a greater reward once they were below, doing their best to make use of every square inch of the cramped berth.

Then he cursed, the sweat stinging his eyes, pissed he'd forgotten to fully close the opening the last time they'd left the boat. Closing it now, reminding himself to give the sharp-eyed night watchman a sizable tip.

Skinny fell in behind the large sedan that was trailing Dancer's lady friend by a few car lengths, having watched as the vehicle squeezed its way into a horn honking line of vehicles voicing their displeasure as they fled the local area, heading to northern environs to escape the oppressive heat of the Delaware river basin. He raised a hand to his jaw, activating a small military issued headset radio, letting Jason know there was something different about their target's activities, the black sedan moving with a more directed intention, staying closer to Cheryl's car than normal. He listened to Jason's hissing reply, then responded. "I don't give a *flying fuck* what you think! There's *something* about to drop. I can *feel* it."

Jason, two lanes over, out in front of the vehicle Skinny was driving, let his partner's remarks land. "Like that time—outside Kawaala?"

Skinny was quiet for a moment, his side starting to ache, his free hand rubbing at a scar beneath his shirt. "Yup. Same vibe. Like looking through their eyes, seeing us coming up the draw. *Fucking Sandies!*"

Jason winced. "Can you close in on them from the left?"

"I can *try*. It's getting tight out here, but I think—*fuck!* Our girl just signaled. Looks like she's taking the exit ramp."

Jason swore. "I'm already *past* it. Try to get *over!*"

Skinny twisted the wheel, cutting into the line of traffic, his sudden move igniting a dozen horns in a blaze of noise and raised middle fingers. He just missed the exit ramp, the other two cars already halfway up it, swearing as he pulled into the breakdown lane and began backing up, forcing several cars to swerve to avoid him.

Cheryl grinned, watching the lights of the car behind her as it managed to make the exit ramp, falling further back now they had left the highway. She set her lips in a determined line, turning right at the blinking red light, aiming for a mini mart whose name had been on a sign a half-mile back. Not in need of anything, just allowing an opportunity for the foreign entourage to make their move. She touched her locket, containing a microchip with an access key to her unique code embedded inside, under a picture of Robert. One that would allow her program to be altered, then redeployed. It had been her idea to expose it to being taken from her, a plan suggested to and grudgingly supported by Cole. Made possible with the help of a team of programming experts he'd requisitioned from the NSA.

"The guys—and the gal, would like to add a tracker, just to be safe." Cole looked at Cheryl with a shadow of concern etched on his face. "Just in *case*."

Cheryl shook her head. "No. They'd find it. An obvious tip-off that someone's watching them. Thinking it's your people or the corporate group. With the same result—rejecting the bait, knowing it's a potential Trojan cow."

"Horse, Cheryl. A Trojan—" Cole stopped, noting her smile. "You *got* me."

"Just wanted to see if Jean filled you in on my—issue with history blindness. Seems he did." She paused. "Down to *every* detail."

Cole blushed. "Not *all* the details. He left a few to my—imagination."

"In your dreams, Don Juan."

Cole looked down, his fingers locked together, betraying his worry about her safety. "We—well *you*, have this planned out, down to every probable outcome. But something could *still* go south." He looked up. "I get you not wanting to let us track your key code, but you need to take the phone I gave you. That way we can cover you, in *observation* mode only." Cole raised his hand, cutting off her response. "No *arguing*. I won't have Jean finding out about this, and my not having someone there to step in if things—"

Cheryl grabbed his hand, squeezing it tightly, then letting go, missing Cole's wince, his fingers aching. "*If* things go south, Cole. Which they won't. This has got to be as *clean* as possible. Right? The same as if you were in *their* shoes. I mean—if there's even a hint of being followed by government agents—it all falls apart. So, no worries on my end, I've got this completely locked down. Have *had* it locked down for a long time, predicting what their next move is going to *have* to be, considering the potential of what's involved."

"Two more things then, before—before you leave." Cole reached out, taking her hand, holding it for a moment then letting go. "I've never been jealous of anyone before. Never had to, considering the company I've kept." He paused, Cheryl waiting, both silent. He swallowed, his feelings for her clear. "Jean—is a lucky man."

"We both are, Cole." Cheryl reached up, tapping him on his cheek. "And the second?"

Cole pulled out his cell phone and swiped the face, pulling up Jean's number, holding it up, letting Cheryl see. "I have to do this—have to get his clearance. To hear him give it to—"

Cheryl's hand flashed out, knocking the phone away, grabbing it as it hit the floor, putting it away, before Cole could react. "Not gonna happen, Senator. Not unless you're willing to put me away. And Jean *too*."

The sedan drifted to a slow stop, their quarry having parked a few spaces down from the door of the small market, sliding into a pool of shadow beneath a burned-out overhead light. The young man behind the wheel pulled into a vacant parking spot to the left side of the compact car. He kept the engine running, hands on the wheel, eyes straight ahead. It was his first active mission, and he was nervous, his hands shaking.

A large, thick-necked man in the passenger seat looked over, a thin smile on his lips. He opened his mouth to offer an insult, catching the look on the senior agent's face in the rearview mirror, sitting in back, her eyes focused, lips taut with concentration. A look he recognized, one the diminutive woman had worn before kicking him clear across the dojo floor during their last training session. He closed his mouth and cracked open his door, the dome light staying dark: the bulb removed. Keeping his hand on the edge of the door, he began preparing himself, ready to spring into action as soon as the agent in back gave the command.

Cheryl paid for several items she'd picked out at random, tucking the change received into the opening of a small jar near the register with a picture of a young girl lying in a hospital bed. She avoided looking outside, knowing her plan had worked, having noted from the corner of her eye that the car following her had pulled in beside her own.

"Anything else?" The clerk gave her a bored look, his displeasure clear at having his call interrupted, his cell phone on the counter, the image of a chubby girl with a pretty face twisting her hair with a finger, smiling back.

"No." Cheryl turned to leave, then stopped. "I can hit the highway north again, right?" The pasty-faced boy shrugged. "Yeah. Just turn left, head back to the first light. Hang a right." He picked up his phone, making a promise of beer if the girl on the other end of the call came by. Cheryl walked away, a grin on her lips, knowing some things would never change. Then she slipped outside, realizing her night was about to take a dramatic turn, hoping it would work out for the best. She held out one hand, palm up, remembering what Jean had said about hoping for the best, deciding to keep the other one at her side.

"What is *she* doing?" The man in the passenger seat forced himself to look away, as if bored. "With her hand? Is that a *signal?*"

"Shut up, fool—and be ready to move." The senior agent slid over to the left, getting out and stopping to stretch, hands on her lower back, the pistol she had tucked into a custom holster in the small of her back, one of American design, its weight reassuring. She glanced at Cheryl as she passed by. "I have a long drive ahead. Too much coffee. Is the restroom inside clean?"

Cheryl stopped, then shrugged her shoulders, the locket swinging from the chain around her neck, catching the other woman's eye. "*Gas station* clean, yeah. But you should use one of the paper seats covers. On second thought—use two." She turned to go, the woman stopping her again.

"I love your pendant. It's lovely."

"It's a locket. With a picture inside. A gift from a friend."

The woman closed the distance, noting the large agent on the other side of the car slipping out, moving like a cat, despite his girth. "May I see it, the picture?"

Cheryl reached up, closing her fingers around the locket, allowing a measure of caution to creep into her voice, along with a look of concern on her face. "I—really need to get back on the road. Like *you* said, a long trip ahead. Heading out of state to try and beat the heat."

The senior agent hardened her voice. "You will come with me, Doctor." Her eyes narrowed in a glare that matched her tone. "We know who you are working with. Your friend, the Senator. Know of his proclivity to provide his *friends* with special gifts. Like the one you are wearing. Inside, please. We need to—"

Cheryl darted away, almost clearing the front of the idling sedan when an arm circled her upper body, compressing her against a chest seeming to be made of steel, her feet off the ground, arms trapped against her side, fingers still clenching the locket. She tried to shout, the woman rushing over, jamming a gag in place. The large man carried her to the back door of the sedan, shoving her in, slamming it shut behind her. The other door opened, framing the woman agent, a small gun in her hand.

"There is only a need to talk, unless you choose otherwise."

Cheryl had already removed the gag, a wedge of silk cloth. She held onto it, her fear real, voice shaking as her adrenal glands kicked in. "Who—who are you?"

"Stop it." The agent sitting across from Cheryl stared at her. "We know who you are, and inane remarks such as that serve no purpose." The agent paused, forcing a friendly smile onto her thin lips. "We simply require the key."

The car was already swinging out onto the road, heading for a reentry to the highway ahead, the driver keeping pace with the posted speed limit, stopping at the traffic light, waiting for the signal to turn green.

"Where are you taking me?"

"To the next exit. Where, if you are amenable to our request, we will turn around and bring you back."

"It's not here. Not *with* me, I mean. I—gave it to Cole. To the Senator. He has it. Forced me to turn it over. A matter of national security. Threatened me with prison if I refused to—"

The agent shook her head. "Why is it so difficult for you people to accept defeat? Never willing to bow your head and walk away. Live to fight—how is it said? Oh, yes—*another* day."

Cheryl dropped the act, leaning back, hands on her legs. "Never learned how to do *that*." The car was back in heavy traffic, speeding up, merging in, the driver easing into the right-most lane. Cheryl wondered if the two men Jean had tasked with over-watch had been able to keep up, or if they'd missed her at the exit. A flurry of butterflies swarmed in the pit of her stomach; her bravado being tested. Not a game, she reminded herself. This is real, with real consequences and not a scene from some movie.

The agent narrowed her eyes, trying to work out what the American woman had said. Before she could ask, Cheryl took a deep breath, letting it out, appearing to come to terms with the gravity of her situation. Then she smiled at the agent, her voice friendly in tone.

"I have a saying in mind. Stop me if you've heard it before. Goes something like this: that when your backs against the wall, hold out your hands. Let hope fill one hand, shit fill the other. See which one fills up *first*." She paused, watching as the woman repeated the words to herself, noting from the corner of her eye that the large man in the front seat was holding out his hands, staring from one to the other. Her smile widened. "Oh, and *another* one. Something I just made up. That when shit finally *does* start to hit the fan, don't be afraid to throw some of your *own!*"

Cheryl launched herself over the front seat, clasping her hands around the driver's head, her fingers squeezing his eyes, her hands, and arms, honed from hours on the wall, impossible for the large man in the passenger seat to peel off, screaming something unintelligible at the driver as the sedan slewed to one side, contacting several cars, going into a spin. The man let go of Cheryl with one hand, grabbing the wheel, fighting to keep the car heading straight.

The senior agent leaned forward, trying to break Cheryl's grip, unable to. She reached for her pistol, using the butt end to bludgeon the crazy American woman on the head. Cheryl held on to the driver's face, determined to keep them from getting the code. Ignoring Cole's advice. Knowing they would be more apt to accept the bait if covered in blood. Her blood. The repeated thud of metal against her temple began to take a toll. Her hands loosening, vision fading, the sounds of horns blaring and metal screeching in protest fading away, leaving her barely aware as the agent tore the locket from her neck. Then silence descended, along with a thick blanket of darkness as she let go, drifting gently away.

Skinny had reversed course back to the beginning of the exit ramp, then began a search for Cheryl's car, finding it as he was passing a gas station, turning around, killing his lights as he swung into the furthest edge of the badly lit parking lot. The large sedan he'd spotted earlier was parked alongside Cheryl's car. Two people standing outside: Cheryl and a small woman who was talking to her. He felt his stomach lurch when Cheryl broke away, a huge shadow rising from the front of the sedan, engulfing her, tossing her in back, the car reversing, then pulling out of the lot.

Skinny radioed Jason, pulled over at the end of the entrance ramp leading back onto the highway, yelling at him to pick up the sedan as soon as it swung into view, letting him know what had happened, that he was tailing the vehicle to the stoplight, waiting for further instructions.

Jason swore, knowing things were not going as planned, Jean having told the two of them someone might follow Cheryl, but no other action would be expected. Words in the effing wind, Jason thought to himself as the sedan approached, just like all the other times when things didn't go as planned, leaving him and men stuck having to take care of the dirty work themselves.

He keyed his mike with a cough, activating the transmitter. "Stay on their bumper, danger-*effing*-close. Be ready to move when *I* do." Jason slammed his foot down, pulling into traffic, staying just in front of the merging vehicle.

Jean's phone rang with the sound of an old-fashioned trilling, answered before it could cycle through second time. The screen displayed Jason's name, eliciting an icy chill in his core, belying the warm air outside the marina office. "What's happened?" He listened as the younger man quickly caught him up, the agitated sound of his voice dropping into muttered cursing, followed by a thud and screech of metal on metal. Jean was already at his truck door, an older model Humvee, key in the ignition by the time Jason got back in touch and filled him in, having to go, cutting the call short.

Jean tore out of the parking area, his fear set aside as he dialed Cole's number, knowing the man's gamble that Cheryl would never be in harm's way had just been called, and raised.

Two FBI agents were almost to the scene of the multiple car pile-up, the road littered with flashing headlights and knots of people slowly moving to the side of the road. Others were surrounding two cars, trying to render aid. One of the agents in the unmarked vehicle, sitting in the passenger side seat, was on his phone, giving directions and best guess assessment of what was happening with their inside man, or woman, in this case. The agent behind the wheel cursed, having to slam on the brakes, jammed in by vehicles stopping to rubberneck. His passenger exited the car, sprinting ahead.

Cole listened to the agent's terse report, one hand on his forehead, his eyes closed in frustration and fear, knowing his back-up phone would be ringing, soon, a pissed off Jean demanding to know what the hell had happened, his own team on the scene, following Cheryl at all times. Nothing he could tell him, having to wait to find out himself. He went with his instincts, ordering a med-evac bird to prepare to pick him up at the nearest agency helipad, with an emergency flight plan filed based on the agent's reported location and a direct route from there to Walter Reed.

Jason helped Skinny pry open the driver's side rear door. They'd watched three figures slip away, climbing down over the edge of a steep embankment, with a small man supported between a larger one and a woman. Disappearing into the night, of no importance now, both men intent on checking the condition of Dancer's woman friend

"She's here. On the floor. Help me get her back in the seat." Jason eased Cheryl's unresponsive body up, her head falling to one side, a black shadow covering one side of her head and neck. He touched her throat, feeling a slight pulse. Then he pulled his hand back, fingertips covered in blood, knowing she was seriously injured. "Pulse is weak."

"Still breathing, but shallow." Skinny had his ear to her mouth. "Not good. She's fading. Gonna need a bird, *asap!*" Jason nodded; his eyes wide, uncertain what to do next. Skinny leaned up, looking him in the eye. "Need to call for a medivac, sir. We're getting hammered out here. Have injured, needing to get out. Now." Skinny kept his voice low, prodding his friend, his former lieutenant, to get back into the fight. Jason recovered, dialing Jean again, knowing he would need to move heaven and a good portion of hell to get a bird headed their way in time.

Jean glanced at the phone, Jason's name showing, again. He waited for the truck radio to connect into the call, then punched the screen, answering it.

"Not good, Major. Need a bird here, *yesterday*. State troopers just showed. Gonna have them secure a landing zone. At mile marker—just a minute." Jean bit his tongue waiting for the seconds to ooze by, each one a moment of searing agony, wishing he could crawl through the phone and come out the other end, able to do something, anything. To be there with her. "I've got the coordinates. Got something to write with?"

"*Give.*" Jean listened, memorizing the numbers, punching them into a message and sending it to Cole's phone, multitasking as he careened down the road, knowing a place where he'd be able to cut over to intersect the highway, just beyond the location sent.

"I'm *already* on the way, Jean. Got a trauma team with me. Be there in ten." Cole paused, expecting Jean to let him have it. "Jean?"

"I'm ETA in *three*. My guy said they have the road closed. I'm heading south now, on the northbound lanes. Multiple accidents got it blocked, so you're good to land north of the numbers I sent you. Meet you when you land. Or someone will."

"I'm sorry, Jean. Don't know what—"

"Just *get* here, Cole. Get that bird on the ground as fast as you can. She's—she's hurt. Bad."

The phone call dropped, Cole left staring at the screen, tethered to the pilot by a headphone cable plugged into the nearest jack. He activated it. "Eta to coordinates?" He listened for a moment, then cut in. "You're authorized to do whatever's needed to be wheels down in *five.*"

CHAPTER FIFTY-EIGHT

TEA SHOP, WASHINGTON D.C.

Mari

Their server bowed, a smile of appreciation on his wrinkled face as he poured tea into Mari's cup. Perfectly done, not a single drop out of place. The final one left hovering for a full second of breathless anticipation before falling into the center of the thin-walled cup, the ripples reaching its outer edge at the same time. Mari returned the man's bow, hands on her knees, forehead almost touching the top of her cup. She held her bow for a moment, hearing the intake of the old man's breath, reacting to her acknowledgment of his skill.

Luther held back a smile of appreciation, the younger woman exceeding all his expectations. He'd known Mari would appreciate the honor shown in being inviting to the tea ceremony. The same cup used as before, in front of her now, a gesture he knew she'd noted when first kneeling, hands folded in her lap, the clothes she was wearing, selected with a thoughtful balance between east and west. Presenting herself as if a rare pearl, balanced on the honed edge of a samurai's sword.

Mari bowed her head to Luther, receiving one in return. Then she lifted her cup, drinking in the aroma, savoring it for a moment before tasting the dark brew, an artful blend of tea leaves. "It is—suitable."

Luther angled his head, her response dictated by the formal setting, without need of western exuberance. Properly done, owed to her mother's training, he assumed. Beyond reproach.

"Sweetener?" When she hesitated, he smiled. "Decorum is no longer required. You have honored the server—and yourself. Please, let us loosen the ties of our kimonos. Figuratively." He reached to a tray holding a selection of small containers of honey, selecting one from the very end.

"Then, yes. That would be good. The flavor is a—bit unusual. Not sweet enough for my taste, at any rate." She paused, then lowered her eyes. "My father would frown, hearing me say that."

Luther glanced over, a small stick of bamboo in his hand, honey coating it. "Not your mother?"

"No." Mari lowered her cup, resting it on the table. "She didn't approve of my father teaching me the ceremonies. The art of showing deference. Maintaining stoicism."

Luther took a step back mentally, reconsidering his earlier assessment of Mari, making a slight adjustment based on her revelation of parental instruction. "Your father's heritage?"

"He's—or rather, he was Scottish. With some Irish blood mixed in on his mother's side."

"A historian? Or a professor, perhaps, with an interest in the Orient and its many customs?"

Mari smiled, her eyes lighting up at memories of her father, his long aquiline nose stuck in books, reading everything he could find having to do with both Chinese and Japanese cultures. "A self-taught philosopher. Of life. Interested in cultural traditions from around the world. Chinese culture, one of his favorites. Thus, becoming one of mine."

She held out her cup, waiting for a drip of honey from the small stick Luther was holding. Surprised when he pulled it back, swapping it out for another. "An error on my part. Honey being as varied in flavor as the flowers from where the bees collect the nectar. This one is from the garden of a remote temple in western China. Prepared for me in a local town, shipped to the owner of this establishment."

Mari watched as the man she still did not have a name for leaned in, stirring her tea with a small wooden wand, then removing it, holding it still, until every drop of liquid had fallen free. She raised the cup and tasted the commingled flavors: the blend stirring memories of her father doing the same, tears rising to the surface of her eyes, not allowed to fall. She looked over, drawn to the energy of the solemn faced man. "Thank you—" She hesitated, stumbling on the moment of connection, unable to show her gratitude in full.

Luther watched her closely, knowing he had chosen correctly. The woman an asset. Still. To him if no one else. His plan unfolding as he had foreseen, with a slight alteration. A white tigress, her destiny now tied to his, sown into its fabric. "Please—call me Luther."

CHAPTER FIFTY-NINE

WALTER REED, MARYLAND

Cheryl

Jean came into the private room, his face drawn, with three days of growth covering his cheeks. Eyes red from lack of sleep, unable to rest, even when he closed his eyes. Woken by the frequent interruptions every fifteen minutes or so as nurses and doctors took turns coming in to check on their special patient's condition.

Isaac looked up, closing the book he'd been reading while Jean took a shower in the doctor's lounge, ate, and hurried back in case of any change in Cheryl's condition. "You get some food into you?"

Jean shrugged. "Some. Don't ask me what it was. Can't remember." He came over and stood beside Cheryl's bed, the smell of antiseptic and fresh bandages covering most of her head, no longer noticeable, his sense of smell having adjusted to the new normal. Adjusting to the routine of eating alone, snatching minutes of sleep where he could, only leaving her side when Jason, Skinny, or Isaac came by, lending their support.

Jean glanced at the book in Isaac's hands, looking even smaller, due to their large size. It had been a gift from Mari during her recent visit. Sun Tzu's, The Art of War, signed by General Ridgway. A gift she and her sister had presented to their father on his last birthday, several years ago. Re-gifted to her as part of his will. Now presented to him, a man she trusted and respected.

Mari had let him know she was leaving, reassigned to another project in need of her talents, asking him to let Cheryl know how sorry she was at the turn of events. Then she gave him a number, letting him know that Cheryl could use it at any time to reach out, once she was back on her feet. A message Jean had promised to pass on as soon as the willful woman lying in her bed could heal enough to be pulled out of the medically induced coma the doctor had put her in.

"She's stable." The doctor checked the readouts on the imposing group of medical instruments, hovering at the sides and head of Cheryl's bed, her body looking small beneath their looming presence. "Touch and go there, I'll admit. But she's strong. *Very* strong, and that's the best we can hope for, until the swelling reduces. The good news is that her vitals are back where—well, not *all* the way back, but close enough that we can start bringing her out."

"That's *good*, right?" Jean's face revealed a trace of hope.

"Better." The doctor shrugged. "Not quite there yet, at the *good* point of her recovery, but yes—you can rest easy knowing—" The doctor narrowed his eyes, studying Jean's face. "Military, correct?"

"Retired, a couple of months ago. As a major—in the Marines."

"Sleeping?" The doctor stared while Jean figured out what he was asking, his bedside manner short, to the point of rudeness. A trait Jean admired in himself, though not as much in others.

"Some."

"Are you still capable of following orders?"

"Ones that make sense and won't get anyone killed for no good reason. Yes."

"Go home. Get some *solid* rest. I'll proscribe you something, enough to knock you out until you can get your senses fully back in operation. You're a zombie, scaring my people. You need rest, like artillery needs munitions. And right now, major—you're firing blanks."

Jean opened his mouth to protest, the doctor cutting him off. "She's in the *clear*, okay? Shouldn't tell you that, and I'll deny ever having said it." He paused, looking at Cheryl, then back at Jean. "And she's sure as hell not *going* anywhere, at least for the next twenty-four hours while we ease her back to *this* side of things. So, do us all of us a favor and get-some-rest. You'll need it once—" He nodded toward Cheryl. "*This* little package of awesomeness wakes up."

Jean nodded, sinking back into the chair, his legs no longer able to hold him up. "Okay. Sir." He closed his eyes, leaning to one side, slipping away into an exhausted sleep, a prescription tucked in his shirt when he woke up, a nurse coming in to check on Cheryl's drain.

"So, I told this guy that he could either move his *effing* tractor, have us haul it away, or watch us flatten it right where it was. Or words to that effect. Neither of us able to understand the other, my interpreter down with a minor wound." Jean paused, then smiled. "Remember how he stood there, anger in his eyes. Not at me, but at the shitty situation he was in the middle of, with no one else to vent his frustrations on. So, like I said, I gave him an ultimatum—"

"Stop—please—for the *love* of god."

Jean froze, hands clamped behind his head, eyes closed, having been regaling Cheryl with tales from his military service, following doctor's orders to keep talking to her. Six hours of solid sleep having helped: his voice strong, mind sharp, or rather, not nearly as dull. Jean waited a moment until daring to look at Cheryl, wondering if he'd heard her voice or only imagined it.

"I'm—thirsty."

Jean stood up to run and get a nurse, then stopped, eyeing a cup of water on the bedside table, used to help ease the dryness in his throat. He headed to the door, shouting for help, then went back to the bed, holding the cup to the side of Cheryl's mouth, tipping it just enough to moisten her lips. She whispered something and Jean leaned down, his ear close to her mouth.

"What was that?"

Cheryl answered him, her words sounding stronger, bringing tears to his eyes. "You should see the—*other* guy."

The doctor nodded as he checked a print-out from one of several monitors tied to Cheryl. "How much do you remember of the endless autobiography he was telling you?"

Cheryl groaned, both the doctor and Jean starting to lean in, concern in their eyes. "Most of it. Unfortunately." She looked at them. "What?"

"Are you in pain? Has your headache returned?" Jean grabbed her hand, waiting for her to reply. The doctor stepped forward, eyeing him with a stern look, grabbing the name tag on his white coat, pulling it out an inch. "Do you have one of *these* on your chest, Major Kelly?" He didn't wait for a response, stepping in, taking Mari's hand away from Jean, checking her grip. "Squeeze." She complied, his fingers feeling the steel-like compress. "*Okay!* Enough already. Don't need you to do any *damage*." He shook his hand, looking at Jean.

"She climbs. A lot. Need's a—firm grip."

The doctor nodded. "Okay. Then *you* hold her hand and let me know if it's as firm as you remember. Need an assessment of her strength, before taking the next step."

Jean complied, feeling Cheryl's grip increase to the edge of his own tolerance, before easing. He looked at the doctor. "She's good. Good to go."

The air was cooler, a breeze from the north-west having scrubbed the local area, clearing away the heavy humidity. Heat was still hanging around, but bearable, bodies able to sweat, helping to reduce the effect. Cheryl rested in the sun, her hair growing back in from the operation performed to reset shards of bone: result from the beating she'd received. They'd removed the drain in the side of her skull, her color improving, though she was still pale. Her legs, arms, and shoulders had lost muscle-tone over the past month, her body thin from weight loss, though her appetite had returned, baskets of fish nuggets delivered daily by special messenger, with enough for the nurses and doctors in the ICU's breakroom to share, the entire nursing staff letting Jean know their appreciation for the deliveries made daily for each shift.

"I'm sorry." Jean's voice was low, sitting on a bench beside Cheryl who was in a wheelchair, still unable to use a walker, residual issues causing havoc with her balance, due to damage to her inner ear. Minor, when compared to her remarkable recovery from severe head trauma. Upsetting to her, wondering if she'd ever be able to climb again. He looked at her. "For everything you've had to go through. I just wish he'd—Cole. That he'd—" Jean stopped, knowing his feelings were of little importance, measured against what Cheryl was dealing with.

"It wasn't his idea—Cole's."

Jean looked at her. "Had to be."

"Are you saying I'm *lying?*" Cheryl looked at him, a familiar glint in her eyes, causing Jean to back down.

"No. Not if you say it's *true*, and you're not just trying to patch things up between us."

Cheryl lifted her arm, mimicking someone using a brush. "Get it? Using the stuff. That white stuff they put on walls to repair cracks. Or holes."

"You mean—spackle?" Jean grinned.

"I guess so. How would *I* know?" Cheryl frowned. "I'm a *doctor*, Jim. Not some *spackle guy!*"

Jean laughed, a feeling of relief coming over him. "You're an—idiot."

"You don't have to yell. Nothing wrong with my hearing. Just my balance. *Jerk.*"

A soft cough from a few feet away pulled their attention to the path. Cole was standing there, looking like a boy called on the carpet by his parents and not one of the more popular, and therefore powerful senators serving in Washington.

"Just wanted to stop by and see how you're doing. Both of you. Was here—visiting a few friends." He wound down, waiting a few seconds before turning around to leave.

Jean called out; his voice clipped. "A moment of your time, Senator." He paused, staring at Cole. "I have something to ask you."

Cole turned back, ready to face the music. "Fire away. The range is *hot*."

"Was it your idea, using my—using Cheryl as a decoy?"

"I approved the plan."

Jean held out his hand, stopping Cheryl as she opened her mouth to interrupt. "And the key to her code, planting it in her locket, knowing it would bring the opposition into the open, taking advantage of any opportunity to take it?"

"Again—my call."

"So, it wasn't *her* idea?"

Cole shifted his eyes, looking at Cheryl, who gave him a short nod. "Yes. It was."

"And you couldn't talk her out of it?"

Cole stared at Jean, his expression stiffening. "Could you? Could *anyone?*"

"Did you even *try?*"

"Had my cell phone *in* my hand. Your number dialed. She slapped it away, knocking it to the floor. Then picked it up—ending the call."

"And you couldn't get it *back?*"

"She put it somewhere—safe. Where she knew I—" Cole's face reddened, his eyes focused on the ground.

"I shoved it in my *panties*, Jean. Switched it to vibrate—hoping you'd call back."

"This isn't a joke, Cheryl. And that—wasn't funny."

"It was a *little* funny."

"Okay." Jean shook his head, looking at her, seeing the grin he remembered, the same look in her eyes from the first time he saw her naked, standing in a shower, asking, and offering herself. "Maybe a *little.*" He looked up at Cole. "You're not *off* the hook." Then he sighed. "But you are off the rack. Lashes earned and delivered. For dereliction of duty."

"Guilty, as charged."

"Charges *dismissed.*" Jean stuck out his hand. "Without prejudice."

Cheryl leaned forward, moving the wheelchair with her arms. "I'm *thirsty!* Which one of you fine gentlemen is going to take me to the nearest bar?"

The evening was the thickness of a windowpane away, Cheryl's fingers touching the glass. So close, she thought as she looked through, picking out stars she thought she recognized. One of her brother's favorite hobbies, locating them, showing her where the constellations were and their names, clearly seen in the high altitude of the New Hampshire mountains. Dim things now, city lights denying them their just due.

"What time is it?"

Jean checked his watch. "Just after twelve. It's late. You should try to get some—"

"Tuesday, right?" She turned and looked at Jean, sitting on the couch, thumbing through a magazine. "The twenty-fifth, right?"

"Yes. Almost through the month." He came over and sat down beside her, both living at her home, the arrangement made without fanfare, Jean moving in to help with her physical and mental therapy. "Why?"

"Because." She paused, looking out at the city lights in the distance. "In four years and—what *time* is it? *Exactly.*"

"Exactly *what?*"

"The time. To the minute."

"Twelve fifteen, as of—now." Jean took her hand. "Once again—*why?*"

Cheryl turned her head away from the window and leaned in against Jean, his heartbeat in her good ear, pressed against his chest. Her balance returning, though frustratingly slow. "Need to know how long until we're on the back trail leading up to the top of the wall. Just you and me. To where the rock juts out, like the beak of a hawk. Hawksbill. That's where I want to be when midnight rolls around in four years, eleven months, twenty-nine hours and—" She took his wrist, checking the face of his watch. "Forty-four minutes"

Jean reached up, cupping the back of her neck, his fingers stroking her hair, growing back in with a tight curl. "It's a *date*." He kissed her forehead. "Why, Cheryl? Why is it so important to know the time, to keep track of it down to the very minute?""

Cheryl leaned back, looking up at him, her cheeks starting to fill back in. "You really want to know?"

Jean considered. "I'm okay with *not* knowing—unless you *want* to tell me."

"It's the day my brother died. When my parent's let him go. Not me, though. I'd have held on to him for as long as it took." Her eyes filled. "I would never have let him go, Jean. Not in a *million* years. Never." She muffled a sob against his shirt. "And it would have been a mistake. A *terrible* mistake, my doing that. Keeping him *here*. Knowing what it's like. Wanting to come back and being unable to. Because I couldn't have reached him. Not then. Making him wait until—"

Jean pulled her in against his chest. "I understand. And so does Robert." He waited, holding her until she stopped shaking, back in control, looking up at him like a tear-stained child.

"That's why I *planned* this. To happen on the same day. The day when he—died. That's when it happens, at one minute past midnight. That's when it all falls apart. When everything I've built, worked on for all these years, when it all goes *splat*. Face-plant. All the way down to where gravity lives, in the ground, always there, pulling and tugging at you when you're climbing. Trying to keep you from flying away—like a bird."

Jean grabbed her by the shoulders, holding her out, staring into her eyes, seeing the look of satisfaction on her face. "What—have you *done?*"

Cheryl shrugged out from under his hands and stood up, reaching out to grab his arm, needing a moment to find her balance. Then she walked over to her laptop and opened the screen, pulling up a timer. It matched her countdown. Three minutes having passed. "I put a kill shot in the code. One that shuts it down. Not just the *original* code, but in every single segment of it. Put it in *every* connection, affecting anything they use it for, even in the pieces they'll be snipping out to use in the smallest applications. Surpassing what current AI programs can ever hope to offer. Programmers by the thousands using the key, breaking my code, and putting it in places even *I* haven't thought of. All of it—rendered useless, with each bit of code eating the next. Like tiny snakes, swallowing their tails. All of it. Everything—" Cheryl looked at Jean, eyes bright, her arms crossed, a smug look on her still much too thin face. "Going to hell in a hand-basket."

Jean stared at her, finally waking up to the fact she was unlike anyone he'd ever known. Still a young girl, challenging authority every step of the way, knowing, deep down in her bones, that anything was possible, if you just looked up and dared make the leap. "They'll come after you. After *us*. Everyone. Governments. Corporations. The entire *fucking* world."

Cheryl smiled, her eyes looking directly into his. "Let 'em. Got to find me first."

"Find *us*, you mean." Jean crossed over and took her hands, holding them, leaning his head against hers, looking into her eyes, his voice a whisper. "Where can we go?"

"Haven't decided yet. But I'm thinking a sailboat. One of those ones with two parts."

"You mean a—catamaran?"

"Yeah. Big one. Big enough to get us to New Zealand. They have mountains there. Lots of 'em. Got a handful of years to figure *that* part out. But I'm sure something will occur to me." She bit her lower lip, lowering her eyes. "You sure you want to be at the pointy end of the—what did you call it—the spear?"

Jean gathered her in, gently pressing her to his chest, his hand gently cradling the back of her head. "Someone has to be there with you, at the bottom of the wall. Ready to catch you when you leap." He leaned down, finding her lips, tasting them, his voice a whisper. "Can't think of any place I'd rather be."

EPILOGUE

TOTTMAN COVE, PHIPPSBURG

Out of the Shadows

David stood a hundred paces out on an extensive bed of compact, brown sand, flecks of mica reflecting the angled rays of a mid-morning sun. It was dead low tide, the rippled shelf warm beneath his bare feet, warmed by the sunlight, heating the slow incursion of salt-water as the tide turned, reclaiming its fair share of the bay.

He stood at the edge of a drop-off, staring into the icy water, knowing how cold it would be. Remembering having testing himself against it, not by choice but shamed into it. Maggie diving in first, screaming from the shock, then laughing. Splashing him, chiding him, until he made the leap, joining her there. The air in his lungs exploding from his throat as the water grabbed him where he lived, squeezing a soprano scream from his throat, one that rivaled hers as he grabbed her and forced her head beneath the surface, bringing her up and kissing her. Salt-flavored water streaming into their mouths as they held onto each other.

There was no reason to stay another day, this visit made on the backs of his legs and the occasional vehicle stopping to offer a ride. Easier to find them once he'd reached and cleared the city of Bath, residents further out on the finger of land in Phippsburg, less leery of those afoot. Stories swapped with them until their journey needed to take a turn away from his path. Thanking each one with a smile and polite decline of lunch or dinner.

David's needs were simple, what he carried in his backpack enough to see him through. He'd reached the end of one journey and was beginning the next, taking him back to the west coast. Back to the life he'd abandoned, waiting for him to return. His mentor breaking down in sobs, promising him, when finally able to speak, that it was all there. House. Vehicles. Job. A future, ripe with promise. The call had ended with a promise to keep the man informed, sending his location now and then so a pin could be placed on a map, starting from the east coast, nowhere left to go but home. Back to a house he'd left unlocked and abandoned. Cared for by the man who'd been his closest friend, outside of Meg. His Maggie. His one and only Maggie Mae.

David felt a nudge against the back of his leg, almost buckling it, a long, wet nose finding his hand, licking between his fingers, tasting the salt from the chilly waters of the tidal cove. He knelt, taking Dawg by the head, looking into his amber eyes, thumbs rubbing the base of his ears. "Figured you'd show up—eventually."

He walked back to the shoreline of sun-bleached white sand, put on his boots, and gathered his pack. He slung it across his shoulder, sticking an earphone in place, listening to one of his favorite songs: an old folk song he'd learned to play on a guitar, always bringing tears, happy tears, to his eyes and a frown to Maggie's face.

Head up, he began walking away with a long stride, waiting until the chorus kicked in, then raised his voice, singing as loud as he could. His life, a shadow stretched before him, pointing the way back home.

"The green grove is gone from the hills, Maggie, where once the daisies sprung. The creaking old mill is still, Maggie, ever since we both were young."

ACKNOWLEDGEMENTS

I would like to thank all the usual suspects who once again waded through the original story, their advice and support instrumental to helping bring this work to completion. I especially am thankful for the support of my older sibling who encouraged me to publish this book. And for being there, through every step I've taken—from the very first one.

I also offer my sincere thanks to my editor, David Aretha. And to three wonderful people he introduced me to, Martha Bullen, Christy Day, and Maggie McLaughlin, each helping to put a professional veneer on the story enclosed.

ABOUT THE AUTHOR

M. DANIEL SMITH is a prolific author of historical fiction, speculative and literary fiction, mysteries and thrillers. He is the author of *The Red Path*, the first book in the *Legacy's Road* series, and his latest technological thriller, *Coalescence: The View Within*.

He particularly enjoys writing about strong-willed, feisty women and the men they love, showing them in moments of emotional turmoil, introspective conversation, and physical closeness. Coming from a blue-collar background, raised with two older sisters and strong female role models, Daniel enjoys exploring the interplay between wives and husbands, siblings, and people meeting, then falling in love.

As a voracious reader who began reading all the books in his parents' library when he was five, he cut his teeth on a wide range of subject matters, covering war, romance, historical novels, and the like.

A life-long Mainer, he is continually inspired by the wild natural beauty of his home state. Now retired, Daniel spends his time writing the type of novels he grew up with, telling his character's stories as clearly and as honestly as possible. Learn more about Daniel and his books at www.bayledgespress.com.